LOVE IN THE BLIZZARD OF LIFE

DR. ERICA GOODSTONE

Dedication

Love in the Blizzard of Life is dedicated to my friend
Barbara V. Schonbrun Wassum
filled with the spirit of love
and the enjoyment of life
who left this world too soon

CONTENTS

ACKNOWLEDGMENTS

Love in the Blizzard of Life was inspired by

Patrick Mascola, Publisher of *Around Town* Newspaper, who called me one week before the local Nanowrimo.org Kickoff Party. As I read his novel, *Hell on East Rock*, I said to myself: "That's how you write a novel. I can do this." And I did!

Willena Flewelling, fellow blogging tribe member and *Mentoring for Free* coach, who introduced me to Nanowrimo.org on November 25, 2011 exactly one year before I completed the first draft of my novel.

My husband, Mark, for calling me Dr. Erica Tolstoy during all those times that he called and interrupted my writing process.

·

1 THE SADNESS OF APHRODITE

Today was an ordinary day, just like so many other days that had passed and so many unlived days yet to come. She walked slowly, deep in thought, her body permeated with melancholy as she approached the path to her apartment.

Aphrodite Maia Morgan had lived in the same townhouse on Ramsey Street in Hawthorne Connecticut for a very long time. Every inch of the environment had been embedded in her brain and embodied within her hyper-sensual anatomy. She walked along the winding cobblestone path, aware of the earth beneath the stones welcoming her home. As she approached the modern cantilevered staircase leading up to her front door, she paused as an expression of gratitude for being alive. Standing perfectly still she allowed her breathing to slow down, consciously counting every inhale and exhale for 5 minutes. She had timed it so often that her body-mind system responded as soon as the 5 minutes was over. A very deep breath filled her body. She held the breath for as long as she possibly could and then she suddenly released it with an intense grunt of relief. The 5 minutes had ended and she knew she was home.

Before searching in her purse for her keys, Aphrodite always checked the environment to be sure it was safe to go inside. Without glancing up, her body said hello to the beautiful bluebird who visited her every day. Aphrodite did not, and could not, adhere to a rigid schedule. Yet no matter what time of day she arrived home and completed her breathing exercise, the little bluebird was right there hovering above her head. The fluttering of her intuitive friend's wings seemed to give her permission to leave the outside world and enter her inner sanctuary. As soon as Aphrodite's glance turned upward, the bird flew to the top of the nearby willow tree watching intently as if to ensure that it was safe for Aphrodite to enter her home.

Today, as she smiled at the bluebird, she could feel a deep longing for love pounding in her heart. Without words, she asked the bluebird to help her to find love, to become love, and to feel the love she so desperately craved. Little cheerful staccato chirps and the sound of wings brushing through the branches caused Aphrodite to look behind her at the golden shimmering iridescence of the setting sun. The sparkle was so intense that she had to squint and close her eyes. As she opened her eyes, she was momentarily mesmerized by the beautiful pastel palette rainbow leading over the hills that stretched for miles behind her building.

As she slowly walked up the 5 steps leading to her apartment door, her senses were attuned to everything around her. Aphrodite found herself communicating with a family of ants that scrambled to bury themselves deep into the ground as they sensed her approaching on the steps above. Without words, she asked them about their world and they sent her their message for the day. Today the word was "Trust." The ants reminded her to trust in the process of life, to trust that the seeds of her joy have already been planted, and to know in her heart that the man of her dreams is already here and loves her.

Sadness seemed to fill her heart as she realized she would be leaving her outdoor friends once she entered her home. But, of course, she knew she could always reach them with her senses since her inner world had no boundaries. Aphrodite knew that nothing, not even cement-filled walls, would ever block her soul from connecting with the cosmos and anyone and anything that exists.

Reaching the top of the stairs she noticed her blossoming Sweet William plant had developed Fusarium Wilt which causes the leaves to curl or droop down. The heaviness of Aphrodite's heart was spilling outward into her surrounding environment. Her natural friend, the bluebird, seemed to have become her supervisor and personal guide. But her Sweet William plant, the one that had just recently blossomed after she had spent an entire year watering it, seemed to be mirroring her current state. She bent over to gently stroke the wilted leaves, inhale the spicy, clover-like scent, and move her lips to embrace the essence of the plant. Sweet William beckoned to her to pluck one flower and slowly savor the taste on her tongue. As soon as her saliva touched the flower in her mouth, the leaves returned to their upright position, and the entire plant appeared to have regained its sense of elegance. Aphrodite's face lit up into a bittersweet smile as she searched inside her purse for her key chain.

There was a gentle breeze that seemed to whisper to her, repeating the words of her friend, the bluebird. All she could hear was: "Trust, trust, trust. Love is here. Love is all around you. Open your senses and feel the love. Remember you are never alone." With that renewed sense of trusting in love, she slowly turned the key to open her door to her inner sanctuary, her home.

And there he was, beaming and energized at the mere sight of her. She could feel his excitement and she knew without an inkling of a doubt that he was all hers and that he knew he belonged to her and she belonged to him. Her very presence brought him obvious delight as he smothered her face with kisses, licked her ear and vigorously rubbed his body back and forth against her. She realized immediately that he had been sitting patiently near the door during her 5 minute exercise, eagerly waiting for the moment when she would turn the key and open the door. His entire existence seemed to depend upon that special moment when she would once more hold him in her loving arms.

Yes, she was totally confident that this handsome, very special, tender and adoring man loved her unconditionally. And he was the true and only love of her life. Although her beloved man was completely content in his overwhelming love for her, she was happy but still wanted and desired more. She longed to be held in the arms of a different man, a tall and powerful hungry man. She longed to be with an adoring, loving and exuberant man whose hunger for life could only be fed by the assurance of her undying love for him.

Fluffy, a Poodle/Pomeranian mutt with soft curly white fur and a sweet angelic face that could melt anyone's heart, continued to lick her cheeks and her neck as his tail wagged rapidly back and forth. And then, just as quickly as he had gotten excited, his exuberance died down and he slowly sauntered away seeking something new to attract his attention. Aphrodite smiled at the unwavering sweetness of this little man who filled her life and her apartment with so much tender love. She watched his white fluffy body wiggle away as his tiny paws made the most delicate sounds on the hardwood floor in the hallway.

As she placed her old designer handbag on the hallway vanity, she momentarily was startled by the image she saw in that beautiful antique mirror, the one she had recently mounted right above the vanity. Her face revealed a combination of loving softness – from that sweet greeting by her beloved man – and a chronic expression of sadness, appearing to represent all the sadness that ever was in her life and in the lives of everyone else who had ever lived on this earth. She knew she was embodying centuries of emotional anguish, inner turmoil, unrequited love and repression of the inner spirit. In this moment she could see literally thousands of tiny lines and crevices appearing on her face, each one representing the anguish of human longsuffering. Her face was not her own but a composite of thousands of unknown faces. Each tiny crevice seemed to ask and even beg her to help them undo their fate and the fate of their descendants through the gift of life Aphrodite had been given to fulfill.

Seeing her time-worn face in the mirror reminded her of why she was here and what her true purpose was in this lifetime. Hers was not meant to be an easy life. In that interim world where souls are waiting, where lifetime decisions are made, she remembers that she had chosen to begin her life in suffering, to experience the dark side of life, to overcome her pain and sorrow, and to gradually become a brave and courageous example of human potential. Her sad eyes told her she was not quite finished with her required painful lessons of life. In fact, one truth she had come to understand is that the further along she would progress on the spiritual path, the greater and more powerful would be her opposition. If she was no longer her own worst enemy, which many people are, then she would surely meet some external enemies, her strongest opponents yet, whose main objective would be to hinder her progress and cause her to give up the fight.

Aphrodite knew she was not a quitter. Often extremely demanding, sometimes overly needy and clinging, she often felt abandoned and unloved. But one thing she knew for certain. She would never give up the fight - no matter how many obstacles she had to overcome or how much pain and sorrow she had to endure. Her inner knowing would keep her focused on the path ahead and she was determined to reach the promised-land of true love, in this lifetime. All of her life, beginning in her mother's womb, she had been longing for the love that she had so often been denied. Not feeling worthy, she did find some semblance or illusion of love in the hearts and minds of so many broken beings who hadn't discovered their own love and had very little to provide for her.

Before preparing her dinner, another of her daily rituals, she opened her new bottle of vintage Pinot Noir that she had bought on Frederico's recommendation. He was the self-proclaimed wine connoisseur at her favorite local liquor store. He had proudly shown her the special sticker indicating a 93 wine rating. As she poured, she silently blessed the wine, inviting the glass to hold and support the essence of the wine with love. Setting the glass aside to allow the wine to breathe and the full fragrance to emerge, she reached for her beautiful notebook to write about today's message she had received from the ants.

This was not an ordinary notebook. The cover had been created by her friend, Jolie Arbor, an up and coming mural artist and "indoor lifestyle designer" (her newly created business description). On the cover was a lovely representation of Aphrodite's face, highlighting those large and brilliant deep blue eyes with a hint of sadness and that flowing light brown hair with strands of golden highlights. Jolie's painted image had captured those lush and rounded lips which had tantalized a large number of men in Aphrodite's 25 years of existence. Her high cheekbones and that long slender nose with a slight slant and gently flaring nostrils added to the intensity and beauty of the painted image. Jolie had known Aphrodite intimately for many years and truly loved her, although Jolie, herself, had always hidden behind a mystique of distance and disdain. She rarely allowed others to get even a glimpse into her inner world, presenting herself as a staunch, unemotional and independent artist.

Jolie Arbor had always poured her heart and soul into her work, actually believing she had no intrinsic worth and that her artistic pieces gave her the only value she possessed. Unbeknownst to herself, Jolie's artistic pieces always revealed her overwhelming fear of personal exposure and her acute awareness of the painful fragility and vanity of human being. Aphrodite, wise beyond her years with centuries of wisdom provided by her uncanny connection with the natural world, had always seen beneath Jolie's veneer but chose to let her friend discover life's truths for herself. Aphrodite prayed often for Jolie's salvation and entrance into the promised-land of self-love and personal fulfillment. Yet Aphrodite didn't realize during her first two decades of life that she, herself, needed to learn self-love and self-acceptance before she could find deep and lasting love with another.

What Aphrodite and her friend Jolie had in common was a sense of being different and of not belonging. Both had been adopted. Jolie had been 3 years old when both parents had died in a car accident. Aphrodite had been adopted only a few days after her mother had given birth to her. She had never been told the true story of her birth, where her parents came from, who they were and therefore, who she was. Both girls seemed to have a deep sense of being unlovable. Both were unable to express their love openly. Jolie poured her heart and soul into her exotic masterful works of anguish turned into art. Although Aphrodite lived in the physical world, she felt much more comfortable, safe and alive when connecting with the spirits of animals, plants and the souls of others. She had deep compassion for the suffering of humanity and her own sense of not knowing who she really is. No matter how loving her adoptive parents, other relatives, friends and acquaintances might be, there was always a bit of sadness in her that nobody could reach until one day when she would finally reconnect with her birth parents.

2 CASSANDRA'S FAMILY

Cassandra Sybil Melanakos seemed to be the luckiest child in the world. She was born to a wealthy and highly influential family on the island of Agapelargos, a tiny island in the Saronic Gulf inlet of the Aegean sea, on the southeast coast of Greece not far from Athens. Growing up in such a powerful and influential family, Cassandra learned to be charming, mysterious and mature beyond her years from as early as anyone could recall. She was treated like the princess of the family, revered by her 3 older brothers, Alexei, Damion, and Stefano, pampered by her loving mother, Lyzandra, and adored by her strong and powerful father, Demitri. Owner of a night club, **The Cyprus Club**, which catered to the seedy side of society, Demitri worked long hours and rumor had it he was a suitor to many of the lady employees and customers. He enjoyed his big business dealings, his alcohol and being surrounded by sexy and voluptuous women. Lyzandra, his wife, apparently adored Demitri, or at least she made an outer display of love. She listened attentively when he spoke, she smiled as soon as she saw him, she rubbed his shoulders, brought him his slippers, and poured him a glass of liquor, tea or whatever he requested. Lyzandra loved her lifestyle. Although she would have to be dumb and blind to not know that Demitri's life was filled with other women, she did not want to make waves, upset Demitri, and give up the lifestyle she had gotten so used to living.

Cassandra adored her father, running toward him with joyful giggles ready to be swept up in his arms on those evenings that he arrived home in time for dinner. He would call her his little babushka, a term he had heard from some of the ladies he knew. He'd open his arms wide and with one whisk of his right arm he'd swoop her up into his arms and spin her around. She was always thrilled by his touch, his excitement and his obvious love for her. Then he would say to her with a most tender expression in his eyes: "So how are you doing today my little babushka? Have you been a good girl? I hope you are not teasing all those innocent boys the way you tease your brothers and your daddy? You know, you are a sexy little girl and your mother is going to have her hands full keeping you out of trouble." At this point she was 8 years old. Cassandra smiled shyly, with a sad and hurt expression, wondering why her daddy always told her she was teasing the boys. She loved her daddy more than anyone in the world and never wanted to tease him or cause him the slightest discomfort. She vowed then and there that she would never do anything to cause him to distrust her. But that was in those early years before the hormones of puberty would take over and that rational decision would be suppressed in the heat of the moment.

Life was simple, happy and so easy in those early years. Cassandra was rarely, if ever, alone. The family lived in a huge 10 bedroom mansion sitting on the top of a hill, the highest point on the entire island. Her youngest brother, Alexei, was 10 years older than her. That year when she had just turned 8 and he was 18, he got his first sports car, a snazzy red Fiat with cream colored leather seats, convertible top and the most powerful sound system available. Alexei loved to show off his beautiful little sister to his many friends around town. He would drive down the windy road that led out from their home to the bottom of the hill and turn left onto Lake Drive, heading for the little quaint town and Cassandra's favorite pastry shop. She loved passing by the lake, feeling the protection and shade from the sun provided by those huge overhanging birch trees – especially in the summer.

As they approached the small downtown, Cassandra's excitement would build. She loved passing by her mother's favorite dress shops and designer shoe stores. Cassandra, with her natural intuitive sense, would always expect Alexei to find a parking spot right in front of the pastry shop – and he usually did. As Alexei drove into town, Cassandra smiled quietly and waved as he called out greetings to his many friends. Alexei loved his little sister and had a different name for her, "manari mou," my little lamb. A proud and macho Greek man, just like his father, Alexei was worried for his little sister's safety. He would often repeat his father's words, but he made it much more personal. He'd look at his little Cassandra with a slight smirk on his face, stare at her chest – which had not yet begun to develop, and he would say: "In a few years I will not be able to take my eyes off you, manari mou.   You are already teasing me with your beautiful little body and the way you move so gracefully. I love you and I want you to remain my manari mou forever."   Cassandra felt that same uncomfortable sense that neither her father nor her brother really understood how pure her heart was.   All she wanted was to please her brother.   She would never intentionally betray her brother's love.   But she had not yet experienced the fire of sexual passion.

Cassandra did not feel as easily loved and protected by her two older brothers.   Both were more distant and yet extremely controlling.   When they were around, she had to be careful not to say something to upset them. Damion, 13 years her senior, had a quick and sometimes violent temper.   Without warning, he would fly into a rage and smack her across the face for disturbing him in some way, perhaps just being too talkative at a given moment when he wanted her to be quiet.   But he was also the one who took care of her when, at 5 years old, she was in bed all day with the measles.   He had gently rubbed cream on her itchy skin and kept telling her she was still beautiful.   A few years later, at 7 years old, she remembered that game he had played with her, asking about her most private parts and telling her they must be itchy and would need him to rub them with cream.   That was the first time he had slapped her, when, at 7 years old, she had asked him why he had put the cream in her "no-no" parts when the itchy measles rashes were only on the outside.   He lashed out at her, yelling: "You little devious tramp.   Don't ever say something like that again. Little girls should be quiet and pure.   They don't think dirty thoughts like that.   You are a bad girl and you better stop talking like this or you are going to cause this family trouble." Again, she felt totally misunderstood because she loved her brother and wanted more than anything to please him.

Cassandra's oldest brother, Stefano, 17 years older than her, no longer lived at home but would often stop by the house with his latest girlfriend to spend the night in his old bedroom. On one of these occasions, Damion joined his brother for a tryst with a girl they had both picked up at their father's nightclub. Hearing some strange sounds, a creaking bed, some distinctive moans, and what sounded like a loud slap, Cassandra went to Stefano's bedroom to see what the fuss was all about. What she witnessed was imprinted on her brain for the rest of her life. Her two brothers had torn the woman's dress to expose her bare breasts, had tied her hands and feet with straps to the bedposts forcing her to lay there with her legs and arms straddled wide apart. Tears streamed down the helpless woman's face as she felt another smack of Damion's belt across her body. Laughing, aroused and obviously enjoying their sense of power and control, Damion and Stefano were using this poor woman's body for their own sexual delight and release. And Cassandra had unfortunately become a witness to their cruelty. When Stefano noticed his little sister standing in the doorway, he invited her in saying "Come here Cassie, I have something for you to play with." Reluctantly, Cassandra walked slowly toward her brother. He took her hand and guided her to caress this defenseless woman's breasts and private parts as he whispered quietly in Cassandra's ear: "This is what a beautiful woman's body feels like. Soon you will be a grown up woman and men will feel your body too. But be careful. Do not go out by yourself to a bar. We decided to teach this young lady a lesson she will never forget. Women belong at home, waiting for their man, or chaperoned by their brothers."

Cassandra ran back to her room, shaking with the horror of what she had seen and wishing she had never seen it. In the morning, the woman was sent away without breakfast, wearing that same tattered dress. Damion and Stefano joined the family at the breakfast table, eating with gusto and talking calmly as if nothing strange had happened. A woman's sense of self-worth and a young girl's innocence and trust had been destroyed and yet Cassandra's brothers felt not the slightest sense of remorse.

Although Cassandra was traumatized and disturbed by this incident, she felt that her 3 brothers loved her and would protect her from this type of danger. Nobody ever mentioned that night again. And she returned to her illusion that she lived in a safe and loving world and that she was the beloved princess of the house. At 8 years old, Cassandra's innocence had been shattered but she managed to hold the fragile pieces together for 8 more years, pretending to herself that she was exaggerating the significance of that night. She even fooled herself into half believing that the woman who had been tied up, beaten with a strap, and raped, had really wanted to play those games with the two men she had just met in a bar, Damion and Stefano.

3 CASSANDRA'S PUBERTY

At age 13, Cassandra had a huge scare. She didn't know what was happening to her body and she actually believed she might be dying. In her family she had been taught to be strong, that illness was often in the imagination, and that she had better have a good reason to call the doctor. Afraid to tell her mother that she was bleeding, she tried to stop the bleeding with paper towels and napkins from the kitchen cabinet. But the bleeding would not stop, no matter how many paper napkins she used to stop the flow. So she chose to wear black panties and black pants in case there was a leakage of blood.

As luck would have it, her mother insisted that she wear her new white dress to church that Sunday morning. Cassandra took some extra napkins and even a kitchen towel to protect against the bleeding. She reinforced that with two pairs of panties before slipping the dress over her body. Her plan was to do a lot of standing and only sit when absolutely necessary. Her plan did not work out well.

Damion decided to drive his brother Alexei's Fiat to church and he invited Cassandra to join him. She tried not to go, saying that she always drove with mom and dad and would feel more comfortable with them. Damion looked at her quizzically and said: "Don't be ridiculous. I'm your brother and you love riding in this car. Please stop your nonsense and get in the car or we'll be late for the services." Being the good and obedient sister that she was, Cassandra sat on that soft creamy leather seat all the way to the church. When she got out of the car, she glanced back at the seat and was relieved to see the pure creamy clean leather.

Once inside the church, she excused herself to go to the ladies room to check whether the bleeding had stopped. To her dismay, it was worse. Gobs of gooey blood had run through all the paper wetting the inside of her panties. So she took as much toilet paper as she could to protect her and she returned to the pew where her brother was anxiously awaiting her return. When he saw her approach he angrily asked her: "What's wrong with you? Are you trying to behave like a spoiled woman, keeping a man waiting while you freshen up? I'm your brother and you better not start playing with men's minds. That can be dangerous." Cassandra did not respond to Damion's anger. She was feeling worried about the bleeding and wanted to be careful not to let him know.

At the end of the sermon, Cassandra started to head for the bathroom again but her brother stopped her. Impatient and annoyed, he told her emphatically: "Stop playing games with me. We have to get home quickly because I have a date with a hot older woman who works at daddy's club. She promised to show me some new moves and we plan to spend the afternoon together." Once again, Cassandra behaved like a good girl and did not protest.

On the ride home, she felt kind of wet down below but she thought she was properly protected. When they arrived at the front of their house, Damion walked around to open the car door for her. Regardless of his ruthless and sometimes cruel disposition, he still had some gentlemanly manners. So he stood there holding the door open for her. As she stepped out of the car he was about to slam the door closed when he saw a stream of bright red blood. Horrified, he yelled at her: "Where did that come from? Did you do something bad with a boy without telling me? You little slut, you just ruined your brother's fine Italian leather car seat. Alexei will never forgive you. And I have a mind to give you a huge whipping. Just wait until I get home later."

Cassandra ran into the house sobbing hysterically. The blood was streaming down her legs and she just wanted to die. She ran up the stairs to her room, rushed to sit on the toilet, immediately removing all the bloody paper. She dumped it all into the sink, removed her dress and sobbed uncontrollably. After wiping herself, she took a quick shower, stuffed her crotch with as much paper as she could put there and put on a pair of black panties. Then she rinsed off the bloody papers that she had dumped into the sink and buried them inside a huge roll of toilet paper. She threw that into the trash bin. Then she looked at the back of her white dress, streaked all the way down with blood. She tore the dress and then threw it into that same trash bin, got into bed and sobbed into her pillow. This was Cassandra's introduction to puberty.

Soon after she had crawled into her bed, she heard a knock at the door and Alexei's noticeably anguished tone. Cassie, he yelled, "How could you do this? You know how much I love my new car; it's the pride and joy of my life. You just ruined that expensive designer leather seat. What's wrong with you? Are you becoming one of those selfish women who just take away what a man works so hard to get? I'm so disappointed in you." And he stormed away mumbling: "Maybe if I really scrub the seat with that new leather cleaner, I can get rid of those awful stains."

Cassandra did not get out of bed the rest of the day and evening, even after her mother had called several times for her to come down for dinner. At about 9 PM, Damion returned home and immediately ran up to Cassandra's bedroom. He didn't knock on the door; he just barged into the room unexpectedly. Cassandra had been sobbing and whimpering on and off the entire day. When he saw her eyes swollen from all that crying, instead of feeling empathy he felt a renewed sense of anger. And he proceeded to remove his belt strap.

What he did next broke Cassandras's heart and spirit. He ordered her to remove her nightie because he didn't want to tear it. Shaking with fear, she listened to him. Lying face down with her head buried in the pillow he lashed her across her butt and her back several times until he caused her skin to bleed. Finally, he decided to stop and he changed his tone to a semblance of caring. Sitting down beside her on the bed, he gently stroked her wounded skin which actually made it burn and hurt even more. Softly he whispered in her ear. "You are my sister Cassie. I want you to be better than those other sluts I meet but I am worried about you." And he left the room.

Cassandra's mother had been oblivious to what was going on. She had no idea that her sweet little daughter had just gotten her period. Lyzandra had not been told that Cassandra's bleeding had stained her brother's expensive leather car seat. And Lyzandra had no idea how brutal and cruel her well behaved sons would treat her daughter when they were upset. Having grown up in a strict and male dominated Greek family herself, Lyzandra knew better than to argue with or confront the man of the house. And in this house, there were 3 men living there and one who visited regularly. Even though she was their mother, Lyzandra was an obedient woman. She respected and honored her sons and had no concept that her daughter needed her protection.

On this night, however, Lyzandra was concerned that her darling daughter had not joined the family for dinner. After washing and drying the dishes, which went much slower without Cassandra's assistance since none of the men ever helped, Lyzandra went up to her daughter's room to find out what was wrong. When she got there, she found her darling daughter Cassandra tucked under the covers and crying softly. Lyzandra walked slowly toward the bed, feeling a deep sadness in her heart. "What's wrong my baby?" she asked her suffering daughter. Finally, finally, someone cared about how

Cassandra felt. She poured out her heart to her mother, explaining that she had been bleeding for two days now and was afraid to talk about it. Her mother laughed and hugged and rocked her daughter, reassuring her that this was a normal part of growing up. Lyzandra used this moment to explain male-female sexual attraction and how sexual contact can lead to the creation of a new human being. They didn't talk about Damion's cruelty. And Cassandra did not tell her mother about that time she had seen her two older brothers rape and beat a woman they had met that night at her daddy's club.

After that painful and embarrassing menstrual beginning for Cassandra, her mother provided an abundant supply of sanitary pads and tampons. Cassandra never again had to worry about bleeding onto her clothing or anyone's car seat during her menstrual period. She had learned the hard way and was always well prepared in advance.

What she was not prepared for was the sudden rush of powerful emotions when her hormones began to rage. It caught her quite by surprise. She could actually recall the exact moment, that very first moment when she felt a strange and unfamiliar tingle in her body. A boy had just smiled at her and she felt a flush spreading through her entire system. This was the tall and lanky boy, Peter, who lived next door. She had known him since they were toddlers. They had played neighborhood games together with her brothers and the other neighborhood boys and girls. Cassandra remembered how funny he had been when she had thrown a softball at him and he had fallen backwards, landing on the ground. When he instantly jumped right back up they all got hysterical laughing. The group used to play wrestling games and they created special hiking contests in the woods. Peter had been her hiking partner on many occasions. He was just the boy next door. She had always liked him, but on this one day something changed.

It was a warm and sunny summer day. She was wearing a form fitting, strapless, stretchy blouse and Peter was in a playful mood. When he got close to her he playfully tugged downward at her top and it temporarily dropped below her budding breasts. Before she could pull her blouse back up, he had stopped to stare. He couldn't believe what he was seeing and she felt his eyes piercing her body. She felt that flush spread all over her. Part of her wanted to run away and hide. Although her mind told her to be embarrassed, what she felt was something very strange and new. For a moment, it was as if she was in a hypnotic trance. Instead of automatically pulling her blouse back up, she let it linger below her breasts enjoying the sensation of his eyes focused on her body. Then her rational mind took over and she adjusted her elastic blouse to insure that it was once again fully covering her chest. She turned and ran home. At 14 years old, she had discovered what every woman sooner or later learns: her body is an instrument of joy for men. She was so happy to have discovered these new and exciting sensations. Cassandra's life as a woman was about to begin and she could not have possibly imagined what lay in store for her in the coming years.

4 CASSANDRA MEETS CYRANO

Cassandra developed into a lovely and quite voluptuous young woman. At 16, she was elected Beauty Queen of the year at her high school. It seemed as if all the local boys were infatuated with her. She had about 20 invitations to attend the year end dance where she was about to be crowned queen. Receiving so much positive attention, Cassandra walked with an attitude of elegance and confidence with a bit of snobbishness thrown in. Men her age were fascinated, intimidated and actually terrified of her beauty and elegance. Girls could often be seen gossiping and even making up cruel lies about the motives behind Cassandra's actions.

Just as she lived to please her father and her 3 brothers, Cassandra also wanted to please all the men at her school and in the neighborhood. When they flirted with her, she carefully flirted back but was always ladylike and even prudish in her responses. The boys loved her even more for that. None of them would even consider attempting to take advantage of her, first because she was such a proper lady and second, because they knew they would have to answer to one of the men in her family. And her father was quite well-connected on the island. Anyone who would attempt to violate someone in his family, especially his beloved and only daughter, would have to face some unimaginably cruel consequences.

The more popular Cassandra became with the men and boys, the less accepted she was by the girls. From an early age, she had always felt more comfortable with boys than with girls. She was a strikingly beautiful child who had inherited large piercing blue eyes, high cheek bones, full and flowing hair with natural golden highlights, and a body that became rounder and more voluptuous with every passing year. At 16, she was in her prime, and she could feel the eyes of all the boys watching her and their hearts pounding as she walked by. The boys, with their hormones raging, had to contain their excitement and be very careful how they approached her.

One boy became the example that nobody else wanted to become. Nicholas Pappas was a handsome young man, standing about 6'2" with broad shoulders and the type of muscular body that artists love to draw. As captain of the high school soccer team, Nicholas was outspoken, aggressive and felt as if he was on top of the world. He was brazen and arrogant and could often be found speaking to women in an inappropriate, even offensive manner, smirking when the girl would blush with embarrassment and turn away.

On one occasion Nicholas walked by Cassandra, stopped to stare at her breasts, and acted as if he was talking directly to her body saying "Hello beautiful ladies." Another time he approached her from behind, gently tapped her butt and told her "Your body is built for pleasure." She was about to turn around and tell Nicholas that he was out of line and ought to watch his words. But before she got a chance to say anything, her brother Damion, the one with the violent temper, had stopped by the school to tell her something he wanted her to do that afternoon. As Damion walked toward his younger sister, he overheard Nicholas' words. But Damion thought he had heard Nicholas say "Your body is built for a penis." Without hesitating even for an instant, Damion punched Nicholas in the stomach, knocked him to the floor and started kicking him until a few other boys jumped on Damion to make him stop. When the principal was informed about the incident, he immediately left his office and rushed to the outer hall to find out exactly what was happening. Seeing Nicholas sprawled out on the floor, obviously bruised and even bleeding, the principal actually gave him a warning, saying: "The young ladies in this school are educated and proper. We pride ourselves on teaching the men to show respect. Your actions are a poor reflection on the school. We trust you have learned an important lesson here."

The principal had been informed, before he left his office, that Damion had gotten out of control, had punched Nicholas and had started kicking him. But nobody would dare to confront Damion and take the chance of losing the large endowment donated each year by Mr. Melanakos, Damion's father.

After that incident, none of the boys would go near Cassandra. The girls had already distanced themselves from her out of jealousy. Now the boys also made sure to stay away from her out of fear that something bad would happen. She held her head up high, added a decisive wiggle to her walk, opened her jacket often to expose her curves in the latest form fitting sweater, and smiled to herself knowing the boys were nervously and secretly excited by her beauty.

Her brothers hovered around her at home or on those rare occasions when she was invited to a party. Feeling smothered and stifled, she would do the only thing she was free to do on her own – ride her pretty pink bicycle for a few blocks. As long as she rode in the neighborhood during daylight hours, her brothers did not worry about her. They knew that all the local boys would never forget what happened to Nicholas, just for saying a few slightly off color remarks to their little sister, Cassandra.

Nobody in the family, at the school or anywhere in the entire town, could have anticipated what was about to happen to Cassandra. She was so youthful, sweet, playful and innocent. The shopkeepers loved to speak with her because she talked about history and geography and politics and all sorts of subjects that most young ladies had no interest in. Yes, Cassandra was highly intelligent, extremely beautiful, and growing sexier every day but nobody would dare to mention that or attempt to touch her.

It was 3 days before Easter. A navy ship had pulled into the harbor to celebrate Easter at this Greek island paradise, a few days early, before heading out to sea again. Cassandra was riding her bike along the water, the same path she had taken every day for the past few weeks. In the distant harbor she got a glimpse of a strange looking, rather large and unusual boat. She had never actually seen a naval ship before. So she decided to go into the park at the end of the road before the turn that leads to town, because the ship was in the harbor right in back of the park. Her curiosity had been aroused so she rode her bicycle through the park in the direction of where the ship was docked. As she looked around, Cassandra was so happy that spring was here. Flowers were beginning to bloom, leaves were starting to fill the trees, and the sun was shining brightly. Looking carefully for a bike rack in the shade, she found one only a few hundred feet from the dock. Carefully, she positioned her bike so it would not fall or get scratched by a nearby bicycle.

As Cassandra walked toward the ship, a group of sailors passed by and waved to her. They looked so handsome and manly in their uniforms. She was eager to meet one of the soldiers and find out why they were in town. Only a few hundred feet from the boat, she noticed a young man sitting quietly on a nearby bench. Unlike her usual standoffish attitude, today she was feeling warm and welcoming. She decided to approach this young man to say hello. As she started walking toward him, he looked in her direction and a broad smile spread across his face. He had not seen a woman in many months and he thought to himself, "She might be the most beautiful woman I have ever seen, maybe even the most beautiful woman in the world."

Standing right in front of him, she reached out her hand in an offer to greet him with a handshake. Eagerly, he touched her hand and she felt electric sparks jolt through her body. He held her hand firmly, with a strong and powerful grip that she found delightful. The words just flew out of her mouth: "Welcome to our little island. We don't often have the privilege of visits from the navy. What is this ship doing here and where are you headed?"

As he began to speak in a kind of broken Greek, she realized he was probably not from Greece. He had an accent she had never heard before and she found it intriguing. In fact, she felt mesmerized by him – his presence, his handshake, and now his words. Her heart was pounding so loudly she was sure he could hear her. He spoke in a soft and inviting tone, stumbling a bit over his words. "I am Greek, my parents are from Greece, but my dad found a business opportunity in Australia and moved there a year after I was born. I can speak a little bit of broken Greek but English is really my language. The ship is here because the captain and a few of the sailors, like me, are natives of Greece and still have some family here. I have been visiting my grandfather, Hermes, and my uncle, Basileus, my father's brother. The commanding officer has given us permission to spend a few days here before we are sent away for an important, scary and dangerous mission to Vietnam, the place where there is a brutal war going on."

Cassandra found herself glued to the conversation. Having heard many stories of atrocities happening in Vietnam, she felt intense concern for this handsome and soft spoken man who was about to embark on a dangerous mission. To her, she had met the man of her dreams and she realized it could only be temporary. It was the beginning of April and she knew her time with this very special man would be limited. She vowed in that moment to make time in the next few days to see him as often as possible until his ship would be departing. Since they both could only meet in the middle of the afternoon at the park, she was confident that her brothers would never find out. All three brothers held an attitude about this park, saying it was for the lower class local people and tourists. They felt it was beneath their dignity to spend any time among the common folk.

Eager to find out all she could about this handsome sailor, she asked him his name. "Cyrano Niles Maniatis," he answered, "but my friends call me Cyrano. And what may I ask is your name, beautiful lady of my dreams?" Cassandra quickly replied "Cassandra Sybil Melanakos - my brothers call me Cassie. I have three very protective brothers. And my father owns the biggest nightclub on the island, **The Cyprus Club**. Have you heard of it?" "Of course," he said. "The guys on the boat dragged me there last night. What a display of gorgeous women."

Cassandra suddenly felt deflated and a bit uneasy. Noticing her bodily response, Cyrano immediately reassured her: "Cassie - may I call you that?" She nodded as if to say "Yes." "Cassie, the women at your father's club are quite attractive but the moment I laid eyes upon you I felt there could never be anyone else in my life to compare. You are the most beautiful woman I have ever seen – and – I can't believe you walked up to greet me. I am truly a lucky man. You must have hundreds of boys just clamoring to spend a few moments with you, to stroke your flowing hair and caress your rounded and voluptuous body. As I speak, I can hardly keep my hands away from you. Cassie, I want you. I feel such a strong desire to hold you in my arms, to kiss you all over and to tell you 100 times that I love you and will always love you. Even though we have just met, I know we share a very deep longing that can only be fulfilled with each other."

Her body felt as if it was on fire. The surging of her hormones made her want to jump into his arms and let him tear her clothes off right out here in front of everyone at the park. But of course she kept her composure and reminded him that she has 3 older brothers and a very powerful, strong, domineering father. She glanced at her watch and a suddenly frantic expression covered her face. "I didn't realize it is getting so late. I must get home immediately or one of my brothers will badger me with questions later, and maybe even beat me again."

She turned to leave and he grabbed her left wrist with a concerned look on his face. "Cassie, my dearest, are you telling me that your brothers beat you? If I ever saw that I would want to kill them. You are so sweet and innocent and beautiful. Anyone can tell by just looking at you that you are kind and loving and live to please a man. Let me be that man. Love me, Cassie. I can't wait to see you again. I will be here tomorrow afternoon, same time, at 2 PM. Please meet me again. My heart is already aching with desire and longing. The hours will move slowly tonight and I will dream about you when I sleep."

Cassandra told him she would try to be there but could not promise. He said, "I will wait for you at 2 PM every day while I am here. If you never return, I want you to know that this has been the best day of my life and I believe I already am starting to love you. Please come back tomorrow my beautiful Cassandra. We belong together. We can make each other so very happy. Sleep well tonight my love."

She walked back toward her bicycle, her legs shaking so much that she thought she might fall at any moment. Once she mounted her bicycle and started riding, she felt as if she was gliding in the air and that feeling lasted the entire ride home. At the house, she took the bike to the back and saw her brother Alexei washing and waxing his beautiful car. He smiled when he saw her and asked "Did you have a nice ride today? Where did you go?"

She couldn't tell her brother she had stopped at the park and met the most incredible sailor. In fact, she didn't want to even mention that she had been riding her bicycle through the park. So for the first time in her life, she lied to her favorite brother, the one who was never cruel to her and always watched out to protect her. She answered him by saying "I rode along the lake path and turned toward the town, and then I turned back and went in the complete opposite direction. The sun was shining. It was warm. The leaves are starting to show on the trees and there were flowers on the side of the road. It really is so beautiful on our island."

"Glad you had a pleasant ride." Alexei responded. "You really love that pink bicycle, don't you? In only a couple of years, you'll have your own snazzy car and then maybe you'll understand why I treat my red baby Fiat so well."

Cassandra reminded her brother that they both ought to freshen up and get ready for dinner. She turned to go into the house and felt so excited inside that she had difficulty putting her key into the keyhole. Once inside she yelled out to her mother. "I'm just going upstairs to wash up. I'll be right down to help you get dinner ready." And then she quickly ran up the stairs to her bedroom.

5 LOVE WITH A PROPER STRANGER

At home only a few hours after her meeting with this stranger at the park, Cassandra's heart was still pounding softly and her body felt tingly all over. She thought a shower might calm her down. It did. She stayed under the hot water for a long time, letting it gradually wash away the strange and new sensations she had been feeling. Lathering her body in a state of hypnotic rapture, she imagined sharing her shower with this new and wonderful man. Smiling inside, she thought about how upset the men in her family would be to know that their little Cassie had erotic thoughts about a total stranger, a sailor from far away.

At dinner she ate voraciously, filling her newly discovered sensual openness with food. Damion noticed that his sister's appetite seemed stronger than usual and he immediately admonished her: "Better watch out Cassie. If you keep eating like that, you'll get fat like the old matrons you see in town. You don't want to be an old maid, do you?" She ignored his comments and took a second helping of the potatoes and vegetables that she loved. And then she ate a big piece of her mother's freshly baked Karidopita cake which she just could not resist. After dinner, she announced that she was tired and would be retiring early. Nobody questioned her and she quietly went up to her room.

Her hot shower, the full meal and that delicious piece of walnut cake had calmed her down. But her mind was still racing. The minutes seemed to be dragging by so slowly. It was still early but all she wanted was to go to sleep and hopefully to dream about being with this new man, Cyrano Niles Maniatis. She really liked his first name because of this play she had seen called "Cyrano de Bergerac" in which the actor had a huge and obstructive nose, felt he was ugly and undesirable, but touched the heart of a woman through his poems. Her Cyrano seemed to possess that poetic quality, yet she found him to be handsome, manly, well-built and extremely confident. She had never before met a man quite like him.

In fact, the only "men" she really knew were her brothers and some of their friends – and then, of course, all the older men like her father and her friends' and neighbors' fathers. The boys at her school were immature, childish, and seemed to be insecure and nervous around girls, especially around girls they were attracted to. Many of these boys were obviously attracted to Cassandra and often behaved strangely in her presence – dropping things, stuttering, or acting silly. She would flirt with all the boys but had never felt the desire to get close to any of them.

Tonight she wished she was a writer or a composer, a poet or an artist. She wanted to capture, in words or music or art, the intensity of these strange and wonderful bodily sensations. Part of her wanted to scream at the top of her lungs, dance like there was no tomorrow, and beat a drum so loudly that the whole town would feel the vibrations. Waiting for this night to end felt almost unbearable. She knew she would have difficulty sleeping but she could not bring herself to talk to anyone, to play cards with her brothers, to watch a program on TV, or to listen to the radio. Nothing could possibly please her between now and the time she would once again be looking at that wonderful handsome sailor.

Cassandra slipped into her favorite pink silk nightie which matched her fluffy pink slippers. After spending extra time on this night washing her face, combing her hair and putting that special night cream all over her face and neck, she finally climbed into bed. Unable to sleep, she tossed and turned and finally went back into the bathroom. There she decided to put some of that sweet smelling cream on her legs and arms and the rest of her body. As she stroked herself, she imagined what it would be like to have this big, powerful and gentle man touch her breasts and stroke and caress her entire body. She imagined that he would love feeling the texture of her skin and that he would express his desire with the most loving words. With her eyes closed, she could almost feel his tender and sensual touch extending to every part of her body. The longing intensified as she spread the cream across her breasts and down the inside of her thighs. Cassandra loved her curvaceous, developing body and she knew that Cyrano would be delighted with her.

After several more hours, Cassandra finally fell asleep and found herself in a beautiful, heavenly garden. And there he was - this handsome sailor who had captured her heart, this specimen of manhood, Cyrano. He reached out to her. She reached out to him. They touched. They embraced. The energy between them was electric. They kissed and vowed to love each other for eternity. Her eyes were closed. She felt ecstatic. But when she opened her eyes, he was gone. Some strange dark figure stood in back of her, ready to grab her. She tried to run away but whichever direction she wanted to go, she could only see another dark figure waiting. Scared, with no place to go, she surrendered. And then she suddenly woke up and realized she had been dreaming. Cassandra was afraid to fall asleep again because that dream had frightened her. She had felt trapped with no escape.

Wondering what the dream meant, if it did have a meaning, she realized that perhaps she was feeling trapped by her family, her 3 brothers always watching over her. She thought that maybe the dream was telling her to just surrender, to let her brothers be who they are, and allow herself to be protected by them. That thought lasted for a little while. And then she remembered. "What about Cyrano, that handsome sailor I just met. If I surrender to my brothers' wishes, then I will never see that man again. And my heart will be broken and uneasy forever. I must see him. I must defy my brothers. They have enjoyed the company of many women. Why can't I enjoy the company of this one man? It's just not fair and I won't allow it. Anyway, they will never know." They say that what you don't know won't hurt you. In Cassandra's case, what she didn't know was about to destroy her current way of life - forever.

When the sunlight entered her room, she jumped out of bed, went to take another shower, scrubbed her hair, styled it with her hair dryer and comb, and created soft flowing curls. She chose her favorite necklace, the one her mother and she had carefully designed with a 24 karat gold heart surrounded by tiny diamonds on an intertwined triple strand gold chain. Since she was planning to ride her bicycle, she could not wear one of her favorite dresses so she chose a pair of navy blue stretch pants with a pink angora sweater. Although it was springtime, the air was still a bit crisp and she loved the way that sweater showed off her curves.

Before going downstairs for breakfast, she turned to the right, to the left and even made a complete turn while gazing appreciatively in the mirror. Yes, she liked this outfit and was sure that her new man, Cyrano, would be quite pleased to see her. She actually threw herself a kiss, then slipped into her pink sneakers, walked into the hall and shut her bedroom door behind her.

On this particular morning, everyone in the family was busy. Alexei was meeting some friends to go hiking. Damion was planning to help his father collect money from a few of their regular customers who had been charging their bills and had not yet paid. Lyzandra had gone to get her hair cut and styled at the local salon. Cassandra poured herself some coffee from the pot that was still warm. She took a milk container from the refrigerator, poured the desired amount, returned the milk container to its previous place, and sat down to eat.

Then she cut open some pita bread and put a few slices of cheese and tomato inside. As she ate her breakfast, she fantasized about the afternoon ahead of her. Since she had slept late and taken a long time to get ready, it was now almost 1 PM. Her plan was to meet Cyrano at the agreed upon 2 PM hour.

She went to the garage to find her bicycle and decided to clean it with a towel. Then she reached for the car wax she had seen Alexei patiently and carefully apply to his beloved Fiat. She waxed her bicycle and wiped it until it shined. Then she went inside, washed her hands, and came out again ready to take her bike for a ride. Little did she know that this bike ride, and the events that would follow, were about to change her life forever. Today, Cassandra felt as if she was on top of the world, that she had the power and capacity to do anything and be anything she desired. And what she wanted more than anything on this beautiful spring day was to spend time with her handsome Cyrano.

Cassandra rode her bicycle carefully down the winding path leading from her home to the lakeside road below. She noticed the flowers had grown a bit larger and the leaves were pushing their way out into the open. It was another beautiful day. She actually stopped at one point to look out at the water and feel the beauty and serenity of her environment. A bit nervous, she wanted to take a moment to gain her composure and prepare for what she knew would be a powerful greeting.

She continued to ride her bicycle along the familiar leading to the park. When she finally arrived at the park she headed in the direction of the navy ship. Cassandra could see the ship anchored in the distance and she noticed several sailors walking around the park, some with ladies they had probably met that day or the night before. When she arrived at the bike rack, she parked her bicycle and looked toward the bench. It had never occurred to her that Cyrano would not be there. But he was nowhere to be seen. Her heart sank. She felt deflated and more than disappointed. Her heart ached so much that she thought she would be unable to bear the pain. She decided to wait at the same bench where she had met him. So she walked over to the bench with her head down, revealing the intense sadness she was feeling at the mere thought of never seeing her new man again.

As she walked toward the bench, she did not glance around her. Cyrano had been chatting with a few of his ship mates and had not noticed that she had arrived. When he saw her headed toward the bench, he walked toward her from behind. As she was about to sit down, she was startled by a hand on her shoulder. But she recognized his touch in an instant by the electric jolt she felt in her system. Standing close behind her, Cyrano whispered in her ear: "I am so glad you came back today," and he turned her around to look directly at her face and into her piercing blue eyes. That broad and confident smile spread across his face. She loved that big dimple in his chin and the slight dimple on his right cheek. Cassandra could not keep her eyes off him. She was studying every crevice of his face, feeling enthralled by his very presence, wanting to remember everything she was seeing in him.

They both sat down at the same time and his right hand slipped onto her left thigh, lingering there for quite a while. Neither of them made any gesture to remove his hand. Cassandra could feel the moisture building in her private parts, a sensation she had never felt before. He imagined what it would be like to touch her more intimately and he kept his hand on her thigh, letting the fantasy build in his imagination. But he didn't have to actually touch her there; she felt his hand directly from his thoughts. She had always had a strange way of feeling other people's energy but this time it was sensual, even sexual, and unfamiliar to her. Outwardly quiet and serene, their insides were burning with desire for each other. Cassandra could not understand why she felt such strong sensations. She had heard her brothers talk about this and she had read about it in some of her brothers' hidden books that she had looked at when they were not around. But now she was actually feeling these strange and wonderful sensations.

Cyrano asked if she would like to take a walk with him and she instantly nodded as if to say "Yes." Together they walked toward a section of the park, not far from the ship, that had a tall hedge surrounding a large weeping willow tree. Behind the hedge, they were in their own private world. Cyrano wrapped his strong arms around her waist, pulled her close to him and pressed his lips against hers. She did not resist. She could not resist. Cassandra, pure and innocent Cassandra, was swept away with passion for this man she hardly knew. He moved his hands down her back to feel the round softness of her firm butt and she let his hands remain there for several minutes. She felt the moistness inside her groin as he leaned his pelvis into her body. Again, she did not and could not resist. For her, this was the most amazing bodily experience she had ever had. She had the sense that she was being devoured by this strong and handsome man and all she could think about was giving him more and more of her whole self. Holding each other firmly, they sat close together for a few hours on the small wooden bench next to the tree. Neither said a word but each somehow knew what the other was thinking.

At one point, Cassandra pulled away from Cyrano and checked her watch. It was already 4 PM and she realized it was time to leave. Cyrano grabbed her and held her close, smothering her face and neck with warm gentle kisses. Then he whispered in her ear, over and over and over, "I want you, baby, I want you. Cassie I want you so much. Let me have you before I leave for this awful war. I may never return and I want to have this one special memory. I know you want it to. I want you, baby, I want you."

Cassandra knew she wanted this man, more than she had ever wanted anyone or anything. Once again, her legs were really shaky as she walked away to get her bicycle. She didn't look back when he called out to her: "See you tomorrow my love. Please be here. I need to be with you. I can't wait till we are together again." She pedaled fast and furiously, attempting to override the intense physical sensations that she could not deny. Her body longed to be with him. Nothing but his strong arms could bring her the joy and release she was craving. She thought about him the entire ride home.

She rushed home knowing that the family would be expecting her to assist with the food and festivities. This was Good Friday, two days before Easter Sunday, and it was a tradition for the whole family to be together. When she arrived home, she put her bicycle away, waved hello to her brothers who were all sitting in the living room, and she said to them: "I'll be right down." They could all feel that something was different about the way their sister was acting. But they were so absorbed in their discussion that they didn't pay much attention to her.

Cassandra quickly showered and changed into a lovely violet and white trimmed chiffon dress with matching shoes and pretty hair clips. She had gotten her clothing ready before leaving on her bike ride. When she came downstairs and entered the living room, Stefano, her oldest brother, who had come to spend the night, was the first to speak. He teased Cassandra by saying: "Wow. My little sister, do you know how sexy you are becoming?" She felt a bit more confident that night, so she did not shy away and look sheepish but she just stood tall and looked at him. Her newfound strength intrigued Stefano, making him more aggressive in his sexual teasing and knowing. He grabbed one of her breasts and said, jokingly with a sense of power and control, "These belong to me. If I ever catch you giving these to someone else, he will be in trouble but you will be in worse trouble. Women have to know their place. My little sister, Cassie, if you weren't my sister I would be bringing you upstairs right now so we could have a go at it. I'm a hot and sexually healthy guy. But since I can't have you in that way, I will certainly not allow some strange man to taste the goodies. Do you understand?" It was as if Stefano had a sense that Cassandra was about to get herself into serious trouble and he was forewarning her.

6 EASTER HOLIDAY

The day before Easter was a busy time in the Melanakos household. Lyzandra was heavily involved with preparing a lavish pre-Easter dinner and the even more elaborate Easter Sunday meal. Cassandra, as usual, was required to set the table and to wash all the fine silverware and those special gold-plated designer plates used only for holiday meals. Once the family and guests were relaxing in the living room, she knew it would be her job to prepare and serve the hors d'oeuvres, the drinks and whatever was needed by anybody. If one of the men, her brothers, her father, or her grandfather happened to notice her take a bite of an appetizer, she knew they would immediately warn her to be careful not to overeat because she could lose that perfect slim body. So she would often sneak a taste in the kitchen before bringing the tray out to the family.

This year, Stefano and Damion had both invited their recent girlfriends, Adonia and Rhea, to join the family festivities. Grandma and Grandpa Melanakos would be arriving mid-afternoon and planned to stay in one of the lovely guest rooms. Lyzandra's parents, Abiron and Theodora Papadakis, had to take care of some family business and promised to get there just in time for dinner. Since they had a habit of arriving later than the other guests, Cassandra's mother planned to start serving dinner at the appointed time, even if her parents had not yet arrived. Demitri's brother, Abrax, and his sister, Loanna, were planning to arrive on Sunday late morning. Lyzandra's two sisters, Chloe and Delia, would be arriving before breakfast to attend the morning mass on Easter Sunday with the family.

Easter was Cassandra's favorite holiday because she felt an intense connection with the spirit of Jesus that was heightened during mass. She could see a clear image of Jesus' persecution and his resurrection. Although she rarely talked about it, Cassandra felt she had a direct connection with the Holy Spirit and the healing powers that Jesus displayed. Late at night she would often go into a deep trance in which she heard conversations and received revelations about people she knew. Cassandra knew things she could not have known any other way and this information often scared her. She rarely told anybody what she had seen. Sometimes she found herself predicting a specific illness or disease, a violent incident or a betrayal of trust but she usually kept this knowledge to herself. She was always amazed when her predictions came true. Nobody would have believed that Cassandra had this rare gift.

She knew she should have told Cyrano that she would not be able to see him the day before Easter or on Easter

Sunday. But she had been so caught up in that intense hormonal rush and those incredibly wonderful thoughts and feelings that she actually forgot for the moment that it was Easter weekend. Now, as she prepared the table and the appetizers and helped her mother with the cooking and other details, her mind was racing. Her body felt as if it was pulling her toward the door. All she wanted to do was to leave the house, get on her bicycle and ride as quickly as she could toward the park to see the man of her dreams. But of course she could not tell anyone in her family that she had gone to the park and she certainly could not explain that she was uncontrollably attracted to a total stranger from another continent.

Her body carried out all the required tasks but Cassandra's mind was a few miles away, imagining a scene that made her feel so sad. She could actually see that handsome man sitting on the bench, looking impatiently in the direction of the bicycle rack, feeling disappointed, hurt and even a bit angry. Cassandra was not just imagining this scene. She could actually see him sitting there and she could actually feel what he was feeling. Since she was a very young child she had been able to see and feel things that other people were seeing and feeling. This unique ability did not bring her happiness. Rather, she felt strange and different from others for as long as she could recall. And still at 16 years old, she had managed to never reveal to anyone else that she had these powerful and unique psychic abilities. At this point she was aching with emotional pain that was not just her own. She knew she was also feeling Cyrano's disappointment and fear that he might never see her again.

Cyrano sat on that park bench for about 3 hours, waiting and hoping to catch a glimpse of that beautiful young lady who would arrive on her pink bicycle. His heart felt so heavy. His head drooped as he thought to himself: "She is very attached to her family. They love her and protect her. Maybe she told them she had met me. Maybe she thinks I'm too old for her. Maybe I was imagining that she felt the same way I did. Maybe I will never see that beautiful young lady again. How can I go off to this war feeling such a great loss? I must see Cassie again. I told her I would wait for her every day while I'm here and I will."

Finally, as the blue sky gave way to dark gray clouds that became thicker and more ominous by the minute, he realized it was about to pour and he ran back to the ship. Cyrano could not sleep that night. He tossed and turned and felt his eyes fill up with tears. He had finally met a lady he could love and she may be gone forever. In the morning he got up extra early, rushed through his chores on the ship and returned to that park bench by 11 AM. He sat there for about 6 hours, not even thinking about food. His heart was aching and his body longed for her gentle, sweet touch. He could not understand why she had not returned after they had shared such a beautiful moment in time together.

When Cyrano finally made his way back to the ship it was already dark. It wasn't until late Sunday afternoon, around 4 PM, that one of his ship buddies wished him a happy Easter. This was the first time he had been made aware of the holiday. While on the ship they rarely focused on holidays or other special events. Birthdays would maybe lead to a pat on the back or some kind words but there were no celebrations. When he realized it was Easter weekend, his heart felt so much lighter. He breathed a sigh of relief and understood that Cassandra could not possibly explain to her family that she had met a sailor from Australia. They would certainly not have allowed her to return to the park. Cyrano thought to himself: "If I had a beautiful daughter or sister like Cassandra, I would not want her to hang out at a local park with some total stranger from another country or continent. I certainly hope she has the good sense to not mention our encounter to her family. If they find out, she will never return to me." He felt encouraged and worried at the same time, but relieved that she was not purposely avoiding contact with him.

Cassandra had felt sad and dejected, worried and heart weary throughout Saturday evening, during Sunday morning and even Sunday afternoon mass. Of course, she put on a smiling face and behaved as if she was content and all was well. But her insides were churning with emotional anguish. And then suddenly, around 4 PM, just as the family began to gather for Easter dinner, Cassandra felt the internal cloud lifting. In that moment, she knew that Cyrano had finally realized it was Easter weekend and that he now understood that she had to be with her family. She also knew that he would be expecting her to be with him the day after Easter Sunday. And she had every intention to do just that. She could hardly contain her excitement once the emotional pain was gone.

Easter Sunday was quite uneventful. Her brothers behaved so gentlemanly and debonair with their lady friends that Cassandra felt as if she must have been a really bad girl to have been beaten by them on several occasions. Only Alexei had not brought a girl, so he sat close to Cassandra and chatted quietly with her through most of this holiday weekend. Right at the point when the emotional pain had lifted, Alexei asked his sister to go for a ride with him. It had stopped raining and with the convertible top down, she felt the gentle breeze cooling her excitement about the adventure she was about to have. She knew the event was coming. She had already seen it happen since she could not only see present events but she could see the future and the past, exactly the way it was going to happen or had already happened. Her sexual innocence and purity was about to be gone – forever - and she knew it before it happened. But what she did not know consciously, even though her dreams were telling her, was that there would be severe consequences and she would suffer a great deal for a long time.

7 ECSTATIC ANTICIPATION

Monday had finally arrived. Cassandra was awakened by the sound of a bluebird chirping sweetly to its companion. Her body felt alive and energized and ready for something new. She had a sense that the ultimate experience of her life was about to happen and that nothing would be able to interfere. Cassandra knew in her gut that her life was about to change – forever. What she did not know on this fateful morning, the dire consequences of her actions, is the only thing that could have stopped her from following her heart's desire. Cassandra's body tingled from head to toe just at the thought of gazing at that handsome man again. She imagined feeling his warm and strong hands gently touching and exploring all the curves and crevices of her body.

Cassandra knew that Cyrano would be there waiting for her at their appointed time. She was relieved to know that he understood that she had been obligated to spend the Easter weekend with her family. Cassandra had seen the whole picture, him sitting on that bench for hours feeling forlorn and betrayed. She saw him finally return to his ship, feeling defeated and lost. And she also saw him talk to a ship mate on Sunday, realize it was Easter and that Cassandra would, of course, be spending the holiday with her family. And she saw his face light up with a renewed sense of anticipation of once again seeing his beautiful Greek lady, Cassandra.

All she could think about was the ecstasy of being with him. She did not allow herself to even contemplate the fact that she was stepping into dangerous territory. Cassandra was beautiful and sexy and so very innocent. She could not fathom the emotional and physical anguish that would ensue from her reckless sensual abandon.

At 16 years old, she was hot and ready to explore her sensuality in a way she had never done before. She could see in her mind's crystal ball that Cyrano was planning to seduce her and persuade her to be intimate with him and that he was, at this very moment, telling one of his ship mates about his plans. Coming from her strict and macho family background, Cassandra should have instinctively resisted this pull to become a full-fledged woman. But she had no resistance. As if pulled by a silent magnetic wave, she could no more easily resist returning to that spot than she could give up being Cassandra. This was her fate pulling her toward her destiny and she was prepared to follow her heart and live her dream, even if the dream would shatter shortly afterwards. This act of family and cultural defiance would have long reaching impact, far beyond her own life and would determine the destiny and life purpose of her yet unborn daughter.

On this ominous morning, Cassandra took a very long time with her personal toiletries. She soaked her body in the bathtub, scrubbing away any rough edges with a loofa sponge her father had given to her from one of his foreign customers at the night club. She used the purest soap to wash her body and her hair, followed by 2 applications of that new cream rinse which would leave her hair soft and supple. As she dried herself with the huge pink bath towel that she loved, Cassandra glanced at her beautiful body in the mirror. Admiring that young lady in the mirror, she threw herself some kisses and smiled at the thought of her upcoming adventure.

The blouse she chose to wear was a purple silk and lace V-neck blouse, almost transparent, with carefully tapered darts to accentuate the lines from her slim waist to her full and rounded bust. To avoid any conflict with her family if they would see her, she slipped a simple camisole under the see-through blouse. But she was planning to remove the camisole before meeting Cyrano in the park. She wanted to absolutely tantalize him so that he could not even attempt to resist being with her. She knew he was a polite and well-mannered man and that he might be reticent to go too far with her because he knew she was a lady with a proper upbringing. So she planned to make her own intentions as clear as possible. The slacks she wore were black elastic with snaps that sealed the crotch area. This was a new style that many women really liked. Cassandra found that it was so easy to use a toilet without having to struggle with pulling down the pants. It was also easy to wear when she was menstruating because the snaps helped to hold the sanitary napkin in place. But on this occasion, Cassandra chose to wear the snap-up pants to make it as easy as possible to enjoy sensual pleasure with this wonderful man of her dreams.

The shoes she chose to wear had very low heels, so that she could be safe and comfortable riding her bicycle. Her purple socks were made of silk and felt smooth and luxurious on her feet. After assessing herself in the mirror and approving of the way she looked in her outfit, she returned to the bathroom to finish blowing and styling her hair. Scooping a small amount of special hair cream into the palm of her hand, Cassandra carefully spread it through her hair with her fingers first and then with a large comb. As she blew and styled her hair, she sprayed it with a special conditioner and hair spray to make it shiny, soft to the touch, and free from frizz. When she had finished, her hair was full and flowing and fluffy with long sensual curls. Cassandra put a small touch of foundation on her face, added a simple black line on her upper eyelids with only a hint of pastel purple eye shadow, and a pinch of pink color to highlight her high cheekbones. She looked breathtakingly beautiful and she knew it.

When she arrived at the breakfast table, Alexei was sitting there. He actually had to catch his breath and blurted out to her: "Oh my God, Cassie. You are so gorgeous. I am going to have to really guard you for the next few years to prevent some unscrupulous guy from doing something bad to you. Oh God, there are so many young boys and even older men who will lick their lips in utter hunger to get a glimpse of you or to be able to touch and stroke your skin. You really had better watch out."

It was as if Alexei had a premonition but was too afraid or disbelieving to question his gut feeling. He said nothing more but watched his sister carefully and waited on her throughout that breakfast. He watched her pour her juice and sit down to drink it. When she reached for the pot of coffee that had just been brewed, he stopped her arm, went to get it for her, and poured it into her cup. Then he opened the refrigerator and asked if she wanted some milk for the coffee. She nodded "Yes." When she indicated that she wanted a piece of toast, he jumped up to get it ready for her and he also brought some butter and jam. Alexei treated his beautiful sister, not like a princess, but like a queen. To him she was queen of the house and he held her on the highest pedestal imaginable. She was the woman of his dreams that he knew he could never have.

Alexei asked his sister if she wanted him to drive her anywhere. Knowing that the convertible top being down, which she usually loved, would mess up her hair in the breeze, she told him: "Thanks Alexei. But today I want to rest for a while and then take a nice long bike ride." Alexei offered to ride with her this morning. She felt a knot in her stomach and a sense of fear. But then he said: "Oh, no. I just remembered I have an important business meeting later in the afternoon. I need to prepare some papers later." Cassandra told her brother: "Alexei, I did not sleep that well last night, maybe it was all that food. So I want to just sit quietly and read and maybe even take a nap. And then if I feel up to it, I will take a short ride on my bicycle in the afternoon." Alexei seemed okay with her response. He reached over, gave her a peck on the cheek, and went back up to his room to get some papers ready for his afternoon meeting.

At age 26, Alexei was still living at home but he was a really good businessman and was always busy creating his next business venture. On this particular day, he was really focused on, and excited about, a very lucrative business deal that he was expecting to finalize this very afternoon. So his mind was not paying attention to the obvious sensual energy his sister was emanating. Alexei did sense this unfamiliar energy in his little sister but he let it slip to the recesses of his mind as his attention was focused on how he would handle the business deal that day. But he would recall this morning over and over again in his mind for the rest of his life. It was the most important day in his little sister's life and he was more focused on business than on protecting her. He would never be able to forgive himself for letting Cassandra out of his sight this day, not until another significant day over 2 decades later.

It was now only 11 AM. She had gotten up late again and had taken a very long time to get ready. Cassandra was relieved that Alexei had an important meeting and would not be home. Damion had spent the night at his girlfriend, Rhea's home. Cassandra was sure that Damion would be spending the afternoon with his girlfriend and her family. She knew that afterwards he would probably go directly to **The Cypress Club** to assist his father, the employees and maybe have another tryst with one of the dancers. Damion, she knew, had a very strong sexual appetite and often needed several different women, sometimes on the same day, to satisfy his intense urges. Today, for the first time in her life, Cassandra wondered why it was okay for her brothers to explore their sexual and sensual desires with many different women. She wondered what it would be like for her to engage intimately with a wide variety of men. Cassandra couldn't even imagine having intense erotic sensations filling her body for many different men. This one handsome sailor was the only man who had ever aroused that much desire in her body. At this point, she had no idea that she would be having this unexpected experience very soon, within only a few months from this fateful day. But today, she was feeling aroused just at the thought of being with that one handsome man. For the first time in her life, she felt lustful toward a man and could hardly wait for the next few hours to pass.

Cassandra sat on the comfortable, soft deep-cushioned living room couch for a few minutes, contemplating how she would pass the next few hours. She felt as if she was about to jump out of her skin. The anticipation was almost too much for her to bear. Her instinct led her to reach for the bible that was sitting on the table on her right side, in front of that antique lamp her mother had purchased on one of her many trips to France. Cassandra usually loved reading the bible because it always provided an answer when she felt some sort of confused emotion or problem situation. Today she thought she had only picked up the bible to kill some time. But what she read disturbed her deeply.

She turned to her favorite section of the bible, Proverbs. The first verse that caught her eye, Proverbs 1:8, said:

"Listen, my son, to your father's instruction and do not forsake your mother's teaching." Although this did not feel good to her, she was able to kind of brush it off because it was directed to a man, to a son. Another verse that caught her eye, Proverbs 15:20, said: "A wise son brings joy to his father; but a foolish man despises his mother." She knew that she was the joy of her father's life and that she loved her mother with all her heart. But somehow she was not making the connection that her defiant action would bring anger and sorrow to both her father and mother, that the action she was about to take was, in fact, "foolish" in the eyes of anyone brought up in her culture. She had not yet thought of it as foolish in the eyes of God. Then she read another verse, Proverbs: 11:29, which said: "He who brings trouble on his family will inherit only wind, and the fool will be servant to the wise." This verse made very little connection to her on this day but she would read it over and over and over again in the months and years that followed.

Cassandra decided to stop reading the psalms. She leafed through the pages to locate another passage that might soothe her in her longing for the next few hours to pass. The passage that seemed to reach out to her was in Matthew 15:4, which read: "For God said, 'Honor your father and mother' and 'anyone who curses his father or mother must be put to death.'" She read this verse a few times, almost shaking with fear at the thought she might be "cursing" her father and mother. But she brushed that thought aside as soon as her mind returned to the image of that incredibly handsome and strong sailor.

It was now 12 PM. Cassandra stopped in the kitchen to

make herself a half sandwich on her favorite pita bread. She filled it with hummus, lettuce, tomato and few olives without pits. She poured a glass of water and sipped it slowly. Her thoughts brought her to the park and to Cyrano's cabin on the ship. Cassandra could actually see Cyrano dressing and getting himself ready to meet with her. In her vision she saw him shower, put on some powder and some special cologne, and comb his shiny hair to the side with one big wave that fell slightly across his forehead. What she could not see was the end result of this coming afternoon rendezvous.

At 12:30 PM Cassandra went back up to her room to freshen up. She brushed her pearly white teeth so much that they almost sparkled. She knew she would not be able to stop smiling and she wanted Cyrano to see what beautiful teeth she had. Then Cassandra dabbed on her neck a bit of her favorite exquisite perfume, the one her mother had brought back from Paris as a gift for her birthday very soon after her menstruation fiasco at age 14.

The time was now 12:45 PM. Cassandra knew it would take only about 15 minutes to drive to the park. But she could not wait any longer. Her loins were tingling and aching. Her heart was pounding in a strange and unfamiliar rhythm. She was unable to relax and sit still. So she filled her purse with some money and her house keys and quickly walked down the stairs and out the door. On this day her mother was attending a local charity event. Her father had left for work several hours earlier and she had heard Alexei finally leave the house and start up his car about 10 minutes earlier. She reassured herself that she could leave freely now and that nobody would know where she was going. This was true. But what she didn't realize is that what she was about to do would leave a serious telltale sign. She could not imagine that her action in the name of love was about to totally destroy her current life and send her into an abyss of horrors, a walk on the seedy side of life. But before this night would end, Cassandra's fate would be sealed and her life as she knew it would never be the same.

8 ECSTATIC FULFILLMENT

"What a beautiful spring day," Cassandra thought as she stepped outside. Looking up toward the sky she saw a little red robin chirping softly on a low branch on the large nearby Cypress tree. Although there was a slight breeze, the sun was shining brightly and Cassandra felt the warmth slowly spreading throughout her body. She had taken another approving glance at herself in the mirror and she was confident that she looked beautiful and sensual and appealing. Just the thought of Cyrano's eyes appreciating her body sent shivers up her spine. The anticipation was building as she opened the garage door and pulled out her pretty pink bicycle.

Cassandra loved the feeling of riding around the island on her bicycle, not having to depend upon anyone else to drive her somewhere. When she was with one of her brothers, or even her mother, she would always have to remain docile and accepting of wherever they chose to go and whatever they wanted to do. She could ask if they would please take her somewhere, but more often than not, her wishes would be pushed aside. And she had no recourse to complain or insist. Her role as the good daughter had been instilled in her for as long as she could remember. And she had begun to hate that role for the past few years.

Before mounting her bicycle, Cassandra stood just outside the garage for quite a while thinking about the time her brother Damion had beaten her for bleeding on Alexei's car seat. And then she recalled, with a sense of renewed horror, the shock and distress she had felt while observing her two brothers brutalize a helpless woman with a belt strap and take turns raping her. Cassandra also thought about how painful and humiliating that experience must have been for the woman. Realizing that that poor woman would probably never be the same again, that she would probably hold on to those memories, even have recurrent nightmares, Cassandra wondered how she would cope with such a horrible nightmarish experience. She couldn't imagine this woman being able to flirt freely and look a good man in the eyes again. The shame would be too intense. Cassandra smiled for a moment, thinking about how much she knew her brother Alexei loved her and how much her two older brothers would protect her. "Yes," she thought, "sometimes they can be really mean and controlling, demanding and a few times they have even hit me, but I know they only want the best for me. They want me to be the woman they can be proud to call their sister. And I am."

For some strange reason, Cassandra could not connect the dots. It really did not occur to her that the action she was about to take would not just upset her family, it would destroy the love and connection and all that comfort and security she had been accustomed to. She did not realize that there was a line that once it was crossed, there would be no going back. Cassandra did not yet understand that a woman's role was not something to take lightly or to transgress without dire consequences. For a long time, she had wondered what it would be like to have a taste, an experience of the sensual and sexual freedom that her brothers often had. And now, she wanted to have her own personal experience, to explore her own sexuality, with this handsome stranger. Believing she could engage in this exciting sensual and sexual exploratory experience and keep it as her own private and personal secret, she could not fathom that anyone would discover the truth.

Cassandra really thought she could have her sexual fantasies fulfilled and then return to her normal life unscathed. She knew that she could never marry Cyrano, no matter how much her love for him would grow. She also knew that her parents intended to arrange her marriage and she would have very little choice. In fact, a few months earlier, she had overheard a discussion her parents were having with her oldest brother, Stefano. He suggested to her parents that there were 3 local boys from very substantial families whose marriage to Cassandra would greatly enhance the family business. Stefano had promised to find out more about the financial background of each of those families. It was decided then that Cassandra's father, Demitri, would not yet approach any of these boys' fathers about a potential marriage. Cassandra had felt like a piece of merchandise, like a commodity to be sold and used for the benefit of others. Yet, whatever fate she thought might be in store for her by marrying a local Agapelargos Island boy she did not love, she did know that whoever was selected would attempt to treat her like a princess. He would buy her fine clothes and expensive jewelry. He would buy her a beautiful home, provide her with children to love, and take her on lavish vacations. She knew her parents would choose a boy from a wealthy family who was brought up with good manners and respect for a proper woman. Cassandra decided at this moment that she would always see herself as a pure and proper woman with this one private secret tucked inside her heart.

She smiled at the thought of creating her own secret fantasy that she could recall over and over in years to come. This day would certainly haunt her memory but not in the way she had imagined. Cassandra mounted her bicycle and started rolling down the winding path toward the road below. Pansies and other pretty flowers were blossoming along the path. She could see the leaves spreading on the trees. The sun sparkled through the branches and the warmth on her back felt so good. This day belonged to Cassandra and she was going to enjoy every single minute.

Riding her bike along the path near the lake, she waved to a friend of Damion's as he passed in his black sedan and then she thought she saw one of her mother's friends in a little red car. When she arrived at the place where she could enter the park, Cassandra stopped to look carefully all around the area to make sure nobody was watching. She had already decided that if somebody saw her there she would keep riding a little further and then turn back later. But the coast was clear and she entered the park. Riding her bicycle through the center of the field she saw some mothers walking with baby carriages, a few little children running ahead of their parents, and even some older couples walking leisurely and talking. The atmosphere in the park was peaceful and people seemed to be absorbed in whatever they were doing, and happy.

Cassandra arrived at the bike rack and carefully placed her bicycle there. She glanced toward the bench and saw that it was empty. Looking at her watch, she noticed that the time was 1:30 PM and their appointed meeting time was 2 PM. Cassandra decided to look for a bathroom, not to freshen up, but to remove the camisole that hid the beautiful shape of her upper torso. Once inside the bathroom, she carefully unbuttoned and removed her blouse. Holding her blouse in her right hand, she managed to lift up and pull off the camisole. Then she put her blouse back on and buttoned it up, leaving an extra button open to reveal more of her cleavage. She tucked the camisole into her purse and started walking toward the bench. A sailor who saw her emerge from the bathroom took one look at her see-through blouse and immediately walked toward her. As he approached, he began asking questions: "How are you doing, young lady? Your body is so beautiful. Will you come for a walk with me so I can show the other men how beautiful you are?" Smiling sweetly, she politely refused. Walking only a few more steps, another sailor approached her. This one stared directly at her upper torso, told her she was voluptuous, and reached out to touch her. She put her hand up for defense and then pulled it away abruptly saying in an annoyed tone: "Excuse me, but I am meeting someone here." Feeling a bit unnerved and not as safe as the last time she had been in the park, Cassandra walked quickly toward the familiar bench and immediately sat down to wait for Cyrano.

At 2 PM, on the dot, that deep and comforting voice could be heard from a few feet away. "Cassandra, my beautiful Cassandra, you have returned to me." Cyrano's eyes lit up when he caught a glimpse of her almost exposed bosom. His expression revealed that he was elated. As he approached, he reached out his hand beckoning for her to offer hers. He lifted her hand ever so gently to his lips and placed a soft moist kiss on the top. Immediately, he explained that he had been sitting on that same bench for hours and hours on Saturday and on Sunday, feeling dejected, sad and abandoned. Finally, when the sun had already started to go down, he had returned to the ship where one of his ship mates wished him a Happy Easter. And then, he explained, "That's when I understood. I thought to myself: 'Of course she cannot leave her family. They are celebrating Easter weekend. She could not possibly get away during this holiday. But she will be here on Monday, I am sure.' And here you are, again, looking so ravishingly beautiful I just cannot take my eyes off you. Come with me, my love. Let's feel the joy of being totally together now, in this romantic garden.'"

Being a gentleman, he would not make an outward display in public. Cyrano beckoned for her to come with him to their private spot behind the hedge surrounding the big weeping willow tree. But when they got there, they discovered they were not the only ones who liked that spot. Another couple was cooing and kissing and oblivious to the world around them.

Without hesitation, Cyrano asked Cassandra: "Have you ever been on a navy ship? Let me show you what it is like. I know you'll find it interesting – the small cabins that we sleep in, the kitchen where we cook our meals, the small bathrooms we all share, and the controls on the bottom level. Come, my lovely Cassandra, come explore my world with me. Then we can come back to this willow tree and maybe then the couple will be gone." But, of course, Cyrano had no intention of returning to the bench near the tree with this beautiful woman

with this beautiful woman. All he could think about was undressing her and caressing her magnificent young and shapely body. His heart was pounding and he thought for sure she could hear.

Cassandra hesitated and felt sort of strange about this situation. A sensation of fear momentarily filled her belly. She wasn't thinking about what her father or mother or brothers would say. She was more concerned in this moment about the looks and stares and attitudes that the other sailors would have about her. Cassandra thought to herself, "What will the sailors on the ship think about me when they see me boarding this ship with a man who hardly knows me? Will they think I am a low class woman without manners and without men in my life to protect me?"

At that moment, Cyrano took her by the hand and gently began to lead her toward the ship. His touch was so soft and strong and commanding that she felt electric energy again flooding the cells of her body. It's as if the energy shot through her brain and cleared up those fears and doubts. Just one touch from this man and she knew he could lead her anywhere and ask her to do anything. Her body had taken over as the hormones surged and the tingling began. She could feel some moistness between her legs and just for a moment she thought: "Oh no, I'm bleeding." But then she realized she had finished her period about 2 weeks before so she was not and could not be menstruating. She wasn't sure why she felt that wetness but it made her have a sense of desire and longing for something more. Cassandra longed to have this handsome and strong man take her in his arms, touch her skin and caress her entire body. And, something she had never thought of before, she also wanted to feel his manhood deeply inside of her.

As they approached the ship, she marveled at the structure and beautiful lines almost appearing to be hand carved. Cyrano explained that the crew worked really hard to keep the ship spotless. He said with pride: "You wouldn't believe how many hours we spend scrubbing and waxing the exterior of this boat. It's really a beauty, isn't it?" Carefully, Cyrano helped Cassandra to step onto the walkway which ended at the entrance. Once inside the ship, she was led along a corridor toward the room at a lower level where all the controls were. Cyrano didn't actually bring her into the control room but she could see it at a distance and felt awed by all the different mechanisms. Turning to Cyrano she said, "You must know so much. How did you learn to handle all those controls? What is it like to be on this ship for weeks at a time? What is this mission you will be going on? And how much longer will you be here at this island?"

Cyrano chose not to respond. He did not want to tell this beautiful lady that he would be leaving the following morning. He wanted to enjoy this night as fully as possible so he allowed her to imagine a more complete relationship with him. His body was craving her touch. He could hardly keep his hands off her as he led her toward his cabin. She was looking at the view of the park from the ship and imagining what it would be like to be on this ship in the middle of the ocean. Then she thought, "What if there were enemies shooting at the ship? How scary. And this man will soon be facing that." That thought made her want to bring pleasure and comfort to this man whose life would soon be in danger.

She was now walking behind Cyrano in the narrow corridor leading to the door to his cabin. Pleased and delighted, she admired the strong masculine shape of his body from the rear. She loved the broadness of his shoulders and the way he held his body upright. She noticed how his muscular back tapered downward toward his firm butt and his long and powerful legs. Cassandra thought this man was the most handsome man she had ever seen. He looked so strong and manly in his sailor uniform.

Cyrano opened the door and led Cassandra into his tiny room filled mostly with a bed and a small sink in the corner. The community toilets and showers were a few steps away down the corridor. He had a small dark dresser with a few items on top. Cyrano invited his guest to sit but the only place to sit was on the bed. She knew, without a doubt, that this man would soon be making advances toward her. But he did not rush. He offered her a few sips of cognac, the liquor bottle he had saved for the possibility of such a moment with a beautiful young lady. Cassandra took a few sips and felt a warm rush going down her throat. The cognac did relax her.

Cyrano had not been with a woman in quite a while since he had been traveling on the ship for weeks at a time and his last trip had lasted a few months. Feeling clumsy and a bit awkward, he just kept talking. He said to her: "I want you Cassandra. I want to take off your blouse and caress those shapely young breasts that I can already see. I want to run my fingers through the middle of them and pull each one up to my mouth for a good strong kiss. I want to suck on your neck and kiss your big round lips. Oh how I want to feel my body next to yours. Come lay with me my beautiful Cassandra."

Cassandra was spellbound with desire filling every pore. When he touched her shoulder, she instinctively moved toward him, sitting up straighter so her breasts would be more prominent and closer to his mouth. With her body movements, she was almost begging him to caress her breasts. His hands slowly moved on top of her blouse, feeling and enjoying the soft silky texture. Cassandra loved the feel of his big strong hands which felt almost hot enough to burn her. The heat of his desire for her had spread to the tips of his fingers. She couldn't tell if his hands were really that hot or if her body was burning with desire.

Cyrano cupped her breasts with his hands and moved his lips to kiss them through her blouse. Without realizing it, she began to arch her back to bring her breasts up to meet his lips. She wanted him to devour her body with his hands and his mouth. Slowly, one button at a time, he began to open her blouse while his hands wandered above and below the silky material. As he touched her raw flesh he could hear her groan with delight. Then he moved his hands down toward her belly. Next, he gently laid her body down on the bed as he moved his mouth all over her chest, down toward her navel and back up to her breasts. All the while his hands were exploring the soft and smooth texture of her skin, the shape of her slender waist, the round curves of her shapely hips leading down to her belly and the moist area between her legs. He wrapped his hands around her back and kissed her naval, using his tongue adeptly to caress her supple and eager body and that milky white soft skin.

As his hands moved down her body to feel the roundness of her firm backside, he enjoyed the texture of her elastic pants. Moving his hand further down, he left his palm firmly resting against her crotch. He could feel the wetness seeping through the snaps in the crotch of her pants. In her mind, she was begging Cyrano to rip her clothes off and to fill her body with his masculinity. But she was forever the lady and could not express those desires in words. Cyrano felt as if he had gone to heaven or struck gold. He could not believe his good fortune at having this beautiful, responsive woman eagerly accepting his caresses. They were both entranced with each other.

Cyrano pulled away from her, stood up and stared for a few minutes. He wanted to photograph in his mind the absolute perfection of this woman and this moment. Instinctively he knew that the joy and pleasure he felt now could carry him through whatever danger and destruction he would encounter on his upcoming war mission. Cassandra wondered why he had backed away. She sat up and leaned over to kiss him. He held her face in his hands, placed his lips on hers and kept them locked there briefly as he began to explore her tongue with his. Very carefully, Cyrano moved his tongue inside her mouth and slowly laid her down again on the bed, their mouths intertwined as they moved together. At this point, her blouse was completely open and his hands were rapidly moving across her torso, feeling one breast, feeling the other, running his tongue and his teeth over her hard nipples that stuck out straight. He was rubbing her belly through her elastic pants, reaching down to feel the warmth and moistness down below.

Now he brazenly undid the snaps at the crotch of her pants, expecting to see a pretty panty protecting her private area. To his surprise, Cassandra had chosen to not wear panties with those elastic pants. She had been anticipating this night and wanted to be really ready. Cyrano felt such a surge of desire that he could not stop himself from getting ready to plunge into her. He took one detour though.

First, he used one of his fingers that had felt so hot on her body and slipped it into her vaginal opening. She let out a loud "Ooh." As he moved his finger in circles she began to softly sigh, "Ahh!" Pulling her body toward him, he kneeled at the edge of the bed, opened her legs and used his tongue to stimulate her through the opening in her pants. His tongue explored the crevices of her private area and she moaned again in utter delight and emotional abandon. He could feel her hips moving upward to meet his mouth and in circles to feel his tongue more fully.

Now she reached up to him with both her arms, inviting him to stand up for a moment. She leaned forward and he once again caressed her beautiful round breasts that fell right into his open palms. Her eyes glued to his pants, he let go of her breasts and reached down, opening his pants just enough to release and free his male organ. Cassandra actually gasped at the sight of it. To her mind, his penis was huge. Although she had seen each of her brothers naked and aroused at different times, she had never seen a male organ that looked so big and wide and smooth as this one. Her hands instantly began to stroke his hot organ and she could feel the moisture oozing at the head. Her desire was so intense. All she could think about was having this man fill her up and bring her body to a state of unbridled ecstasy. She had no doubt that Cyrano could fulfill her fantasy.

He reached for her head, held it between his palms, and gently directed her mouth toward his organ. She had never done this before but she was so aroused and felt such desire for him, that she let his organ fill her mouth to the point where it was actually choking her. But as she relaxed and allowed the arousal to fill her throat, she could actually feel her throat opening wider to accommodate his huge male organ. In that instant, she thought about fire eaters and how our throats are amazing and supple, more than most of us realize. She sucked on his organ and enjoyed every moment of it.

Soon he lifted her head because he did not want to end this before entering her and feeling her insides. Now the moment had come. He poised his penis at the opening to her vagina and he started to move inward. The moistness oozing from both of them helped him to enter deeper inside. She felt some unexpected pain. She had no idea that she had a hymen, that extra skin protecting her internal vaginal walls. She did not know that this piece of skin would be broken through this act and that a man might later know that she was no longer a virgin. Cyrano did not realize she was a virgin so he started to pummel into her. She groaned. Cyrano thought she was groaning with pleasure when actually what Cassandra felt was intense, ripping pain as her hymen was being ripped away from her internal walls. He kept on moving in and out and he also circled his hips to fill her as completely as he could. Soon the pain stopped and she felt better. That's when she began to move her hips in rhythm with his. Her body was in a total state of ecstasy as she felt his heat spreading into her. And then it happened. She felt several, intermittent waves of contractions spreading up through her insides and down her legs. And he let out a loud gasp as he shot his load of sperm all the way up into her accepting vagina. They lay together on the bed afterwards, wrapped in each other's arms - both totally content, both feeling more alive and more connected than they had ever felt before.

Suddenly, Cassandra looked up at the clock and saw that the time was already 4:30 PM. She knew her family would be wondering where she was. Instantly, she became the good girl and good daughter again. Taking the camisole out of her purse, she quickly slipped it over her head and down onto her chest to cover her beautiful body from her lover's view. Then she put on her blouse and buttoned it up. When she touched her oozing vaginal fluids she was surprised to see some blood. Cyrano soaked a towel in the sink and rushed back to clean her private area before he helped her to snap her pants closed.

When Cassandra stood up, she could still feel some of the fluid dripping down her legs. They kissed once more and he told her he would walk her back to her bicycle. They walked silently, not as romantically as before. He didn't attempt to hold her hand and she didn't reach for his. When they got to the bicycle rack, he reached out to shake her hand gently and he said: "This was the most beautiful afternoon of my life. I will never forget you, my beautiful Cassandra. My wish for you is that you have a long and beautiful and happy life with a wonderful man. Have several beautiful children and maybe you can name one of your sons, Cyrano, so you will always remember me."

Surprised and noticeably upset, Cassandra asked him: Why are you talking that way. Can't I see you again tomorrow and the day after that?" She had planned to be seeing Cyrano every day for the next 2 weeks. And that's when he finally told her the news: "My ship is leaving in the morning and I could not bring myself to tell you until now. Please forgive me. This has been the most incredible day of my entire life and I will remember it always. I will remember you and this beautiful Agapelargos Island for the rest of my life."

Tears filled Cassandra's eyes as she realized this would be their only time together and she may never have this kind of ecstatic experience again in her life. But she did not know that this one ecstatic experience would destroy her happiness and cause her to live a life of unimaginable pain and anguish and suffering for many years to come. This moment was bittersweet but her future would soon become merely bitter. He kissed her gently on the cheek and softly whispered in her ear: "Goodbye my beautiful Cassandra. Live a long and happy life for me. I will often think about you and dream about you and long to be with you. We may never meet again but who knows, maybe someday we will. Goodbye Cassandra. Goodbye my beautiful Cassie."

Cassandra turned, mounted her bicycle, and could hardly see where she was going because her eyes were blinded with tears. This experience had been everything she had ever dreamed about and more. She would have liked to be with him at least a few more times. She wanted to see his handsome smile, those broad shoulders and that huge organ again and again. But in this moment Cassandra believed that all she would ever have, for the rest of her life, was the memory of this one ecstatic afternoon with the most handsome and gentle man she had ever known. And that memory did sustain her through many years of lost self-esteem, lost sense of integrity, and lowered social status in her life.

9 AFTER THE ECSTASY

Cassandra rode her bicycle past all the people in the park but now she could hardly see anyone. With tears streaming down her face, her eyes were blurry and her heart felt heavy. She had expected to enjoy this afternoon, reminisce about it all evening, dream about her lover at night, and return to see him the following day. The sky was turning gray as the breeze picked up. She knew a storm was coming and she pedaled quickly to get home soon. The ride took her about 20 minutes so it was almost 5 PM as she approached the hill leading to her home.

When she reached the garage, Alexei was busy finishing his latest waxing of that car he loved so much. She waved to him, expecting his usual bright smile. Instead he responded gruffly, saying in a loud voice, much louder than usual: "Where have you been all day? Mother came looking for you. She's making that lamb stew that we all love so much and she needed your assistance with the sauce and the vegetables and setting the table. Damion was about to get in the car to go out searching for you. Did you go into that park? Where did you go and why are you arriving home so late? Cassie, it's not really safe for a woman to be out all alone. And look how sexy your outfit is. Are you looking for trouble or what?"

Cassie didn't know what to say. She couldn't let on that she had gone into that park. Her brothers would have been furious with her and then they would restrict her movements and maybe even beat her. She tried to think about a good excuse but nothing occurred to her. Finally, she blurted out: "I went to that little church at the other side of town. I went there to be by myself. I sat down just to think for a while and I found myself sitting there for hours. It was such a peaceful and spiritual place for me to be still and think about my life. I didn't even realize what time it was. You know, Alexei, I have been worrying about what I will do with my life after I graduate from high school."

Alexei responded with a quick flick of his wrist, indicating that what she was thinking and worrying about was nonsense. He explained in quite a condescending way: "Women brought up in a good home like ours do not need to think about such things. Remember Cassie, the most important thing for you to focus on is how to become the ideal wife for a good man that your family will choose for you. Even if you do continue your education, you will not be supporting your family. Your husband will have the financial responsibility. Your job will be to give him a good home, take care of his children and keep him happy so he won't have to stray."

When Alexei saw that his little sister had tears in her eyes, he thought his words had been a bit too harsh for her. So he walked over to give her a hug. That's when his nose detected a familiar odor but he couldn't quite recognize what it was. He told Cassie, "I think you were riding that bicycle too much today and must have really gotten sweaty. You could use a good shower. Run along and freshen up before dinner. Don't let the family get too close to you before you shower. See you at dinner."

Alexei felt sick to his stomach. He sensed that his sister had done something unforgiveable. But he loved her so much and he did not want to believe she would stoop so low. Instead of dwelling on his thoughts or questioning his sister until she was cornered and had to admit the truth, he chose to ignore the signs that had been so obvious. Her hair and clothing, usually so precisely styled, were a bit disheveled and there was no reason for that. The weather had been beautiful all day. She had been riding on her bicycle which she did almost every day. Usually, he recalled, his sister would look just as neat and lovely when she returned home as she did when she started out.

Alexei was always thrilled to see his sister's beautiful smile, those lovely curves and the way she walked with an air of elegance. But he realized that on this particular evening his little sister looked different. He thought to himself: "Her hair is messy, her body has an odor, sort of familiar but I'm not sure what it is. And I thought I saw some stains on her blouse." Alexei decided that maybe he was reading too much into this, that maybe she had just taken a longer bike ride than usual and maybe there had been much more wind than he had realized." Then he had another thought: "Maybe Cassie had stopped for lunch and spilled something on her blouse. She has done that often since her body has been developing into a more womanly shape." He let those unwanted thoughts recede into the back of his mind as he returned to the task of shining up his beloved Fiat.

Luckily for Cassandra, when she entered the house nobody was right near the door. She caught a glimpse of Damion sitting in the living room watching TV and she heard her mother bustling around in the kitchen. Without even saying hello because she didn't want them to see her, she ran upstairs and immediately removed her clothing. She went into the bathroom, locked the door, and put some soap suds into the sink to soak and wash her pants. She put her blouse and camisole directly into the hamper she used for clothing she would later clean and iron. Then she took a nice long shower, washing her body and her hair thoroughly. When she emerged, she toweled herself carefully and tenderly, recalling Cyrano's touch and crying softly. As she started to style her hair with the blow dryer, she heard her mother calling from downstairs: "Cassie, where are you? I need your help. Please come here NOW!" Cassandra yelled back, "I'll be right down mother." And she quickly finished blowing her hair without doing too much to style it. She dabbed some powder on her body, especially around her crotch area which felt a bit sore. Then she sprayed a bit of perfume to make sure she smelled good for the family.

When Damion saw her, at first he responded a bit angrily, saying: "Why are you so late? Where were you? I almost went out driving around to find you. Good thing you made it home in one piece. It's not safe for a young girl to be out on her own all day, especially a beautiful shapely girl like you from such a prominent family. You have a reputation to maintain and don't you forget that, Cassie. Now go help your mother already. She's been in a frenzy wondering where you've been."

Lyzandra turned as soon as she saw her daughter and exclaimed: "You are never late like this. Are you becoming like your brothers? You do realize, it is okay for men to hang out around town, to ride around by themselves, but young ladies have to be careful. You need to always remember that what you do as a woman reflects upon your family. We sometimes worry about you. Now come help me get the dinner ready. Everyone is hungry and waiting. Your father will be home soon and he needs you to get him his slippers and serve him his drink. I am so glad you came home before he arrived. I don't even want to think about how angry he would have been if his only daughter was not here to wait on him and show him that special respect he deserves from his little girl."

For the next few months, Cassandra's life appeared to continue as usual and she was truly enjoying her final year of high school. Assuming her family would find a good match for her, she had no real plans for what she might do after graduation. Thinking her life was soon to be set in an orderly and comfortable way, she felt relaxed and realized she didn't have to think much about her future. But she did knew that she had found true love with Cyrano and that no man would ever replace him in her heart. Often she would notice one of her male classmates staring at her with a sense of passionate desire in his eyes. Smiling to herself she would think: "Only one man has had me and you will never have that same opportunity."

Knowing that a guy was aroused by her presence would trigger in her a need to make his desire stronger. So she would purposely lean over in such a way that he could get a brief glimpse of her full breasts. Or she would drop something and then bend over to expose her round butt covered with a G-string panty. All the while she would pretend to be totally innocent and unaware of the boy's reaction. Enjoying the power she knew she possessed to arouse men so easily with her body movements would often cause a warm rush to spread throughout Cassandra's system. She loved showing off for men and teasing them as only a beautiful woman can.

Lately, however, a wave of nausea would overcome her whenever she bent over. If she felt the gaze of a nearby boy on her body she would often respond by feeling slightly sick. Not knowing what was happening, she began to worry: "Maybe I am just turned off by these young and silly boys," she thought. "Or maybe there is something physically wrong with me and I need to see a doctor." Just as she had been totally naïve about that first day of menstruation when she had bled threw her white dress onto Alexei's special leather car seat, she was also unaware of the effect of her one evening of ecstasy almost two months earlier.

At graduation, Cassandra managed to make it through the

ceremonies but had to run to the bathroom to throw up before going home. Her whole family was there to celebrate with her. Lyzandra was so proud of her beautiful daughter for completing her education. Many Greek women were not so fortunate. But there was no preparation for Cassandra to continue in her studies. Now, after graduation, the family would put all their efforts into selecting the appropriate potential mate for her.

Knowing this was the plan for her future created mixed emotions in Cassandra. At times she would feel so good, relieved that there is nothing more expected of her until her future husband is selected. She understood very well that once betrothed her womanly work would begin. She knew she would be totally responsible for keeping her man sexually happy, for creating and providing a beautiful well-kept home, for giving birth to several babies and hopefully several boys, and for remaining emotionally calm and always supportive of her husband and family. Sometimes Cassandra envied her brothers who were free to explore their sexuality, continue in their education, get involved in business, travel the world and then have their young and virginal wife chosen for them when they were ready. At times she wished she could run away and escape from the fate that awaited her. In a strange and totally unexpected way, Cassandra's wish would soon come true.

10 CASSANDRA'S CRUCIFIXION

The moment Cassandra had recently been dreading had arrived. Everyone in her family finally knew that she was pregnant. When they asked, Cassandra would refusd to tell them who the father was so they did not know if it was one of the local boys, an older man, or even a relative. Lyzandra was beside herself, obviously feeling unnerved, humiliated and extremely angry. She had carefully instructed her only daughter on the way to be revered in this upper class Greek society. Lyzandra had expected her daughter to marry a suitable young man from a respectable family. She dreamed about pampering her grandchildren and showing them off at her many church and civic and private events.

Lyzandra's mind was racing as she wondered to herself: "What will I tell the ladies at our weekly luncheon? What will I say when one of their husbands asks me how my beautiful daughter is doing? How do I explain this to my parents and to Demitri's parents? How will I manage this household without the help of my only daughter? Why has she done this awful thing to me? She has disgraced this family and we may never recover. I warned her over and over again that women must be strong and pure and preserve their virginity at all costs. Her father has often lectured her and her brothers have also disciplined her when she even attempted to step out of line. I can't even look at her. I don't want to ever see her face again. As far as I'm concerned she no longer exists. I do not have a daughter. Now I will devote all my attention to honoring the 3 sons I am so proud of. They have been so well trained by their father. They behave with impeccable manners, they treat women in style, and they show that they are always men and that they are in control. My boys have never dishonored this family the way our little selfish daughter has done. I am mortified. I don't know if I can go on."

Cassandra had been hiding her growing belly by wearing looser clothing than usual. Each of her brothers had commented. Damion, on several occasions, had tapped her belly in front of the family and jokingly warned her to stop eating so much because she was getting fat. Even her father, who rarely made those types of remarks, stared at her belly a few weeks earlier with an unexpressed fear that this may not be the result of overeating. But he dropped the thought from his mind because it was too unbearable to even consider.

It was a Friday afternoon in the middle of September. Cassandra, who had turned 17 a few days earlier, was attending the Sweet Sixteen birthday party of one of her younger friends. The party was joyous. The girls were laughing and joking, opening presents, sharing funny and even some raunchy stories. One of the girls commented on Cassandra's weight and about the fact that she was wearing such a loose pink blouse, unlike her usual form fitting signature silk and cashmere sweaters. They didn't realize she was pregnant and was merely hiding her very slightly bulging belly. She laughed it off, saying she had been eating too many sweets and intended to be much more careful starting right now. So Cassandra refused to even the taste the delicious chocolate layered, strawberry filled whipped cream covered cake. The other girls bought her story and she felt relieved, for the moment. What Cassandra did not know was that this would be the very last time she would spend time with her childhood friends. In fact, this was the very last time for the next few decades that Cassandra would have a laughing, joking and totally happy afternoon with good friends. Life as she had known it was about to end – forever.

The trauma began when Damion picked her up at her friend's party. In his usual style, he went around to her side of the car and opened the door for her. But as she approached he literally shoved her into the car seat. She knew there was about to be a storm. Her heart racing, her fear at a fever pitch, she held her breath and didn't dare to speak. Damion spoke as soon as he got into the car and had started the engine. He yelled at her: "You slimy little tramp. What have you done? Yesterday Stefano went to see Dr. Christakos, the urologist, for his annual checkup. You know that Dr. Christakos shares an office with mother's gynecologist, Dr. Athanas. And you know how Stefano likes the ladies. So he was talking and flirting with Doria, the office assistant at the desk. Doria told Stefano that she saw you sitting there the day before, waiting to see Dr. Athanas. And she innocently asked Stefano if you were okay.

So, feeling concerned about you, his little sister, Stefano stopped by Dr. Athanas' office to find out why you had been there to see him the day before. He was worried that you might be really sick. Surprised by the question and not thinking much about it, Dr. Athanas said he had done a pregnancy test and you are definitely pregnant. Dr. Athanas had thought it was wonderful news and that you had married someone quietly in a small private wedding. Stefano thanked him for his concern and said nothing. Last night Stefano was really busy at work so he came to tell us this morning, right after you left to be at that Sweet 16 party. Sweet 16, that is something you are not. By the time Stefano got to our house, as you can imagine, he was in a total rage. You are lucky you were not at home because he might have killed you. Women in our family do not behave like that. We have all cared for you, watched over you and protected you against all harm. Now you will be cast out on your own to fend for yourself. And none of us will give a damn."

Damion's words shot through Cassandra's body like a cannon ball filled with poisoned daggers. At this point she was terrified about what she was about to face. There was no time for her to think about how to respond, what she might say or do, or even to ponder what her fate has in store for her after today. Cassandra felt as if she had stopped breathing as her body braced itself for the coming storm.

When she arrived home, Damion did not go around the

car to open the door for her, as he usually would do. Instead, he yelled out loud to her: "From now on you will open your own car doors, that is, if you are ever invited into a man's automobile again. Women who are sluts do not get treated so well. Remember that woman Stefano and I beat up and used for sex. That is what will happen to you for disgracing the family that has done nothing but love and protect you and keep you safe."

Hearing Damion's car pull up to the front door, Cassandra's father emerged from his usual seat in his office and rushed to greet her at the front door. He didn't wait for her to open the door. Instead, he pulled it open so she almost fell into the room. Looking at her face with an expression of total disgust and rage, he lifted his right hand and whacked her across the face as hard as he could. Cassandra fell sideways and held on to the wall for balance. He looked at her as if this would be the last time in his life that he would see her and he yelled in a loud and scary voice: "You are nothing more than a low class slut. You have disgraced this family and from this day forward you are not only disinherited but you are disowned. You are no longer welcome in my home. I do not have a daughter. Perhaps my 3 fine sons will one day produce children and then I will have a granddaughter to love the way I have showered you with my love all these years." Demitri then turned his back on his daughter and intended, in that moment, to never lay eyes on her, or even mention her name, again. But that was only in his temporary moment of fury. There is a saying: "Hell hath no fury like a woman scorned." And Cassandra's fury would soon leave a long lasting trace of shame and sorrow on her entire family.

Reeling from the physical and emotional impact of her beloved father's words and behavior, Cassandra felt dazed and sick to her stomach. She knew that her life would never be the same. And then, as soon as her father had left the room, Damion emerged from the living room. His demeanor was hostile and cold, his body language indicating that she was so low that it wasn't even worth his while to talk to her or touch her. He spit on the floor several times, staining her favorite pink designer silk covered dress shoes with the sexy pillar shaped 2 inch heels that she had happily displayed at her friend's' party. Knowing that she loved those beautiful shoes he went over and purposely stepped on each shoe, making sure to leave a big dirt mark on the top of each. He thought, in that moment, that he was through with his little sister for the rest of his life. Damion spit on the floor in her direction one more time and then he walked away muttering cuss words to Alexei who had just entered the room. Then Damion looked at Alexei and loudly informed him: This is your task, your job, to beat some sense into this little tramp who used to be our sister, before we throw her out of the house for good."

Alexei made a dramatic scene, shoving and then yanking Cassandra by the hair. Angrily screaming at her, "Tsoula," meaning 'you dirty little slut,' I will give you what is coming to you. We are going upstairs right now. He grabbed her right arm to pull her up the stairs with him. He didn't have to work hard since she was already so emotionally defeated she could not possibly resist. Cassandra was too shell shocked to respond. What nobody saw was the tears welling up in Alexei's eyes. He had always had a soft spot for his beloved sister and he knew she was a kind hearted, gentle and loving girl. He was the only one who understood that her heart had been opened and her hormones were raging. So he acted as if he would beat the daylight out of her, but it was all an act.

He kept yelling at her as he pulled her up the stairs, saying the same types of nasty insults that his brothers and his father had screamed at her. And when he got her into the room he slowly removed his belt.

Cassandra was terrified. Alexei was the one brother she had counted on to protect her and to never harm her. She cowered and protected her head as he got ready to smash her with his belt. But to her surprise, he began beating the bed and yelling obscenities at her. He built himself up into a frenzy and beckoned to her to start screaming and begging him to stop, pleading for forgiveness. Without hesitation, she let out a wail. "Ow, ahh, oh. Alexei please stop. Please, I love you. I don't want to hurt anyone. I made a big mistake. Please. Ow. Stop. You're hurting me. Please stop. Please. Please."

At this point Cassandra was sobbing loudly and gasping for breath. Alexei came closer to her and ripped her blouse open with his bare hands. Luckily, the material was so strong that he could only rip it part way. Her cleavage was revealed but her breasts were basically still covered. Then he grabbed her beautiful lace trimmed designer skirt and tore at it piece by piece. Her sophisticated outfit was being torn to shreds and she continued sobbing, begging Alexei to stop. He was relentless. He stroked her legs, making sure to tear her expensive silk nylons with his nails, leaving several gaping holes and running tears.

For a few minutes, Alexei stopped his raging behavior and whispered into Cassandra's ear. "I am so sorry my beautiful little sister Cassie. I have always loved you and protected you. I only wish I could have protected you from this situation. But you didn't tell me and my hands are tied. Please always remember that I do love you. I do not want to hurt you. You see how I have not hit you the way our father and Damion and Stefano would expect. I know how kind and loving and gentle you are. I know that you would not have done what you did if you did not fall in love with this stranger. But I must obey my family and our ancient traditions. If I do not show my rage at you, they will not only disown me but they will beat me to shreds, maybe even break my bones. I have no choice but to make it appear as if I am brutalizing you for getting pregnant and dishonoring our proud and prominent family. Please forgive me my beloved Cassie for what I am about to do. I must spank you with the belt and smear your panties with your blood so I can show them what I have done to you for disrespecting our family."

Her eyes filled with tears as she gazed into his kind and caring eyes. She reached out to hug him and he pushed her away, put his hand underneath her skirt, between her legs and he pulled down her panties. Next, he threw her down onto the bed face down and immediately lifted her skirt with her panties halfway down. He rubbed her butt for a moment as if to prepare her for what was coming. And then he began to lash her with his belt. This time she was screaming for real as the belt hit her over and over again, across her butt, across her back and against her legs. Then he shoved her to turn her body over so that she would be lying on her back. Now he was ready to continue his physical punishment of her. He put down the belt and chose to use his hands instead. He smacked her hard across the face, first with the inside of his right hand smacking the left side of her face followed by the back of his right hand smacking her right cheek. He smacked her across the face several times from right to left and left to right. Finally, he reached once more for his belt and proceeded to whack her across her pregnant belly yelling "You bastard baby. Go to hell. You don't deserve to live."

Finally, when he saw that she was bleeding in many places, he stopped his brutality and once again became the docile and loving Alexei she had always loved. He went to the sink in the bathroom, soaked a towel in warm water and returned to caress her bleeding skin on her belly, on her legs and on her back, on her arms and on that beautiful rounded butt that so many men had admired. Then he ordered her to slip out of her panties and give them to him so he could show the family that he had completed his task as a proper man would do. Without giving her a moment to glance back at the room which contained her whole life, all those precious mementoes of her beautiful days on this island paradise, he commanded her to go downstairs and to leave the house. All she could grab was her purse, with only a few dollars in it, her shoes, and the light sweater she had been wearing that day.

When she reached the bottom of the staircase, her teary eyed mother, Lyzandra, was standing there looking staunch and serious. In a cold and distant tone of voice, Lyzandra said to her daughter: "We cannot allow you to remain in our home. As soon as you walk out that door, we will no longer know you. You are disowned. There will be no money for you and we want no further contact with you. You have dishonored this family and we will not tolerate that. From this point forward, I have only 3 sons. Sadly, I no longer have a daughter. But my sons will fill my heart with the love I feel for them. You could have married a prominent and prosperous man. You could have provided this family with many beautiful grandchildren to continue our legacy. But you chose to act like a whore and give your body to a total stranger. Goodbye Cassandra. May God be with you."

Cassandra felt as if she had stepped into a nightmare that would end when she awoke from her sleep. She pinched herself to see if this was real. Without looking back, she opened the front door and stepped out into the world beyond – totally alone. Then Cassandra walked toward the garage and saw that the door had been locked shut giving her no access to her beautiful beloved pink bicycle. All she had was her two legs so she started walking. Not knowing where to go she headed for the park where she had experienced such wondrous love several months ago. Her body ached from the beating she had received and from her emotional devastation. But she had no choice. She had to just keep walking away from the home, the only home she had ever known, and the family that she had always loved so dearly.

11 AFTER THE FALL FROM GRACE

Cassandra walked down the hill on the winding path that led from the home she had always known. Stopping midway toward the bottom of the hill, she turned around to take one last look at the home and the life she was leaving - forever. Dazed, emotionally numb and in a state of complete shock, she viewed the house from a distance and felt, for the first time in her life, like a complete stranger. "Whose home is that," she thought. "Did I really live here and love that family? Did they know me and love me, Cassandra – or was it all a total illusion?" Tears welled up in her eyes as she bid farewell to her beautiful pink bicycle which had given her the freedom to ride around on her own and lose her sexual innocence with the man of her dreams. And she thought, "Dreams are just that. Dreams. My life is over, at least the life I have lived until now. My dream is gone too. That handsome sailor, so strong and masculine and soft-spoken, was he a dream too? Did I imagine his passion for me or was this also a total illusion? I really don't know what life is all about but I have a feeling I will soon learn a lot more than I have ever known."

Transfixed for a moment, not wanting to believe this was really happening, Cassandra stood perfectly still gazing intently at the home she was leaving. In disbelief and denial, she stood there wishing beyond hope that someone in her family would soon come running out, begging her to return and pleading for her forgiveness. Although she might pretend to resist, she knew she would immediately go running back to the house and to her family no matter what abusive behaviors she might have to endure. "This is my island. I love living on Agapelargos Island. This is my home. This is my family. How will I manage without them?" Cassandra wondered in a bewildered and frightened state of mind.

As the sunlight started to diminish and the breeze began to pick up, Cassandra felt a bit chilly. She turned away from her home and continued her descent down the winding road. When she arrived at the street below, for the first time in her life she walked along the shoulder of the road. Not thinking clearly she just headed in the direction of the park that had brought her such joy and had now become the demise of her life as she had known it. The park was further away than she had realized because, she thought, "It's so much easier to get there on my bicycle. I feel tired and a bit chilly and I am all alone in the world." Cassandra did not even think about her rising hunger. Usually she would eat a hearty breakfast, a sandwich or salad or soup for lunch, and then a fairly large and filling dinner with her family. Today she had been at that party and had eaten less than usual because she had been pretending to her friends that she had merely gained weight. It was way past her dinner time by now and her stomach was beginning to growl. She had only a few dollars in her wallet, no place to go to stay for the night, nobody to rescue her, and no place to even get some food. Cassandra just kept walking forward, putting one foot in front of the other, trusting that her life would go on and somehow her current dilemma would be solved.

Keeping hope alive, she figured one of her brothers would eventually come looking for her. She thought they would get upset that they had left her all alone, a young woman alone, to fend for herself in a world full of dangerous men. Actually, Cassandra thought correctly because later that night and the following day Alexei and Stefano began searching all over town for their little sister. Together the two brothers scoured the town to find Cassandra, stopping at the church, the police station and even the park, to no avail. Then they contacted Damion and asked him to invite some of the tough guys who were regular customers at **The Cyprus Club**. Together, as a group, they all went looking for Cassandra hoping beyond hope to locate her somewhere. But the 3 forlorn brothers could not find their little sister. She had vanished. "Where could she have gone?" they wondered. The following day, they contacted the police again and checked to see if there was any new news about their missing person report. Although the detectives used all their best techniques to track her down, they came up empty after receiving many leads from local townspeople. They even searched through the park, asking around to find out if anyone could give them some information about their sister. Yes, a few people thought they might have seen her on her pink bicycle, but that had been a few months ago. Nobody said they had seen her on the day her family had beaten her and had thrown her out of the house. Lyzandra and Demitri, Stefano, Damion and Alexei lived for the next two decades regretting their harsh behavior and unloving attitudes toward their beloved daughter and little sister. Each of them suffered intense guilt and sorrow about what they had done to her. Each one suffered separately, causing lots of pain in their relationships with each other and with their own intimate partners.

Cassandra walked and walked. It felt to her as if she would just be walking for the rest of her life. But eventually she approached the entrance to her beloved park. Standing perfectly still, she gazed at what she could still see of the open field, the tall Cypress trees, the Olive trees, the flowers and the people. There were still a few couples walking in the distance. She imagined that they had found love and passion and romance as she had. For a moment, she envied their togetherness. In her previous life, her life before that awful beating by her brother and the humiliating rejection by her whole family, she would never have entered that park or any other place at night, in the dark, all alone. But tonight was different. Cassandra felt not much better than the dirt under her shoes. She felt worthless, dirty, and undeserving of life. As she entered the park she didn't seem to care what might happen to her. In fact, she was kind of hoping to be beaten to death by some violent stranger. Cassandra wanted this awful nightmare to be over.

What she didn't expect and could not have imagined, was that her full nightmare had actually not yet begun. Being thrown out of her house by her family was a trauma, a one-time horrible event. But what was about to happen would be recurring, over and over and over again for many years to come. She was about to meet the dark knight of her soul and she had no defenses left to guard against him.

In the distance she saw that bench, the one where she had first met her beloved Cyrano. In her imagination she saw him sitting there, smiling at her, beckoning for her to join him on the bench. She even managed to walk toward the bench, for a few minutes being led by her imagination. His deep voice tingled in her ears. That handsome face beamed as she approached. He reached out his hand to her, inviting her to join him. As she got closer, her heart started pounding loudly as she thought: "Maybe Cyrano did not leave town. Maybe he came back to the bench hoping I would return. Maybe my nightmare is already ending." So she reached back to hold his hand and he spoke to her in a deep, but slightly harsher voice.

"Hello young lady. Who do I have the pleasure of greeting on this cool and dark night?" He spoke in a different language that she did not recognize. His hand felt rough and his tone was harsh, but she still clung to the hope that this was her beloved Cyrano. She replied: "Cassandra. I am your Cassandra, the one you loved and caressed all over all night long. I'm the one who took your organ into my mouth and felt it swell within me. I am the one who brought you to ecstatic ecstasy. You are my beloved."

The man on the bench, Dietrich Danjel Skold from Sweden, understood only a few words in Greek but he thought he recognized a few things she was saying. He heard her say words that sounded like "loving and caressing," "his organ swelling," and "giving a man ecstasy." The man on the bench was thrilled. He thought to himself: "She is perfect. This is exactly the type of woman I have been looking for. I'm not sure what she looks like but I will check out her body to see if it is rounded and firm the way men prefer." And then he pulled her toward him, not to kiss her but to fondle her body and determine if she was as good as he was hoping. He pulled her close to him with his big rough hands grasping each of her hips. "Yes, he thought, they are round and firm." Quickly, he moved his hands to cup her buttocks and feel their texture and firmness. Pleased with how high and firm they were, he moved his hands down her thighs to feel her calves. Her legs were quite long with a tapered sexy shape. He was already delighted, thinking he had found the perfect woman and had struck gold, literally.

Before she could even think about pulling away, he had wrapped his strong right arm around the back of her waist and used his left hand to stroke her belly. Disappointed that she had a round belly, he thought that meant she was a bit overweight so he planned to put her on a strict diet. But then his left hand moved upward to explore her breasts. He could not believe his good fortune. Those breasts felt like honey covered gold in his hands. He was thrilled. Her breasts were incredible – large, round, natural, soft, firm and full with nipples that stuck straight out. Aroused, he couldn't help himself from sucking on her nipples through her blouse. She tried to resist but he was much stronger than her, especially in her current state of emotional and physical exhaustion.

Reaching down to feel her crotch he had another exciting revelation. She had no panties on and he could test her out right here and now, before spending another moment or a single penny on her. Still holding his right arm firmly around her waist so she could not escape, he very quickly unzipped his pants, released his organ and pulled her body down until she was sitting directly on top of his penis. Now he lifted his palms to her shoulders and pushed her body downward using tremendous strength to enable his penis to enter her wet, unwilling, yet ready vagina. Literally lifting her up and down, up and down, he used her body to satisfy himself. As he shot his sperm into her he let out a very loud gasp. Cassandra was not even crying. She felt so worthless that her mind believed she deserved this type of treatment. Not even attempting to resist, her body responded and she moaned into an unexpected orgasm.

"How much do I owe you," he asked in his attempt to say it in Greek. She shook her head, indicating to tell him she was not a prostitute. But when she didn't accept payment, he thought she meant that she had enjoyed the sexual encounter so much that she would not charge him. He thought she was giving him a free sample so that he might become a regular customer and tell his friends about her. Smiling to himself, he was thinking excitedly: "This woman is so perfect. Tonight is my lucky night. I can't wait to tell Roffe about her. We can really start that business we had talked about. She is perfect for the job."

12 DIETRICH STRIKES GOLD

Today was Dietrich Danjel Skold's 25th birthday and he had big plans for his future. Cassandra seemed to fall into his lap, just as he had been visualizing the creation of a new business venture. He had recently decided to take a short and much needed vacation on Agapelargos Island near Athens where he had checked out some disappointing business opportunities. Dietrich felt that he was on the verge of creating something new and exciting but did not yet know what it was going to be. So he decided to spend a few days alone, contemplating his life, clearing his head and perhaps discovering a way to implement his dream of financial freedom. He had toyed with multilevel marketing schemes. He had watched and learned about the ins and outs of business from his older twin brothers and his father, often having been invited along with them to their business meetings. Inside, he had been feeling as if he was about to burst. Something had been bubbling up and he had wanted to be completely ready when the opportunity presented itself.

In fact, it was just this morning that he had spoken on a long distance call to Roffe, a friend of his older twin brothers, Hannes and Leif. Hearing that Dietrich had just turned 25, Roffe, now 33, provided some fatherly advice and Dietrich was eager to listen. Roffe told him emphatically: "Now is the time to create that business you have talked about for years. You are at perfect age, young enough to take big chances and old enough to not be totally foolish. I have spent the past two years commuting back and forth between my home in Sweden and my business meetings here in Lucerne, Switzerland. I have discovered that the Swiss are ready to do business. But they are very smart and you have to offer them something new and exciting and lucrative. What do you have in mind?"

Responding with an air of uncertainty, Dietrich replied: "I have a dream in my mind but I am not yet ready to talk about it. I don't yet have all the players I need to start setting up the business. And I don't really want to do it in my home town in Sweden. For me it would feel so much better, so much freer, to start my business venture far away from home, away from the scrutiny of my father or the doubting concerns of my mother. My goal is to strike it rich in another country and then return home carrying the goods."

Roffe responded like a caring and concerned relative: "Dietrich, I know how well you have done in your school studies – all A's, honor roll, awards. I know how popular you have always been with the ladies and also with other guys. And you have proven, many times, that you're not afraid of hard work. I have seen you put in long hours to help your brothers in their fur business. I even heard that you would sometimes help your father to compose his lectures and handle some of his basic correspondence. You definitely have what it takes to succeed in business. Now come up with a good plan and maybe I'll find a way to help you set it up and get it going."

Born into a large family in a small town in Sweden, Dietrich was the middle child. He had two twin brothers 3 years older, Hannes and Lief, one sister a year older, Carina, and 3 younger sisters, Evelina, Gertrud, and Henrika, each one about 2 years apart. Needless to say, Dietrich was familiar and comfortable around women from his earliest years. His sisters took good care of him. The older sister protected him and his 3 younger sisters looked up to him, admired him and may have even been secretly in love with him. Dietrich was oozing with confidence around women and he had a flair for enticing women to do his bidding. He had the natural ability to lead and control and dominate. Women loved Dietrich and he had them literally eating out of his hand. One woman would eagerly come to clean his apartment. Another young lady would bring him home-cooked meals, even knowing he was about to share those meals and make love to another woman. Women were always calling him on the phone, begging him to come back to them when he had had enough of their relationship. Yes, Dietrich was a true ladies man and he loved his life. But he wanted to prove to his family and to himself that he could make it on his own and make it big.

The males in Dietrich's family, his father and his two old twin brothers, were highly educated, productive and successful in business. His father, Angul, was a well-respected nuclear scientist whose worldwide travels introduce him to the business world which he loved. Angul had established a lucrative speaking career which brought him into frequent contact with influential, wealthy and globally successful businessmen. His friends and colleagues taught him how to acquire wealth, through their example, through their connections and through sharing their knowledge and experience. Over the years Angul had purchased stocks and properties and even invested in building several different international companies. Dietrich had been introduced to the business world at a very young age and felt ready to start his own business at this point.

Dietrich's mother was a celebrity in her own right. Working at a local TV station, she was seen throughout the country as the most well-spoken and knowledgeable female TV anchor. With seven children to raise, both parents managed to travel regularly for business and for romantic getaways, leaving the children in the care of nannies, relatives and neighbors. When Dietrich reminisces about his childhood, one nanny immediately comes to mind. She was tall and blond and shapely and used to carelessly allow her body to be exposed to him. She wore flimsy cotton dresses and when she bent over facing him he would glance down her blouse at her beautiful round breasts, never covered with a brassiere. One time, while the nanny was cleaning, she bent over to pick something up and he got a full view of her naked bottom – she had no panties on. That moment became imprinted in his mind. Whenever Dietrich would find he was alone in a hotel room, instead of leafing through sexually explicit magazines or watching a sexual movie on his TV, all he had to do was think about that one nanny and he could easily bring his arousal to complete fulfillment.

Having spent the past 2 days on this small and beautiful Agapelargos Island, Dietrich was feeling very relaxed and confident that his business opportunity was about to appear. Sitting on this park bench, he had been silently imagining what type of business could bring him pleasure, excitement and financial freedom. That's when the idea of a brothel first occurred to him. "That's it," he thought. "I will create a sexy and exciting place for men to unwind, feel manly and have all their fantasies fulfilled. Hmm! What would father and mother say about this? Hmm! I know they would not be happy. But my business has nothing to do with my parents. This will be my baby, my brain child, my adventure. Maybe Roffe can help me set it up in Switzerland. I hadn't thought of that country but why not? True, I don't speak the language but I will be able to learn enough words to get by in business. I wonder how I will find the right girls to satisfy the men?"

Lost in deep thought, at first Dietrich did not see Cassandra approaching him. But then he realized this young woman was walking toward him. He reached out his hand to her, smiled, and beckoned for her to join him on the bench. She walked toward him and offered her hand as she got closer. Dietrich could see that she was tall and slender with long flowing hair but she looked quite disheveled. Her blouse was torn and stained with what looked like mud or dirt. He saw that her skirt was also torn, her face was all puffy and her eyes were bloodshot. Dietrich assumed this young lady was a prostitute, high on drugs, and looking for a handout.

When this young woman started talking to Dietrich in Greek, he thought he recognized the meaning of a few of her words. He heard her say words that sounded like "loving and caressing," "his organ swelling," and "giving a man ecstasy." Dietrich thought to himself, "Am I imagining this or has God sent me the first woman to get my business off the ground? She looks as if she could be quite attractive once we wash her up and give her some clean and form-fitting clothing."

As Cassandra got really close to him, Dietrich decided to check out her body to find out if it is rounded and firm the way men might like it. He grasped her hips to pull her close to him. Dietrich was delighted that her hips were round and firm. Next, he moved his hands to check out her buttocks and was again happy to feel the strength and firmness there. Then he moved his hands down her legs to feel the shape of her calves and her thighs. When he stroked her belly, he felt a bit upset, thinking to himself: "She's a little overweight. I will restrict her diet so she can lose this excess fat. Now let me check out her breasts." Dietrich was so thrilled to feel the bulges of her big, soft round bosom and the nipples that stuck straight out that he couldn't stop himself from sucking on her nipples through her blouse. At this point, he had a firm erection and wanted to test her out to see if she would be as pleasing as he had begun to imagine. Thinking it might be difficult to remove her panties, he gripped her body harder with his right hand as he reached down to touch her crotch. That's when he discovered she was not wearing panties so he immediately positioned her on top of his penis and pulled her onto him.

When she moaned as if in ecstasy, he thought to himself: "Oh she's good. She makes it seem so real. The men are going to love her. I can't wait to bring her with me to Switzerland and offer her first to Roffe and then to some of his friends. Once we train her to behave the way we want, the men will be coming in droves to have this special experience with her. Then we can gradually find a few other women to join our harem. I can't believe my good fortune. I am so excited I will not be able to sleep tonight."

Then Dietrich had a disturbing thought. "I wonder if her pimp will come looking for her. That could be really dangerous for me. So I'd better bring her to my hotel room immediately before someone finds us here." And so he zipped his pants, loosened his grip on Cassandra, took her by the hand and led her to his hotel. By this point, Cassandra was in a delirious state and offered no resistance. When they arrived at the hotel, the doorman, the concierge, the woman at the desk and some of the guests looked at her strangely. Everyone thought she was a hooker and did not like her messy appearance. Dietrich decided he would provide a bath for her and ask the front desk to send up another terry cloth bathrobe for his guest.

When they reached his room, Dietrich opened the door and invited Cassandra to come in. Willingly, she entered the room. He pointed to the bathroom telling her that he would make a bath for her, let her clean herself up, and the hotel management would be providing her with a bathrobe. Then he said he would buy her a new dress in the morning for their plane ride to Switzerland which he planned to schedule for that afternoon. He also told her he was going to order some food with room service. Just for tonight, he was not going to enforce her special diet. That would begin after their flight to Switzerland and once they have settled into their business arrangement.

Cassandra did not understand his words, since he spoke in Swedish, but she felt relieved that she was now in a comfortable hotel room and she would be able to take a bath or a shower. Her life had become unimaginable to her. Realizing she had no control over her fate, she chose to focus on what was good in the moment. And in this moment, now, she was about to take a soothing bath. Cassandra had no idea about what would happen after this evening and about Dietrich's big plans to use her to have sex with men for large sums of money to begin the creation of his own fortune.

13 DIETRICH'S BUSINESS PLANS

Dietrich filled the tub with hot water and threw in one of the small shampoo sample bottles to create a bubble bath. He wanted to make sure his lady was pampered, relaxed and happy on this special evening. He was about to call his father's secretary to book a flight for two for the following afternoon from this little Greek island to Lucerne, Switzerland. Cassandra had been sitting in the desk chair, oblivious to anything but her confused and hazy thoughts. Feeling as if she was dreaming and this could not possibly be real, she wondered when her family would have a change of heart and begin looking for her. She figured her brothers might need a day or two to calm down and come to their senses. And she knew that Alexei would have difficulty sleeping. Cassandra figured that Alexei would begin looking to find his sister in the morning. She had no idea that her brothers had already started searching for their little sister all over the island. But they could not find her. It was already too late. Nobody in her family could possibly have imagined, not even Cassandra herself, that by the following afternoon she would be on a one-way flight to Switzerland. To her family, the local townspeople and the local police, it appeared as if Cassandra had vanished into thin air.

When the bath was ready, Dietrich motioned to Cassandra to take off her torn and dirty clothing and clean herself well in the bubbly water. She obeyed his motion to enter the bathroom. Seeing the tub filled with beautiful bubbles, she immediately closed the door, eagerly removed her torn and soiled clothing. She carefully hung her skirt and blouse on the hook on the back of the door. But as soon as she had entered the tub and sat down to relax in the warm water, Dietrich opened the door and quickly removed her clothing from the hook. He told her he would throw away her dirty clothes and buy her some new outfits in the morning. Of course, she did not understand so she started yelling: "No, no, no! I have no clothes to wear. I won't be able to go anywhere. Please, please, please – don't do this. My whole life is already ruined. How much worse can it get?" And she burst into uncontrollable sobbing.

Although Dietrich came from a powerful family and was himself quite a shrewd businessman, he did have a heart. He was not a cruel and unfeeling person. When he saw her burst into tears, he sat on the edge of the tub and rubbed her shoulders saying softly that it was going to be all right. He believed she was afraid that he would keep her as a prisoner or physically harm her. So he reassured her with his tone of voice, since she didn't comprehend his words, that he would not hurt her physically. In fact, his plan was to take very good care of her – to dress her up, pamper her body with massages, wraps and special oil treatments. He was going to have her hair colored and styled professionally and her makeup artistically applied. Then he planned to have an exotic photo shoot of her in many different degrees of nudity, from being fully clothed wearing provocative, revealing outfits, to being almost fully unclothed with her private parts exposed. Still believing that Cassandra was a common street hooker, he imagined that she would be thrilled with the arrangements he was planning for her. Dietrich did not understand until several months later what type of background his "employee" actually came from.

While Cassandra was soaking in the warm bubbly bath, the hotel attendant arrived with a freshly washed and folded pink terrycloth robe and slippers to match. Dietrich brought them into the bathroom, hung up the robe and placed the slippers on the small bathroom chair. He could see Cassandra's face light up when she saw the clean and fresh pink robe since pink was her favorite color. She thought immediately about her pink bicycle that she had loved so much and would probably never ride on or see again. Tears welled up in her eyes but the hysteria had calmed down. The bath had done its wonders and she felt better than she had felt in many hours.

To her surprise, when Cassandra emerged from the bathroom Dietrich was about to open a beautiful designer bottle of champagne. She heard the loud popping sound of the cork. Then, holding the champagne bottle in his right hand and a crystal glass in his left, he turned to face her and handed her a beautiful crystal champagne glass. For a moment, Cassandra felt like an elegant princess about to be treated to a high quality glass of champagne. She temporarily forgot the circumstances that had led to her being here.

When Dietrich saw this previously dirty woman all cleaned up and wrapped in that pink terrycloth robe with her hair bundled high in a towel, his eyes opened wide in astonishment. Dietrich thought to himself, "I have never seen such a beautiful woman. She is magnificent to behold and she is mine to offer to all the men who will be thrilled to be with her. I can't believe how beautiful she is. How in the world could this dirty little tramp be so quickly transformed into such a beautiful specimen of a woman just by having a hot bath? Wait until I tell Roffe about my good fortune today."

Cassandra accepted the beautiful and delicate long stemmed glass, holding it steady as this strange and foreign man poured just enough champagne for it to bubble up but to not spill over. Then Dietrich lifted his glass to make a toast. She could feel the confidence and excitement in his voice but she had no idea what he was actually saying. Dietrich told her: "We are going to build a huge business. You are my lucky charm young lady and you don't even know it. Wait until you get a taste of the life I am about to provide for you. Living on the streets will be a thing of the past. You will sleep in a comfortable bed, after you have entertained your quota of men for the night. In the morning you will be able to sleep as late as you like. We will provide special baths, herbal wraps, massages and all sorts of treats for you. And you will be wearing the most exotic and sensual clothing. So tonight we celebrate. Drink my sweet lady. Drink to a bright and lucrative future."

Feeling his exuberance and obviously happy attitude, Cassandra was careful not to upset him. She vowed to herself that she will do everything she can to keep him happy so he won't be angry with her. Recalling the way Stefano and Damion had beaten and raped that poor woman they had brought home from the night club, Cassandra feared that this strange man might be violent with her. She did not yet understand that he had big plans for her but these plans did not at all include violence. What this man wanted was to have Cassandra act as his sex slave. He planned for her to share her shapely body freely with him and with her many customers who would pay a high price for their intimate experiences with her.

As they both sipped the champagne, there was a knock on the door. Room service had arrived. The waiter rolled a table into the room with several ornate silver platters on top. The aroma of food stimulated her long-forgotten appetite. As the waiter lifted the lid, she saw a variety of delicious Greek food - beef souvlaki, spice-flavored rice, sautéed vegetables, hot pita bread, hummus, baba ganoush, olives, salad with feta cheese and onions and green peppers. She had not realized just how hungry she was. And, as she was about to taste this delicious and familiar food that she loved, she did not know that it would be about 25 years before she would enjoy her favorite Greek dishes again.

Dietrich tipped the waiter and then picked up two plates, offering one to Cassandra. Without hesitation, she filled her plate with all the wonderfully displayed food. He thought, as he watched her: "No wonder she has a belly, she likes to eat and she eats too much. We'll have to fix that - but not tonight. Tonight we celebrate the start of a wonderful new business. And this beautiful lady will be the star attraction."

After the meal, Dietrich told her he wanted to pamper her with oils. Of course she did not understand what he was about to do. He had gone downstairs while she was in the bathtub to locate some oils. The young man working at the front desk gave Deitrich a bottle of a fragrant Greek oil that the young man explained was often used by the hired hotel masseurs. Dietrich's intention was to be kind and loving toward Cassandra because he wanted to have a loyal and happy employee. So on this first evening together, he was planning to pamper her body with oil, powder, massage and a loving sexual experience.

When they had both finished eating, Dietrich poured another glass of champagne and they both sipped quietly. Cassandra was sitting in the desk chair where she had eaten her dinner. He motioned for her to sit beside him on the bed. But before sitting on the bed himself, he started to take off his belt. Cassandra cringed and looked away. Noticing how suddenly terrified she had become, Dietrich walked over to her, touched her right shoulder and said very softly: "Young lady, I don't know what your pimp has done to you in the past, but I am not going to hurt you. I have no intention of ever hurting you. All I want to do is build a big business and make lots of money. And you are already a good hooker. I tried you out earlier this evening and I was quite pleased with you. We are going to do this together. You are my ticket to success. And I am your ticket out of hell. We are a good team. Soon you will realize that."

Taking her right hand, he gently led Cassandra to the bed. He rolled back the top sheet and the coverlet and then motioned for her to lie face down. At first, she stood there frozen in her tracks, her body actually shaking in fear. Again he reassured her with soft and gentle words and a soothing hand on her right shoulder. Standing behind her, he massaged her shoulders lightly. Without her consent he reached around to untie her robe and he slowly slipped that comfy pink terrycloth robe off her body. And that's when he saw all those strap marks that her brother, Alexei, had lashed upon her body earlier that same day.

He turned Cassandra around to face him. Looking directly into her eyes he asked: "Did your pimp do that to you? Is that the way you've been treated? Please little lady, do not worry. I will never hurt you. You are never going to be hurt again. I will see to that. I am now here to love you and protect you. You are my lucky charm and I will be the same for you."

Seeing the tender look in his eyes and the kind expression on his face, Cassandra felt a little bit safer and a little more relaxed. The next time he motioned for her to lie down on the bed, she listened. Standing at the side of the bed, Dietrich gazed down at this incredibly beautiful body which he had felt with his hands earlier that evening but he had not yet seen with his eyes. Scanning from top to bottom he saw her long neck, her well-shaped shoulders and her long slender arms leading to perfectly manicured nails. That detail surprised him. His image of a street hooker did not include perfectly manicured nails. But he figured that maybe he was wrong and maybe that was part of the prostitution culture. Looking at Cassandra's protruding round and muscular behind, he immediately reached down to stroke her. Cupping both of her buttocks in his hands, he massaged them with his hands moving in circular motions. Then he reached over to the table and poured some oil into his hands.

Rubbing his hands together to warm them and spreading the oil into his palms, he palmed each of her buttocks letting one finger slowly probe the opening below the crease. He poured some extra oil into his hands and started massaging her entire body. Dietrich was very aware of all the red streaks and newly formed scabs. He stroked those areas very lightly as he spread the oil all over her body. Working his way down her thighs to her calves, he spent some extra time massaging her firm and strong calf muscles. He thought to himself, "She obviously works out. Her body is so fit."

When he reached her feet, he was surprised to see they were neatly polished and the color matched her manicure perfectly. Having always felt a particular interest in women's feet, he could not resist an urge to feel her toes in his mouth. Knowing she was perfectly clean now, he rubbed and played with each of her toes, first massaging them with his hands and fingers, then caressing them with his tongue and lips, and finally pressing them into his mouth.

Every part of Cassandra's body pleased this man. He felt as if he could not get enough of her. And just as she had become so relaxed that she almost fell asleep, he climbed on top of her, placed some oil on his finger, lubricated her opening and then entered her body from the rear. He moved quickly in and out, holding onto her hips for leverage. Without providing any physical resistance, Cassandra complied with Dietrich's movements, allowing him to control her body at will. When he finished, he got off her, cleaned himself off in the bathroom and returned with a hot towel to wash her bottom. He cleaned her thoroughly, returned the towel to the bathroom, shut the light as he came back into the room and crawled into the bed next to her.

Thoroughly exhausted from her traumatic and stressful day, Cassandra fell asleep immediately. That night, her dreams were filled with family. Sitting at the family table, her brothers, her father and her two grandfathers raised their glasses repeating several times: "Cassandra, beautiful Cassandra, you are the treasure of our hearts. Men will always love you. Choose wisely. Your man will provide a beautiful life for you if you choose the right man." She slept soundly and at least in her dreams she was still living at home on her beloved Agapelargos Island, with her family that adored her. In her dream, nothing had changed and she was still the Cassandra she had always known herself to be.

14 THE MORNING AFTER

Morning had arrived. Cassandra was awakened by the sunlight streaming through the window. Dietrich had quietly gotten out of bed, showered, dressed himself and had gotten prepared for all the activity that lay ahead. As soon as Dietrich opened the curtains, Cassandra was immediately awakened. Smiling at her, he said in Swedish: "Good morning sunshine. Today will be a very busy day. You must get up and get yourself ready while I go downstairs to the dress shop. I will bring back some clothing for you to try on.

Of course, she did not understand what he was saying but his motions suggested that she needs to start getting herself ready. He contacted room service to order a small breakfast for her. When he left the room, Cassandra walked over to the window staring down at the beautiful island she had always loved. It was all so familiar to her and in this room she had a panoramic view of the park, the water and the road leading toward her parents' home. Still half disbelieving what had happened to her the day before, it took her quite a while before she could bring herself to get ready. Startled by the sound of a loud knock on the door, her very first thought was: "Alexei has found me. I knew he would come looking for me." She ran to the door to open it and her heart sank when she saw a strange man standing there with his rolling table. He said in Greek which, of course, she understood: "Room Service my lovely lady. Where shall I place this?" She motioned to the desk near the window. The room service delivery man placed the covered dishes on the desk and left the room.

Before eating anything, she went into the bathroom where she found a new toothbrush and a fresh tube of toothpaste sitting on the counter for her. She ripped opened the plastic covering and was pleased to see a pink toothbrush. Pink had always soothed her in the past and it was just the right touch on this strange and surrealistic morning. After brushing her teeth, she took a long hot shower, washing her body as thoroughly as she could. The scabs across her back and her butt hurt slightly but she applied the soap slowly and gently, enjoying the sensation of washing away whatever had been negative and unpleasant the day before.

After rubbing her body with the towel, she wrapped herself in that warm and cozy terrycloth robe. And then she realized that she had no clothing to wear. "What will I do?" she wondered. "Is this man going to keep me a prisoner? Will he make me into his sex slave and not allow me to leave this room? Is this going to be my fate?" Somehow her mind thought about the famous American man who had created Playboy Magazine. Her brothers used to read those all the time, struggling with the English but leafing through to see those beautiful naked women. She thought about that man, the publisher, who she had been told invited hundreds of guests to his wild parties but he was always dressed in his pajamas and bathrobe. "Is this what this strange man has planned for me?" she thought as she emerged from the bathroom.

Since she realized the food would soon get cold, Cassandra removed the lids and smiled when she saw her favorite omelet with spinach and feta cheese. There was fresh fruit on a plate (sliced apples, strawberries, pineapple and even banana) with a huge dollop of Greek yogurt. As she sniffed the pleasing aroma of fresh brewed coffee, she poured the coffee into the cup provided for her. There was also a small container of milk and a bowl of sugar. She added a teaspoon of sugar and a few drops of milk to her coffee. Life in this moment felt good. Cassandra decided on this very day that she would only focus on what is good in every moment of her life. Right here, right now, life felt good. She had just taken a wonderful hot shower. She had just brushed her teeth with a pretty pink toothbrush. Her body felt warm and comfy in her pretty pink terrycloth robe. And, in this moment she is eating her favorite delicious food for breakfast. Sipping her coffee, she was actually smiling. Cassandra had not even noticed that her little purse containing her identification papers was missing.

Without knocking, Dietrich quietly opened the door and saw Cassandra sitting at the desk, sipping her coffee and looking out the window. He thought to himself, "I have to pinch myself to remember that this is real. She is really here and my business venture is really going to happen. This girl has such a nice long slender back and pretty wavy hair. Wait until I have a good stylist create some exotic hairdos for her. And now, I can't wait to see how she looks in the new clothes I just bought her."

Placing her purse he on the bed, he walked quietly toward Cassandra and reached out to tap her on the shoulder. Surprised, he saw her jump and quickly spin around to see who was there. Sensing danger, her body had instantly contracted and she felt frozen with fear of the unknown. Seeing Dietrich standing there with a few shopping bags on his arm, she did not at first realize the packages were for her. Placing the bags onto the bed, he pulled out a beautiful pink silk dress. Her eyes lit up at the sight of it. Somehow he instinctively knew that she liked that color. Maybe it was because she had been wearing a flimsy pink blouse the night before. He held the dress up to her, indicating that she should stand up. As he held the dress next to her tall body, he sensed that he had chosen the correct size. Although he could not locate a bra for her, he did find some lace trimmed pink silk panties.

Handing the dress and one pair of panties to Cassandra, he pointed to the bathroom for her to try it on. But then he changed his mind. Seeing her sweet expression and her tall and elegant stance, he decided he wanted another look at her beautiful body. So he reached to the ties that held her robe closed, slowly opened it and stared at her incredible bosom. Reaching out with his hands he couldn't help himself from caressing them and tweaking those firm taut nipples. Knowing there was no time to play around and that he did not want to take a chance of staining her new clothing, he decided that now was not the right time to be sexual with her again. He knew he would have lots of free time to enjoy the pleasures of her body in the days and weeks and months to come.

So he lifted the dress over her head, helping her to raise her arms and slip them into the long lace-trimmed sleeves. Her firm breasts filled out the dress just perfectly. Dietrich could not believe his eyes and felt so proud of himself for judging correctly. He had selected just the right size dress for her. This dress was made of a soft and clingy material, with a neckline curved into the shape of a V revealing a small amount cleavage. The top portion was just loose enough for an eager man to glance down from the top and get a full view toward her belly. He thought again to himself: "Hmm! She will have to lose that belly."

Cassandra reached out for her new panties and he watched carefully as she lifted each leg to pull the panties up to cover her private area. As he watched her struggle to pull her panties up, he thought to himself: "Last night I was so thrilled when I reached down to remove her panties and she wasn't wearing any. We will have to provide her with panties that are easy to open. I remember seeing some with open slits at the bottom in a magazine a few months ago. One panty had snaps and another had a small tie that could easily be opened."

Dietrich had also purchased a pair of pink sandals with a slight heel. Again he had guessed her size correctly because Cassandra's feet easily slipped into the sandals and they fit her perfectly. She looked down and smiled at her new pretty pink sandals topped with a black and white polka dot bow. The dress felt wonderful on her body and she moved around in a circle to show her new outfit to this man who had given it to her. Smiling approvingly, Dietrich put the empty clothing bags in the bathroom garbage bin and proceeded to gather up his belongings which consisted of a briefcase and his jacket. As he hung his jacket on his arm, Dietrich thought to himself: "Uh oh! She doesn't have a jacket and it is much cooler in Switzerland." But then he smiled with an impish thought: "Oh yeah! When she gets chilled those nipples will stand out and excite me. I will buy her a warm jacket as soon as we reach our destination."

At that moment the phone rang. Cassandra thought once more: "Oh finally, Alexei has come looking for me and I will be freed from the control of this strange foreign man." But then she heard Dietrich mumble: "Ne" meaning 'Yes' in Greek, followed by "Efharisto" meaning 'Thank You' in Greek. And she realized that this man would not be thanking Alexei or the police if they were on the phone. She knew that her chances of being freed from this man were running out. Since she had very little money and no place to go, Cassandra felt she was in no position to attempt to leave him and go anywhere alone. She also had never gone anywhere totally by herself except when riding on her pink bicycle. Once again, Cassandra decided to find the good in every moment. Wearing her new pretty pink dress, her soft and comfortable pink panties and her new pink sandals, she felt okay and smiled as she passed the mirror in the hallway.

When they reached the lobby, Dietrich immediately led Cassandra toward a back entrance so that nobody would see her face. There was no doorman in the back, just a taxi cab sitting there with the engine running. When they entered the taxi, the driver asked where they were headed and Dietrich said, in Greek: "Airodromio," meaning airport. Cassandra knew then that she would be leaving her beloved island for a long time, maybe forever. During the short ride to the small island airport, she watched the scenery along the way silently memorizing the sights and sounds and the internal sensation of being at home. Cassandra knew it would a long time, if ever, before she would be riding on this road again.

At the ticket counter, Cassandra stood by as Dietrich supplied two false IDs, one for himself and one for her. He had taken her purse with him in the morning, found a photo of her, and had cleverly superimposed her photo image onto the fake ID he had prepared a few weeks earlier in anticipation of creating his new business. Although he hadn't planned to create a false ID for himself, thinking that her pimp might come looking for him and find him on the passenger list, Dietrich chose to not take any chances. The ticket agent provided Dietrich with two boarding passes and he quickly headed with Cassandra toward the security gate to check in.

To insure that they would spend as little time as possible waiting at the airport, Dietrich had arranged for them to arrive only a few minutes before the plane was scheduled to depart. All the while he was looking over his shoulder, worried that Cassandra's pimp might be following them. Little did he know that if Cassandra's father and brothers had found them, it would have been a much more serious danger for him. He could not have comprehended their ensuring rage and they probably would have killed him, without a second thought, for raping and kidnapping their beloved Cassandra. But fortunately for Dietrich, he did not have to experience that trauma. When they arrived at the gate, the plane had already begun boarding and he heard the stewardess on the loud speaker announcing the final boarding call. After handing the two tickets to the boarding agent, Dietrich and Cassandra were led to the outside terminal area where they were directed to walk toward the plane to board it.

Climbing the stairs up to the airplane entrance, Cassandra felt a sickness rising in the pit of her belly. She had no idea where she was headed and what might be in store for her. At the top of the stairs, before entering the plane, Cassandra looked back at the terminal building with tears filling her eyes. Silently she said to her island: "Goodbye my darling Agapelargos Island. I may never see you again. But I will always love you for having brought me such a beautiful life until now. Goodbye and stay as beautiful as I remember you today. Maybe good fortune will bring me back to you someday." Then Cassandra turned and stepped into the airplane which would take her toward her new life in a new country.

15 THE MELANAKOS FAMILY SEARCH

That evening, after Cassandra had been asked to leave the house alone, was quite solemn in the Melanakos household. Lyzandra spent her usual time in the kitchen preparing one of her delicious meals, lamb stew, a delicacy and favorite of the men in the family. But as she stirred the soup and broiled the potatoes with vegetables, tears filled her eyes so she could hardly see what she was doing. The men were focused on their individual activities. Demitri was on the phone in his office talking to his stock broker. Lyzandra could hear her husband talking loudly, almost yelling in the distance, obviously upset about some financial transaction he did not like. Damion was sprawled across the living room couch making plans to test out the sexual skills of that new exotic dancer at *The Cyprus Club*. He was also talking quite loudly but using seductive words and sexual innuendoes, a style that he was often teased about by his slightly envious brothers. Damion had a way with women that quiet and soft spoken Alexei just did not have. Even Stefano, who was himself quite a ladies man, was often impressed with Damion's commanding presence with women. Alexei was in the garage, as usual, cleaning every corner of his beloved Fiat convertible.

At 7:30 PM, Lyzandra called her husband and her two boys to sit down for dinner. Stefano, still quite upset by his discovery at the doctor's office earlier that day, suddenly showed up at the door to join the family for dinner. He could sense that something was not right and he asked, "Where is Cassie? Is she in her room? Have you given her a good hard beating? That little slut has ruined our good name in this community. What are we going to tell our friends and neighbors? What will the priest, Father Petrides, say? Are you going to send her away somewhere to have this baby so we are not embarrassed and humiliated by her growing belly? What is this family planning to do?" Looking first at his father's stone-faced expression, then his mother's teary eyes, then Damion's angry expression and finally the bewildered look on Alexei's face, Stefano knew the family had done something rash.

Lashing out at all of them, he screamed. "What are you all crazy? Cassie may have done something terrible but she is still part of our family and we have always loved her. She has always been such a good girl until now. I'm sure she can explain to us how this happened, with whom and why she let it happen. Maybe this unscrupulous man raped her. Maybe she tried to resist but his strength overpowered her. Maybe she actually did the worst thing imaginable, gave herself freely to a man who inspired passion in her. Haven't we all done that with women? I know I was crazy with rage a few hours ago but I talked to a few of the women at *The Cyprus Club* about a hypothetical proper sister of a friend of ours who had gotten pregnant. They certainly set me straight and reminded me that a family has to love and protect all its members, no matter what."

Lyzandra served the meal and they all ate in silence. Finally, while eating dessert, Alexei announced that he would go searching for Cassandra. He explained: "She could not have gotten too far since it has only been a few hours and she was walking. We locked the garage door so she had no access to that pretty pink bicycle that she loves. Does anyone want to come with me as I ride around town searching for Cassie?" Both Damion and Stefano volunteered to join him but since his sports car could only accommodate two passengers, Stefano insisted that he wanted to come. Damion, somewhat relieved, was now free to go hang out at **The Cyprus Club** and enjoy some sexual ecstasy of his own with that new exotic dancer. He figured his brothers would easily locate his little sister. "Where could she possibly have gone," he thought to himself. "Maybe she walked to the church. Maybe she went into town. Maybe she actually walked into that park that we always taught her to stay away from. I'm sure they'll find her easily. How many young women are walking around town all alone at this hour?"

As Lyzandra began clearing the dishes from the table, Demitri actually lifted a few plates himself and carried them into the kitchen. That was the first time she had ever seen him lift a finger to help her with a family dinner. Amazed, she turned to him and asked: "Demitri, What has gotten into you? You have never helped me with my cooking and cleaning. That is my responsibility. You are a good man and good husband. You provide so well for our family. And I am proud to serve all of you. But thank you for this special gesture of caring that I see."

Demitri sighed, "Ah my wonderful Lyzandra, you have been a good wife. I have not always appreciated you and I have flirted with many other women. But tonight, for the very first time, an emotion has stirred up inside of me. Even when we first married, I did not feel this emotion. I love you, my Lyzandra. I have grown to love you. And tonight, for the very first time, I know that this is true. And the reason I know is because my heart is aching over the pain I have caused our beloved daughter, Cassandra. All I could think about was how she shamed us by giving her body to a strange man without being married by the church. But she has been such a good girl, the light of my life, and I do truly love her with all my heart. I am glad my sons are out there looking for her. I'm sure she could not have gone too far on foot. I hope she's not cold tonight in that flimsy little lacey blouse and skirt. Oh my Lyzandra, what has this family done to our beautiful Cassie?"

Alexei drove down the winding path to the highway that ran along the water. It was now quite dark and there were only a few street lamps providing dim lighting along the road. Alexei and Stefano talked about where to begin and where she could possibly have gone after being humiliated, beaten and emotionally distraught. Both immediately thought about the church and blurted out in unison: "She probably went right to Father Petrides to ask him what she should do?" Stefano continued: "Father Petrides probably sat with her, asking her to repent for her sins. But maybe he shunned her and sent her away also. We are all taught to think that way and to treat our women badly if they misbehave."

When they arrived at the church, Alexei and Stefano got out of the car feeling quite hopeful. The church door opened into an almost empty room with only 2 elderly men sitting and praying. Father Petrides saw the two boys and motioned for them to come toward him. As they got close, he asked: "To what do I owe the pleasure of seeing both of you at this late hour. I have only seen the two of you at Sunday services, and not recently I might add."

Stefano spoke first. "We are looking for our sister, Cassandra. She ran out of the house this afternoon after we had a family quarrel and she has not yet returned. The whole family is really worried about where she could possibly have gone. Did she come to see you, Father Petrides?" The priest shook his head, saying: "I have not seen your beautiful sister but I am sure she could not have gotten too far." Alexei said, before turning to leave: "Father Petrides, if you see her please tell her we love her and we want her to come home." "Will do boys," said the priest, thinking to himself as he watched the two brothers walk away: "I wonder what happened in that family?"

Once outside the church doors, Alexei turned to his brother and said: "What do we do now? Where could she be?" Stefano suggested they check out the local restaurants in town, especially Cassandra's favorite pastry shop. "But they would all be closed by now," Stefano replied. "I know, I know" said Alexei, "but maybe she stopped there and stayed outside for a few hours figuring we would come searching for her."

So Alexei drove toward the little town, slowly making his

way past all the stores including the pastry shop. They stopped at the quaint little restaurant on the corner where the family had shared many lovely dinners. Seeing that the lights were on indicating that the restaurant was still open, Alexei parked the car right in front. Both boys eagerly walked into the restaurant that was so familiar to them. Chloe, their favorite waitress greeted them at the door, inviting them to choose a table. Stefano immediately asked her: "Have you seen our sister Cassandra? She's been missing for a few hours and we don't know where she has gone." Chloe shook her head, wondering to herself what could have possibly happened that Cassandra would be missing. But she dared not ask. The boys left as quickly as they had arrived, both feeling a sense of disheartened dread. They didn't know what to do next.

That's when Stefano suggested they go into the park. Alexei was a bit resistant saying: "I can't imagine that our little sister would have wandered into that lower class park all by herself. Yes, there are some average people that go there but there are also some derelicts and aggressive men. The wrong man could easily have mistreated or harmed our beautiful little sister. Hopefully it is not too late to save her and protect her. I will never be mean to our little Cassie again in my life. She has been the jewel of my heart. Any other woman will have a big act to follow in order to gain my love."

Parking the car in the parking lot adjacent to the main entrance, Alexei and his brother walked into the park. It was quite dark but there were many standing lamps lighting the path. They walked toward the water and actually arrived at that very same bench where their sister had been sexually molested only a few short hours ago. There were a few couples walking around in the park. They stopped to ask everyone they saw if they had seen a beautiful young lady in a flimsy slightly torn pink blouse and a lace trimmed designer skirt. Nobody seemed to have seen their beloved Cassandra.

Discouraged that nobody could tell them what had happened to their sister, the two brothers decided they should go to the police station to submit a missing person report. . Fearing the worst, that she had been raped and murdered or beaten and left to die somewhere, they didn't say a word to each other. When Alexei pulled up in front of the local police station, he greeted the officer on duty and told him they wanted to report a missing person, their 17 year old sister, Cassandra Sybil Melanakos. They told the officer there had been a family fight, that their sister had gotten enraged and stormed out of the house. They both lied to prevent the possibility of being charged with a crime. By now, both brothers feared the worst and prayed that their fears were in vain.

They returned home to find their mother waiting impatiently in the living room. "Have you found her boys?" she optimistically asked. But when she saw their forlorn faces, she knew that her beloved daughter was missing and may never return. Nobody in the family could have imagined the fate awaiting their beloved Cassandra.

For the next few days and weeks, the three brothers scoured the town, posting photos of Cassandra everywhere. Somehow nobody seemed to have seen her on that fateful night. What the Melankos family did not realize is that Cassandra had looked so disheveled, like a homeless person or street hooker, that nobody had really paid attention. Even the clerk at the hotel, seeing her shabby unkempt appearance, had assumed that Cassandra was a local street hooker. When Dietrich stood with her at the counter to check in the staff kept their distance and wanted nothing to do with her. And when they were leaving the hotel the next morning, Dietrich had taken Cassandra swiftly toward the back door so that none of the daytime staff at the hotel had actually seen her face. Even the room service waiter had not paid much attention to her because he was rushing to return to the kitchen.

It wasn't until a few days had passed that it even occurred to anyone that Cassandra could have been taken away from Agapelargos Island on a boat or an airplane. So the family hired a detective to check the passenger lists on all the boats and the planes that had left on the days and weeks following Cassandra's disappearance. Every search led down a futile path. Cassandra had disappeared and was nowhere to be found. The search for their sister usurped the energy and emotions of her 3 brothers for many years to come. But Demitri and his three sons never gave up hope that they would one day find their beloved Cassandra. Lyzandra's heart was broken and she never quite recovered. Sadness permeated her days and most of her upper class friends grew weary of her negative attitude.

Nobody in town ever learned the true story about why

Cassandra had left her family. Rumor had it that she had always been wild and defiant. In fact, several of the boys bragged dishonestly about their secret conquest of her, knowing she had never given herself to any of them. It wasn't until several decades later that one of the brothers would have an accidental brief encounter with his much more sophisticated and mature sister during his travels to investigate a new business opportunity in Switzerland.

16 DIETRICH AND ROFFE'S SEX SAMPLER

Although he had maintained an outward appearance of being calm and confident, inwardly Dietrich had been terrified for many hours. He had been expecting that someone, presumably this young lady's pimp, was out searching for her and would eventually find them together. Dietrich imagined that the pimp would be in such a state of rage that Dietrich's life would definitely be in danger, that he would probably be beaten badly or maybe even killed. So when he and his newfound lady, Cassandra, were finally seated and the plane left the ground, Dietrich breathed a huge sigh of relief. Cassandra noticed his response and realized he had not been as secure as he had pretended to be. When the stewardess passed by, Dietrich ordered a strong drink and invited Cassandra to order one for herself as well. This was to be the last time Cassandra would understand what people were saying for a very long time to come. She wanted to say something to the stewardess about her precarious situation but Dietrich kept a firm eye upon her. Even at one point when she motioned to get up to use the bathroom, he followed her there and waited outside the door, making sure she had no opportunity for private contact with the stewardesses or anyone else on the airplane. Nobody on this flight had the slightest suspicion that this beautiful young lady was, in fact, being held hostage and being kidnapped at age 17 by this Swedish man who had been a total stranger to her the day before.

When they deplaned at the airport in Switzerland, Dietrich looked around uneasily, nudging Cassandra to walk quickly with him toward the exit. Relieved to see his friend Roffe waiting near the exit door, Dietrich's face lit up with another sigh of relief and obvious joy. "Yes," he thought, "It IS going to happen. Everything is working as well or even better than I had anticipated. Luckily for me, Roffe was available. We are free and clear now and about to create such an exciting and lucrative business. Roffe and I will soon be rich."

Cassandra looked at the signs along the walls, written mostly in German and in French. Overhearing conversations in these strange languages, she did not understand a single word. Then she felt a cool chill shoot up her spine. She didn't realize that she was now in a country, Switzerland, which had a completely different climate from her beautiful little island in the sun. Shivering in her light weight dress, all she could think about was that she needed a jacket. Dietrich was excitedly sharing his business plans with Roffe, not even noticing that Cassandra was cold. Finally, Roffe interrupted the conversation when he turned to look at Cassandra and saw her body shaking. Roffe asked, in a concerned and caring voice: "Don't be scared, young lady. We are not going to hurt you. Or are you cold, is that why you're shaking? Dietrich, can't you see she is shivering? Give her your jacket. This beautiful young lady looks elegant and yet fragile. She certainly doesn't appear to be a street hooker, but if you say so, we have ourselves a real beauty to put on display." Dietrich removed his jacket and placed it around Cassandra's shoulders. Roffe continued: "I have already started checking out various locations and I think I spotted just the right place to begin our business. I'll tell you all about it during the ride to the hotel."

While riding in Roffe's car and looking out the window, Cassandra noticed that the streets and the buildings seemed narrow, dark, old and cold – very different from her warm and lovely island. This new city did not make her feel welcome. In fact, she had never felt so all alone in her entire life. Since nobody around her spoke Greek, she could not explain anything she was thinking or feeling, wanting or needing. All she could do was to make gestures, like a little baby, and these two men would either pay attention or not depending upon their own moods and interests. Having grown up as the token female surrounded by demanding, abusive and controlling men, Cassandra was used to being in this position of not having much say about what will happen next. She realized that she certainly had very little control over her life at this moment, even less control than she had known in the past. So, in her usual matter of fact way, she once again made the decision to look for and discover what is good about the present moment. She refused to think about the life that she had left behind.

When they arrived at the hotel, it was already quite late. Cassandra and Dietrich had not eaten for many hours.

While Dietrich headed toward the front desk to check in, he instructed Roffe to take Cassandra to the hotel restaurant and order some drinks and food before the restaurant might stop serving for the night. Roffe motioned for Cassandra to walk in front of him so that he could observe her body from the rear. Watching her long legs move in a rhythmic, sensual glide, her hips moving slightly from side to side, and her long wavy hair flowing gently down her back, he decided then and there that he wanted to sample her wares before inviting other men to try her out. He held himself back from grasping both her butts and squeezing them before she reached a chair to sit down. Of course, Cassandra was totally oblivious to what was going on this man's mind. She was happy to be in an elegant restaurant at this hotel, ready to eat a tasty meal that she knew would be nothing like her familiar Greek dishes.

Roffe spoke in his choppy Swiss-German to the maître di, asking for a corner table in a booth. Before sitting, he asked for a bottle of champagne to be brought to the table along with some fresh appetizers. While waiting for the waiter to arrive, Roffe sat down to the left of Cassandra and quite close, almost immediately placing his right hand on the inside of her left thigh. Her body froze as she cringed at his touch. Moving his fingers up her thigh toward her crotch, he felt arousal already beginning in his body. He knew he wanted her and the desire was growing within him. If Dietrich had not suddenly arrived, Roffe would have begun exploring Cassandra's private area right there at the table. But Roffe managed to contain himself once his long-time friend appeared.

When Roffe released his grip on Cassandra's leg, she let out a deep sigh. But when she heard the pop of the champagne bottle cork, it startled her and she actually jumped about an inch off her seat. Dietrich laid his left hand on her right shoulder to calm her down. He quietly whispered in her ear, in Swedish, "It's going to be okay little hooker lady. Nobody is going to hurt you. We are both going to make love to you tonight. I want Roffe to have a taste of what I have already experienced with you. We are going to make so much money and you are about to become a sex star. So eat up little darling. You are going to need your energy. We will help you work off that little growing belly of yours." Dietrich had no idea that Cassandra's belly was not growing from overeating but from a fetus developing within her.

Roffe ordered some of his favorite Swiss food for the table, explaining what each dish was. First came the appetizers: a beautifully displayed plate of various local cheeses including Emmental, Gruyère, Vacherin and Appenzeller served with homemade bread and rolls. One of the dishes that Roffe had grown to love was Zürcher Geschnetzeltes - thin strips of veal with mushrooms in a cream sauce served with rösti, a popular potato dish. Another dish was a favorite from the French part of Switzerland, Papet Vaudois, a filling dish of leeks and potatoes served with Saucisse au chou (cabbage sausage). A third dish included cut meat Zurich style with Raclette – hot cheese dribbled over potatoes, served with small gherkins and pickled onions.

Having finished off almost 3 glasses of champagne, Cassandra momentarily forgot where she was and the fact that she was actually a captive of these two men. She found herself gobbling down this delectable gourmet Swiss food. Having never tasted anything like this, her taste buds were being stimulated to high intensity. And then the chocolate fondue arrived. Using a long fondue fork, she was instructed to stick one end into a strawberry and then dip it into the chocolate. Absolutely loving the taste of the food, Cassandra was actually laughing together with these men at how sloppily they were all dripping chocolate onto their faces. At one point, Roffe leaned over to lick the dripping chocolate from Cassandra's chin and he started nibbling on the side of her lips. She actually didn't mind. At that moment, being already quite drunk and feeling so sensually stimulated by the food, she didn't even flinch. In fact, she kind of enjoyed this strange man's attention.

Dietrich asked Roffe to order some strong freshly brewed coffee for the three of them, explaining that they were about to engage in some exciting and highly strenuous activity. Cassandra had no idea what these two men were secretly planning to do with her that night. And this would be only the beginning of a sexual adventure that would become a continuous cycle of pleasing a variety of different local men - travelers, businessmen and even young boys having their first sexual experience.

Asking to be excused, Dietrich headed for the front desk to request some sample hotel bottles of body creams and lotions. Roffe asked the waitress to bring him a container of freshly made chocolate fondue. Waiting at the table for the check and the container to arrive, Roffe again began to fondle Cassandra. His right hand slipped around her back, grasping her right hip. He lifted her slightly off the chair to allow her butt to sit firmly in his right palm. And he moved his fingers slightly to fondle her uncomfortable butt. As his fingers edged toward the inside of her leg toward her private area, the check arrived. So once again, he removed his hand, signed the check with their room number, and he pointed for Cassandra to take the container with her.

When they walked out to the lobby, Dietrich had just finished collecting his goodies – several bottles of body lotion and body cream. He had already asked, as he checked in, for an extra supply of huge bath towels and wash cloths. Roffe, Dietrich and Cassandra walked toward the elevator down a long corridor to the right of the front desk. Dietrich pushed the button to the eighth floor and led his group to Room 808. He happened to have a preference for the number "8." It had always been his lucky number and so he was thrilled when the hotel clerk assigned him to that room. To Dietrich it had been an auspicious omen, a good luck sign for the ambitious enterprise he and Roffe were about to begin. And tonight was going to be their first sampling of an adventure that he believed was going to build to ecstatic heights in the months and years ahead.

When Dietrich opened the door to Room 808, Cassandra let out a gasp. She had not expected to be taken to such a lavishly furnished penthouse suite. The center room was huge and there appeared to be 2 separate rooms that could not actually be seen from the main area. On the coffee table in the center, next to a beautiful ornate gold trimmed white and floral silk covered couch, was a large basket containing fruit and cheese, crackers and nuts. A bottle of champagne was nestled in a tray of ice next to several crystal long-stemmed champagne glasses. Along both walls were mahogany tables upon which were vases and baskets filled with an assortment of lovely looking and sweet smelling flowers.

Reaching into one of the flower baskets, Deitrich handed a beautiful pink rose to Cassandra. He whispered in her ear softly: "You are my lucky charm, my princess of fortune. Roffe and I are going to make so much money with you. And you are going to be our sex star. I can't believe my good fortune to have met you. And it was only last night that I had my first taste of your sweet ambrosia. I am ready for more. And tonight I will be sharing you with my friend and new business partner, Roffe."

Turning to Roffe he said quite excitedly: "I can't wait to have a piece of her again. She was that good. But first, I want to watch you delve into her and tell me if she is all that I believe she is. I believe we have struck gold but I want you to tell me if I am just exaggerating or if she is everything I say she is. Wait until you see her naked. Her body will really excite you. Those long legs, round firm butt, large firm breasts, nipples that stick straight out.... Oh my God, my dick is already hard. I can't wait to have her again. But I want YOU to have her first. Enjoy her. Play with her. I will get even more aroused watching you and anticipating my turn with her. But I just realized we need to take showers. I will go into the bathroom on my right. You take this young lady into the bathroom over there and wash her up good in the shower so she is sparkling clean and ready for both of us."

It didn't take much convincing for Roffe to immediately take Cassandra's hand and lead her to the bedroom on the left. Removing his shirt and tie, he placed it on the back of a nearby chair. He had been wearing a business suit all day and had removed his jacket immediately after entering the suite, a few minutes earlier. Cassandra watched as Roffe proceeded to remove his pants. Watching him stand there in his jockey shorts she could see that he was actually quite attractive. She liked the muscular shape of his chest and shoulders with a thin layer of hair trickling down the center. It was obvious to her that he was already aroused because she could see a big protrusion down below. Pointing to the bathroom, he indicated that she should remove her dress. She stood there without budging so he moved closer, pulling her body against his so that his firm erection could press up against her. His arousal was already quite intense and he was afraid he might let go too soon, before having a chance to feel himself inside her. So Roffe released his grip and slowly lifted Casssandra's dress over her head. She did not resist. Just as Dietrich had done the night before, Roffe found he could not help himself. He just had to suck on her nipples that stuck straight out, even before he had totally removed her dress. As he continued to lift her dress over her head he fondled and caressed her beautiful round breasts that were not being held in place by a brassiere. Realizing suddenly that she did not yet have any other clothing to wear, he stopped what he was doing and carefully laid her dress across the top of a big leather lounging chair in the corner of the room.

Before removing his jockey shorts, he reached over to Cassandra and slipped his right hand down the front of her belly, inside her panties. Playing with the hairs that led down to the opening below, his fingers gently massaged her vulva. Soon she could feel one of his fingers moving up inside her vagina. The finger felt big and strong and it was moving in circular motions, stimulating her in a way she had never before imagined. As he moved his finger rapidly toward the front inside of her crotch, she felt her body suddenly convulse into a series of powerful contractions. Her legs felt weak and she had the sensation that she might fall down.

Roffe, now beside himself with desire that felt almost painful, actually shoved Cassandra onto the bed, opened up her legs and without removing her panties, just pushing them to the side, he inserted his penis into her and rapidly ejaculated with a strong and powerful contraction that led to a few more. He laid on top of her for quite a while, allowing his body to gradually ease back down to normal. Instead of taking her into the bathroom to shower with her and wash her up, he decided to let Dietrich enjoy washing her while he was still feeling hot and ready. Roffe thought to himself. "That was incredible but my night with her is just beginning. I want to take a nice hot shower, relax, drink some more champagne and then have her stimulate me in different ways before I explore her body again."

So he called out to Dietrich who was still in the shower in the other bathroom. Since Dietrich was not responding, Roffe leaned over Cassandra to remove her panties. Then he lifted her by the shoulders and pulled her up off the bed. He nudged her gently to walk in front of him toward the bathroom at the other end of the suite. Roffe wanted to get a good look at her totally naked body as she moved so he could describe it to his new customers. He was a bit disturbed when he saw the scabs and remaining redness from the welts on her body. He knew that he and Dietrich would help her body to heal and would certainly never physically beat her.

Hearing the shower as they approached the bathroom, Roffe pointed and then nudged Cassandra to go join Dietrich. Since she was now a bit chilled and felt dirty with semen dripping out of her, she eagerly entered the shower not quite realizing that Dietrich was still in there. His face lit up when he saw that incredibly voluptuous body coming toward him. His first move was to fondle her beautiful breasts and right there with the water dripping on his head he lifted each breast to his mouth to suck on the nipples. Then he began to wash her body, every inch of it, putting a large amount of soap on a washcloth and continually rinsing her crotch clean. He even probed her anus with the soap-filled wash cloth.

Then, handing her the washcloth, he indicated that he wanted her to caress and clean his organ that was now sticking straight out toward her. After she had washed his organ, he pushed her head down to place it into her mouth. Moving her head up and down with his strong palms holding her cheeks, the pressure in his organ built and he shot his semen into her throat. Cassandra gagged and spit it out into the shower floor. This is the first time Dietrich raised his voice, yelling at her: "Don't ever do that again! When you are working with a customer you make sure he believes you are enjoying his body, his semen and whatever he decides to do with you. I will teach you to be an obedient hooker. Maybe that's why your pimp has beaten you. Maybe you were not behaving properly and his customers were getting upset. We will have to fix this tonight. I'm going to tell Roffe to make sure he gives you some practice with your mouth. Our business is starting in just a few days and we need you to be up to par!"

Upon emerging from the shower Dietrich handed Cassandra a huge bath towel to dry her body and he pointed to a white terrycloth bathrobe hanging on the door. When he finished drying himself, he left her alone in the bathroom while he went to tell Roffe what they needed to teach their new sex star. While Roffe and Dietrich planned their next moves with Cassandra, she reached for the mouthwash on the counter, rinsing her mouth over and over again, but to no avail. These two men were planning to fill her mouth with their semen many times that night to teach her how to swallow it and appear to enjoy the process.

By the end of this first night, Cassandra had become a full-fledged prostitute. There was no denying it. Her body had been entered from different directions. She had been led to pose and move and even dance in different positions. And these two men had given her a lot of practice to improve her oral sex skills. But – the part that surprised her and that she had least expected – is that she actually found herself thinking: "I had been saying for the past 2 years that I envied Stefano and Damion for having so many exciting sexual adventures.

Well, my beloved brothers, your little innocent sister is no longer innocent. I am having my wish come true, maybe not in the way I would have imagined, but I am certainly having some different sexual experiences. And I am actually enjoying them. Who would have believed that?"

This first night, only moments before the sun rose, Cassandra's job as a working prostitute had finally ended. All three of them were totally sexed out and exhausted. Each of the men slept on one of the beds leaving Cassandra to sleep on the couch in the main room. Feeling totally wiped out, she would have easily slept on the floor if needed. Sleeping quite soundly, none of them awakened before almost noon the following day. The two business partners were quite pleased that they had taught their sex star how they expected her to behave with their customers. Their next task was to create the proper environment and invite the men who would be eager and willing to pay the high fees they would charge for a taste of their sex star's sensual delights.

17 CASSANDRA THE HOOKER

Dietrich was the first to wake up on this new day. He opened the curtains and smiled as he looked out over the city where he believed he was about to make his father proud. Not planning to ever explain exactly what type of business he had created, Dietrich intended to return home for visits with his pockets filled with Swiss francs, easily turned into Swedish cash. At first his mind was wandering but then he realized: "This beautiful young lady, our prize asset, has no clothing except for the dress she wore yesterday all day, on the plane and during dinner. I must go out to find her some new clothes. How can she begin serving men if she doesn't look stunning when they see her outside this room?"

Quietly, he walked across the main room so that he would not disturb Cassandra who appeared to still be sleeping soundly. He did not realize she was pretending to be asleep because she did not feel ready to accommodate more sexual activity. Her vagina was sore and her body felt as if it had been through a really strenuous workout. Dietrich nudged Roffe and said: "Wake up, Roffe. We have work to do. I am going to go shopping for some pretty, sexy dresses for our young lady. We can begin making money with her almost immediately, even before we have actually opened up officially for business. I will see if I can find some local customers."

Roffe reached for his robe, wrapped the belt around him and walked into the main room. Seeing Cassandra lying on the couch he could not believe his eyes. He thought to himself, "She looks gorgeous, even after having been through such an intense night with Dietrich and me. She seems to be a real natural beauty. I can't wait to get our business going and share her with our customers. Today I'll contact the landlord of that large loft-like space I saw advertised." And then Roffe noticed the container of chocolate fondue. Opening the container he said out loud: "We forgot all about this. Weren't we going to experiment with pouring this chocolate and some whipped cream on her private parts? Damn, we forgot that in all of our excitement to explore her body. Hmm…Too bad."

Staring intently at the basket of fruit still sitting on the table in the main room, Roffe was lost in thought when Dietrich asked: "Do you want me to order room service for both of you? It's really lunch time now and you're probably hungry. But we can't take her down to the restaurant with us. Remember, this beautiful young thing has no extra clothing, just the one dress she wore yesterday. Don't we want her to look exceptional for all the men to start desiring her? You know, she can actually start working tonight in this hotel room, even before we have acquired our business location. In fact, we may be able to entice some of the staff right here in this hotel to try out her wares on their breaks. We can offer a substantial discount to them as our in-house beta testers for this new business. You know, that's not a bad idea because if the guys working here get a piece of the action they will want to keep it quiet. Nobody wants to ruin a good thing. And we certainly do not want anyone complaining about us to the authorities...."

Interrupting Dietrich, Roffe blurted out "Oh wow! I have an idea that I think you're going to love. It starts with that chocolate fondue and what to do with it. We can create special delicacies, special treatment packages for varying fees. Hee! Hee!" He laughed deviously. "We can give our treatments enticing and titillating names with a specific theme. Maybe the themes will change over time or for specific events and holidays. But after eating that sensually magnificent dinner last night, here are my thoughts for our special **Sexual Delights Delicacy menu.** What do you think of this unique and enticing menu of sexual delights?

- **Chocolate Nips Delight**. Get a taste of those big firm nipples in your mouth dipped in hot melting chocolate fondue.
- **Whipped Butts.** Spread the whipped cream in the butt crease and rub yourself between the cheeks.
- **Lollypop Heaven.** Give her a mouthful of you dipped into warm melting cheese or chocolate fondue.
- **Banana Victory.** Insert a fresh and firm banana (dipped in chocolate or plain) and then eat the whole banana and more.

- **The King's Throne.** Sit on the throne and get the royal lap dance treatment."
- **The Oil Well.** Dip yourself into the warm oil, drip it into the oil well and enter the rear at your own risk.
- **The Queen's Chamber.** Enter the chamber using any of the open doorways.
- **The Kitchen Sink.** Enjoy a sampling of any or all of the appetizers and entrees.

And we can charge different prices for each one. Of course, we will have to set some really strict rules. If they only pay for the **Chocolate Nips Delight**, they can only ejaculate between her breasts. If they order **Whipped Butts**, they cannot enter her rear opening but they can use her butt cheeks to stimulate their release. For **Lollypop Heaven** they will receive oral sex and for **Banana Victory** they can only perform oral sex. In the **King's Throne** they will receive a lap dance but touching her body is taboo. Now it gets interesting and much more expensive. If they choose **The Oil Well** they can enter her from the rear only. And if they choose **The Queen's Chamber** they can only enter her from the front in missionary position. Finally, the most expensive item on the menu will be **The Kitchen Sink,** an opportunity to sample our young lady in any combination of these delicious sexual delights. What do you think about this Dietrich? I think I'm on to something great!"

Dietrich's eyes were wide and bright with a sense of wonder, excitement, anticipation and absolute delight. He reached over to grab Roffe and they both were literally jumping up and down and in circles hugging each other and laughing in pure ecstasy. Together they knew they were about to create something incredible.

Before leaving to shop for some new dresses for Cassandra, Dietrich called room service to bring to the hotel room an assortment of sandwiches, soups, pastries, fruit and a pot of fresh coffee. As he left the room, Dietrich thought to himself: "I will invite some of the guys on the staff to come for a special treat in our room, ½ hour of the special delight of their choice." Since Roffe had just introduced this incredible menu of sexual delights, Dietrich was impatient to test out this menu with a few excited paying customers. So, before investing a single penny in creating a sign, a menu, an advertisement, or a business card, Dietrich knew they could start their business this very evening. So he put on his networking businessman cap as he sauntered out of the room to go shopping for the young lady's dresses and a few new customers.

Too excited to spend time eating in the restaurant, Dietrich got a cup of coffee and pastry to go. He was hungrier to fill his wallet with money from paying customers than he was to fill his stomach with food. As luck would have it, while standing at the restaurant take-out counter waiting for his coffee, Dietrich overheard two men talking. Although he understood very little German, he did understand some of the cuss words. His ears perked up when he heard one of them say: "vögeln-to." Some of his father's German business associates had used that word before and he knew it was a vulgar way to say they wanted sex. So he motioned to them that they could come upstairs. Pointing to his watch he indicated they should come to Room 808 at 7 PM and he showed them a menu while pointing to their male organs. They appeared to understand and both looked quite happy. He did not quote prices but had a plan to entice them once inside their hotel suite, especially after getting a glimpse of their sex star's body. He would have Cassadra show just enough of her wares to have them hungering to pay for the highest priced delights.

Asking at the front desk where he might find a good dress shop, Dietrich headed for Miss Inger's Place a few blocks away. "Perfect," he thought when he saw the lady standing behind the counter in the back. "That lady working here has a build something like our little hooker lady. This salesgirl can find me a few beautiful dresses and a few pairs of sandals for now. Once we have our business established, I will take our young lady shopping and she can try on some sweaters and pants and more form-fitting, sexy outfits. For now, we just need her to have some simple, clean and pretty dresses to impress our potential customers."

The owner of the shop, who had just emerged from his office in the back room, was a heavy, loud speaking man with a slightly protruding belly. He had a big laugh and would often take the liberty of patting one of his sales girls on the rear. Dietrich thought to himself, "This man might be a perfect customer." So very casually, in a really broken German since he knew very few words, Dietrich attempted to invite this man to meet Cassandra. Pointing to the hotel, Dietrich made the hourglass shape of a woman's body several times and then pointed to his own penis as he moved his hips forward and back. This big man was already licking his lips in anticipation. Although he wanted to see a photo, Dietrich said he did not have one. He did not want to show Cassandra's fake passport which did, in fact, display her photo. He invited the man to arrive at Room 808 at their hotel at 8 PM.

Having purchased several different dresses in various colors and styles, Dietrich was ready to return to the hotel. As he walked along the street he gazed into the shop windows and suddenly saw a reflection of himself. He noticed he was standing noticeably taller and straighter, presenting an air of confidence that he had not felt in a very long time. Having started and failed at several small businesses in the past, Deitrich had the strong belief that this business venture would be a winner. And it was going to start bringing in money this very evening.

At the hotel, he said hello to the doorman who had greeted all of them the night before when they had arrived. The man made an off color remark in German, which Dietrich understood, describing Cassandra's breasts as full and round and easy to grasp in his hands. Dietrich took this as a sign that the doorman might be their third customer. So he boldly asked when this guy would have a break and if he would like to enjoy some sweet delights in their room at 10 PM. Dietrich had thought it might be good to give the hooker lady a long break between customers, especially on her first night in business. But the doorman smiled, saying: "No, my break is at 9 PM. Would that time be okay? I am often hungry for something sweet at that hour." Dietrich nodded his approval and told the doorman to knock on

Room 808 at 9 PM.

Pleased with his shopping and business canvassing for the day, Dietrich stopped at the restaurant for a late afternoon lunch or early dinner. Noticing a house phone on a counter near one wall, he called the front desk asking to be connected to Room 808. Roffe answered immediately and said: "Where have you been? I've been stuck here all day so far. Can you come upstairs and relieve me of my responsibility for a little while?" Dietrich responded: I'm in the restaurant. I bought several dresses for our young lady to wear. I'll have someone bring the dresses up to the room. Have her put one on and bring her down to the restaurant with you. We do not want to take a chance of leaving her alone at any time because she could possibly run away." I have some good news. Seems we are in business. Three different men have agreed to come to our room tonight. I know they will be thrilled when they get there. Then we will invite them to partake in one of our expensive sexual delicacies. See you soon."

Dietrich asked one of the waiters to contact the front desk and have these shopping bags delivered right away to Room 808. A young lady from the front desk arrived in the restaurant a few minutes later and assured Dietrich that she, herself, would bring the packages up to the room immediately. As she started walking away, Dietrich noticed she had quite a nice body and a pleasing style of walking. He was already thinking about expanding the business to include additional hostesses to provide sexual delicacies for more male customers.

About ½ hour later, Roffe and Cassandra arrived at the table where Dietrich was sitting. The time now was 5:30 PM and Dietrich knew the first customers, those two boys, would be arriving at 7 PM. "Not too much time," he thought. So he signaled to the waitress and asked Cassandra and Roffe to order their food quickly because work was about to begin. As soon as the food arrived, he asked the waitress to bring an extra container of chocolate fondue. He couldn't wait for this evening to begin. He and Roffe would be orchestrating the sequences, the sexual movements and the timing of each activity for Cassandra and for her customers. Dietrich encouraged everyone to finish up quickly so that they could be back in the room no later than 6:45 PM.

At 7 PM, 2 young men could be heard talking quite loudly in the hallway. Sure enough, it was those 2 young men that Dietrich had met at the hotel restaurant. When they knocked on the door, Cassandra greeted them in her white terrycloth bathrobe wearing nothing underneath. Before they entered the room, she untied her belt and opened her robe for just a moment, causing the eyes of these two men to light up and she could see them licking their lips in excited anticipation. She invited them to enter the room and their eyes opened wide as they observed the opulence of this room, the ornate carvings on the furniture, the full display of beautiful flowers, the fruit and cheese baskets and the champagne bottles on ice.

Roffe invited both men to join him on the couch to discuss the business side of this event. He provided a price list, which he had written up earlier that day while sitting alone with Cassandra. The two young men were told that they could be alone with her, each one for only ½ hour, and they needed to quickly decide who would go first and which delicacy each one wanted to indulge in. One of them quickly chose the Chocolate Nips Delight after having had that glimpse of Cassandra's round firm breasts and those hard nipples that his body had instantly responded to. He was told by both Roffe and Dietrich that there would be no privacy in this hotel suite. He was informed that his activities would be observed and if he did not obey the rules he would be banned from ever working with them again. The young man agreed and eagerly entered the bedroom where Cassandra was waiting. Roffe brought a bowl of chocolate fondue, freshly made and still warm. He motioned to the young man to remove all clothing so he would not stain anything but he was reminded that for the minimal fee he had paid he was only allowed to play with the woman's breasts.

In a flash, their very first customer had removed his clothes and was standing there stark naked staring at Cassandra as she slowly let her robe drop to the floor. In advance she had removed the bed covers and had laid several large bath towels on top of the bed sheets. The bowl of chocolate fondue had been placed on the night table next to the bed. Cassandra sat down on the bed leaning back against the headboard with a few pillows behind her back for support. She pointed to the fondue, indicating that it was time for this customer to enjoy his chosen delight. First he put his mouth into the bowl of chocolate and went directly to her nipples to start sucking. Then he got more brazen and dipped his hands into the chocolate, rubbing it all over her breasts, then licking and sucking and enjoying the delicious sweet taste. She reached down to his penis and indicated that he could put it between her breasts. Rubbing chocolate on his penis, he beckoned for her to use her mouth but she shook her head saying: "No, no. Not what you paid for." When Dietrich heard her say "No, no," he ran into the room and reminded this young man that he had only paid to fondle her breasts and not for her to fondle him in any way. So Cassandra lowered her body to sit on her knees to allow her breasts to be right at the level of his penis. With both of his hands he cupped her breasts and rubbed his organ between them, letting out a strong sound as the fluid shot out of him. He was then directed to the other bathroom across the main room to wash up and then leave. Cassandra went into the bathroom closest to her to clean up all the chocolate and whatever else had gotten onto her body.

Removing the towels covering the bed sheets, Cassandra replaced them with clean towels and then prepared to greet the second young man. His request had been for the Lollypop Heaven. So he was asked to remove his pants and indicate what position would be most comfortable for him. He chose to lie flat on the bed with his head elevated almost to sitting position so he could watch as she pleasured him. Cassandra indicated that if he wants her to pour warm chocolate or whipped cream or oil on his organ he would have to pay more money. He decided to enjoy the sensation of her mouth without any additions. She climbed onto the bed, straddled his body with her knees wide apart so he could glimpse the opening in her crotch and she covered his organ with her mouth, moving up and down, using her tongue in swirling motions, and squeezing his organ with first her right and then her left hand. His excitement was quite intense and his release came quickly. This time, Cassandra did not spit the fluid out of her mouth. But she also did not swallow it. This second customer was immediately instructed by Dietrich to go to the other bathroom to clean up and then leave. Waiting until the man had left the room, Cassandra ran into the bathroom, spit the fluid into the sink and rinsed her mouth repeatedly with mouthwash.

Cassandra had very little time to relax and freshen up between customers. The man from the dress shop had already arrived. She quickly removed the towels she had been laying on to pleasure her previous customer. Then she replaced the old towels with fresh clean towels. She took a few moments to rinse her mouth again before returning to sit casually on the bed to meet her next customer. The man with the big belly had requested Banana Victory because he was embarrassed about his weight. He preferred his own touch when he was aroused since he knew exactly how to make it happen quickly. When he entered the room he was handed a banana that had been opened enough to make the process easy for him. He was instructed to remove his clothing so that he would not dirty anything. Cassandra was sitting on the bed with her bathrobe closed when he entered the bedroom. She invited him to put her into whatever position he wanted for him to enjoy penetrating her with the banana followed by eating the banana and enjoying a further taste of her.

He beckoned for her to lie down with her crotch near the

edge of the bed with her feet wide apart. He removed 2 pillows from the bed to sit on them. First he checked her out by placing one finger inside. To his delight, her insides were oozing fluids. That's when he opened the banana and shoved it inside her opening as far up inside as it would go. Holding her thighs to keep them spread open he began eating, one of his favorite past times. He bit off a piece of banana, chewed it and then bit off another piece and then another until his tongue was reaching inside of her for the next piece and the next. He was chewing away, catching some pubic hairs, licking the whole area and feeling his organ grow and throb. Keeping his mouth glued to her open vagina, he began stimulating his organ quickly and just the way he knew would get him off. He ejaculated onto her body and she cringed for a moment in disgust and then immediately changed her facial expression to a huge smile. Roffe immediately told the man to bring his clothes and go to the other bathroom to clean off. Cassandra washed her body with a warm wash cloth, replaced the dirty towels, and came back to the bed to rest in her robe before the next customer arrived.

When the man with the big belly had left, Roffe and Dietrich, sitting on the couch began laughing as they counted their money. They could not believe their good fortune and how easy this business seemed to be. At 9 PM, on the dot, the doorman appeared, eager to taste one of the delights he imagined would be great. Being a mere doorman and not often feeling respected, he chose The King's Throne for his sensual delight. So he was told to remove his clothes and to sit on the big comfortable leather chair. Cassandra had already placed towels on that chair too. He sat on the chair wondering what to expect. Having seen the topless dancers many times at her father's night club, she knew exactly what to do. Slowly and seductively removing her robe, she let the doorman get a glimpse of one breast and then she covered it. She let him glimpse the other breast and then she covered it. Then she turned herself around, bent over bringing her head to her knees as she lifted up the back of her robe for him to get a different view. After a while, she let her robe drop completely to the floor as she moved and undulated to stimulate his imagination. When she saw his penis rise in response to her movements, she moved closer and reached out as if she was going to touch him and then kept her hands a few inches away. She moved her breasts close to his mouth and he reached with his tongue only to have her pull away again. When she rubbed her breasts on his chest and up toward his mouth, his hands couldn't help but reach around to grasp her butt. She yelled, "No, no." and Dietrich came running to warn the guy that he would never be allowed back if he disobeyed the rules of his particular delicacy. In this delight he was not allowed to touch her body. So he obeyed and let her move her hips forward and back and up and down, leaning against him, with her different body parts. As she rubbed vigorously against him, his body convulsed and he suddenly enjoyed his happy ending. This time Roffe came into the room to escort the customer out and point him toward the other bathroom to clean up.

Work was finished for the night. Cassandra started to remove the towels when Dietrich motioned to her saying, "No, no. You have finished with your customers and now you are mine. I have been hungry for you all night. Hearing those men grunt in pleasure and seeing their eyes light up when they saw your voluptuous body made me want to interrupt their fantasy play and have you right then and there. But I held myself back until now. I want you my little darling and I want you right now. I think I want to try the Whipped Butts delight. Roffe...." Dietrich called out. "Where is the whipped cream? Is there any left on the table?"

Roffe brought a bowl of whipped cream into the bedroom, hungry himself to enjoy Cassandra's body again. Dietrich instructed Cassandra to lie face down on the bed placing two pillows under her belly. He positioned her body so that it would easy for him to rub his organ along the crease between her two butts. Spreading the whipped cream on his penis, he changed his mind and asked Cassandra to sit up and pleasure him with her mouth – which she did obediently. His arousal was intense and he was about to explode. That's when he turned her back onto her stomach, spread the whipped cream onto both of her cheeks and began to rub his organ along the crease. His ejaculation was almost instant.

When Dietrich had finished he was surprised to see an eager Roffe waiting for his turn. Roffe chose to enter the oil well. He had already placed his bowl of oil scented with mint and basil and sweet honey on the night table next to the bed. He told Casssandra to remain in that lovely position with her beautiful round rear end facing him. Roffe went into the bathroom and returned with a warm wet wash cloth to clean away the whipped cream and whatever else remained on her backside. Then he proceeded to dip his fingers into the oil and slowly and methodically penetrate her rear opening. First he used one finger and then two. Almost pouring the oil into her, he was able to insert 3 fingers and almost a 4th. He knew she was ready for him. So he quickly rubbed the oil onto his organ and began to insert himself into her. The opening was ready for him so he slipped inside with ease and began moving in and out while holding onto the front of her hips. At one point he reached his hands further up her body to fondle her breasts and to squeeze her nipples. His body soon convulsed and he smiled with pure delight as this episode came to an end.

Dietrich and Roffe were now in business, for sure. But they also enjoyed perks that any man would be thrilled to have. And they could have it whenever they wanted. Cassandra was living her fantasy and actually felt quite good about it since nobody wanted to hurt her. She felt safe and over-protected by both of her masters whom she called her bosses. Each night Cassandra would provide the specific delights requested by each man. There was a detailed list of sexual delights to be made available by her. The rules were clearly written and each customer signed an agreement before indulging in the goodies. All customers were strictly limited to receiving exactly what they had paid for and nothing more. Cassandra knew what was expected of her and this enabled her to feel safe and secure and even somewhat in control of her life.

After two months, business was thriving for the two business partners. They had contracted to purchase a large space and were in the midst of planning a dramatically themed environment. Focused intently on setting up the space and figuring out how to induce additional ladies into the fold, neither Dietrich nor Roffe had realized that Cassandra's belly was becoming noticeably larger. It wasn't until one of their regular clients reacted negatively upon seeing her growing belly. Dr. Albrecht Kuhn, a distinguished visiting medical doctor and professor from Munich, Germany with a specialty in gynecology and obstetrics, reacted strongly one evening when Cassandra opened her robe. In front of everyone, Dr. Kuhn exclaimed aloud: "My God, young lady, I do believe you are pregnant. All these weeks, all these visits, I have enjoyed your body so much that I did not realize this. Yes, I did feel your belly and I would often think to myself that it was rather round, but it felt so firm and smooth. I had even wondered at one point if you might be holding a fetus but I ignored that thought because I didn't want my enjoyment with you to end. But now I cannot continue having sex with you. I do not want to be responsible for causing a miscarriage at this late stage of pregnancy for you."

Dr. Kuhn stormed out of the bedroom and into the main room obviously quite upset. On this evening, which he had been anticipating for hours, he was not going to have the satisfaction of indulging in his favorite delights - Oiling the Well or Entering the Queen's Chamber. He had just spent several long and grueling days presenting a series of research paper presentations at the Grande Rounds of 3 different local hospitals. During many of his talks, right in the middle of a slide, the image of Cassandras's naked body would flash through his mind and he would feel his organ expanding. Roffe put an arm around Dr. Kuhn's shoulder and reminded him that there were many other delicacies he could indulge in. Dietrich jumped up, brought the list to Dr. Kuhn, and excitedly suggested he would enjoy the **Lollypop Heaven** because that would not be harmful to Cassandra's growing fetus. Delighted that he would not have to leave unfulfilled, Dr. Kuhn returned to the room for this special sexual delicacy.

Before leaving, Dr. Kuhn asked the two men if they had any plans for this very pregnant young lady to get tested and treated. He asked them: "Does she have a doctor? Where will she give birth? She appears to probably be in her 7th month of pregnancy, quite far along. And with all that activity she has engaged in, the baby may arrive before the full 9 month term. I would advise you both to get prepared and to find a new sex star to please your many male customers. As a matter of fact, I may have a solution for both of these problems. There is a very beautiful young nurse-midwife who has assisted me in many deliveries at my former hospital in Munich. I will invite her to be Cassandra's full time nurse and assistant. And, I am quite certain she will also be a perfect fit for your business needs. Wait until you see her body and the way she moves. And I'll let you in on a secret. In Germany, she has a private service that she provides for many of the husbands of the near-term pregnant women she serves. Her skills are excellent as both a midwife and a man pleaser, if you know what I mean. But I will only invite her to join you if I am brought into your business as a full partner."

Dietrich and Roffe immediately conversed with each

other in Swedish, trusting that Dr. Kuhn would not understand. Dietrich reminded Roffe: "We don't have a legitimate passport for Cassandra and we don't want to give the police any reason to investigate her and any of our business matters." Roffe quickly responded: "We are going to need a doctor in case there is a medical problem. So I guess we have no choice. And this woman Dr. Kuhn talks about may help us to begin our business at the new space."

Turning to Dr. Kuhn, both Dietrich and Roffe shook his hand, slapped him on the shoulder and informed him they would draw up a contract for him to sign in the next few days. Both Dietrich and Roffe did not have any time to feel upset about Cassandra's pregnancy and the impending birth. Instead, they felt elated that their business was about to expand and grow to a higher level. Cassandra's official duties as a sex star providing sexual delights for men had officially ended that night. Dr. Kuhn was to be her final customer but she would choose, of her own volition, to remain in the business for many years in a different, more managerial, capacity.

18 CASSANDRA GIVES BIRTH

Having worked with Roffe and Dietrich and all the male customers for a few months, Cassandra had gradually begun to communicate some words and phrases in a few languages. For those clients who spoke German or French, she had learned to ask some simple questions and to respond to what they told her about their professional life, their intimate relationships, their body needs, etc. Dietrich and Roffe had assumed from the very start that Cassandra was a street hooker, controlled by her pimp. Up until this day when Dr. Kuhn had informed them that she was definitely pregnant, neither had ever considered that her background had not been the way they had imagined it. As soon as Dr. Kuhn had left, Dietrich rushed over to Cassandra's room where she was showering to get ready to presumably entertain one or both of her bosses before being allowed to go to sleep.

To Cassandra's surprise and bewilderment, for the very first time Dietrich sat next to her on the bed and did not reach out to touch and fondle her. Instead, he turned to face her and deliberately asked: "Cassandra, tell me about your background. What was it like for you to be working with your pimp on that Agapelargos Island? Tell me where you originally came from, what happened to you in your childhood, and how you got involved in the sexual pleasuring business?" Expecting an interesting and possibly arousing story, Dietrich was thinking he might indulge with her one last time before she receives her physical checkup. Dr. Kuhn had promised to arrange for one of his assistants to provide a pregnancy test and a full blood workup for Cassandra the following afternoon in the hotel room.

What Dietrich heard next broke his heart, causing him to instantly fall to the floor on one knee, profusely begging Cassandra for her forgiveness. As she explained that she had been brought up in a strict and Orthodox Greek home on the beautiful, peaceful island of Agapelargos, tears flooded her eyes. She explained to Dietrich that she had been trained from as early as she could remember to always be a really good girl - obedient, loving, and a complete servant to all the men in the family. She would bring them their slippers, their drinks, their food and anything else they might request. For every meal, it had been her responsibility to assist her diligent mother to cook and serve the food, to later clean up the table and then wash and dry the dishes. Her brothers, she explained, had no such responsibility. They would each engage in their favorite activities: Alexei washing his newest sports car, Damion contacting some woman for a sexual exploit, Stefano making a business deal, and her father, Demitri, discussing his investments with his current broker.

Cassandra, now crying profusely, took a deep breath and explained something that shocked Dietrich, bringing him immediately to the floor on his knees. Cassandra told him: "I was so jealous of my 3 brothers. They could go out with as many women as they desired. Then something happened that changed my attitude and has brought about my downfall. One day, when I had just turned 8 years old, I heard Damion and Stefano beating and raping a woman in one of the bedrooms down the hall. We lived in a huge mansion on the hill. When I heard a woman screaming and crying, I ran to see what was happening. I thought somebody had gotten hurt and that one of my brothers was probably helping her. What I saw caused me to freeze in shock. When my brothers saw me standing in the doorway, one of them called me over and invited me to fondle this woman's body. They even pushed my finger into her vaginal opening which was very wet. And then Stefano whispered into my ear these words I will never forget: *"This is what a beautiful woman's body feels like. Soon you will be a grown up woman and men will feel your body too. But be careful. Do not go out by yourself to a bar. We decided to teach this young lady a lesson she will never forget. Women belong at home, waiting for their man, or chaperoned by their brothers."*

At this point, Dietrich's eyes were also filled with tears. He had grown to deeply care about this beautiful woman who he no longer considered a stranger. Having been brought up as a gentleman in Sweden, he had never been the type of man to take advantage of an innocent woman. Reaching out to hold Cassandra's right hand, he asked her to continue talking and explain to him how she ended up in the park that night, who had beaten her and why she was not wearing panties.

Hardly able to talk because the sobs were continuous now, Cassandra very slowly told Dietrich more of the details of that fateful day. She explained that her family had been wonderful to her, most of the time, yet they were all extremely controlling. "I was not allowed to go anywhere by myself. One of my brothers or one of my parents would take me where they wanted to go at the time. I could ask but very often my request would be ignored. I really had no control over my life. Secretly I had fantasized about being free to be me. But I continued being the good girl until puberty and menstruation hit me and once again destroyed my sense of love for one of my brothers. I started bleeding and not knowing what had caused it, I didn't dare tell anyone. After church, my brother did not let me use the bathroom again because he was in a hurry to go have sex with some woman from my father's night club. When I got out of the car, I had dripped blood all over my brother Alexei's fancy new leather car seat. Damion had borrowed Alexei's car and is the one who had driven me to and from the church that morning. When I got home, I ran upstairs, removed my badly stained white dress and panties and threw them away in the garbage. I stayed in bed crying into my pillow the rest of the day. When Damion returned home that night he beat me with his belt strap. At this point I was 13 years old. But my hormones had begun to flow strongly and I felt strange sexual feelings for one or two, not many, of the boys at my school."

Dietrich looked up at Cassandra's tear stained face and reached over to kiss her left cheek. Sadness and remorse filled his heart when he realized the ordeal he had put this sweet and lovely woman through. He thought to himself, "I'm no better than her abusive brothers. In fact, I'm no better than that imagined pimp that I thought had beaten her up and would be coming after me to possibly kill me."

Dietrich asked her again, "Oh my dear Cassandra, I am so sorry. I had no idea that you came from a high class family and that you were not usually alone at night like you were that evening. So, why were you there? Why was your blouse so torn and dirty and why didn't you wear panties? I was positive you were just a street hooker looking for some action – and I was happy to oblige in that moment. If I had only known...."

As Cassandra talked about her favorite pretty pink bicycle, her face temporarily lit up in that innocent teenage smile that brightened her entire face. She explained how that bicycle had been her very first vehicle, offering her the sense of freedom she had craved for years. She said: "So on this one beautiful sunny day in spring, a few days before Easter Sunday, I took a leisurely ride with my bicycle along the road that wrapped around the lake. I had passed that park many times in one of the family cars and even on my bicycle. But on that fateful day I decided to explore the park. My family had always told me not to go in there, that there were too many common people and that a woman alone could be raped or physically harmed. They often told me that the park was a dangerous place. They expected me to stay away from there."

"This was such a beautiful day," Cassandra continued. "The flowers lined the edge of the grass along the road. I could see lots of couples walking arm in arm and children giggling and running around. That park felt safe to me and I just wanted to explore something new, a place I had never been before. And then I saw him sitting on that same park bench where I met you. Do you remember my calling you Cyrano? When I saw you that evening, just for a moment I actually thought I was seeing Cyrano. Anyway, Cyrano and I met and were instantly attracted and maybe even in love. We vowed to meet again the following day at 2 PM. I came to see him that next day and we kissed and fondled behind the bushes near a big willow tree. We promised to meet again the following day at the same time but it was Easter weekend and I could not leave my family so I did not return until Monday. By that time we were both so hot and wanted each other so badly, that I did not resist when he invited me to join him on the ship. He was a Greek Australian sailor about to go on a dangerous mission to Vietnam. We made love that late afternoon. Then, as I was leaving, he told me he would be departing in the morning. I never saw him again and I have no idea what has happened to him. I don't even know if he's still alive."

Dietrich was mesmerized by his sweet Cassandra's story, this woman he had foolishly mistaken for a prostitute. Thinking back, Dietrich realized he had recognized that she exhibited class and he had chosen to ignore the signals because of his greedy desire to create a business with her as his sex star. All he had thought about was his own needs and desires. He vowed that he would beg for her forgiveness for the rest of his life if she remained near him. But he decided he would not keep her against her will ever again. If she wanted to leave, he would provide for her basic financial needs indefinitely.

"So," Dietrich asked, "What happened next?" Cassandra continued talking: "I seemed to be fine for the next few weeks but I started feeling really nauseous. I'd rush into the bathroom wherever I was and often just throw up. I had no idea what was wrong with me. Just as my family had not taught me about menstruation, they had also not informed me about the signs and symptoms of pregnancy. After 3 months had passed, my friends started to joke about my wearing looser blouses than usual. They thought that maybe I was putting on some weight. A few days earlier, I had paid a visit to my mother's gynecologist, Dr. Athanas. Informing me that I was pregnant, he congratulated me and told me my husband was a lucky man to have married such a beautiful young and fertile woman. I did not dare to tell him I was not married. That is a complete "no-no" in my culture. Unfortunately, my oldest brother, Stefano, happened to visit his urologist, Dr. Christakos, for a checkup. While flirting with the office assistant he discovered I had been at the office for a visit the day before. Stefano asked Dr. Athanos what was wrong with me and why I had come to see him. The doctor, thinking I was married, told Stefano I was pregnant and shook his hand. Stefano told my other brothers and my parents about his visit to the doctor's office. So, when I arrived home from my friend's wonderful Sweet 16 party, it turned out to be the last time I would ever see my friends or my family again."

Whimpering now and finding it harder to talk, Cassandra tried to continue by saying: "When I came home, my father was waiting at the door. He told me: 'You are nothing more than a low class slut' and 'I no longer have a daughter.' Then he slapped me hard across the face that almost knocked me to the ground. My brother Damion spit on the floor a few times, staining my beautiful designer shoes. Then Alexei, the brother I had been closest to, volunteered to give me my beating. Damion was in such a rage that he might have actually killed me. So Alexei walked me upstairs, first beating the bed with his strap and then finally hitting me with tears in his eyes. He made sure I had welts all over my body and he purposely tore my clothing and dirtied it with my own blood. Then he pulled off my panties to show the family later that he had caused me to bleed and had humiliated me properly. But what I didn't expect is that when I came back downstairs, my father had already turned away, but now my mother showed me a stone face and told me I was no longer her daughter. Then she insisted that I leave the house now and never return.

I was sure that one of them would come running outside but nobody did. The garage door had been locked so I had no access to my beautiful pink bicycle that I had loved. So I walked down the winding path leading to the road and I just kept walking. When I got to the park, I automatically headed toward that bench where it had all begun. And there you were, sitting on the same bench that my beloved Cyrano had occupied only a few short months earlier. And the rest you know."

Dietrich climbed onto the bed next to Cassandra and she expected him to begin fondling her as had been his style. Instead, he hugged her strongly for possibly an entire hour, allowing them both to cry in each other's arms. That's when he offered to give Cassandra money so she could go somewhere else. She replied: "Oh my dear Dietrich, I have always known you are a good man and that you did not realize who I was. I know you have never intended to hurt me. And you have never hurt me. I felt beautiful and sexy and desirable in a way I had always fantasized about. You gave me the opportunity to really express my female seductiveness. Now I do not want to leave you. Maybe I can help you to build your business."

Thinking aloud, Dietrich said to her: "You know, Cassandra, we are going to need a manager for our new business space. Would you like to be the Madam, the manager, the director and the one person with all the control over the behavior of the many employees we plan to hire?" Cassandra smiled and hugged him, feeling known, accepted and loved for who she really is for the very first time in her life.

Dr. Kuhn sent his physician's assistant to take Cassandra's blood and to give her an internal exam. The results proved that she was indeed pregnant and that she was quite healthy. Her two bosses had fed her well and had provided her with a comfortable place to shower and rest and sleep. They had given her numerous breaks during her working hours so she had rarely felt overtaxed. Fortunately, Cassandra's body had been strong enough to withstand the many different actions and movements and positions it had been put through.

For the remainder of her pregnancy and for a long time after the birth, Cassandra was pampered – massaged with creams and oils by her lady assistants and provided with whatever food she desired. The nurse-midwife who had worked with Dr. Kuhn arrived two weeks after Cassandra's final evening as the sex star. To Cassandra's surprise, this proficient midwife, Britta, was a slender, shapely, buxom blond German girl in her mid 20's. Her midwife assistants, Heidi and Frida, were also naturally blond, tall, and slender with less curvaceous breasts but high, firm and round butts. Even before anyone had told her that these women would soon be invited to become the new sex stars, Cassandra had already planned to get them ready.

Her hand maidens took Cassandra everywhere, catering to her every need. They took her to movies and concerts, sporting events and lectures. As soon as she requested something, one of these ladies or Dietrich or Roffe would quickly find a way to get it for her. Once again, Cassandra felt like the princess of the house. She finally felt at home in Switzerland. And she was excited about the upcoming birth and her new task as Madam C., manager of the business.

As the birthing time came closer, Cassandra scoured through books with baby names. She could not decide what to name her baby. Not knowing if it was a boy or a girl, she looked through as many names as she could find. To honor her own nationality, she finally chose the Greek name "Aphrodite," the Goddess of Love, for a daughter. In fact, she felt intuitively that she was carrying a girl because the baby did not kick as much as she had been told a boy might do. For the middle name she decided upon "Maia" which she had been told meant "Illusion" in

Hindu. And for the baby's last name, she wanted something beautiful. She thought long and hard about it and finally decided to use Dietrich's middle name, Danjel meaning "God is My Judge" as the baby's last name. Knowing that Dietrich could arrange false papers because he had done that for them at the airport in Greece, she asked him to arrange for her baby's birth certificate to read: Aphrodite Maia Danjel.

Cassandra knew it was coming. She had felt a few contractions earlier that day. Dr. Kuhn had reminded her many times to start getting herself ready once the contractions would start. Her assistants were all right by her side. They made a warm bath for her to climb into. Then they took turns massaging Cassandra's body - her belly, her lower back, her butt and even her breasts. One of the ladies inserted two fingers into Cassandra's vagina to stimulate the area to dilate further. And then the intense pain began. Thrashing about in the water, Cassandra could not bear the pain so her assistants helped her to stand up and walk around, squatting occasionally. The pain was becoming more and more intense as the contractions happened at quicker intervals. The midwives helped Cassandra to keep moving as they continued to massage her body. Britta kept reminding Cassandra to breathe in that forceful way she had practiced. Heidi and Frida continued massaging Cassandra's legs and belly and chest as Britta kept almost yelling at her to breathe. The crowning began. Her assistants could see the baby's head. Cassandra let out some wolf like screams which scared Dietrich and Roffe who were waiting impatiently in the other room. Finally, Cassandra gave one final push and the baby was released into the waiting arms of both Britta and Heidi. Her assistants were about to cut the umbilical cord and take the baby away to wash her up when Cassandra insisted she wanted to hold the baby immediately, all wet and dirty. They placed the baby girl, Aphrodite Maia Danjel, in her mother's arms for the one and only time for both mother and daughter. Cassandra looked deeply into her daughter's eyes and quietly whispered: "I love you my baby Aphrodite. You will grow up to be the most beautiful and loving woman in the world. Maybe one day we will meet again. Remember, I will always love you and not a single day will pass by that I do not think about you. But, my beloved angel, I know what I am about to do is best for your life. You do not want to grow up in a brothel with a mother who is a madam. For you, I want the finest family and a top education."

With tears in her eyes and feeling choked up, Cassandra continued talking to her newborn infant. "Dietrich, Roffe and Dr. Kuhn have many fine connections. They will find a perfect home for you my little darling. I do not want to see you all washed up because it will break my heart and I will have a harder time letting go of you. Goodbye my precious angel. I will always love you with all my heart and I will pray for your safety and love and forgiveness. Maybe one day, a long time from now, we will meet again. I will then beg you for forgiveness and explain to you that this was my only choice for my beautiful, precious Aphrodite. Go my angel and live the life of your dreams. My loving prayers go with you."

Cassandra called to Britta to wash up this beautiful baby and to take good care of her. Britta thought she meant to take care of the baby for the next few minutes or hours. Britta cut the umbilical cord and handed the baby to Heidi and Frida to be bathed. As the midwives were washing the baby, Cassandra called Dietrich into the room, sobbing and telling him to please take the baby into the other bathroom, have her washed up, clothed and taken away. She begged Dietrich through her tear-filled eyes to please create a birth certificate with her beautiful daughter's new name: Aphrodite Maia Danjel. And then she pleaded with him to find her baby a substantial and loving home.

She begged him to take this helpless child away from this hotel room so that she would not be tempted to keep her baby. Dietrich, with tears in his eyes as well, at first attempted to persuade Cassandra to keep her baby daughter. But when he saw that she had made up her mind, that she was convinced that this would be the most loving thing she could do for her daughter, Dietrich complied with Cassandra's request. As soon as the baby was washed up, Dietrich ordered the midwives to take the baby to a different hotel a few miles away. Promising to provide the midwives with money and whatever they might need to take care of the baby, he asked them to keep her with them until he could find a suitable family to adopt Aphrodite.

Britta remained with Cassandra the rest of the night to comfort and console her. First, she helped Cassandra to get herself cleaned up in the shower. She brought Cassandra some fruit from the table, offering to dip it into the chocolate fondue. Cassandra had no appetite that night nor was she hungry for several days afterwards.

That night Cassandra cried into her pillow for a long time before finally falling asleep. In a vivid dream, she saw her beloved Cyrano and cried out to him: "I had to do it. I had to send her away so she could live a beautiful life with a real family." And Cyrano, with a smiling happy face answered: "Do not fear my beautiful Cassandra. One day we will all be together. I promise my darling. Our daughter will grow up to be as beautiful as her mother and she will have special gifts that will bring us all back together again. Do not fear. Keep the love alive. Don't ever forget to love." Cassandra suddenly recalled the words spoken by Peter Pan in one of her favorite childhood movies from America. She could actually hear those words spoken to her by Cyrano: "You know that place between sleep and awake? The place where you can still remember dreaming? That's where I will always love you. That's where I will be waiting." She felt her heart smiling as she slept more soundly and deeply than she had ever slept in her life before or after that night.

Cassandra never saw her baby again. The memory of those optimistic, loving and promising words of her beloved Cyrano, were buried deep in her memory for decades after that night. In Cassandra's waking life, she felt as if there was no past and no future. She was now living only in the present moment as Madam C., the Manager and Director of the *R & D Pleasure Palace*.

19 CYRANO'S MISSION

Cyrano Niles Maniatis had returned to the ship after walking Cassandra to get her bicycle at the bike rack. He had kissed her goodbye and watched her walk away, feeling a mixture of joy in watching the way her body moved, sadness that this could be the very last time he might ever see her, and a sense of sweet warmth filling his heart as he recalled the thrill of her touch. Walking back to the ship, he felt as if he was walking on air. Cyrano knew he had just enjoyed the love of a princess, his princess. He thought to himself, "If my life would end right now I feel as if I have been fulfilled. I have lived." And he returned to his cabin emotionally prepared to get ready for battle.

Although the captain had told the crew they would be departing the following morning, he did not warn them that they would be heading directly toward the war zone in Vietnam. That day started out exactly like many other mornings but life as Cyrano had known it would last for only a few more days. Before arriving at the shore of this strange and foreign land, their ship would be captured by a dangerous-looking army of Vietcong soldiers carrying rifles and bayonets.

During the trip, which took several days to complete, the crew ate good food, sang lively songs, bantered and teased each other and behaved in their usual somewhat male-confined abusive manner. But they all had a great deal of respect for each other having worked together for long periods of time. During the trip they listened intently to broadcasts about the dangerous fighting in the place they were headed toward. But of course, nobody on the ship really believed that their ship would be targeted and captured. They had the powerful group intention of invading this foreign island and being the captors, not the prisoners.

As their ship approached the island, it suddenly became eerily silent and then they heard some strange language on a loud speaker. They discovered later that the Vietcong were telling them to surrender their arms or they would be dead at once. Surrounded by submarines that had just risen to the surface, the sailors had no place to hide. A swarm of Vietcong climbed on the boat, yelling loud incomprehensible words at the terrified sailors. Each sailor had his arms raised high overhead but the invading soldiers took no chances. Armed with strong ropes, they wrapped each prisoner in rope leaving only enough leg room for them to walk. Once the ship was anchored at the shore, the sailors were marched off the boat in single file, smashed in the head or back or any body part with the side of a rifle if they even attempted to speak. A few of Cyrano's ship mates had been brutally smacked during this terrifying walk onto the open beach and then into the jungle. Although they had been taught about what they might expect in the jungle, none of them had ever experienced anything quite so terrifying.

During that first night in enemy territory, the sailors were frisked and thoroughly searched to remove any weapons. Then each man was isolated from the others and positioned on the campground with a rifle bearing soldier sitting at his side. Any sign of resistance and the sailors knew they would be shot. Just to terrorize their new captives, the Vietcong made it a point to torture and murder a few of them to prevent any uprisings. They brought one unfortunate man into the center of the camp as a horrifying example of what these dangerous warriors could do. Cyrano flinched when he saw that the man chosen for this first torture was his confidant and friend, Nelson, the one who had reassured him that Cassandra had not come to meet him because it was the Easter holiday. They brought Cyrano's friend into the center of the campground and poured oil over him while everyone watched with eyes wide open and in shock. The soldiers stood around for a while smoking and lighting each other's cigarettes until one of them flicked his lighted match at Cyrano's friend. As this poor unfortunate man screamed in pain, his body burst into flames. He tried to roll on the ground to put out the fire, which he did to some extent. But then another soldier threw a match at him and the fire burst out again. The sailor was jumping, screaming and rolling around until his flesh had burned and his body collapsed onto the ground. As this poor man's body burned to cinders, the Vietcong soldiers stood around joking and laughing. To them it was hilarious the way this man had to jump around while being burned alive.

Before turning in for the night, the Vietcong soldiers decided to use another sailor as bayonet practice. Dragging a screaming terrified sailor into the center of the campground, they first used the bayonet to scare him and tear off the ropes that bound him. But as they got going they took turns, one after another, poking him through the heart, through the groin, through the belly, through his back and into his sides. They just kept coming at him from every direction, his blood spurting out everywhere and his screams so loud that the screeching sound caused a sharp pain in Cyrano's ears. And this was only the first night of hell for this group of formerly cheerful and fun-loving sailors.

In the morning, each of the sailors was given a small portion of rice with water. They did not know if they would be poisoned but they were so hungry they did not resist. If a fly or insect had flown into their rice and they reacted in any way, a soldier would grab the bowl and that hungry sailor would be fed no additional food for that day. The sailors learned very quickly to be totally obedient and to willingly accept their fate. Cyrano obeyed the commands without flinching. He had been well trained about how to handle being a captive. Yet he had never really imagined that he might end up in such a dangerous and life threatening situation.

After having witnessed the horrific murders on that first night, the men certainly did not have a good night's sleep on the ground. And they were not prepared for the next horrible torture that would end up lasting for 21 months.

Each soldier was instructed to start digging in a certain location. Cyrano's spot was the closest one to the main camp area where the soldiers had their tents. The sailors all believed they were digging their own graves and were about to be shot so they lingered and dug as slowly as they could, hoping, wishing and praying to be rescued. The mean and angry looking soldier assigned to Cyrano inspected the hole his prisoner had dug and insisted it needed to be a little wider. At first Cyrano thought the man was being abusive but he later realized that this man was actually being kind, wanting Cyrano to make his space larger so that he would have more breathing room. Expecting to be rescued at any moment, these did not yet know that these holes they had just dug were going to be their private dungeons, without being able to walk around or see a full daylight, for what would soon feel like an eternity.

Before nudging Cyrano into his manmade hole in the ground, his Vietcong guard offered him a small portion of rice and water. Then, with a rifle nudging him from behind, Cyrano and his remaining ship mates were pushed into their private holes. This underground cell was dark and warm. The temperature on this island would sometimes reach over 100 degrees Fahrenheit. Sweaty from wearing the same uniform and watching those horrifying murders, Cyrano was certainly not comfortable. But he had a strong will to live, to survive his ordeal and to one day return to that peaceful, idyllic Greek island to see his beautiful Cassandra again. He had no idea if she would be waiting and still available for him. And he wondered if her feelings had been as strong for him as his feelings were for her. Regardless of what his future might bring, Cyrano was convinced that the memory of that one evening with Cassandra would help to save his life and preserve his sanity. During those endless hours underground, Cyrano carefully recreated in his mind every inch of Cassandra's body, her facial expressions and the clothing she wore. He repeated her words over and over again in his head. He imagined her beautiful loving smile. Images filled his mind of her big round breasts and the pleasure he had felt when he touched them. In this hole in the ground he would often imagine that Cassandra was in there with him, making sweet love to him. And this imaginary sense helped to pass the time, keeping his mind rational and giving him the strength and purpose to remain live.

One night, Cyrano imagined that his beloved Cassandra was giving birth. It had been about 9 months since that wonderful evening they had been together. He could not possibly have known that she was pregnant. After all, they had only made love one time. But he imagined that she was going through labor, screaming in pain with loving assistance around her. And then he got an imaginary glimpse of his beautiful daughter, all bloody and messy from the birthing process. But then he saw some ladies take his daughter away and in his vision he saw his beloved Cassandra crying. Cyrano actually heard her words. He clearly heard Cassandra say: "I had to do it. I had to send her away so she could live a beautiful life with a real family." And Cyrano, with a smiling happy face heard himself answer "Do not fear my beautiful Cassandra. One day we will all be together. I promise my darling. Our daughter will grow up to be as beautiful as her mother and she will have special gifts that will bring us all back together again. Do not fear. Keep the love alive. Don't ever forget to love." And then he recited a line from his favorite childhood movie from America, Peter Pan, when Peter Pan said: "You know that place between sleep and awake? The place where you can still remember dreaming? That's where I will always love you. That's where I will be waiting."

Cyrano was haunted by that conversation for the rest of the time he was a prisoner underground. At some point, almost two years later, sirens blasted and he could hear scrambling feet and the sounds of the Vietcong being captured by Allied Forces. He heard someone speak into a megaphone with a message repeated in English, French and Spanish: "We are here to save you. Do you speak English? Do you speak French? Do you speak Spanish?"

At first Cyrano was frightened, thinking these may be captured soldiers and that if he was taken out of his cell in the ground he would be shot. But the message was repeated over and over again and finally

Cyrano found the courage to call out to tell them, in English, that he was buried underground.

The Allied soldiers began digging and it took three of them to pull and lift him out of his prison after 21 months of a living hell. At first he could not see anything. His eyes burned and he could not even open them without feeling severe pain from having been in the darkness for so many months. To his surprise, he was unable to stand and he collapsed onto the ground.

That's when he discovered that several of his ship mates

had survived and were also sitting on the ground around the camp. All of them were crying in disbelief that their long ordeal was finally ending. None of the captured sailors had talked to another human being for the full 21 months. The food they had received, the small daily morsels of insect strewn rice and water, had paid a toll on their nutritional health. Each of the freed prisoners had to be carried on a stretcher to the airplane that they thought would take them home.

However, before sending the sailors home, they were first transported to a special hospital in Lucerne Switzerland, for rest, recuperation, physical evaluations, nutritional and physical therapy and emotional debriefing. What both Cyrano and Cassandra did not know is that the hospital where Cyrano was recuperating was only a few miles away from where Cassandra was now working as Madam C. Fortunately for both of them, it was not yet time for the star-crossed lovers to reunite.

20 APHRODITE'S ADOPTION

Cassandra had just informed Dietrich that she wanted him to have her new baby washed and taken away so that she would not see little Aphrodite all cleaned up. After a few minutes of attempting to change Cassandra's mind, Dietrich finally complied with her wishes. He called out to Frida to please take the newborn baby to the other bathroom to bathe her. As soon as Frida had finished washing baby Aphrodite, she and Heidi wrapped the baby in a bath towel. Heidi ran into Cassandra's room and motioned for Dietrich to come into the main room for a few minutes. She asked quietly: "Dietrich, is there any clothing for the newborn baby to wear?" Dietrich reached into the closet for the little suitcase Cassandra had packed a few days earlier. It was filled with adorable pink baby outfits and lots of baby toiletries, diapers and other supplies.

Cassandra and Britta had spent weeks gathering up all sorts of clothing and dangling crib objects, soft and cuddly stuffed animals and play toys, and different paraphernalia they knew would be needed once the baby arrived. What Britta, Frida, Heidi, Dietrich, Roffe and even Dr. Kuhn had not expected was that Cassandra did not plan to behave like the baby's mother or act as her caretaker. Cassandra had made this decision during that complete physical exam with Dr. Kuhn's assistant when the assistant, assuming Dietrich was Cassandra's beloved husband, said to her: "How lucky this baby is to have two parents that love her and plan to take good care of her." Cassandra knew in her heart at that very moment that she wanted more for her baby girl than the life of living around nightclubs and prostitutes. With a very heavy heart and a strong determination to do what she knew would be best for her daughter, Cassandra chose to not tell anyone about her decision until they had no choice but to take care of this helpless newborn baby.

Frida and Heidi finished drying tiny little Aphrodite and patting her private parts with powder. Heidi chose an adorable, frilly baby outfit with material that was delicate and soft to the touch. But Aphrodite wanted no part of this. She wanted to go back to her mommy. Screaming and kicking and resisting, Aphrodite was no match for the two young and strong nurse midwives. After a great deal of struggle, Frida and Heidi managed to squeeze Aphrodite into her new outfit. Her tiny feet fit snugly into the footsies and the snaps around the bottom would make it quite easy to change her diapers in a few hours. Then they wrapped Aphrodite into a beautiful thick pink blanket and strapped her firmly into her new baby carriage.

As soon as the baby was in strapped into her carriage, Roffe led Frida and Heidi to the back service elevator down to the garage level where he had told the taxi driver to meet them. Roffe and Dietrich had agreed it would be best to avoid making a big scene in the middle of the lobby with these two ladies taking the newborn baby with them in a carriage never to return with the baby. When Frida, Heidi and Roffe were outside the hotel, Roffe folded up the carriage and placed it into the trunk of the taxi. Frida got into the back seat and moved over to make room for Heidi and the baby. Heidi, holding precious little crying Aphrodite in her arms, quickly joined Frida in the taxi. Roffe sat in the front seat to provide directions to the other hotel where the two ladies would be staying temporarily with the baby.

When they arrived at the other Swiss hotel, Dietrich paid the driver, re-assembled the baby carriage, and escorted the 2 midwives to the front desk. While registering for the room, Roffe reminded the clerk at the desk to make sure there was a good sized refrigerator in the room. He paid in advance for an entire month. Rofee wanted Heidi and Frida to be able to just concentrate on taking care of the baby so that Roffe and Dietrich could spend their time seeking an appropriate family to adopt Aphrodite. Roffe escorted these two ladies from Germany, who were now Aphrodite's primary caretakers for the foreseeable future, to their room. Before leaving, Roffe told the midwives: "Heidi and Frida, please order room service, towels and whatever else you need for now. Tomorrow Dr. Kuhn will provide you with a substantial supply of baby food to last at least for the rest of this week."

Aphrodite was still crying, but more softly now. Heidi and Frida knew that soon the baby would get tired and would eventually fall asleep. They agreed they would take turns showering once baby Aphrodite was sleeping. Both nurse midwives had spent the past few years assisting laboring mothers, helping in many deliveries, and often taking care of the newborns for the first few days. Thus they were prepared for a series of sleepless nights ahead. Both ladies felt heavy-hearted as they watched this innocent little infant struggling to make sense of what was happening to her. They knew they could not replace the mother, Cassandra, whose heartbeat Aprhodite had heard while still developing in her mother's womb. Fortunately for Aphrodie, both Heidi and Frida were warm, caring and basically loving women. They both gave continual attention, affection, soothing words, pleasing smiles and gentle massages to this precious little baby girl.

The following day, Roffe contacted a few adoption agencies while Dietrich created a legally viable birth certificate for Aphrodite Maia Danjel. Both men enlisted Dr. Kuhn in their efforts to locate an appropriate adoptive family. The process didn't take very long. Serendipity brought the adoptive parents to Dr. Kuhn before he had even begun to ask around. As luck would have it, that very weekend, only a few days after Aphrodite was born, Dr. Kuhn was scheduled to be the keynote speaker at a 3 day international conference being held at the local conference center where he often organized lectures and special events. The conference theme was *Parenting: Creating and Finding a Good Home for Your Baby.* Speakers included a variety of medical professionals (gynecologists and obstetricians, urologists, nurses, endocrinologists, etc.), psychiatric professionals (psychiatrists, psychologists, social workers, counselors, graduate level interns), attorneys, representatives from adoption agencies, and some local parents seeking information.

Dr. Kuhn arrived extra early at the Thursday night open cocktail hour to reach out to his colleagues for some advice on how to locate an appropriate adoptive couple. Glancing through the conference schedule, Dr. Kuhn noticed that an American psychologist, Dr. David Morgan, who Dr. Kuhn had met briefly at a conference in New York many years earlier, was planning to speak on the topic: **"The Dangers of Adopting: What to Look For and What to Avoid."** He thought to himself: "I will have to find Dr. Morgan. Maybe he has some suggestions for how I can quickly locate a suitable couple to adopt this baby."

Serendipity was surely at work. Before speaking to anyone at this opening party, Dr. Kuhn approached the bartender to get a glass of his favorite red wine. Someone tapped him on the shoulder saying "Albrecht." When he started to turn around he first caught a glimpse of this tall stunning blond standing next to the man who had tapped him. "David, David Morgan, remember we met at that conference in New York a few years ago. I told you then that I was single and really wanted to find a life partner. Let me introduce you to my lovely Swiss wife, Chiara. We've been married almost 2 years now. She is the one who kept pushing me to send my application in early to insure that I would be speaking at this conference. She was born here in Lucerne, not too far from this hotel, and she was anxious to return to her hometown, meet with some of her childhood friends and show me a little about her life before we met. We are so much in love, but unfortunately, after getting tested by the best doctors in Connecticut and New York, we discovered that my sperm count is very low and my wife has some gynecological problems. We have been unable to conceive and we both want a child so badly. Isn't it ironic that I had chosen this topic, all about adoption, before my wife and I had seriously begun planning to adopt our first child. You know, they say that once you adopt, perhaps your body becomes more relaxed and sometimes, that's when your wife finally gets pregnant."

Dr. Kuhn stood there with his mouth hanging open for almost a minute. Dr. Morgan became uneasy, saying to him: "Are you all right? You look as if you've seen a ghost." After paying for his drink, Dr. Kuhn asked Dr. Morgan to come talk to him privately. Waiting patiently while Dr. Morgan paid for a cocktail for himself and his wife, Dr. Kuhn sipped his wine in anticipation of a very special business deal. Dr. Morgan told his wife he needed to speak in private with Dr. Kuhn so he excused himself and reassured her that he would be back in just a few minutes.

Dr. Morgan started the conversation by asking: "Are you all right? You seemed to have such a shocked expression on your face when I told you our dilemma. I don't mean to lay all my problems on you each time I meet you at a conference. It's just that our desire to adopt has gotten really strong and we're not sure where to begin. Should we adopt an American child or a Swiss child? And which agency is best? Will we go through the whole process only to be disappointed if the mother changes her mind? I have all these thoughts and worries and concerns. I don't want to seem so confused when I give my talk tomorrow. But this adoption issue has been weighing heavily on my mind and it's been affecting my work recently. I just don't know what to do."

The answer Dr. Morgan received gave him a chill down his spine. Dr. Kuhn explained: "One of my local patients here in Switzerland, a beautiful young woman, has just given birth a few days ago. She told me she cannot possibly provide a good home for the baby and her parents agree. She and her boyfriend are too young and still in school, not ready to handle the responsibility of taking care of a child. She asked me, actually begged me, to take this beautiful, precious newborn baby girl, Aphrodite Maia Danjel, and find a perfect adoptive home for her. David, you and your stunning wife, would make absolutely perfect parents for this beautiful little baby. She needs you. And she needs you immediately. As soon as you sign the papers Aphrodite will be yours. You can actually take her home a few days after the conference." Dr. Kuhn allowed David to assume that this little baby girl was born to young Swiss parents. He certainly did not describe the mother's recent activity as a hooker.

Noticeably excited, David said to Dr. Kuhn: Oh my God! I can't believe this. Please wait here for a few minutes while I speak to my wife Chiara. This sounds almost too good to be true." As soon as David told his wife about this sudden good news, Chiara rushed over to speak to Dr. Kuhn asking: "Where is this beautiful baby? When can I see her? If we like her and she responds to us, when can we take her home?" Dr. Kuhn realized that Chiara could see the baby at any time. But he decided to act a bit coy and he told her: I will have to check with her current caretakers to see when they might be available to bring the baby to this hotel, maybe even as soon as tomorrow." Chiara's face lit up and she gave her husband a big kiss and broad hug. She was too excited for words.

Both of them trusted Dr. Kuhn, having seen his name as a leading presenter at many international conferences. He was well known and quite respected among his colleagues. Dr. Kuhn asked Dr. Morgan for the couple's room number and promised to call them either later that same evening or first thing in the morning with more information.

After making his rounds at the opening cocktail party - greeting familiar colleagues, meeting some new conference attendees, and even saying hello to a few graduate students and interns, Dr. Kuhn made his way back to the front desk downstairs. He asked the attendant at the desk to call the Swiss hotel where Frida and Heidi were staying. Heidi answered, feeling relieved to hear Dr. Kuhn's voice on the phone. "Dr. Kuhn, she said, the baby has finally quieted down. We have been hugging and massaging her and saying soothing words for hours. She is such a beautiful little thing. I hope you find her a good home very soon." In an excited voice, Dr. Kuhn responded: "It may be sooner than you think. I just spoke to a couple here at the conference who have been thinking about adopting and were not sure how to begin. When can you bring the baby here to this hotel where I am speaking? It's only a short distance from your hotel?"

Frida suggested that she and Heidi could bring the baby to the hotel the following morning but not tonight. Frida explained: "Aphrodite has finally fallen asleep. I would not want to wake her. She has been traumatized enough being taken away from her mother. We need to handle her very carefully and gently. We can bring her to the hotel tomorrow morning. Tell me what time to have her ready and we will be there."

Dr. Kuhn made arrangements with Frida to bring the baby to the front desk of the hotel at 11 AM and ask them to call Chiara Morgan in her room. Then they could ask Chiara if she wants them to come upstairs or if she would prefer to meet the baby downstairs in the lobby. After finalizing the details with Frida, Dr. Kuhn called the Morgans in their room. David answered saying: "I didn't expect you to call me so soon. What's up? Did you speak to the baby's mother? When can we see this little girl?" Expecting Dr. Kuhn to say that it would probably be a few days from now, both David and Chiara where surprised when Dr. Kuhn said: "Tomorrow at 11 AM. Can Chiara meet the two nurses, Heidi and Frida, at the front desk?

Excitedly, David turned to his wife who was anxious to know what had just been said: "Darling, you are going to meet the baby tomorrow morning at 11 AM. You will spend some time with her, maybe all day. So by the time I finish my lecture, you can tell me all about her. It's going to be hard for me to stay focused on my presentation. If you like her, I think we can really do this. I can't believe it." Chiara was so excited she just grabbed David and tried to kiss him all over his face while he was still on the phone.

David, feeling really optimistic, said: "Albrecht, if this works out I have no idea how I could ever repay you. This is incredibly exciting news. Where do you want Chiara to meet the two nurses with the baby? Ado you want her to wait near the front desk?" Dr. Kuhn replied: "Yes. Perfect. Then, if Chiara likes, they can all go up to your room or walk around the hotel grounds or wherever she wants to go. Good luck to both of you. I know you will fall in love with Aphrodite."

The following day, while Dr. Kuhn was speaking and sharing his knowledge on 2 separate panels, Frida and Heidi were getting baby Aphrodite ready to meet her potential new mother. Chiara had eaten a good breakfast, had walked around the hotel grounds for about a half hour and returned to her room in anticipation of meeting this little newborn baby. She thought it might be a good experience but she was not prepared to be so emotionally overwhelmed at the sight of this precious little baby girl.

Heidi and Frida arrived at the front desk of the hotel at exactly 11 AM as promised. They asked the clerk at the desk to contact Chiara Morgan in her room. Chiara excitedly answered the phone saying: "I will be right down." When she walked across the lobby toward the baby carriage, Chiara looked stunning in a white silk dress with pink trimmed ruffles, a pink shoulder bag and pale beige delicate heels. On her neck she wore a special magnetic heart, supposedly containing magnetic energy to keep her body feeling calm and relaxed. Aphrodite was wearing a white jumpsuit with pink laced trim with those little snaps down the bottom. She had a light pink bonnet on her head and the sweetest, brightest smile when Chiara arrived. Baby Aphrodite responded to the softness of the colored trim on this strange new lady's dress and she actually had a faint smile on her face, or it appeared that way to Chiara, the woman who would soon become the baby's new mother.

Chiara's heart was immediately filled with love. She could not believe how beautiful and precious this little girl was. Instantly, as soon as she saw Aphrodite, Chiara knew that she wanted to adopt this baby and bring her home. Chiara also knew that David's heart would melt when he looked at this little darling. She asked Frida and Heidi to please bring the baby up to her room and wait with her for the next few hours, until her husband would return from his day with his colleagues. A few hours had passed and Chiara was entranced with this little baby. When David opened the door, he saw this precious little angel clinging to his wife. And he saw the most angelic, loving and peaceful expression on Chiara's face. David knew then and there that this would be their new baby girl. Aphrodite was about to have a wonderful family of her own.

Dietrich and Roffe were informed that evening that their worries would soon be over. Dr. Kuhn promised to handle the adoption arrangements as long as Dietrich would provide an accurate birth certificate to give to the new parents. Dr. Kuhn also promised to provide a full health report of the baby from the day of her birth to the present time. Dietrich, Roffe and Dr. Kuhn agreed that the payment received from the Morgans for the adoption would be split equally among all three of them.

After spending Friday afternoon and evening with Aphrodite and her two caretakers, David called Dr. Kuhn. Excitedly, Chiara got on the phone and told Dr. Kuhn: "My husband and I are so thrilled. We will definitely adopt this precious baby. However, I am planning to attend a very special *Loving Truth Teachings* meditation course this very weekend, all day on Saturday and Sunday with a powerful healing teacher, John Upright Fuller. I have been planning to attend this event for many months. He travels all around the world and he happens to be speaking right here in Lucerne Switzerland, this week. Can you have the papers ready for us on Monday morning?"

Dr. Kuhn reassured Chiara and David that he would speak to his colleagues and assistants and have the proper paperwork ready for them to sign on Monday morning. Back at Cassandra's room, Roffe and Dietrich ordered champagne for everyone. They toasted to the successful handling of the adoption and the imminent opening of their new business venture, *The R and D Pleasure Palace*.

21 APHRODITE IS TAKEN TO AMERICA

To all outside observers, Chiara and David Morgan were living an ideal and wonderful life. They lived in a huge home on a private estate in a small exclusive town in Connecticut. Dr. Morgan's career had been flourishing for many years. As a local psychologist, his practice was filled beyond capacity with a long waiting list of eager new patients. A prolific researcher and writer, he had developed a world-wide reputation, often invited to keynote at prestigious professional conferences around the world. He had done a lot of research on early childhood development, learning about the long term effects of "**good enough mothering,**" a term coined by one of his favorite mentors, an English pediatrician and psychoanalyst, Donald Woods Winnicott. David was enamored of the work of Hungarian physician, Dr. Margaret Schönberger Mahler, who co-authored a book: ***The Psychological Birth of the Human Infant: Symbiosis and Individuation.*** Dr. Mahler and her co-authors had observed the bonding process of mothers and infants from the child's birth until about 3 years of age. This book profoundly affected Dr. Morgan, causing him to be resistant for years about bringing a child into the world for fear that he might fail in his task as a parent. And understanding how essential the mother-infant bond is, he certainly did not take marriage lightly. He had been involved with numerous women who did not meet his high standards of personal excellence - those qualities he thought were needed to be an exceptional mother.

And then he met Chiara, a beautiful, sophisticated Swiss woman. David was dazzled by her. She epitomized his educated view of the physical beauty, charm, sensitivity, warmth and family background of a woman who would be the best mother for his child. He had met Chiara at a conference but she had not been attending his intellectual, professional presentations. She had been seeking spiritual enlightenment and had found this little known healer whose words felt like magic to her. John Upright Fuller, author of *The Loving Truth Teachings* and many other spiritual books, had revealed his fantastic ability to create healing through his consciousness alone. He did not have to know the exact issue or problem. He did not have to meet the person seeking help. He did not have to touch the patient nor did he have to touch the friend or relative who was asking him to assist in healing the patient. Joel practiced a deep type of meditation in which he would clear his mind of all thoughts and allow a message to reach him, usually a clear biblical statement. He had often explained to his loyal followers that once he heard or expressed the appropriate "truth" about who we really are as spiritual beings, a healing would naturally occur.

David and Chiara, very different in their attitudes and approaches to life, discovered deep and lasting love in each other's arms. He was the scientist, the researcher, the author and the logical, methodical person. She was the artist, the free spirit, the sensitive and emotional being and the one who focused most on nurturing their relationship. From the moment they met, they became inseparable. David never traveled without his beloved Chiara. Their love and affection and sexual relationship brought deep internal satisfaction to both of them. Their marriage was like a fairytale. He agreed to come to Switzerland, where she had been raised, to marry her in a quaint ancient castle. They spent their honeymoon in Australia where she introduced David to her teacher and mentor, the healer John Upright Fuller, who happened to be offering a workshop nearby right at that time.

David had never before believed in spirituality. Although he had grown up in quite a religious family, at the time he married Chiara, he had only been attending church on Sundays and not every week. He had a basic belief that there is probably a God, but he did not have a real conviction about it. However, he adored Chiara and was willing to endure what he thought would be a boring lecture just to please her. This special spiritual awareness course, taken for a few days during their honeymoon, set the course for a wonderful marriage. David actually read several manuscripts and books of **The Loving Truth Teachings** for years to come, transforming his inner life in ways he could never have imagined.

Chiara was thrilled to share her spiritual teacher with the man she loved. Together they sat in council with John

Upright Fuller and felt as if their marriage had been anointed from on high – which it actually was. Toward the end of their first year of marriage it was David, the one who had been so resistant for years, who brought up the idea of having a child with Chiara. She was absolutely thrilled at the thought of it. She loved this incredible man and had no doubt that he would be a wonderful father.

But after months and months of trying, this happy, loving and romantic couple was unable to conceive. At that point they both visited their doctors where they discovered that each one had a problem which was preventing conception from occurring. Chiara cried in David's arms many nights. He really tried to console her but his own heart was also aching. Having read and researched so much about babies and mother-infant bonding, he had wanted to have the unique experience of being a father. When he read about the importance of a father's loving presence and emotional support, he knew he could now provide what his child would need. So when he discovered that Chiara was unable to conceive and he could do nothing to change the situation, he felt sad, even depressed, and somewhat impotent.

That's when David began to start researching adoption – practices, procedures, difficulties, potential later problems, child rearing practices, etc. Becoming quite an expert on this topic, he eventually convinced Chiara that this would probably be a good move for them. After much initial hesitation and resistance, Chiara finally agreed that through adoption they could create the family they both wanted to have together.

Since David was scheduled to present his paper **"The Dangers of Adopting: What to Look For and What to Avoid"** in Lucerne a few weeks later, Chiara was thrilled to discover that John Upright Fuller would be presenting a special class in Lucerne Switzerland, that very same week. She wanted to get her spiritual teacher's reassurance that adopting a child would be a good move for them. She also wanted to hear from him some words of wisdom that might stay with her and guide her to be a good mother. Neither David nor Chiara had expected to have their wish fulfilled so quickly and during that same week.

While David was involved with his colleagues and peers at the conference, presenting his well-received paper and listening intently to many others, Chiara was meditating in John's special class a few miles away in a small meeting room at a local hotel. The title of the lecture, she later discovered, would be: "Meditating on Your Inner Self is a Form of Prayer." Chiara had, in fact, been praying regularly for a beautiful healthy child. But her way of praying, asking to receive something, is not what John talked about in his lecture. Chiara, herself, did not quite understand the meaning of his words at the time, but as she continued to study his teachings she was able to impart her growing knowledge to her spiritually gifted adopted daughter, Aphrodite.

Although Chiara wanted to remember everything this inspiring mystic said, she would often find herself drifting into a state of half dreaming while he was speaking. Then she would suddenly pop back into conscious awareness thinking she had missed something important. But her body mind system had listened and had stored John's soul searching words in her memory. In one of those suddenly conscious moments she recalled the words: "Joy comes only from the inside." He wasn't sure if he had even said those words during this particular class; she may have read this before in some of his letters and other writings. This statement would take Chiara many years to truly comprehend. On this day she thought to herself: "I was so unhappy when I was told that David and I could not conceive a child. How could I have felt joy inside when my dream of a family was being shattered? And now that I will be adopting this precious little girl, Aphrodite, now I feel so happy. Joy does not come from inside. Joy comes from the outside world and the people around you. Maybe John is wrong about this one thing."

Then Chiara caught some other words that stayed in her mind long after this class had ended: "God is Good." She heard John explain that it is a beautiful world, that there is no such thing as lack and limitation. He advised his students to see past the appearances in the moment and to trust that God is always providing for us. He taught that we do not really know what is in our own best interest. What appears to be evil and painful and lacking in some way is often just the hand of God at work, clearing the way for you to manifest your life purpose.

Chiara asked for some private time with John to sit and meditate alone with him. She could feel his healing thoughts spread calm and acceptance and loving trust throughout her body. Chiara felt a unique sensation of emotional release during this private meditation. She knew then, without any doubt, that this baby girl would become the love of her life.

Bright and early on Monday morning, at 10 AM, Dr. Kuhn arrived with the adoption papers, Aphrodite's official birth certificate that Dietrich had carefully created as well as her medical records released from Dr. Kuhn's office. David and Chiara Morgan became the proud parents of Aphrodite Maia Danjel Morgan. They shortened her name to read: Aphrodite Maia Morgan. The return flight to Connecticut had already been booked by David for Tuesday morning. Chiara invited Frida and Heidi to spend this last night in their hotel suite to assist for one more night with caring for this newborn baby. That night Chiara hardly slept. She was so excited, and at the same time terrified, of bringing home this little precious baby girl.

On Tuesday morning, Dr. Kuhn drove Frida, Heidi, David, Chiara and baby Aphrodite to the airport. When David and Chiara got out of the car, Dr. Kuhn helped with the luggage, wished them well and gave Chiara a big warm bear hug. David put his arm around Dr. Kuhn's shoulder and then shook his hand, thanking him profusely and saying: "How can we ever thank you for this amazing gift that will surely change and transform our lives? This little angel is truly a gift from heaven. Thank you. Thank you. Thank you. We will see you soon, I am sure, at one of our future conferences. Take care, Albrecht. You're a good man."

What David and Chiara did not know at that time is the true story of their adopted baby daughter's birth. Dr. Kuhn had told David that Aphrodite's mother was a Swiss teenager whose boyfriend had gotten her pregnant and that her parents had insisted that the girl give the baby up for adoption. He did not explain the true story. He did not tell them that Aphrodite's Greek mother, after having gotten pregnant by having an affair with an Australian Greek sailor, had been beaten and thrown out of her house. And he certainly did not want them to know that the baby's mother had been kidnapped, brought to Switzerland, and thrust into prostitution for the next few months. It wasn't until Aphrodite had grown into a beautiful young woman with unusual psychic and spiritual gifts, that the truth would be revealed to her in a dream. But David and Chiara would only know the truth after Aphrodite had finally reconnected with her birth parents and their extended family.

Before leaving the hotel in Switzerland, Chiara had been provided with that suitcase filled with baby clothing and supplies. She wondered how quickly they could get their home set up for their new baby and whether it would be difficult for her to take care of her new baby. But Chiara was immediately reassured when tiny Aphrodite smiled at her with a sweet sense of deep wisdom. It was as if Aphrodite knew that this was to be her mother and that this mother would be wonderful. People walking by in the terminal caught glimpses of Aphrodite and smiled or made baby sounds and faces toward her. David and Chiara felt so much love coming toward this baby and toward them as the parents. Their dream was about to be fulfilled. They would now be a full-fledged family. And Chiara was excited about her role as this beautiful baby's mother.

The plane ride went quite smoothly. Aphrodite was quiet and slept most of the time, waking up only a few times during the flight. Knowing she was safe and attended to, the baby quickly fell asleep again. When they finally arrived at Bradley International Airport in Connecticut, David's brother and sister-in-law, who lived nearby, greeted them as they left the terminal. His brother, Jim, spoke first: "Congratulations bro. Let me see her. Oh my God is she adorable. How did you get her? We didn't even know you were looking for a baby." And Jim's wife, Arlene, chimed in: "I know what it takes to care for a baby. Let me come and help you out, at least for the first few weeks. I won't take no for an answer. You are both going to be exhausted and you will need some additional arms to hold this little baby and to help you handle some of your household tasks – at least until you hire a nanny you can trust. This is so exciting." Chiara could not stop smiling and neither could David. They both felt as if they had struck gold and they were elated.

22 APHRODITE GROWS UP

The Morgan home was bustling with activity for many months after the arrival of Aphrodite. Friends and relatives visited often just to get a glimpse of this darling infant. Chiara's parents came from their home in Switzerland to stay with their daughter, her husband, and their beautiful new granddaughter for the first month. David's parents, currently living in Florida, visited for 2 long weekends. Then, when Chiara's parents had returned to Switzerland, David's mother came for a long weekend and stayed for another 2 weeks. The grandmothers took pride in handling all those mothering details that Chiara would gradually come to learn. And David's sister-in-law, Arlene, filled in the gaps, helping Chiara and David as needed in the early weeks and months and then as needed over the next few years.

Baby Aphrodite was delighted with all the loving attention, beautiful baby clothes, pretty and soft toys and dolls, and satisfying food. She quickly grew to love her new family. Nobody could understand, not even Aphrodite, why, many years later, she would continue to harbor feelings of inadequacy, unworthiness, a sense of not belonging, and even a certain amount of anger and rebelliousness. In her early years she appeared to be the happiest little baby and everyone adored her. Yet as she grew older, she became more restless and uneasy. Something deep inside seemed to bother her. She would not know until her mid-twenties exactly why she had felt so uncertain about her life and her place in the world.

In her pre-school activities, Aphrodite would easily get along with the other children pay attention to others, to not only be concerned about herself and to share whatever she has with those who might benefit from her gifts. Aphrodite also learned, from a very, very young age, that she was not just a physical being. Her spiritually-focused mother continually taught her little daughter about a world beyond her senses, beyond her thoughts and emotions and body experiences. Aphrodite developed a keen sensitivity to the essence of all living beings. Her connections became so intense that she actually received messages from animals, plants and spirits that could not be seen. She knew without a doubt that she was a spiritual being living inside of a physical body, having physical experiences in this world.

Although it may have begun earlier, before she was able to talk and cognitively understand or explain it, at around 4 years of age her unique psychic abilities became quite intense. One morning, while sitting in her classroom she saw a vision of one of her classmates falling off a bicycle, bleeding and then having stitches sewed onto his face. She went over to tell him: "Don't ride your bicycle today, you might get hurt." But the child did not listen to her and the next day he came to school with a bandage on his face. Another time, when her attention was drawn to a certain child, she suddenly had a vision of an adult passing out on the floor, losing color and appearing whiter than normal. The next day the teacher explained that this same child's mother had just passed on.

Aphrodite not only saw these terrible incidents before they happened but she also saw some good things. She knew when a boy was interested in her no matter how he might disguise it. If she listened intently, she could actually hear his thoughts: "She is so pretty. I wish I could carry her books and walk her home. But she's too smart for me." Then she would purposely go over to that boy and ask him to carry her books and walk her home. He would be beaming and she could internalize his happy energy and feel so good about herself for the moment.

Nobody could fool her or lie to her because Aphrodite could feel the energy and hear the unspoken words. With such a strong psychic and energetic awareness, it became difficult for Aphrodite to sit still in a classroom. Her mind would sometimes feel as if it was invaded by everyone else's consciousness. When she told her mother, Chiara, about her psychic gift, her mother immediately understood and gave her a beautiful gold necklace with a heart shaped pendant. She told Aphrodite to wear that necklace at all times. "When your mind feels full with other people's thoughts and those very strong, very real images, then take off your necklace and dangle it in front of you. Allow it to move from side to side or in a circular motion. Let the necklace gather the energy so that you can later shake the necklace and send the energy back where it came from." Aphrodite wore that necklace every day for the entire time she attended school. As she grew bigger, her mother would buy her a bigger chain to hold her magical gold heart that kept the energy swirling in front of her and not inside her own system.

During her elementary school years, many of Aphrodite's friends would play stick ball, soft ball, basketball and even tag football. She loved playing these active team and even contact sports - throwing balls, catching them, running, and tagging each other. Chiara, however, thought these types of sports are not ladylike and she discouraged Aphrodite from playing outside with the other children. Then she enrolled her daughter in ballet and tap dancing classes. David insisted that his daughter also take gymnastics since David had been a gymnast and knew how important it was to be strong and flexible and able to move your body with ease. Both David and Chiara also wanted their daughter to have some musical training so they gave her piano and singing lessons.

On Wednesday afternoons, when her classmates would play team sports and fun group games in their physical education classes, Aphrodite was sent for her religious training. She hated having to study religion instead of developing and improving her sports skills. And since she had never been given the opportunity to develop her throwing, catching and running skills or her eye-hand coordination, she became a scape goat during afternoon recess activities. Embarrassed and humiliated by a few of her so-called friends, she vowed to one day get even with them. And a few years later, Aphrodite would learn how to channel her special psychic abilities in ways that could benefit or temporarily harm others. But as her spiritual skills reached higher levels, she lost that intense desire to get even with anyone.

With her long slender torso, long legs, and dark tan-looking olive complexion, Aphrodite was often affectionately teased by her classmates with the nicknames of Olive or Olive Oyl. Unlike her birth mother, Cassandra, who had long legs and a curvaceous, voluptuous body, Aphrodite also had long legs but a less curvy, more angular body. Popeye the Sailor, a popular comic strip hero at the time, was known to eat his spinach to build his strength. Then he would use his renewed power to fight the local villains. And often his goal was to protect Olive and win her heart. When Aphrodite showed how clumsy she was in sports activities, like throwing or catching a ball, the other children would laugh and say something like this: "Of course she can't catch and hold onto a ball. She's a slippery, slimy olive. She's Olive Oyl." And they would laugh hysterically. Being highly sensitive, she would feel so hurt but she would rarely let anyone know what she was feeling. Inside, she vowed: "When I grow up, I will find a way to get even with anyone who treats me badly or hurts me."

The name Olive and Olive Oyl stuck with Aphrodite for a very long time, creating in her mind a deep sense of insecurity, unattractiveness and unworthiness. However, as uncoordinated as she had been with basic sports activities, she was the opposite with her dance performances. Her teachers marveled at how quickly she caught on, how elegant and graceful and smooth her dancing was. Aphrodite loved tap dancing. The sound of the taps on the floor and the special tap shoes she had to wear intrigued her. She also loved swinging on the gymnastics bars and rings, and she loved vaulting and even the balance beam. Aphrodite had only been allowed to continue her gymnastics training because her father had insisted. But even though she kept saying how much she loved tap dancing, her mother pushed her into intensive ballet training which ended Aphrodite's tap dance classes. Chiara's childhood dream had been to become a ballerina, but her family had not supported her dancing.

Chiara's mother had wanted her daughter to focus on her studies and to find a good husband. So Chiara wanted her daughter to do what she herself had not been allowed to do, become a famous ballerina. In spite of Aphrodite's angry protests, her tap dancing lessons ceased and her ballet classes increased in number. Toward the end of each year, Aphrodite would be presented as the most promising up and coming ballet dancer. She would perform her solo dance routine to perfection. All those children who had made fun of her clumsy sports maneuvers finally became impressed with her because of her obvious talent for dancing. By the time she finished junior high school she had become a star. All the girls wanted to imitate her and all the boys wanted to be her boyfriend.

Everyone assumed that Aphrodite would become a professional dancer. She did apply for a dance position, eventually, but not with a ballet or dance company. In her junior year of high school, she was invited to model for a furrier in the famous Garment District on 7th Avenue in New York City. Sometimes she would only attend half a day of classes so that she could catch the Metro North railway into Manhattan and be at her modeling assignment by 2 PM. Sometimes she would model on a Saturday morning. Aphrodite loved going in to "The City." She loved seeing all the different huge department stores, like Macys, Saks Fifth Avenue, Lord and Taylor, and all the little dress shops along Madison Avenue and Fifth Avenue. People walking by and speaking in different languages amused her. She also loved the sights and sounds and smells of the city. Sometimes she would stop at one of those handcart stands to get a sweet smelling hot dog or a steaming egg roll. Occasionally she would step into the lobby of one of her favorite hotels and imagine meeting her prince charming there.

The furrier shop where Aphrodite modeled luxurious dresses and furs was owned by two Swedish men, Hannes and Leif Skold. They would sometimes proudly talk about their younger brother, Dietrich Danjel Skold, who had opened a successful restaurant business and high end nightclub in Lucerne, Switzerland. It would be many years later that Aphrodite would finally discover who these two brothers were - the older brothers of the man who had kidnapped and prostituted her birth mother, Cassandra.

The two brother furriers loved Aphrodite. Each one would often tell her: Aphrodite, you are beautiful and so sweet. Soon you will need protection from men because they will be want to be with you and some of them are not so nice." Unlike the stories Aphrodite had heard about lecherous bosses in the garment center, these two men behaved with honor and respect toward all of their employees. Having relocated from Sweden to America and having built a solid business based on hard work, neither of them wanted to cause problems for their employees or for their happy homes. Both men loved their wives and their children but they also enjoyed teasing the young and innocent and beautiful models that worked for them.

As high school graduation approached, Aphrodite decided she would like to attend a college in New York City because her parents did not want to send her far away to an out-of-town campus. Chiara would have preferred to find a good college nearby in Connecticut but she didn't mind her daughter commuting as long as she knew that Aphrodite would return home every night. Together, mother and daughter researched all the colleges in the tri-state area - New Jersey, Connecticut and New York – within about a 1 hour commuting distance. Aphrodite told her mother: "I really want to keep my modeling job at the Furriers because those two owners treat me like family. And they give me a small steady income and those wonderful yearly bonuses so I can cover my extra expenses."

After researching all the local colleges and also talking with friends and acquaintances at the country club and wherever she went, Aphrodite's mother discovered a very special small Liberal Arts College, Harlington College on West 23rd Street in New York City. The school was located in an area toward the lower part of Manhattan called Chelsea. Chiara was first told about this college during an unexpected chat with Jeffrey, a young waiter at her favorite restaurant in town. He told her: "My older sister is currently a student of comparative languages at Harlington College. What a great school that is. It's really small, less than 1200 students, so they give their students a lot of personalized attention. And my sister loves her program of studies there. Oh, and they have lots of visiting professors who bring new ideas and make the learning process exciting. My sister loves that school."

When Chiara told her daughter about this college, Aphrodite was thrilled. The major she wanted to take was comparative languages. Although she felt she would have to continue with her French (which she had studied in high school), she planned to begin learning Spanish and German. And, for some reason that she didn't yet understand, she wanted to also learn how to speak Swedish and Greek. It wouldn't be until many years later, during an intense meditation revelation, that she discovered her Greek heritage and the fact that her natural mother's kidnapper, pimp and later benefactor, had been born in Sweden. During her 4 years in college, Aphrodite managed to learn all five languages and to communicate adequately. She didn't know why she had been drawn to learn all these different languages but she felt compelled to become fluent in each one.

About one month after passing her exams and submitting her application for admission to Harlington College, Aphrodite was accepted as an undergraduate student. Before the semester started, she and her mother, Chiara, attended the college orientation session at main big Harlington College building on 23rd Street between 8th and 9th Avenue. Both mother and daughter were excited about the language program Aphrodite would be taking. Her mother, born and raised in Switzerland, was fluent in 3 languages: German, French and English, and was thrilled that her daughter wanted to study and learn different languages. Chiara thought that particular major would open doors for Aphrodite to secure an interesting and high paying job after graduation.

A week after orientation, Aphrodite took the trip all by herself into Manhattan to register for her classes at the college. Her mother drove her to the train station and waited until she had boarded the Metro North commuter train for the trip into Manhattan. Once the train arrived underground in Manhattan, Aprohrodite followed the other passengers from the train into the terminal building. Once inside the Grand Central Station building she asked someone how to find the Shuttle train that would take her from east to the west side of Manhattan. She felt pushed along and hurried by all the people rushing to catch the next train and all those coming toward her who were rushing in the opposite direction. Aphrodite was surprised at how quickly the train transported all the passengers from east to west. But then when she left this train she was confused until someone asked her where she wanted to go. Soon she found the west side train line that would take her directly to 23rd Street and 7th Avenue. Then she walked up the stairs which opened out onto the streets of Manhattan. She was in awe. Only a few blocks away from the college, she enjoyed walking along this wide 23rd Street, observing all the small shops, a grocery store, and all the different types of people.

When Aphrodite reached the building and saw the big sign outside saying Harlington Liberal Arts College, she took a big sigh and prepared herself to enter this new world. Two big black doors with ornate gold trim and small sculptured images led into a beautiful circular and spacious central room with very high ceilings. There were about 14 desks arranged in a semi-circle toward the perimeter with one or two people sitting behind each desk facing a long line of students waiting to register. An information booth appeared to her immediate right as she entered the big room. A tall lanky older man with a kind of loud, shrill voice greeted her when he saw that she looked confused. He said: "Good morning young lady. Are you here to register? Tell me what you major is and I'll tell you where to get on line."

Aphrodite thanked him as he pointed to one of the middle lines. She had a very good feeling while standing on line in this big room. Aphrodite knew in her heart that she had chosen the right college to help her follow the best career path for her. After waiting online for almost an hour, Aphrodite finally spoke to a very helpful assistant. A young graduate student, only a few years older than Aphrodite, asked her some questions and helped her to select the appropriate beginning classes and to complete all of her registration forms for this first semester. She thanked the young lady who had assisted her and was told to head over to the bookstore to purchase her required textbooks immediately, just in case the store might run out of copies. At the bookstore directly across the street, Aphrodite spent some time searching through titles of books in different sections of the store. Then she asked someone for assistance and found and bought all of her required books, thinking to herself as she walked out of the bookstore "I am going to need a good solid briefcase to carry all these heavy books."

For Aphrodite, this was such an exciting time. She was about to embark on an education but not just the one she had anticipated. After buying her books and before going back into the subway for her return ride to Grand Central Terminal to catch her commuter train back to Connecticut, Aphrodite stopped at a nearby coffee shop. Her mind had been filled with all the energy of the people around her. She needed to go someplace quiet, to collect her thoughts, to relax, and to let her system calm down. As she sat in a corner booth which had a floor to ceiling window, she was able to watch the crowds of men and women rushing by, going wherever they were going, very quickly.

While sitting and sipping a cup of tea, totally absorbed in the newness of this environment, Aphrodite noticed a strikingly attractive young lady carrying a huge shoulder book bag, enter the coffee shop. Since there were no seats available at this hour, this girl, a total stranger, stopped to ask Aphrodite if she would mind some company at her table. Since Aphrodite had not yet spoken to any of the other students, she was delighted to meet a fellow classmate.

"Hi, I'm Sandorita Marquez," this exotic looking young woman said directly to Aphrodite. "And what is your name?"

"Aphrodite Maia Morgan," Aphrodite quickly answered. "Are you a new student at Harlington College? I just bought my books and I can't wait to read them," said Aphrodite.

"What are you studying?" asked Sandorita, glancing at

Aphrodite's books. "Looks like you have a Spanish book there. Hablo espanol? Estudio les artes."

"No, no." replied Aphrodite. "I am just beginning to learn these different languages. I studied French in high school and now I plan to study Spanish, German, and possibly even Greek and Swedish. I love languages. Each one represents a certain culture and the words in each language show us a different way of expressing life."

"And I am fascinated with the arts, especially interior design and fashion. I love dressing up in exotic outfits and tantalizing the men." said Sandorita in a teasing and confident tone in slightly broken English. Aphrodite asked her new acquaintance: "Why did you choose this college since it's a Liberal Arts College and you say you are interested in design and the arts?

Sandorita explained: "I moved here with my family - my parents, my two older brothers and my younger sister - from Chile just a few years ago. My parents thought it would be a good idea for me to first get my liberal arts courses and then maybe transfer to an art and design school. So here I am, for now."

Sandorita ordered a bran muffin with coffee and settled in to chat with her new acquaintance. As they talked, Sandorita explained: "I was looking for a job for several months, but nobody would hire me because I did not speak English very well." Aphrodite immediately suggested that Sandorita might get a job as a model for a Furrier or for another clothing outlet since the school was right near the "Garment District. Ahprodite told her new acquaintance: "There are so many clothing manufacturers, dress shops, accessory shops and Furriers nearby. I am sure you could find a job here. Many of the owners come from different countries and don't speak such great English themselves."

But Sandorita quickly brushed aside Aphrodite's suggestion and responded: "Thank you sweet lady but I didn't finish telling you what has happened to me. One night, a few months ago, I had a date with an attractive older man and he brought me as his guest to this exotic dance club. To my surprise, women came onto this big dance floor, one at a time, and started dancing. Nothing seemed strange until I saw the first woman slowly and seductively begin to remove her clothing. She kept on dancing using more and more provocative and sexy movements wearing less and less clothing. My date and I were fixated upon her. I couldn't believe how beautiful she looked and I wanted to be her. So I asked my date how I might be able to do that."

Sandorita continued: "That guy had obviously been coming to this club for quite a while since everyone who worked there seemed to know him by his first name. In a few minutes, he brought this stocky, brusque, cocky and arrogant man to the table. Louie, I found out later, was one of the owners. He stood in front of me staring at my chest. I was wearing a tight sweater that showed off my rather large breasts and he was looking down the cleavage. I felt as if he was about to grab my breast but he refrained because I'm sure he realized my date was rather tall and quite strong and might have created a fuss about it. Anyway, Louie asked me to come with him to the back room for a brief interview while my date waited at the table for me."

Sandorita described what happened next: "In that back room, Louie asked me to turn around. He sized up my body and asked me to try on one of the outfits he had there. It was a one piece bathing suit which barely covered by crotch leaving my rear end cheeks exposed and only a thin strip of material covering my naked breasts. To me it felt quite sensual to wear that outfit but I did feel a bit self-conscious in the presence of this highly energetic and arrogant man. He asked me to turn around, to bend down so he could observe what I looked like from behind, and then he asked me to do some dancing for him. Having loved dancing all my life and with a little modern dance training, it was easy for me to impress him with my agility. He hired me on the spot and I have been working there ever since."

Wide eyed and curious, Aphrodite asked: "But aren't you embarrassed to wear such skimpy outfits? And aren't the men dangerous? Do they grab at you and touch you in private places? Aren't you scared that someone might hurt you?"

That's when Sandorita put her arm around Aphrodite for just a moment and told her: "This is a very well-run establishment. Nobody messes around with the women working there. Louie and Sal make sure we are all safe. The money is incredible. All I have to do is look in the eyes of the men watching me, then turn around and reveal my round butt cheeks and my shapely legs and when I turn back again they are coming up in droves to fill my bathing suit with large bills, sometimes hundred dollar bills.   I know there are some back rooms and a champagne room upstairs, but I have not yet been there so I'm not sure exactly what goes on in those rooms. Some of the girls seem to make an awful lot of money at this club. And I made enough in the first two months to put a down payment on the apartment I'm now living in by myself."

She looked quizzically at Aphrodite and asked her: "Why don't you stop by this evening and see for yourself? Since you like to model, maybe you would enjoy dancing for men who are eager to give you some of their money. It's an amazing experience. I never could have imagined what this would feel like. It gives me a sense of control over men that I never had before. And I never want to lose that feeling again."

Aphrodite explained to her new acquaintance who would soon become her best friend: "My mother is expecting me at home in Connecticut. I have about a 45 minute commute after I take the west side train to 42nd Street, transfer to the shuttle to Grand Central Terminal, and get there in time to catch my commuter train."   Looking down at her watch, Aphrodite said: "I really do have to get going so I don't miss my train. It was really wonderful meeting you and talking with you. Have a great semester."

Feeling intrigued by this exotic and different young lady from Chile, Aphrodite was also a bit apprehensive and wanted to leave quickly.   But Sandorita repeated her invitation saying: "You are a beautiful looking young woman and I know the men will love you. And you will not believe how freeing it is to work there. Please come to visit one night. You won't be sorry."

Aphrodite motioned to the waitress to bring the check as she explained: "My parents will not let me stay out so late. My mother waits for me at the train station. She would be worried sick if I came home really late."

"But this is your life, Aphrodite, and you get to choose the way you want to spend it. Just visit one time, maybe on a Friday night, and I think you will be hooked the way I have been." Sandorita ended by saying: "Have a wonderful semester at school. And if we don't run into each other, please stop by the club." Then Sandorita scribbled the address of the club on a napkin and handed it to Aphrodite.

As Aphrodite walked out the door, she crumbled the napkin and actually threw it away by the time she had reached Grand Central Station. Her first instinct was to just ignore this chance meeting with a strange and exotic woman. Aphrodite thought to herself: "I guess that dance club is good for her, she's from another country and wants to be free here in America. And she had a really hard time getting any type of job. But my life is fine the way it is. I make a little extra spending money modeling for the Furriers. Anyway, for the next few years I plan to spend all my time studying so I can get really good grades. Then maybe I can work as a Translator or find some other interesting job." Aphrodite pulled her jacket tighter around her collar because she could feel a bit of a chilly breeze outside as rushed toward the subway station to begin her journey home.

23 APHRODITE WORKS AT THE CANDY BAR

Aphrodite had been enchanted by that strange and exotic young lady she had met at the coffee shop near Harlington college right after she had registered for her Fall semester classes. She had never before met such an eye-catching and unusually beautiful young woman as she found Sandorita Marquez to be. Aphrodite was intrigued and wanted to get to know that young lady better. She hoped she might run into Sandorita again at the college or maybe at that same coffee shop.

Growing up in Connecticut, Aphrodite had been subjected to a proper etiquette that had been instilled into the women and even the men. Of course, the men were allowed a bit more freedom to express their natural inclinations. But she could see that even the men were brought up and instructed to live and behave in a certain conforming way. They were certainly not the Haight-Ashbury and Woodstock variety. Even if some of the men and women indulged in smoking marijuana or had pre-marital sex, it was all kept hushed up and private. In public, everyone tended to behave in a quite civilized manner. Aphrodite's mother, the mother she had known all her life, seemed to fit right into this Connecticut society. Her mother loved to do the "right" thing.

Aphrodite's parents belonged to an exclusive country club that did not allow Jews or Negroes or any ethnic groups from other countries. They only allowed members who had been invited by other members and approved by the board of directors who followed and enforced the rather stringent rules.

Aphrodite had endured the humiliation of being teased during many of her younger years. She had often felt tormented by her classmates and so-called "friends" for being tall and skinny with olive skin. But by now she had blossomed into an elegant beauty with an upright elegant stature from her ballet and gymnastics practices that none of the other Connecticut ladies could match. And many were downright jealous of Aphrodite's beauty, charm and seemingly hypnotic effect upon the local boys and men. Some of the women even thought she was evil and gossiped about her, sharing statements that were either exaggerated or completely false. Being an attuned and highly sensitive psychic, Aphrodite could feel their critical energy even when they were not in her presence.

For a long time, Aphrodite had been mildly depressed because she knew too much and felt everyone's negative emotions weighing upon her psyche. That beautiful gold heart pendant did not seem to have the same capability to block the negativity as she got older. But at one point, Aphrodite made an astounding discovery. Without trying, just by thinking about something, she could cause an effect. It began with something simple. In the morning, before taking the train into New York to attend her classes, she would think about wanting to eat a certain type of food. When lunchtime arrived, she would be invited by a classmate to have lunch together at a local restaurant a few blocks away which served exactly that type of food. This type of coincidence began to happen so frequently that Aphrodite could not deny that her thoughts had magical powers. What she didn't realize is that her thoughts were affecting the energy within her body that is connected to the energy of everyone and everything around her.

Soon Aphrodite began to practice using her energy intentionally. She would think about a girl in her class that she might like to talk with. And that day, sure enough, that very girl would come right over to her and ask her some questions. Then Aphrodite began to create little experiments. She would think, "I wonder if that girl will wear a pink blouse tomorrow." And sure enough, the girl would show up wearing something pink – a blouse or a sweater or maybe her jacket. Then Aphrodite would focus on a different girl thinking, "That girl has such straight hair, I would like her to make her hair curly for a day." And sure enough, in the next day or two, that girl would come to class wearing a brand new curly hairstyle that she had just decided to try out that week.

Then Aphrodite experimented with affecting people's relationships. On this one day, she watched a young couple sitting affectionately in the student lounge, smiling and laughing together. Aphrodite thought to herself: "I wonder what it would take for those two to have a big fight." Within a few minutes, the girl suddenly jumped up, slapped her boyfriend across the face and stormed out of the lounge. Since Aphrodite knew that particular couple from one of her classes, she ran out of the room to ask the girl why she had done that and what her boyfriend had done to deserve that slap. To Aphrodite's amazement, the girl answered: "Honestly, I have no idea what caused me to react to his comment so strongly. I love him so much. We were having a wonderful afternoon. But I felt this strange energy come over me and I just had to lash out at him. I hope he can forgive me." So Aphrodite thought to herself: "I wonder what it would take for him to forgive her?" And then she saw him come running out, begging for his beloved girlfriend's forgiveness, having absolutely no idea why she had gotten so angry and why he was so ready to forgive her. Aphrodite finally understood the power of her own thoughts.

Looking back on her earliest years, Aphrodite realized that her thoughts had always guided her life. Her memory seemed to go so far back that she could recall the thought she had as a developing fetus in her mother's womb. She remembered thinking: "Something is wrong here. I want to be adopted by a beautiful woman and a loving man so I can grow up in a happy, loving family." Aphrodite was sure that her thoughts had brought to her this beautiful mother, Chiara, and her successful and kind father, David, to take her away from a bad situation. But Aphrodite did not yet know what that situation was. She only she knew that in the womb she had wanted and needed to get away from the life her mother was living.

One evening, during her long commute on the Metro North Train back to Connecticut from Manhattan, Aphrodite was reading a local newspaper she had brought with her that morning. Turning past the articles and latest news, she found a section of advertisements that intrigued her. On one page, there were many ads for 900 numbers, inviting men to make a phone call to speak to a sexy woman. In small print she saw that those phone calls could become quite expensive since the charge was by the minute. Aphrodite thought to herself: "I wonder who would be calling these numbers. It must be some strange men with some sort of kinky habit." But as she turned the pages she saw that these 900 number ads continued for several pages, along with some enticing ads for "sensual massage" and "sexual role play" and "exotic dancing."

Now Aphrodite thought to herself: "Who are these men that are calling these numbers?" For several minutes she sat there wondering: "Who in the world would want to call a woman just to talk with her? I guess some lonely men might want to receive a sensual massage. The men on this train reading this newspaper are successful businessmen and many of them are married. When I see them with their wives and children at the club or at the beach or at church they seem to have such happy families. So who is calling these numbers?"

She stopped reading to look at the people sitting in the seats near her on this train. Noticing several of the men reading this same local newspaper, Aphrodite suddenly got it. The realization hit her like a bolt of lightning. Aphrodite's thoughts were spinning: "The men who are calling these 900 numbers and paying for sensual massages and going to watch naked women dance at exotic dance clubs are right here on this train! These men work hard in the city, they make good money, they support their families and they have enough extra money to go out and play. And somehow they want to go and play even though they have a wife and children at home."

Feeling perplexed and upset, Aphrodite wondered to herself: "Why?" And in that very moment she decided: "If that's the way men behave, I never want to get married."

Now, during this same train ride going home, Aphrodite thought to herself: "I would really like to see that strange and exotic young lady again. What was her name, Sandora, Sandista? Oh, I remember – Sandorita - such a pretty name." And then Aphrodite let the thought slip from her mind.

A few days later, after one of her classes, Aphrodite stopped to freshen up in the nearby Ladies Room. She heard a familiar voice call out to her: "Aphrodite, I knew I would see you one of these days at the college. How are you enjoying your classes?" Startled and not recognizing this other person for a moment, Aphrodite started to ask: "Do I know you?" Then she suddenly recognized that tall slender unmistakable body and the penetrating dark brown eyes that had made her a bit uneasy in their first meeting. To Aphrodite, Sandorita looked even more beautiful than she had seemed before. She had a tall, slender stature with full round breasts, curvy hips and a firm round butt. And the outfit Sandorita was wearing accentuated her exquisite shape and her curves without being too ostentatious.

Aphrodite responded: "I was thinking about you the other day and I wondered when I might run into you again.

Let's stop at the coffee shop. I have something I want to talk to you about." They headed to the same coffee shop together and chatted over sandwiches and cappuccino. Aphrodite told her new friend about her realization on the train. She said: "I was looking at the men on the train who were reading one of the local Connecticut newspapers which is filled with pages and pages of 900 number ads. At first I wondered to myself: 'Who could be calling these numbers?' And then it hit me like a bolt of lightning: 'These men on the train are some of the men who call those 900 numbers.'" Aphrodite continued: "When I realized that many of these seemingly happily married men are secretly hanging out with other women - on the phone or in-person - I decided then and there that I do not want to get married so quickly. I want to go out and have a good time myself. That's when I thought of you and what you had told me about how much you enjoy working at that club. Please tell me more about it."

Delighted that Aphrodite might be interested in visiting the club, Sandorita said: "I told one of my bosses, Louie, about you and he can't wait for you to come to watch me dance. He is always looking for a new beautiful employee to excite the men and bring him more customers and more money. I know you will make a huge hit with him." And then Sandorita asked, a bit hesitantly: "Do you know how to dance?"

Aphrodite laughed, reassuring her new friend that she was quite an experienced dancer and an acrobat, having taken ballet and gymnastics since she was a very young child. Then Aphrodite explained; My mother wanted me to become a professional ballerina. But even though I knew she would be really disappointed, I told her I have no interest in pursuing a dance career, traveling with gay men, and struggling to make a sub-standard income." Then she told Sandorita: "I know I do want to make a strong impact on the world but I don't know yet know exactly how or what I can do." The two girls got along together easily, chatting as if they had known each other for years.

Finally, as they got ready to pay the check and leave, Sandorita insisted: "Please, Aphrodite, come to watch me dance just one time. I know you will fall in love with the place just as I did. It's an amazing environment. You feel so alive, such intense energy and excitement. The place is vibrant. The male customers love to drink and eat and spend their money on the girls. Our job is to keep them happy and keep them opening their wallets. Of course, they also want to open their pants and get off on the girls. But that is strictly forbidden. I think there is some hanky-panky that goes on in the back rooms or upstairs in that champagne room, but I have not seen it and I have not yet heard much about it."

Sandorita continued: "Louie and his partner Sal, the doormen and the body guards keep the men away from the women. The customers are only allowed to put money into your outfit. They are not allowed to touch the women. Even if you move close to the man to give him a lap dance, he is still reminded not to touch you and severely reprimanded if he does. Any man who blatantly breaches the rule is very harshly escorted out of the place and banned from ever returning.

Sandorita handed a small card to her new friend saying: **The Candy Bar: Come and Enjoy Some Sweets Tonight**, 245 12th Avenue, NYC. Aphrodite told her friend she could not stay out late on a weekday night. But, excited to have a new adventure, she decided she would plan to visit the club the following evening because it was Friday. On the train ride back to Connecticut, Aphrodite opened one of her local Manhattan newspapers and there it was, in bold and intriguing words: *Visit the Candy Bar Tonight.* Turning the page, she saw another ad: *Want some? Come and Get It Tonight - at The Candy Bar.* Then, a few pages later she saw a third ad: *Beautiful Hot Mama – She's Waiting For You at The Candy Bar.*

Aphrodite was intrigued and excited about her upcoming visit to *The Candy Bar*. She put on many different outfits, trying to find one that she could wear to her classes at Harlington College and somehow transform it into a sexy and revealing outfit at night. Of course, she did not tell her mother about her plans.

In the morning, Aphrodite told her mother that she was planning to stay late at the school because she was invited to participate in a school play in which she would be dancing. She promised to take an 11:07 PM train back to Connecticut which was one of the latest trains available at night. Chiara offered to pick her up at the train station because she didn't want her daughter to arrive at the station alone late at night. It was actually her mother's overpowering concern and need to create safety and security for her daughter, which precipitated Aphrodite's early departure from her parents' home. She was coming into her rebellion mode and soon nobody would be able to stop her or control her actions and whereabouts.

That Friday morning at the college, Aphrodite had difficulty containing her excitement while listening to her French teacher talk about the use of various nouns and verbs and special sayings. Her ears were later tuned out as her history teacher talked on and on about the historical reasons for the current economic growth. Aphrodite wanted to build her own economic growth and she had a feeling this new venture might help her get started.

After hanging out in the student lounge for a few hours, she stopped at the nearby coffee shop for a light dinner and then she walked all the way west to 12th Avenue. Walking along this wide avenue which had more apartment buildings, warehouses and fewer shops and restaurants, Aphrodite looked carefully at the numbers. Soon she found building number 245 in bright Neon lettering, with **"The Candy Bar"** appearing in big flashing letters above the number.

At the door, a huge burly muscular man with thick black hair, a mustache and a dark blue suit greeted Aphrodite. He asked: "Young lady, do you work here? I haven't seen you before." She replied: "My friend, Sandorita Marquez, invited me to come to watch her dance. Do I need a special pass?" He answered with a seductive smile: "Young lady, any woman who looks as sexy as you can enter this club any time she wants. Right this way." And he made a motion that he was stepping out of the way to let her enter.

Once inside, the invigorating energy shot through Aphrodite's body. She felt electricity moving rapidly in and out of her cells as she perused this new and exciting environment. To her left was a coat check room attended by a buxom brunette wearing a low cut, uplifting bra type upper garment that invited men to place their tips inside her cleavage – which many of her customers did. There was a narrow staircase leading down to a room with a long bar, lots of small tables, a few booths and couches along the outside. There was a rather large slightly elevated dance floor in the midst of all the tables. Some women were practicing their dance moves. One of them was using a pole, doing leg stretches. She brought her head down to touch one knee while her other leg extended straight up into the air. Aphrodite thought to herself: "I can do that. And with my long legs my movements will look really good. I think this man, Louie, is going to be impressed with me."

As Aphrodite walked toward the bar to speak to the bartender, an attractive young blond stopped her. This woman, Blanche, was the current overseer and manager presiding over the women dancers. Her job was to get the girls out on the dance floor in time, to keep watch over the customers and report any breaches of the rules. She was also a good sales person, often encouraging those who seemed most ready and willing to upgrade to private lap dances in the back room. For the men who were spending quite freely, Blanche would attempt to get them intrigued with the Champagne Room. She would entice them by introducing them to the hottest women, the most seductive and desirable at the club, who she knew would be willing to make the men happy in that private room upstairs for a very high hourly fee.

But Blanche never pushed them to make those expensive decisions on their first or second night at the club. She knew it was best to prep the men, to entice them with what was possible and to invite them to call the girls or to have the girls call them at a phone number they provided. For some of the men it took a very long time before they were ready to splurge on a Champagne Room event. But a large number of the men did partake in receiving private lap dances and tended to tip quite heavily during the experience. The clever dancers would always encourage the men to open their wallets and hand over the money while they were still filled with hot and heavy desire. Once a man's passion cooled down, the women knew that their willingness to part with their money would also diminish.

When Aphrodite explained to Blanche that Sandorita had invited her to watch her dance and to meet Louie, Blanche pointed to a gruff looking man smoking a cigarette at the end of the bar. Then Blanche motioned for Aphrodite to follow her. When they were a few feet away from Louie, Blanche said to Aphrodite: "He's all yours. Show him your stuff and you'll be hired."

"Hello young lady," Louie said. He had been licking his lips in anticipation from the moment he saw her enter the room. Her energy was so intense and healing that he could feel it instantly. The contrast between her spirituality and the lower level energy of the customers and the staff felt palpable to this outwardly gruff, but inwardly quite sensitive man. Aphrodite explained that her friend, Sandorita Marquez, had invited her to come to the club, to meet Louie and to watch her and some of the other girls do their dances.

In his usual style, Louie immediately invited Aphrodite to join him in the back room for a private interview. "Come with me," he said, "and show me what you've got." He asked her to walk in front of him so he could watch the way she moved. Sizing her up in the back room, he asked her: "Please turn around a few times for me and then I'll choose an outfit for you to try on." Already Louie liked what he saw. He chose a pink fluffy trimmed skimpy outfit that zipped up the front with snaps across the bottom. He told her: Leave on your panties and in this outfit you can also wear your bra. Although once you start dancing you are going to have to remove that. I want to see how you dance and move in this outfit. Then I want to see you slowly unsnap and remove the garment while you continue to move and dance seductively. Can you do that?"

Aphrodite felt excited and confident, not even slightly nervous, as she nodded: "Yes." She quickly changed into the outfit right in front of him, because he did not bother to leave the room or look away. He wanted to make sure that the women working for him were not shy and hesitant about unclothing. As soon as she had finished putting on her new outfit, Louie said again: "Okay, show me what you've got. Move that sexy body so I can feel what the other men will feel when they watch you dance."

Without hesitation, Aphrodite began doing a beautiful

and sensual dance, twirling and moving her body in a way that made his mouth fall open. Louie's eyes were captivated by Aphrodite's twirling arms and legs. When he blinked again he couldn't believe that she had already removed the outfit. Her dancing was flawless and entrancing to this man who had seen many young ladies perform for him and for his customers. He asked her to try moving with the pole and she readily obliged. Using her gymnastic moves, she was able to climb up and down the pole and extend her legs to create a straight line from top to bottom. There was no question in his mind that this woman could bring in a slew of customers and make him a lot of money.

When she finished showing him her dancing capability, he said to her: "You're hired. I'm sure my partner, Sal, will agree. Your dancing is breathtaking. The men will love watching you bend over with those long, exotic legs. When can you begin working?" That's when she told him: "I just started attending Harlington College and since I am commuting back to Connecticut, I can only work on Friday and Saturday nights." He told her that was fine with him and she could start working the following night. He promised to provide some outfits and music for her so she would have no immediate expense. Actually, the outfit he had in mind would reveal her body in such a way that he was sure his customers would be begging for more. "Of course," he thought to himself, "We never let our new girls go into the back room or the upstairs upgrade room. They have to prove they are reliable, trustworthy and are willing to give a little more of themselves to please the men. But I can see that this beautiful young girl has some great potential. She will bring us a lot of business."

Before turning to leave this private interview, Aphrodite put her right hand on Louie's shoulder and said: "Don't worry Louie, your wife is not cheating. She loves you very much. Don't believe those people who say bad things about her. They are jealous of you and they want to sleep with your wife who keeps rejecting them. She knows she can trust you, even though you are surrounded by so many beautiful and sexy women. Your wife trusts you and it is time for you to trust her too. Not everyone is lucky enough to find a special love like you have found. Show her how much you care. She needs to hear that from you."

That was the first time Aphrodite had ever blatantly shared her inner knowing with another person, let alone a man who was about to be her new boss. After the words were spoken, she got worried that he would think she was intrusive, crazy or out of line. She was afraid at this moment that he might decide not to hire her. Instead, she saw tears well up in his eyes and he said softly to her: "How did you know I was concerned about that. Nobody else here knows how sensitive I really am. They don't know how much I love that woman. I try to let the girls think that I want to sleep with them so they continue to feel appreciated when the competition gets strong. But how do you know that what you are saying is true?"

Aphrodite replied: "I have had this special internal knowing since I was a young child." She explained how she had known all sorts of details about her classmates and friends but she had rarely told people what she knew about them because they might get upset and make fun of her. She told him: "I always felt different and like a stranger in this world, as if I have been living between worlds."

Unlike his usual behavior with the women at his club, Louie reached out to Aphrodite and gave her a long nurturing hug. He thanked her for sharing her insight and told her: "I am really happy to have you join our staff. The men, our customers, are going to love you. But please don't tell them all those secrets you know about them. Keep that to yourself." Aphrodite made a promise to Louie that she later could not help breaking as she began helping her customers to heal some of their most difficult emotional problems.

After the interview was finished, Louie walked out with Aphrodite and told the bartender to give her a glass of wine and let her sit there to watch her friend perform. Aphrodite's eyes lit up when she saw the beautiful Sandorita appear in a stunning red and black sequined outfit with fur lined gloves and a fluffy fur trim on her outfit. While her friend danced for the crowd, Aphrodite looked into the men's eyes and saw each one's story in depth. She knew she would be doing a lot of healing while working at this club. The bartender called a cab for Aphrodite to take directly to Grand Central Station. Then he handed her a $20 bill that Louie had provided for her so that she would not have to take the subway at night.

When Aphrodite returned the following night for her first evening on the job, she was exhilarated about having her opportunity to perform her special dance moves for a crowd of mostly men. Louie had not expected to have such a strong reaction to this young lady's dance routine, a young woman who had been a total stranger until the previous evening. After watching Aphrodite's elegant and incredibly sexy floor and pole dance on Saturday night, Louie looked at the faces of the men in the audience and saw the lust and lechery in their eyes. Having seen Aphrodite's sweetness, how she understood his love and his concerns about his marriage, and having had a sense of her highly spiritual nature, Louie became rather fatherly toward her.

When she finished her performance that first Saturday night, Louie rushed up to Aphrodite and told her in a powerful, no-nonsense tone: "Put on your street clothes. I cannot allow you to dance on this stage again." At first Aphrodite felt rejected and hurt, thinking that somehow Louie thought her dancing was not quite good enough. Once again he reached out to hug her and with tears in his eyes he said: "Aphrodite. If I ever have a daughter I would like her to be just like you. I cannot allow you to expose your beautiful body to these lecherous men. You would be casting your pearls before swine. What I would prefer is for you to become the new supervisor, the manager and director of all the women at this club. You can invite the men to partake in their lap dances and maybe upgrade to a few hours in the Champagne Room. But your pure body and spirit will never be tarnished or seen or touched by these men in my establishment. Welcome to *The Candy Bar* Miss Morgan."

Aphrodite took the long train ride home that night feeling

warm and protected. She knew that God was with her in all her activities. With a renewed desire to increase her spiritual connection, she closed her eyes in deep meditation for the rest of the trip. When she saw Chiara at the train station, Aphrodite smiled sweetly and gave her mother the biggest hug she had ever given before. Chiara wondered what had brought this on. She was so pleased to be the current object of her beloved daughter's love and attention.

24 APHRODITE USES HER MYSTICAL POWERS

During her first year at Harlington College, Aphrodite's life was extremely busy. On Friday afternoons she would show up at the Furrier to model the latest styles to their prospective customers. As the Thanksgiving and Christmas holiday season approached, she was required to make several additional appearances to satisfy the needs of her bosses. But since her college was not that far away, Aphrodite was able to manage to attend all of her classes, study in the student lounge and the college library on her breaks, and appear for all of her modeling appointments. Her bosses, Hannes and Leif, were very happy with Aphrodite's modeling style and they basked in the continual praise of her audiences. Although her salary was not great, each of her bosses would often surprise her with a huge financial bonus during the holiday season. And then, on special occasions they would provide her with a free sample of one of their high priced popular fur jackets, fur-lined and fur-trimmed hats, fur lined gloves, and fur scarves. Aphrodite was fully protected from cold weather, especially during some of those freezing New England winter days.

During the very first Christmas season that Aphrodite worked with the Furriers, while she was still in high school, Leif had given her a full length fox coat that she treasured for many years. He never told her that the gift had come from someone else. Prior to the official start of the Christmas holidays that year, Dietrich Skold, the younger brother of Hannes and Leif, was visiting from Switzerland to learn more about his older twin brothers' successful Furrier business. While sipping a glass of champagne and flirting carelessly with one of the other models, as soon as he saw Aphrodite he almost gasped. She looked so much like her mother, Cassandra, that Dietrich knew in an instant exactly who she was. He stared in disbelief as she strutted up and down the center carpet, looking beautiful, elegant and confident.

"So much like her mother," he thought. "One day soon I will tell Cassandra that her daughter is alive and well and thriving in New York City. She will be so happy to hear that. But right now Cassandra seems content and I do not want to stir her up and get her really upset. When the time is right, I will tell her what I learned today." From that day forward, he religiously sent money to his brothers specifically to be given to that beautiful and elegant model, Aphrodite. More than a decade would pass before Dietrich would tell anyone, including his two brothers exactly why he was providing that money for Aphrodite. And he did not explain to Cassandra that he had met her daughter until after the mother and daughter were finally reunited on their own a few decades later.

Aphrodite's work as supervisor and manager of the other girls at **The Candy Bar** was only for the two nights every week, Friday and Saturday. Blanche was jealous since she was suddenly relegated to a lesser commanding position on the two most popular nights. The rest of the week, Blanche was fully in charge. But as soon as Aphrodite appeared, Blanche had to switch gears from director to follower. When Aphrodite was working, she gave the directions, the rules and set the standards – standards which followed her employers' rules without attempting to change anything. Blanche, on the other hand, would allow some of the girls to keep their money without revealing the amount to their bosses. Blanche would also allow some of the men to fondle the girls as long as they first provided Blanche with a hefty tip. And she would sometimes make deals with local drug dealers to supply her and some of the girls with drugs in exchange for a free sexual exploit in the back room. Aphrodite would never consider such breaches of her contract with her two bosses.

As the year passed and time moved on, there were certain exotic dancers and certain male customers who stopped coming to **The Candy Bar** on a Friday or Saturday night. Louie didn't think much about it but his partner, Sal, was really concerned. "Why," he wondered. "Why have some of our girls chosen not to work on the weekends and why are some of customers staying away on those same nights?" Are these girls working somewhere else and taking our guys with them? Hmmm! I'll have to check out some of the other clubs and see if I can figure this out."

Every weekend Sal began to spend a considerable amount of time and money at many different Exotic Dance Clubs, often called Strip Clubs, in the tri-state area (New York –

including the 5 boroughs, Connecticut and New Jersey). While at these other clubs Sal would have himself a really good time. He'd indulge in special lap dances with beautiful young ladies from many parts of the world. He didn't care what verbal language they spoke. All he cared about was how they looked, how they moved their body and how easily they could arouse him – and – often, how quickly and willingly they would give him a happy ending.

During Sal's weekend visits to all these other clubs, he did not find a single one of his girls or his male customers. What he didn't know was that a local pimp had set up a prostitution ring using those girls to entice those interested customers for more satisfying weekend pleasures. The girls would return to dancing at **The Candy Bar** from Sunday through Thursday nights. And these same men would also return to the club to get sensually stimulated and aroused in anticipation of their weekend adventures in sexual fulfillment.

Aphrodite's mother, Chiara, became concerned, upset and eventually quite angry at Aphrodite for staying out so late on Friday and Saturday nights. Chiara had no idea where Aphrodite was going and how she seemed to have a lot of money at her disposal. The more that Chiara questioned her beloved daughter, the more resistant and angry Aphrodite would become. After opening a secret bank account, Aphrodite began depositing large sums of money every week. She had no need or desire to purchase clothing, gadgets, or toys. Her plan was to save enough money to buy an apartment or a home and then to accumulate enough money to start her own business. She had spent a lot of time in the presence and company of big business owners - Hannes and Leif's Furrier business, Louie and Sal's Exotic Dance Club business, and the many clients and customers she would chat with at both places. Observing the details of the way each business was handled, she knew she could set up her own successful business when she was ready. With her customers, especially those at **The Candy Bar** whose sexual arousal got them to be extremely verbal and open about their personal business skills and practices, Aphrodite learned the ins and outs of business success.

While studying at college and working on her two jobs, without realizing it, Aphrodite was developing and honing her unique psychic and mystical skills. In her spare time, usually on Sunday afternoons after returning from the morning church ceremony, she would sit silently in her room listening to one of her mother's favorite saved *Infinite Way* audiotapes of a live Joel Goldsmith lecture that her mother had attended. Aphrodite knew that her own consciousness was extremely powerful but she had not yet understood how to control it or the fact that it can really only be used for the higher good.

Some of the women she had known from high school who attended the same local church on Sundays would often speak in a demeaning and even insulting way to her. Aphrodite's astounding beauty, stature and sexy appearance disturbed these "proper" Connecticut housewives. Since Aphrodite was single and incredibly beautiful, many of these women would overhear one of the husbands, and sometimes their own husband, making lewd or seductive comments about Aphrodite's sex appeal and unique "charms." Naturally, these women became more guarded and sometimes rude when Aphrodite was present. What they did not know is that Aphrodite had seen some of their husbands at **The Candy Bar**, on those rare occasions when she would visit the club on a weekday night. Aphrodite would try not to make eye contact and tried her best not to be recognized. But she observed some of these "happy husbands" putting dollar bills into the dancers' skimpy outfits and walking toward the back room for a special lap dance or maybe something more. Aphrodite wondered whether any of these men had seen her there but she doubted that they would tell their wives because that would indicate that they had also been there. None of these men had ever seen Aphrodite dance since she had only done that on her first night working there. So she quietly smiled to herself when she saw these same husbands behaving affectionately in public with their wives.

Wanting to get even with the women who had been rude and judgmental toward her, Aphrodite purposely decided to test out her mystical powers to do something naughty. She sat in church one Sunday wondering to herself: "What would happen if someone accidentally poured a glass of cold water onto Sarah's blouse?" Sarah had been particularly rude to Aphrodite the week before, saying: "Yes, my dear Aphrodite, you do seem to have lovely breasts but do you have to show them to everyone?" Aphrodite had been wearing a form fitting low cut sweater that revealed a substantial amount of cleavage but it was not in bad taste. So, smiling to herself through the sermon, Aphrodite just waited to see what would happen. Sure enough, while the congregation was gathering downstairs for some juice and wine, fruit and cookies and biscuits, one of the children accidentally slipped toward Sarah pouring a full glass of ice water onto her blouse. That day Sarah had been wearing a fine silk and gauze blouse that suddenly became completely transparent when wet. All the men's eyes were fixated on Sarah's naked upper body. Her nipples had hardened from the icy cold water. That's when Aphrodite got even. She quickly walked right up to Sarah repeating Sarah's exact words: "Yes, my dear Sarah, you do seem to have lovely breasts but do you have to show them to everyone?" Sarah was noticeably mortified. Her husband, on the other hand, felt aroused by looking at her for the very first time in many, many months. That night he made beautiful love to his wife and Sarah thought to herself: "Maybe I ought to thank that Aphrodite. She's the one who had the right idea. Men like a woman with some sexiness and I have been completely avoiding that."

Blanche had been a thorn in Aphrodite's side from that very first evening when Aphrodite had taken Blanche's place as head supervisor of the women on Friday and Saturday night. Aphrodite wanted so much to get even and did not know what she could possibly do that would teach Blanche a lesson. Since Blanche had stopped performing at **The Candy Bar** for the past 2 years, Aphrodite thought that forcing Blanche to unwillingly put on a performance would do the trick. Since Aphrodite's consciousness was so powerful, she did not have to figure out the mechanics. She just had to hold the thought briefly, let it go and wait to see the results. This thought occurred to Aphrodite one Friday night.

Blanche arrived early the following night, Saturday, expecting to share some drinks with the men and convince them to select a sexy dancer for a financial upgrade of private services. What she didn't expect is that she was going to be the desired service provider for that evening. The night before, Friday, after thinking about getting even with Blanche, Aphrodite had quietly mentioned to every male customer standing at the bar that Blanche was planning to provide a special gift for him in the back room, just for being a loyal customer.

The men seemed particularly excited to see Blanche that Saturday evening. She wondered what was attracting so much attention to her. As she began to talk to the men at the bar, most of whom she had seen just the night before, each one asked her what she had to offer him for the night. When she started suggesting another dancer, the guy would attempt to fondle her, causing her to say: "Not here, honey. Come with me so I can show you something special." Each man seemed eager to spend time alone with her. She thought to herself: "I haven't done this in such a long time. Maybe tonight I'll make an exception because it will bring me a huge sum of money – and I could use that to buy a whole new wardrobe." So she took one man after another into the back room to give them each her most provocative lap dance. Expecting a huge tip from each man, she was mortified when they would tell her: "Thank you so much Blanche for this very special gift. I was looking forward to being with you again after all these months. And for free. Wow! Let me know when you will be offering this again. I'll be first in line to sample your performance."

When Blanche finally emerged from the back room after providing 10 of these private dances, she looked noticeably upset. Making eye contact with Aphrodite and seeing that glint in her eyes and smile on her face, Blanche knew how this "free" lap dance performance series had been orchestrated. At first Blanche was fuming with anger. But as her anger subsided, she felt that old sense of sexual power. She had reconnected to that internal sense of being a beautiful and seductive woman. Even though these men had not paid her for this experience, they had praised her and admired her sensuality. Inside, Blanche felt really good about herself. Toward the end of the night she actually walked over to Aphrodite, hugged her, and said "Thank you."

Aphrodite had often used her special mystical abilities to get even with someone, usually another woman who had hurt her in some way. But always, the end result would be an emotional and psychic expansion followed by forgiveness and an expression of gratitude by her psychic victims. One of her most memorable experiences in high school immediately came to mind. She recalled the time that the pretty blond and extremely popular cheerleader, Maggy, had convinced the entire cheerleading team to reject Aphrodite, even though her dancing was magnificent, and not let her join the team . Maggy, the star performer at the time had felt threatened. She did not want to be outclassed by this long-legged ballerina and acrobat, Aphrodite. So Maggy managed to convince her entire team that Aphrodite would be detrimental to the cohesiveness of their group. Privately to each team member, Maggy suggested that she had seen Aphrodite flirting with that girl's boyfriend and that Aphrodite seemed intent on getting him interested in her. To protect their own personal relationships, each team member chose not to accept Aphrodite as a fellow cheerleader.

It happened one fateful weekend in late spring of that same year. Aphrodite was thinking about the weather, the atmosphere and the fact that she had heard there were people adding some chemicals into the air which might affect cloud formations. Pondering about this for a while, she looked up to see the shapes and colors of the clouds above. In this very same moment, Aphrodite thought about how much she would have liked being a cheerleader. And then she remembered the way Maggy had maliciously convinced the entire team to veto her acceptance. That's when Aphrodite wondered: "What if there was a chemical so powerful that it could instantly render all hair color innocuous. Imagine all those beautiful 'unnatural' blonds with their hair instantly losing the dye, returning it back to their natural base color. Wouldn't that be something! I wonder what would happen if this chemical reaction lasted for an entire month." Aphrodite let her thought go out into the ethers and she didn't think about it again.

That evening was the final banquet dance of the year. Aphrodite was planning to attend alone. None of the boys had invited her to be their date, not because they didn't find her attractive. It's just that her magnificent beauty was intimidating to most of them and they were afraid she would reject them. Those who might have been a bit more confident were already dating someone else.

That night, each boy arrived at his date's home expecting to see the beautiful blond or the stunning redhead he had been dating or even thought he was in love with. But what greeted each guy at the door absolutely shocked him. Maggy's date, the football team captain David Roark, knocked on her door eagerly waiting to see how beautiful she would look. But when she opened the door with a look o disgust he immediately asked: "Where is Maggy?" Instead of that long silky wavy blond hair, what greeted him was a frizzy mop of light brown hair. He thought it was a different person who had answered the door. Again he asked: "Where is Maggy?" Not realizing what had happened to her hair, she angrily said to him: "What are you talking about? I'm right here." That's when he pointed at her hair, turned his head away and yelled "Ugh! That is really ugly. I can't take you to the dance looking that way. I'd be the laughing stock of the crowd. I have a reputation to keep up. You're gonna have to go by yourself, if you're willing to show up looking like that. I would recommend that you just stay home tonight. Maybe by Monday morning your hair will be back to normal. But you are not prom queen material tonight. We'll have to quickly find a new model for prom queen. See you in school on Monday. I have to go now."

Maggy didn't know what had hit her. She ran to the first mirror she could find in the little bathroom near the stairs. She almost gagged when she saw that her hair had been stripped of color and style. Immediately, she called one of her teammates, Carol, and before she could say anything Carol bawled into the phone saying: "Philip arrived with a bouquet to take me to the prom but when I opened the door and he saw me, his face turned white.

Then he handed me the flowers and he made some lame excuse. He suddenly turned around and rushed back to his car. Philip left without taking me to the prom. I couldn't believe it. Then I looked in the mirror and saw that my strawberry blond hair is now mousy brown. My seductive waves are now stringy straight with not a bit of curl. What happened?"

Maggy and Carol agreed to spend the night together, alternately crying and expressing their rage at these two uncaring guys who they had thought were so special. Both of the girls vowed to give up on men for a while. They shared a bottle of wine and sulked in their tears of betrayal.

Many of the guys showed up at the prom without their lovely blond and redhead dates. Most of the women who were there had naturally brown or black hair. Aphrodite stood in a class by herself. Her light brown hair with naturally golden highlights caused the men to rush over, surround her, and beg her to be their date for the night. Both Maggy's and Carol's boyfriends were among Aphrodite's suitors that night. Aphrodite's wish had been granted. She was finally teaching Maggy, and the other "fake blonds" and "fake redheads" who had rejected her for the cheerleading squad, a lesson they would never forget.

The hair color of all the women in that town had been washed out by a certain unusual chemical in the air that lingered for an entire month. The hairdressers worked hard to help these women re-dye their hair, but after a whole long process the color would last only about ½ hour, just enough time for the girl to leave the salon and drive home. Relationships were torn apart. Men who had vowed to love their woman forever were now fleeing from the mousy brown, frizzy haired woman who had replaced his sexy blond or sexy redhead. But that's when the real kind-hearted, loving and sensitive men were finally given an opportunity to find love.

Maggy had been put on a pedestal by Harry Condor since the first time he had seen her. But Harry was just a scientific nerd, not a football star by any means. He had always seen the kind and caring person Maggy could be beneath her outer attitude of bravado and even mean bitchiness. He had attempted to have lunch with Maggy many times before, but her aggressive boyfriend, David, would suddenly show up and shove himself right next to his Maggy. He would confidently crowd out any nearby men. Now Maggy was alone and Harry took his opportunity to show her the beauty that he had always seen emanating from within her. Having been so devastated by this sudden change in her outward appearance, Maggy now revealed a softer and more approachable outward demeanor. For the first time in her life, she was willing to accept the kindness and attention of a truly sensitive and caring man. Maggy finally was able to appreciate Harry's genuine caring. As she allowed herself to spend more time with Harry during the next few weeks, to her surprise and Harry's delight, she began to actually feel sexual desire toward him. But he was skeptical of her true intentions. He was afraid that when the chemical problem was resolved, and he was sure it would be solved soon, that Maggy would once again become that arrogant, unreachable bitch that he had often observed. So he chose to wait patiently instead of jumping at the chance to get physically intimate with her. That only increased her desire for him and he found her reaching out, touching him and seductively indicating her sexual interest.

Carol had also been admired by a kind and sensitive guy, Peter Gray. Peter had never approached Carol before because as a stunning strawberry blond and cheerleader, she seemed to be way beyond his reach. He would often fantasize about being with her, about revealing to her that he could see beneath her outer beauty to the soft and precious child inside. Now he was able to talk with her and console her about the change in her outer appearance. He showed Carol that he could see beneath her hair, that he loved looking at her face and her beautiful smile, and that he knew how clever and interesting her thoughts and expressions were. Slowly he won her heart and she warmed up to him as no woman had ever done before.

Exactly one month later, as Aphrodite had expected, the hair dye problem had been solved. Helicopters spread across the region spraying a special formulated antidote to the potent chemical, instantly neutralizing its devastating effect. It was as if a miracle had occurred and the smiles returned to the men and women of this town. But many had been changed forever. Maggy and Carol and many of the other cheerleaders and attractive young women had lost interest in the popular, self-centered and arrogant men. They were now able to properly discern the character beneath the outer appearance. And, as a bi-product, each of the women had gained an inner sense of self-worth.

Aphrodite's initial intentions for using her thought power had often been to get even with someone who had in some way mistreated her. But in every case, Aphrodite's loving nature would create a positive effect. The end results would always bring the highest good for all involved. Aphrodite's connection to God, her higher power, the universal law, was so intense that even her momentary negative thoughts had very little effect on the final outcome. Everyone who knew Aphrodite for any length of time would become enamored of her and impressed with her natural mystical qualities and powers. The customers and staff at *The Candy Bar* would eventually have a direct personal experience of Aphrodite's intense transformational energy. The healings that occurred at the club did not necessarily improve the club's bottom line of increasing financial wealth and did not lead to the security of Aphrodite's job.

25 HEALINGS AT THE CANDY BAR

Aphrodite was very happy during the five years it took for her to complete her bachelor's degree in Comparative Languages. She continued modeling for the Furriers on Friday afternoons and working as managing hostess on Friday and Saturday nights at **The Candy Bar**. During this time she regularly deposited a good portion of her substantial earnings into her bank account. Her two jobs had provided so much income that by the time she got her degree, she would be able to purchase a small 2 bedroom apartment in Connecticut. She had grown tired of having to make excuses to her mother about where she was spending her weekend nights. Luckily, she had been able to stay in New York on Friday and Saturday nights while she was attending college and working the weekend shift at the club. Her friend, Sandorita, had invited Aphrodite to stay at her apartment on 22rd Street near 8th Avenue. That turned out to be good for both of them. They would leave the club together at the end of these nights and walk the long city blocks, sometimes empty and a bit scary, toward Sandorita's apartment

Chiara, quite concerned about her daughter's whereabouts, would often call the phone at Sandorita's apartment on a Friday or Saturday night to speak to

Aphrodite and, of course, nobody would answer because both girls were working their shifts at **The Candy Bar**. It was Sandorita who figured out that they could forward the phone message to the phone in Louie's private office and he agreed that it would be okay. Aphrodite had told her mother she was working at a restaurant and cocktail lounge so that when Louie would answer the phone, he would graciously tell Chiara that her daughter was busy waiting on tables and would call back on her break – which Aphrodite would always do to ease her mother's worries. Since Chiara did not drive a car and did not like to do anything on her own, including taking a commuter train by herself into New York City. In all the time that Aphrodite worked at **The Candy Bar**, Chiara never did come to New York to actually see where her daughter was working.

Aphrodite's father, David Morgan, was usually too busy for her. He seemed to be always working, focused on talking with his local patients, getting their stories, and writing about them in his many research projects. When David was at home he was often on the phone or at his typewriter and later his computer, oblivious to the requests or needs of his wife and his only daughter. Aphrodite's mother, Chiara, on the other hand, seemed to be always available, always wanting to know exactly what her daughter was doing and where she was spending her time. Aphrodite often felt as if her mother's overbearing concern was stifling her natural wonder, her desire to enjoy different life experiences and her need to allow her spiritual essence to freely evolve. She vowed to herself: "As soon as I graduate from college, I will move out on my own. If I save up enough money, which I think

I can if I keep working on these 2 jobs, I will be able to actually buy my own apartment." After deciding that one weekend, that Monday morning Aphrodite went to a bank near Harlington College to open her first savings account. She did manage to save a large portion of her very substantial income every single week for the entire four years.

While Aphrodite was commuting to college and David was working really hard, Chiara would often feel lonely and no longer needed by anyone. During the early romantic years of their marriage, David and Chiara had been intensely connected. At that time, Chiara would go with him to every conference and he would be by her side at the end of every meeting he attended. But once Aphrodite entered their life, inevitable changes occurred. It became more difficult for Chiara to just pick up and join David in a distant state or country. At first it was difficult because Aphrodite was a baby, requiring all sorts of baby paraphernalia to be brought on the flight. And then the baby needed lots of attention and care, preventing Chiara from being available to join David at the cocktail parties and other fun events. Yes, they would hire an assistant, sometimes even bringing one along from their home town, but Chiara was not comfortable leaving the baby alone with anyone else for too long.

After struggling to please David by bringing the baby along to many conferences and events, eventually Chiara insisted on staying at home while he traveled. This, of course, did not lead to greater closeness and intimacy. In fact, David seemed to become increasingly distant as the months and years passed by. As Aphrodite began her pre-school classes, then kindergarten, and finally entered the regular elementary school system, Chiara would always make herself available. She would get up early to drive her daughter to school. Then she might spend the day meeting a friend for lunch, playing tennis or golf (weather permitting) or attending a dance, exercise or yoga class at the country club sports area. But she was always ready to drop whatever she was doing to pick her daughter up someplace or respond to her daughter's current needs. Chiara was truly a devoted and caring mother.

The more that David became involved in his outside work, often neglecting the sweet intimacy of the early stages of their relationship, Chiara became more protective and smothering of her growing daughter. Chiara was fearful of letting Aphrodite experiment or decide for herself what she wanted to do. For example, although Aphrodite loved her tap dancing, Chiara pushed her daughter into more ballet classes because that was what Chiara would have preferred. Aphrodite listened to her mother, loved her dearly and went along with her mother's demands and wishes for her – until – that first year at Harlington College when she became friendly with a strange and exotic young lady, Sandorita Marquez.

Chiara usually allotted a portion of every day to sitting quietly and listening to a spiritually enlightening audiotape. Every few months she would attend another consciousness raising or spiritually awakening class or weekend workshop. On those occasions that she planned to spend two days away from her precious daughter, she would enlist her sister-in-law, David's sister, or her mother-in-law, his mother, to babysit. Knowing a family member was watching Aphrodite allowed Chiara to have the peace of mind to fully involve herself and her consciousness in the weekend teachings. Chiara would often arrive home with new books, cards with special sayings, magnetic stickers to place on the refrigerator or on the corner of the television set. When Chiara finally purchased a computer, many years later, those stickers could be found along the edges of her monitor. Sometimes Chiara would light candles and burn incense inviting her growing daughter to participate in a spiritual ceremony. Aphrodite, from as early as she could remember, had practiced sitting in silence, contemplating, meditating, chanting, drumming and praying silently for the wisdom of the ages to fill her consciousness. She read many of her mother's spiritual books and would often seek out her own special books by many well-known mystics and healers.

Although her father, David, had become more distant, Aphrodite had grown fond of the two Furriers, Hannes and Leif, and often turned to them for their fatherly advice. Her experience with *The Candy Bar* owners, Louie and Sal, as well as their employees and customers, taught her about the way men think and how women can use their seductive sexual skills to gain control and power over men. Aphrodite discovered that both men and women often manipulate their lives causing themselves and others to endure a great deal of unnecessary drama and unhappiness. Her work, on both jobs, introduced her to international customers. Aphrodite's language training helped her to communicate in several languages. Although she was most well-versed in English, French, and German, her many international customers helped her to develop additional skill in speaking and being understood in Spanish, Greek, and even Swedish. Her language dexterity helped her to develop immediate rapport with her non-English speaking customers at the Furriers' events, as a manager at **The Candy Bar** and in her later private business as a Healing Mystic.

Over time Aphrodite became aware of herself as an embodied spiritual being whose consciousness could instantly influence the lives of others around her. It took her many years to finally understand that she had been tapping into the universal source of all creation. Knowing that her thoughts were powerful influencers of the thoughts of everyone around her, she wondered why others did not seem to know this. She had often felt powerfully affected in both positive and negative ways from the thoughts and beliefs, attitudes and actions of others. But what took her many years to understand is that many of those whose thoughts most affected her had been totally unaware of the power of their own thoughts. Aphrodite knew, without a doubt, that she could influence other people's thoughts. She realized over time that as their thoughts and their perspective would begin to change, something great would happen. The appropriate circumstances and relationships would somehow appear in their lives, forcing them to self-reflect and change an attitude or behavior that no longer served their higher good.

Without intending to do this, Aphrodite began to focus her spiritual and psychic thoughts upon her fellow employees as well as the customers at **The Candy Bar**.

She loved being in a managerial position. She enjoyed guiding the dancers to improve their seductive approach so that they would attract more money from their audiences. As she began to help Blanche, she felt a special sense of accomplishment. Her goal was to enable Blanche to understand that authenticity, honesty and following the rules would be so much easier on her emotions and level of stress than pretending and sneaking around with some hidden agenda. Most of all, Aphrodite loved helping the male customers reveal to themselves their most private fears, insecurities and hidden spiritual strengths.

One of the regular customers, Jimmy Pollack, who had spent thousands of dollars enjoying sexual bliss in the Champagne Room with younger and younger strippers, was caught off-guard one day when Aphrodite took him aside. She asked him a few pointed questions about his mother. Right there, at the end of the bar, he burst into tears. Aphrodite had pulled out of him his core issue in life. His mother had died while giving birth to him and he had spent his whole life feeling guilty as if he should never have been born. For him, intimacy with a real adult woman had been impossible. His father had brought him up to "be a man." From a very early age it was instilled upon little Jimmy that he should never let women get to him, that he will be heartbroken just as his father was. He also was taught to be careful and never get a woman pregnant because giving birth is dangerous and could lead to her death. For Jimmy, it became suddenly clear that he felt safe only in a strip club environment where he did not have to get close or intimate with any of the women. He could choose the ones that attracted him, play with them, have a sexual release, and then have no further involvement. But when he returned home each time he had been at the club, he had experienced a wave of sadness and a sense of deep emptiness. Somewhere inside he knew there could be more to his life.

With Aphrodite's guidance and encouragement, Jimmy found a caring psychotherapist to help him explore his hidden fears, emotional blocks and sexually compulsive fantasies. Jimmy visited **The Candy Bar** less and less frequently until one day he brought his fiancé to meet Aphrodite, explaining that he no longer had any desire to be with other women. He spoke affectionately saying: "Because of you, dear Aphrodite, I have discovered my ability to love and I have now found the love of my life. We are so happy. I can't thank you enough." Jimmy never returned to **The Candy Bar**, costing Aphrodite's bosses and his employees thousands of dollars in payments that would no longer be received.

Tommy Morello used to regularly bring his many international business associates to **The Candy Bar** for meetings, dinners, entertainment and to entice them to do more business with him. Tommy's wife, that he loved dearly, had no idea about his nighttime activities with the dancers. As a regular customer, Tommy had taken every one of the dancers into the back room to experience her unique lap dance skills. Over time, he began to prefer certain dancers. One of his favorites was the beautiful, exotic and shapely Sandorita, Aphrodite's friend. He would often pay for Sandorita to undulate on his lap and to secretly give him a blow job for which he compensated her extremely well. The first time he had asked for this special treat, he dangled in front of her the gift she would receive for providing these favors. He held up an exquisite 2 carat, high quality, diamond necklace on an 18 carat gold chain. Although he never brought her such expensive jewelry again, he did give her a hefty tip each time she complied with his wishes which would always bring a huge smile to her face. Sandorita loved money and material things.

On one of Tommy's regular visits, while waiting at the bar for Sandorita to complete her dance and join him in the back room for a "special" lap dance, he happened to start chatting with Aphrodite. He had no idea that just one conversation would alter the course of his life. Aphrodite took one look at his energy field and she knew something that she just had to tell him. She told him in a very matter of fact way: "Tommy, I know you don't want to hear this but I know something that I feel compelled to tell you." Surprised, he asked her with a look of curiosity: "What, my dear Aphrodite, do you know about me that I don't already know?" She lowered her voice so that only he could hear and she told him: "Oh my dear Tommy, did you know that your wife has been very unhappy for a long time. You think she doesn't know what you are doing with other women. You think she is oblivious and that she just has a low sex drive. You think you can have your cake and eat it too. Well, my dear Tommy, your wife has been having an affair for almost two years now. Your beloved wife, the woman you say you love, has found love and pleasure in the arms of another man while you are here at the club ogling and fondling younger women. You have a few choices here. You can pretend you don't know and keep living separate lives. You can confront her and continue to lie about your own sexual escapades. Or you can be truthful with your wife, for probably the first time in your marriage. And, if she is willing, you can find a qualified marriage therapist or sex therapist to help you re-create the intimacy and passion in your marriage. Go home tonight and think seriously about this. Do you want to break up your family with those two beautiful children that you adore? Do you want your children to feel as if their mother was betrayed by their father's sexual compulsions or that their father was betrayed by your wife's sexual affair? Tommy, this can be a turning point in your life."

Dumbfounded, Tommy asked Aphrodite: "How in the world do you know such a thing? How did you know I have two young children? I never told anyone here about my private life. I never even told anyone I was married. Did you somehow meet my wife? I don't understand." Tommy appeared noticeably angry and upset. "No," Aphrodite quickly replied, "I just happen to have psychic abilities that I have developed over the years. I am a mystic and I see and feel things in the energy field that surrounds us. Your energy patterns have revealed this truth to me. What you decide to do is your own choice. I just shared with you what I see and know to be true. This revelation is a turning point in your life. You get to decide which direction you will choose to go."

When Sandorita's dance had ended and she smilingly approached her favorite sugar daddy, Tommy's face turned white. Suddenly he could not bear to look at this woman who had previously given him so much pleasure. Turning away he told Aphrodite: "I am leaving now and I will probably never return. You have either ruined my life or have provided the opportunity for me to create true love with my wife. I do not know and I must go home immediately." Tommy never returned to **The Candy Bar**. A few months later, Aphrodite accidentally sawTommy with his wife in the Macy's lingerie department. They were laughing and holding hands as he helped his wife select a few different styles of sexy nighties.

Not knowing what had happened, Sandorita sensed that Aphrodite had caused Tommy, her regular client, to turn away and literally run for his life. "What did you say to him, Aphrodite, that made him leave so quickly?" asked a visibly upset Sandorita. "He was my best paying customer. He gave me so much money every single week – I was thrilled. And you know, I've gotten so used to seeing him and I've actually become quite fond of him and that pleasant way he looks at me and talks to me. But today, he looked at me as if he had seen a ghost. What the hell did you say or do? Did you use some sort of mystical trick to cause him to lose his sexual drive? Are you trying to play a nasty trick on him or on me? What's up with you?"

Aphrodite explained: "Sandorita, you know I have psychic abilities and mystical awareness. I know things about people that they don't even realize. Did you know he has been married for several years and that he loves his wife dearly? Did you know that he has two beautiful children that he loves coming home to? Tonight I saw all of that in his energy field and something more. I told him that his wife is having an affair and that he is at a turning point in his marriage. And I suggested they can go together for marriage counseling or sex therapy."

At this point Sandorita exploded at Aphrodite: "I brought you to this club. I introduced you to this lifestyle. I have provided a place for you to stay every weekend after work. You didn't have to start working here. You could have been more honest if you really felt there is something wrong with men indulging their fantasies with beautiful young and sexy women like me. Tommy was my highest paying customer and I treated him extra special. In fact, I sent some of my other regular customers to be with the other girls because I wanted to give Tommy more attention. Tonight he had promised to take me up to the champagne room which costs $1,000 an hour. You caused me to lose out on all that money. How can I ever forgive you?" Sandorita broke down into uncontrollable sobbing.

"What am I going to do now?" she said. Tommy was my ticket out of this place. I have been saving up money to continue my studies in Fashion and Design. I have been thinking I might one day create my own line of clothing. Did you know I love to sew? Remember those sexy outfits with all those removable pieces? I created the removable pieces so I could slowly take them off, one at a time, to enchant and entice the men to give me more money? Tommy used to put hundred dollar bills in my clothing and invite his friends to do the same. And he would bring hoards of men with him. He gave us all so much business. Louie and Sal are not going to be happy about this."

Sandorita turned to talk to a new customer who was

sitting on a nearby bar stool. Aphrodite tugged at her shoulder saying: "Sandorita, I am so sorry to upset you like this but I know your time at this club is limited. You have such talent that you haven't even begun to explore. I know your mother would often tell you that a woman's place is in the home and she would laugh at you when you said you wanted more out of life. I know that your father and your older brother sexually abused you and that you thought your only value was to attract, excite and please men. I know you were taught to expect men to provide for you. And I also believe that there is a part of you that knows you can provide for yourself. Let me help you strengthen that place inside of you that is longing to come out and live your life freely."

Sandorita walked away in a huff and remained quite angry with Aphrodite for several weeks. During that time, Aphrodite returned home to her apartment in Connecticut, not even suggesting that she might spend a night in her friend's apartment. But one day a few months later, a year after both had graduated from college, Sandorita announced to Aphrodite: "I was just accepted into a special 2 year combination program in Fashion and Interior Design. The school is not far from my apartment and not far from the *The Candy Bar.* But I am quitting this job tonight. You were right. I have talent that I am ready to develop into a successful business venture. Thank you, my dear friend Aphrodite, for seeing in me the strength and capability that I did not realize I do possess."

That night, after Sandorita told Louie she planned to quit her job, Louie knew it was time to speak up. He walked over to his favorite girl in the club, Aphrodite, put his arm around her shoulder and guided her to walk with him toward the exit door. With his eyes a bit glassy, he said to her in a fatherly way: "You know, my dear Aphrodite, both Sal and I and the girls and so many of our customers are quite fond of you. No matter what the problem is, you have a way of bringing people together, helping them to see the positive side of things, and you always manage to resolve problems quickly.

Unfortunately, you have begun to cross the line. It seems to me that you are becoming a psychic therapist helping our customers and dancers discover their inner well-being and their true capacity for self-love. That may be good for them but it is becoming disastrous for **The Candy Bar**. As much as Sal and I love the way you stick to our prescribed rules, because of that strictness we have actually lost many customers to a prostitution ring that Blanche had set into place. She informed us the other day that if you leave and stop lording your honesty and authenticity, that she will come back to our club on the weekends and bring her entourage of male customers with her. We need the money. We need the customers. You are sending away our highest paying and most in-demand dancers. And tonight, one of our best dancers, your friend who brought you here, Sandorita, just told me she is quitting tonight."

Louie continued: "Dearest Aphrodite, I must ask you to leave. With a sad heart, I am firing you. You have brought me peace of mind and a sense of undying trust in my marriage and for that I am eternally grateful. But your presence at this club has been gradually causing us to lose customers. Remember, we are businessmen and we thrive on creating and expanding our business. Goodbye dear Aphrodite and live a good life. We will miss you."

Louie walked Aphrodite to the door without letting her turn back to say goodbye to her co-workers and customers. He knew it was best to avoid giving her an opportunity to explain to anyone, the other dancers or the customers, why she was leaving. Louie just wanted Aphrodite to stop working there so that he and Sal could continue building their loyal, and sometimes sexually addicted, customer base. He did not want to encourage his customers or dancers to engage in a soul searching spiritual quest that would turn them away from the darker side of life. Louie and Sal loved money and together they had been making a lot of money at *The Candy Bar*, until Aphrodite had begun using her psychic spirituality on their customers and staff.

26 APHRODITE'S HEALING PRACTICE

Two months before her college graduation, Aphrodite was fired from the job she had enjoyed for almost 5 years. As she walked out of **The Candy Bar** for the last time, she noticed that the street seemed particularly empty and the night exceptionally dark. Her heart was filled with a sense of sadness and personal rejection. Yet, at the same time, Aphrodite also felt a stirring sense of relief and renewed energy to follow her destiny and live her dreams. Trusting that God was on her side, Aphrodite knew her life was about to take another turn. She walked swiftly deep in thought for several long blocks until she reached the nearest subway entrance. When she arrived at Grand Central Station, she felt happy to be heading home to Connecticut. Sitting on the commuter train during the trip, she looked around and saw the men in her car reading the Wall Street Journal, the New York Times, a big novel, or some business journals and newsletters. It seemed to her that all those men who might have been customers at **The Candy Bar** had chosen to sit in a different car that evening, away from Aphrodite's intense spiritual energy. She smiled to herself when she realized, once again, that her consciousness controls her life and affects the lives of all those around her.

When she arrived home and told her mother that she had just quit her nighttime waitressing job, Chiara was elated. Her mother told her: "Oh Aphrodite, I've been worried every single weekend about your safety, staying and working in the big city until such late hours. You know, on the news I've seen such scary stories about young ladies being mugged, raped, kidnapped or even murdered. I'm so glad you're okay."

Chiara hugged her daughter and told her: I am so happy that you will finally be back at home with your parents on the weekends." Chiara had been quite concerned about her daughter's seeming lack of interest in meeting a man to marry. Her mother had big plans to take her daughter to the country club to introduce Aphrodite to some eligible, wealthy, educated and classy bachelors. The mother-daughter country club visits would last for only a few months, until 3 months after graduation, when Aphrodite would move into the new apartment condo she had secretly purchased.

Aphrodite dearly loved her adoptive mother, Chiara. Her mother was a caring, nurturing, and very kind woman who studied and practiced powerful spiritual principles. But both her father and mother had their own ideas about what Aphrodite should be doing with her life. They wanted her to get a substantial job, with a good pension, one that would utilize her diverse language skills. Her father, David, reassured her that he had many good connections and would find her a suitable job as soon as she graduated. Her parents did not know that Aphrodite had different plans.

The week after graduation, Aphrodite began to research the local real estate market in Connecticut. She kept looking for two months until she found the perfect apartment condo to purchase, not too far from her parents' home so she could easily visit. Aphrodite then enlisted the help of the real estate agent to find her a decorator who could set the home up for her without her having to be there. Aphrodite did not want her parents to interfere in any way. Three months after Aphrodite's graduation from college, her new home was finally ready. It was fully furnished with 2 lovely bedroom sets, a comfortable living room convertible sofa, a 25 inch TV set, a large substantial mahogany dining room table, and a well-supplied kitchen. The decorator had helped her select the best blinds, curtains, lamps and chandeliers as well as pleasing paintings to fill the many walls. Aphrodite had made several visits to the apartment to check on the progress and to approve or disapprove of her decorator's choices. The night before the moving truck arrived, Aphrodite told her parents about her imminent move. She could see the sadness in her mother's eyes, but Chiara once again revealed that she was truly practicing the spiritual teachings she had studied. She hugged her daughter, promising to help her and to be available for her whenever needed.

Both of her parents had always shown Aphrodite total love and acceptance, except maybe in those moments when they had insisted that she follow their advice and live according to their standards. Compared to the parents of most of her friends, Chiara and David were quite caring and exceptional. So Aphrodite could never understand why she had always felt a deep sense of being unworthy, not good enough and different from others. She had grown up in very comfortable surroundings in that beautiful small town, Hawthorne Connecticut. She had acquired many caring friends. Her relatives were always showering her with gifts and hugs and tender loving words of praise.

At a very early age Aphrodite had been told that she was adopted. David and Chiara reassured their daughter, over and over again, that they had chosen her from among many choices of available children. Chiara often explained that the moment she saw Aphrodite's warm smile, she knew this was the little girl she would love for the rest of her life. And Aphrodite was told very often that almost everyone who who would see her when she was an infant had that same delicious feeling of wanting to love her.

Knowing that her parents had always loved her, Aphrodite wanted to find out why she often felt inadequate and different from others – not quite fitting in with any group. When she was modeling or dancing or being a proper managing hostess, Aphrodite felt she was playing a role. When it was a role, she would feel confident knowing she could easily handle the situation without revealing her inner doubt and insecurity. During her really busy college days Aphrodite did not spend much time focusing on her feelings. Absorbed in her studies and wanting to please her teachers, her bosses, her co-workers and her customers, she remained in an emotionally calm and neutral state. She had no interest in dating or having an intimate relationship. Talking and flirting, hugging and occasionally being fondled by her male customers seemed to satisfy her need for attention from men. She found that many men would talk in a demeaning way about women and could easily justify cheating on their most intimate partners. Aphrodite was happy to avoid getting personally involved with any man, especially the men she had been meeting.

Graduating from college, buying her new home, supervising the decorating process and then going through the actual move took up most of her emotional and thought energy for several months after the loss of her weekend hostess position at *The Candy Bar*. Three months after graduation, Aphrodite was finally completely settled in her new home. She was now 22 years old, still as beautiful as ever, and beginning to feel so lonely that she would crawl into bed and cry herself to sleep on many evenings. Her good friend, Sandorita, would sometimes come to spend a night at Aphrodite's new apartment. However, at this time Sandorita had quite a busy schedule. She had found a job as a designer's assistant while attending her special 2 year combination fashion design and interior design program at a local college in Manhattan. Sandorita was taking a full load of courses for her first semester with so many assignments to complete that she found herself working into the wee hours of the night just to stay on track. She did not have the spare time to visit her friend in Connecticut.

During her 5 years of commuting to Harlington College and working at the Furrier and *The Candy Bar*, Aphrodite had not been in touch with any of her local friends. So when she was finally finished with college and had stopped working at **The Candy Bar**, Aphrodite had nobody to talk to, to share her thoughts with, and to support her in following her life dreams. The Furriers, Hannes and Leif, were the only people she knew she could talk to about setting up her own business, but she was not quite ready to decide what exactly she would do.

On one of her Friday morning commutes to her modeling job at the Manhattan Furrier's office, which she continued to do for many years after finishing college, she happened to pick up a local newspaper to read on the train. That's when she saw those 900 number ads again. "That's what I can do," Aphrodite thought. "I can create a 900 number and talk sexy to men. I've had so much practice handling men that this will be easy for me." At the garment center office of the Furriers, she asked some of the men and the women working there what they knew about 900 numbers, whether they knew anybody who had called them. One of the male customers took Aphrodite aside and told her: "Let me tell you a secret. I have called some of those numbers and these women, I have no idea what they actually look like, but they sound so tempting and seductive on the phone. So I was calling some of these numbers for a while, enjoying my little phone trysts. But boy, when I got my phone bill, my wife had a fit. I'm lucky she didn't divorce me after that. So I stopped calling those numbers. But sometimes, even now, I do get tempted but my relationship is doing okay so why do something to ruin it. And they charge such high fees. It's really a big business." Aphrodite's eyes lit up at the prospect of creating her own personal "big business."

That weekend she called several of those 900 numbers to investigate. She would hear a sweet sounding voice on the phone, beckoning for the caller to speak up, to tell her what he wanted and needed. The woman who answered would usually not waste any time. She might begin by saying that it was so late and she had just taken off her blouse and was rubbing cream all over her big round breasts. Then she might ask the caller if he or she - there were some gay women who called these numbers - would like to see her breasts or to touch them. The woman would go into great detail about the sexy structure of her body and the sexual movements she was making while on the phone. Aphrodite knew she could do this easily.

On Monday morning, Aphrodite contacted one of the companies that would get her set up with her own 900 number. She created several enticing ads and placed them into about 20 different newspapers in different townships located in Connecticut and upstate New York. Aphrodite was soon in business, slowly developing it into a big business. Men were calling her at all hours of the day and evening and the money started to roll in. She was having so much fun, teasing the men, getting really graphic about her body and her actions. Often she could hear a man breathing heavily into the phone. She knew he was getting off on her words.

Soon, however, unable to stop her powerful psychic abilities and knowing the most intimate details about her callers' lives, she would start giving them advice. She would tell them such things as: "Stop cheating on your wife. She loves you. Teach her how to speak to you the way I am talking and you will have a hot and heavy love life."

Her exploration into the spiritual realm had started at a very young age when she would meditate and chant and sometimes drum with her mother, Chiara. Then she started to read the writings of different spiritual leaders to help her to understand how to best use her special psychic gifts. Then, she started waking up feeling various aches and pains in her body. To alleviate her physical discomfort, at first Aphrodite went to see different men and women to receive traditional Swedish massages. Often a new massage therapist would show her a sample of some other type of body therapy. And then she would go for a session to receive a different kind of touch. Over a period of about 3 years, Aphrodite had received sessions in many different types of touch therapy, including Acupressure, Acupuncture, Reiki, Polarity Therapy, Craniosacral Therapy, Trager, Alexander Technique, Therapeutic Touch and an intense Rolfing series.

Then she discovered that the mind is not separate from the body. She learned that some of her physical symptoms were the result of memories stored in her body, unresolved emotional trauma that had occurred at a very early age. So she began exploring the mind-body-spirit connection. While working with several advanced healers and somatic therapists, Aphrodite began to uncover and recall details about her birth, her adoption, and the life of her natural parents. She eventually recalled details from before she had been able to speak, facts that later proved to be true that nobody had ever told her.

David and Chiara had explained to Aphrodite: "You were been born in Switzerland to a young Swiss high school student who could not afford to keep a baby, you." That's what they had been told by Dr. Kuhn. They reassured Aphrodite many time" Aphrodite honey, you know that your birth mother had loved your birth father but they were both too young to take care of a little girl. Your birth mother's parents had asked Dr. Kuhn to locate a suitable family." David told his daughter: "My beautiful wife, Chiara, had wanted a little girl so badly. She was thrilled when Dr. Kuhn brought you to meet her in the lobby of the hotel where I was speaking at a conference about adoption. You were only a few days old. Chiara thought you were such a beautiful and responsive infant. She was so excited and couldn't wait to tell me how perfect you were. And I took one look at you and fell in love instantly."

During her exploration into her own mind-body-spirit connection, Aphrodite's night-time dreams seemed to become more vivid. Prior to this period of time she had rarely remembered her dreams. But as she delved more deeply into her own unconscious memories, she started keeping a dream journal next to her bed to capture her dreams each morning before they faded from her awareness. Often she had a dream about working in a brothel providing sexual favors to men. She brushed it off as just a memory of her work at **The Candy Bar**, where she had seen some of the dancers walk toward the back room or upstairs to the Champagne Room. She did not know until it was revealed to her in one of her most intense meditations, that the woman in the brothel was not her, but her birth mother Cassandra.

Another of her recurrent dreams was quite puzzling to her. She knew the war in Vietnam had been escalating but she did not know anyone personally who was fighting there. In this dream, she would see a group of Asian military men in the center of what looked like a camp ground. And she would see them stabbing a man with a bayonet. Sometimes she saw herself captured and standing defenseless in the middle of the camp with about six of these Asian soldiers pointing their guns at her and laughing. In her dreams, although she was frightened, she had kept her emotions calm. She would often look directly into the eyes of one of the soldiers and ask him with her eyes: "Why are you doing this? We are all one and the same. We have one God. We are not separate from God. There is only one source of power and that power is love."

In one of these recurrent dreams, a very handsome sailor who was not Asian, not Swiss, not American, but spoke English with a strange twangy accent, started digging a hole near where Aphrodite was standing at the edge of the camp grounds. Then he told her, with no uncertainty, that she would be safer if she climbed down into the hole and stayed there until the Allied Forces arrived to free all the prisoners. He told her he had come out of his own hiding hole just to help her get into her safe hiding place. This handsome, strong and gentle man reassured her that he was right nearby and would always protect her. Aphrodite brushed this dream off as a reaction to all the news she had been seeing on TV and reading in magazines about the horrors of this war and the agonies of those taken as prisoners. She did not know until it was revealed to her in a powerful meditation that this handsome man, this protective soldier, was her natural father. She later discovered that her birth father had been living in a hole in the ground as a prisoner of war in Vietnam at the same time that she was having that night-time dream.

Aphrodite would sometimes talk about these two recurring dreams but, of course, nobody could have imagined that she was psychically and clairvoyantly seeing beyond her current reality. Nobody knew that her natural mother was working at a brothel in Switzerland and that her natural father was living in a hole in the ground in Vietnam. Even her adoptive parents did not know the truth about Aphrodite's beginnings until many years later. It was actually Dietrich who, after providing money and gifts for Aphrodite for 25 years, finally told the truth to Dr. Kuhn and insisted that he explain it to David and Chiara. At an upcoming conference, Dr. Kuhn took David aside and explained what he had just learned about Aphrodite's birth parents. At that point, David did not want to upset and confuse his daughter (not realizing she had already discovered the truth on her own). He chose not to say anything to Chiara or to Aphrodite. But there is no stopping the truth from eventually being revealed. It took a series of "accidental," "serendipitous" events for the story to unfold.

Aphrodite's 900 number advertising business began to flourish yet it seemed to be evolving into something else. She could not help sharing with her callers what she knew was happening psychically and emotionally to them in their lives at the current time. Without being asked, she would recommend what she considered to be the most appropriate healing method for each client to resolve their underlying issues. Sometimes she would discover that a caller had a nutritional deficiency so she would recommend seeking a nutritionist to develop a new dietary plan. Sometimes she would know the caller's body needed more physical activity. In that case she might recommend starting on the appropriate exercise regime or attending a dance, yoga, aerobics or other type of class to improve bodily strength, endurance and flexibility. In many cases she would suggest that the caller go to have a session of one of her favorite types of body therapy. And then there were the callers who she knew had mental and emotional problems. Depending upon the severity, she would suggest that they see a psychiatrist (if they needed medication and/or in-patient treatment) or a psychologist or another mental health practitioner.

Sometimes she would find herself talking to a man with a strange fetish. One of the men asked her to tell him she is wearing diapers that just got dirty and to beg him to change her diapers now. One of these men begged her to talk about how she would remove his diapers, spank him and clean him up. She said to this second man: "Your nanny did something bad to you when you were only a baby. She molested you when you were 2 years old. I think you should go to have a deep somato-emotional release session and some craniosacral therapy to help you jog your memory and recall the incident. This can help you heal from your early trauma." The man seemed upset and hung up the phone abruptly. Aphrodite never found out if he had followed her advice.

After running her thriving 900 number business for less than a year, Aphrodite received a phone call one day from a radio producer who had been one of her callers and was actually in the process of healing from a long term sexual compulsivity. He had always loved to call young ladies and talk dirty to them but he was at risk for being caught and getting arrested. When he had originally called to speak to Aphrodite, she had told him what she saw was about to happen to him if he continued his illegal activities. He had listened to her advice, had invested in regular psychotherapy sessions and also many deep, heart expanding, mind body therapy sessions. Having learned the power of the inner workings of his own mind and how this strange woman at the other end of a phone line had helped him to heal his life, he wanted to help her to grow her business.

Based in Chicago, Leo Strathmeyer operated a chain of radio stations around the country. After quite a long talk on the phone with Aphrodite, he offered to meet with her in New York City to have her sign a contract for her own empowering radio show: **Aphrodite's Healing World**. Without hesitation, Aphrodite agreed to meet with Leo the following week. Dressed in a streamlined pale pink form fitting silk suit, her appearance was feminine, elegant and striking. When Leo saw her walk into the room, he was enthralled. He knew that together they could create a huge business. He also thought that in time he would help her to become a TV celebrity because he knew instantly that she had exactly what it takes.

Aphrodite's healing practice began growing rapidly. Each week she would present her theories and psychic insights on her radio show and respond to the questions and requests of her many callers. Clients would contact her from around the world for a brief phone consultation for which they paid very high fees. Many wanted to receive private healing sessions in person which required much higher fees. Aphrodite's home became a healing sanctuary. Clients appeared at her home office from all around the globe. Spending just one hour, sometimes less, with this beautiful mystical phenomenon, would help people from all walks of life to change and transform their current life situations. All sorts of problem scenarios would appear at her office. Many clients would complain of depression, anxiety, and physical pains. Others would cry about having been a victim of childhood abuse, spouse betrayal, or inability to meet and connect with an appropriate love partner. Some wanted to overcome their sexual and intimacy concerns. And many came to see this mystical psychic to heal from serious physical injuries, ailments and sometimes life threatening diseases.

Leo Strathmeyer would call Aphrodite and fly to New York to meet her about once every month to discuss business and help her to grow into a much sought after celebrity. At first the contact between Leo and Aphrodite involved strictly business meetings. Leo was seeking ongoing help for his own sexually compulsive desire to call young girls, under the legal age. He knew this was a dangerous practice of his and that it could result in serious consequences. Over a period of several years he continued attending private counseling sessions as well as group therapy.   Then, at Aphrodite's suggestion, Leo found a good therapist who combined deep intuitive counseling with somatic body oriented psychotherapy. He uncovered his earliest sexual molestation issues that had occurred when he was very young. His mother had died when he was born. Suffering deep emotional pain, his father had quickly remarried. Leo's stepmother at the time, who his father had later divorced, played seductive sexual games with Leo when he was an infant. She would change his diapers, play with his penis, flash her naked breasts and laugh as she tried to cause this tiny 2 year old to get an erection. His stepmother had thought it was all very funny but she no idea how she was affecting and imprinting images on Leo's psyche as a baby. The first time he had uncovered and understood what had happened to him, at 32 years of age, Leo had curled up into a fetal position and fell into a state of hysterical crying. Prior to that moment Leo had rarely, if ever, shed a tear in his teenage years, his twenties or his early thirties. Crying hysterically like that he thought he was having a nervous breakdown. But luckily his wise and compassionate therapist responded by reassuring him that this was a normal response to intense grief, grief for the loss of childhood safety and a sense of his own goodness and worthiness.

As Leo's healing progressed, he began to grow increasingly attached to the beautiful Aphrodite. She also grew to like and trust him more and more as his hardened exterior gradually softened. Over time, she shared with him the teachings of many of her favorite psychics and mystics and healers. Leo would often read the books she had recommended, listen to the tapes and even attend workshops when available. And together they felt they were making great strides in life. At this point, Leo had never attempted to be physical at all with Aphrodite. He may have given her a peck on the cheek or a quick hug when they greeted or parted. There had never even been a sexual overtone between them until he had invited her to join him on a very special trip to a little known island on the southeast coast of Greece, Agapelargos Island. From the moment he thought of inviting her, his mind began to see her in a new and more sexual way. And when he called to invite her, she also suddenly thought of him in a new way.

It happened one morning, while Leo was in Chicago working diligently at his desk. He received a phone call that would lead to a total change in his life and lifestyle. The man on the phone said to him: "Hello Leo. You don't know me but let me introduce myself. My name is Dietrich Danjel Skold and I am reaching out to you because I know you can help."

Leo, quite busy with a few deadlines, was impatient and responded by saying: "Why would I want to help you? I don't know who you are and my schedule is totally full right now." He was about to hang up the phone when Dietrich pleaded with him: "Please, Leo, hear me out. I think you will want to help when you understand what I tell you." So Leo sat back in his chair to listen to what this man had to say.

Dietrich went on to explain: "My two older brothers, Hannes and Leif, are the Furriers where Aphrodite has been modeling for many years." Leo responded: "So what does that have to do with me?"

Dietrich continued: "Do know that Aphrodite has never met her birth mother? She does not even have the correct information about her birth mother: who she is, where she comes from, what happened to her and why she gave Aphrodite up for adoption. I want her to meet her birth mother. This is not easy for me to coordinate. Her mother is currently living in Switzerland but she was born on a little island on the southeast coast of Greece, not far from Athens. Have you ever heard of Agapelargos Island? Well, it turns out that when she was 17, Aphrodite's mother, Cassandra, had gotten pregnant. When her macho Greek father and brothers found out, she was beaten and thrown out of her house. They went searching all over the island later that night and the following day, but it was too late. Cassandra had been kidnapped and brought to live in Switzerland where she has remained. Not a day goes by when Cassandra, Aphrodite's mother doesn't wonder what happened to her daughter and how she is doing. Her mother really wants to see her again and I want to create a surprise reunion. But I need your help."

Since Leo had grown really fond of Aphrodite and he knew she had been having strange recurrent dreams, he suddenly realized she had been intuitively connecting with her birth parents. Leo asked: "How can I help?" And Dietrich explained: "I will send you airline tickets for two to take a special trip to Agapelargos Island a few days before Easter Sunday this year. We can pretend that you won a contest and you have chosen to take Aphrodite to show her a different part of the world. Or whatever you want to say to convince her to take this trip with you. I will even pay for the flights and an additional fee. How much would you like?"

Leo answered a bit embarrassed: "Dietrich, I have grown quite fond of Aphrodite. She is a really special young lady with a heart of gold and a psychic ability that surpasses understanding. I would not think of taking money from you to help my sweet Aphrodite find love and closure in her life. She has been struggling with disturbing almost nightmarish dreams and she has not quite understood what they mean. Suddenly her dreams are making sense to me. She may be psychically connecting with her birth parents. I will invite her to come with me to a little paradise island in Greece." Thanking Leo profusely, Dietrich asked for Leo's address to send him the tickets, and gave him his own private phone number in case Leo would need to call.

27 ALEXEI ARRIVES AT THE PLEASURE PALACE

Cassandra enjoyed her new role as Madame C, the head mistress of Dietrich and Roffe's growing **D & R Pleasure Palace**. She enjoyed meeting potential customers wherever she happened to be – at the local grocery store, dress shop, post office or even at her hair dresser. Cassandra discovered there were men everywhere and many of them were curious and eager to find out more about the intriguing place where she worked. She had become quite good at advertising the services provided by writing ads for local papers or just in the midst of a casual conversation.

The ads which had brought in the most new customers were short and to the point. She did not waste words since additional words would cost more money. But she also found that short catchy phrases would cause the men to become curious, get interested and show up at the door without even calling first. Many were shy or reticent about making the phone call so they just took a chance and knocked at the door. The **D & R Pleasure Palace** was located in a rather large building at the edge of the downtown area. Dietrich and Roffe, with Cassandra's feminine assistance, transformed an old warehouse into an amazing center for sensual and sexual activity and private gambling setups.

Cassandra was always trying to figure out a new angle, a new way to advertise. She would sometimes find herself laughing as she wrote the words for the current week's ads. Some of her favorites were:

- *This Hot Baby Wants You.* ***Call Now*** *or Stop By Tonight.*
- *Want Some. Come and Get It.* ***We are Waiting*** *for YOU.*
- *One Night of Ecstasy. Are YOU* ***Ready****?*
- *Who Says You Can't Have It? We Will* ***Give it to YOU****.*

While talking to a prospective customer, Cassandra would often find a way to accidentally reveal a part of her body that he should not be able to see. Wearing a see through blouse with a jacket covering, she would say out loud: "It is so hot in here." And then she would turn toward the man so only he could see as she started to remove her jacket. His eyes would bulge when he got a glimpse of her naked round breasts with those firm nipples sticking straight out. As soon as she had exposed herself to the man, she would quickly close her jacket saying: "Actually it's not that warm in here." Then she would hand the man a card and without fail, that man would show up at The *R & D Pleasure Palace* within a few days. Often, these men would act quite disappointed when Dietrich, Roffe or the bouncer at the door would make it clear to them that Cassandra was the Madam and was strictly off limits for the customers.

If a new customer that Cassandra had invited to the club seemed very upset, she would bring him into a private room telling him she would show him the menu and give him a taste of what to expect. Thinking he would get some action with Cassandra, he would eagerly follow her. But right behind him would be one of the working girls wearing a very straight and not form fitting outfit. The man would assume she was just a secretary or an office assistant. As soon as the man would enter the room the show would begin. This very prissy looking woman would act silly and clumsy, purposely dropping the book onto the floor so that she had to bend over. And that's when the man would get an unexpected glimpse into her private opening without the covering of her panties. And she would wiggle her behind in a silly and provocative way while supposedly struggling to pick up the book. Then she would come over to the man, sit very close to him and put her hand on his thigh as she opened the book right on his lap.

That's when Cassandra, the business woman, would begin her negotiations. She would say something like: "You liked our little display, didn't you? Well we have a whole big menu of sensual and sexual delights for you. Tell us what you like and it is yours for the night. And we have some special daily treats not listed on the menu because they change each day. Choose what you like.

- Monday night we let you **Bite the Buttons**. Delicious M&M buttons are placed in strategic places on our 3 models. Your task is to bite the buttons off of one model's body as fast as you can at the same time as a few other men are biting the buttons off the other models. The winner, the one who bites the most buttons in that time period, gets to play with all the button models at one time. Usually we have 3 button models scheduled. The losers get to sit in the room and watched for a while before returning to the main room where they can buy drinks for the dancers.

- Tuesday night is **Scrub the Tub**. We have 3 handmaidens, each assigned to one man. Each man's task is to let himself get so stimulated that his handmaiden finishes her job first before the others have finished. The winner gets to remain in the room at the end, share a free drink and be stimulated again by his favorite of the 3 women.

- Wednesday night is **Lick the Lollypops.** In this event we have 3 women who love to suck on lollypops. But they like to do it quickly. The man who lets her lick the lollypop and lets her finish before the other two, wins. The winner gets to sit with the 3 women, have some drinks, watch them dance privately for him until he is aroused again and then he receives a second lollypop reward. Of course, you can always pay extra to get additional favors from our dancers, as you will see on our regular menu.

- Thursday night we have the **Heartless Hooker.** We have three tough ladies who don't want to be touched or spoken to in a disrespectful way. These sexy ladies love to show you their private parts, tease you, and sometimes touch you. The first two men to get a full erection receive the punishment. The other man gets to play with the one woman of his choice while watching the performance. For the punishment, if you are one of the losers, you are tied to a chair and teased with a sexy display and no way to satisfy your urges. Of course, any man can always pay extra to get additional favors from our dancers, after the punishment period has ended. He can then choose anything from our regular menu.

Observing the man to insure that his body is already signaling desire, Cassandra would sometimes sigh and open her jacket again as she would continue to explain the *D & R Pleasure Palace* policies:

"On weekends we do not play those games because we have too many customers eager for immediate action. And boy do we provide the action."

At this point, there are very few men who would willingly resist Cassandra's trained negotiation process. Very shortly after entering her private room, each man would predictably take out his wallet, hand her the cash for his chosen activity or provide a credit card to pay his bill in advance. As soon as his payment was completed, he would be swept away toward the appropriate room for the activity he had selected with the woman of his choice. In some cases, he may be invited to have a drink at the bar – sometimes complimentary depending upon the menu item or daily treat he selected.

Over the period of about 5 years, the club expanded to a staff of 25 women working on different shifts, 5 bouncers to insure the safety of all the women, 2 accountants, an investment broker and many different service people with varying consultant contracts. Cassandra managed all the daily details, devoting most of her waking hours to the smooth functioning of the *D & R Pleasure Palace*. Dietrich and Roffe paid their Madam a large percentage of the income which she deposited into a savings account every week. Not really happy but also not visibly unhappy, Cassandra spent most of her days working hard, maintaining a business-like state of mind. She lived in the present moment not daring to look back at her past or imagine her future. Cassandra seemed to be stuck in a time warp which ended suddenly when one of her brothers arrived at the club.

This day was no different from any other. Cassandra had arrived at the *D & R Pleasure Palace* about a half hour before the rest of the staff. She had organized her paperwork, revised any current ads that needed updating, fixed the menus when there were some needed changes and spent about 5 minutes sitting quietly and connecting with her inner self and allowing herself to feel the presenced of God. She did not attempt to find answers. She was not seeking anything past the present moment. Her inner spirit had been broken several few times – when her friends had called her Olive and Olive Oyl as a child, when Cyrano had to suddenly leave the day after their ecstatic time together, when her gentle and kind brother, Alexei, had beaten her and torn her clothing, and especially when her entire family had thrown her out of the house without showing an ounce of compassion. But the final breakdown came before giving birth when she had made the decision to give her love child away to be adopted by a loving family she thought she would never meet and know.

A few months earlier, Cassandra's three brothers had decided to start a new business selling antique clocks, cuckoo clocks, designer watches and other related time-keeping devices. Stefano had been in contact with a watch manufacturer in Zurich, Switzerland. But then Alexei told his brothers that he had a friend who had recently moved to Lucerne, Switzerland, to expand his family's telecommunication business. Alexei's friend, Victor, had told him that Lucerne had a very low corporate tax rate and that it was the home of the exotic watch industry. Damon and Stefano agreed that it would be beneficial for Alexei to explore this business opportunity by visiting with his friend and finding out, first hand, whether this might be a viable business to bring back to Agapelargos Island.

From the day that he had beaten his beloved little sister and the family had thrown Cassandra out of the house, Alexei had sworn that he would never allow himself to love a woman again. He felt so much pain and guilt about what he had done to hurt his beautiful, trusting and kind sister that he believed he was no longer worthy of a woman's love. Instead, he frequented local massage parlors, strip clubs and paid for the company of high class prostitutes. He would enjoy sensual and sexual pleasures and often choose to be punished by a

Dominitrix. His heart had turned to stone as he lived out his fantasies of someone punishing him for his sins against his sister.

Alexei's friend, Victor, had been a frequent visitor of the **D & R Pleasure Palace** before getting married a few years earlier. The last time Alexei had spoken to his friend, Victor had raved about the treatments he had received at this exotic club in downtown Lucerne. When Alexei arrived in Lucerne, he unpacked his bags, met with his friend for some drinks and asked about that club Victor had mentioned on the phone a few years earlier. Victor's face lit up and he immediately said: "Oh, I used to love going there. The women are so hot and they give you just what you ask for. But now I am married and I really love my wife – and she is pregnant with our first child. My days at **The Pleasure Palace** are over. But I recommend that you go there and have a good time. I warn you, though, you will get hooked on that place and want to keep coming back. They're good at convincing you, especially Madame C." Intrigued at the thought of meeting Madame C, Alexei walked with Victor to the front door of the hotel where the two friends shook hands and patted each other's shoulders. Victor said before leaving: "Let me know what you think of **The D & R Pleasure Palace**. I can't wait to talk to you tomorrow." They had arranged to have an early lunch together at noon the next day followed by several scheduled meetings with clock and watch manufacturers, dealers and shopkeepers.

A few hours later, when Alexei arrived at the **D & R Pleasure Palace**, he was greeted by Frida, one of the 3 nurse midwives who had helped Cassandra give birth and were now all working full time at the club. Cassandra had been sitting in her office orchestrating one of her famous negotiations with a new customer. Britta and Heidi, the other 2 nurse midwives, were busy displaying their personal wares to an unsuspecting and vulnerable new customer.

Since this was a Thursday night, Alexei chose **The Heartless Hooker** game and allowed himself to feel helplessly aroused with no way to get relief for about 2 hours. Finally, he asked his dominatrix if he could pay an additional fee to receive a happy ending. She refused, playing the game to the hilt to entice him to beg her for more, perhaps getting him to pay for a tryst in the expensive Champagne Room. So she encouraged him to stay a little longer, dangling a carrot of hope as she continued her heartless teasing. At one point he got down on his knees and begged her to satisfy him. His body was actually in pain before he finally decided he had had enough and left the room.

When he got up to leave he could hardly walk because the pain caused by congestion in his pelvic area was intense. Squinting and keeping his head down, he almost left without seeing his sister. But then he remembered Victor's words and he asked the girl behind the coat check counter if he could meet Madame C. The coat tall, slender check girl wearing a very low cut V neck sweater and a push up bra, said to Alexei, "Why Madame C is right behind you." Wearing a high fashioned, stylish form fitting yet professional pink and gray silk suit with pink stiletto high heels, Cassandra looked authoritative and elegant. She was, at that moment, walking toward the coat check room to tell the attendant to get a jacket ready for one of the clients who was about to leave.

When Alexei turned around to meet Madame C, he almost fell to the floor. His mouth stayed open and the words refused to come out. Cassandra looked at him in total disbelief, frozen in her tracks, not sure what emotion was stirring within her. Her first thought was to just ignore him, to pretend she didn't know who he is. Her next thought was: "I ought to hate him for what he did to me." But her gut reaction won out. She leaped toward him, wrapped her arms around him and broke into sobs for the first time in 22 years.

Alexei, too, found himself uncontrollably crying and finally the words spewed out of his mouth: "My darling, dearest, beloved little sister Cassie, how can you ever forgive me for being such a fool, such a brow beaten boy who had to prove he was a man like his older brothers? Only a few hours after you left the house, I went searching for you, ready to beg you for your forgiveness. Stefano came looking with me but the others weren't quite ready until the following day. But it took less than a day for the entire family to be sorry about what we had done. We are such brutish men and your mother was just trying to please the men in the family. She didn't realize how much you needed her protection and love. You needed our mother to stand up for you. We went looking all over the island for you for days and we posted your photos everywhere we could. We hired Detective Kappas who spent months searching for clues about what had happened to you. He must have interviewed every person on the island to find out if anybody who had seen you on that awful evening. You seemed to have vanished into thin air. Where did you go?"

Cassandra told Alexei she would take the following night off. She promised to meet him that next evening at his hotel at 7 PM to catch up on their lives and make amends with each other. Before saying good night to her brother, she whispered in his ear: "I have always loved you. And now I am ready to forgive you for that awful night, a night I have not been willing to think about for these past 22 years. Tonight it is all rushing back and I know I will have a really hard time sleeping. Please do not tell our brothers or our parents or anyone else that you have seen me. This would be another betrayal by you and I could not forgive you a second time. Please keep our meeting and my business practices private - just between us."

Alexei promised he would not divulge to anybody in the family that he had reconnected with his beloved little sister. But he also made a vow to himself that now he had an even more compelling reason to create this watch and clock business that he had been researching here in Lucerne. He was determined to get his little sister out of the brothel business and into a legitimate money-making business she could be proud to tell her family about. He knew that if he could get her into a successful, legitimate business, and show how much he does care for her, that one day she might be ready to reconnect with her brothers and her parents. Alexei's smiled sadly at the thought of all of them being together again. What he did not know is that he had a niece, Cassandra's daughter, who would one day join them at an unexpected and delightfully healing family reunion.

Waiting impatiently in the lobby of his hotel, Alexei began to doubt that his sister would show up. He was afraid she would recall his cruel beating of her, the way he had forced her to remove her panties and had sent her out of the house forever, with torn and bloody clothing and no undergarment. Worried that she would not be able to bring herself to talk with him and would certainly not forgive him, his heart was pounding, his mind and body filled with anxiety. And then she appeared, exactly on time at 7 PM. He immediately recognized that sweet, open, innocent and caring smile that he had always loved in his little sister. They greeted cordially with a light hug and she placed a polite kiss on each of his cheeks. Hope filled his heart as Alexei asked her if she would like to join him for dinner in the elegant hotel restaurant at the top of the building which overlooked the entire city of Lucerne.

Standing near each other in the elevator, both brother and sister were silently absorbed in their own thoughts. Each was ondering what they would talk about after all these years, wondering how this strange meeting could have occurred and wondering if they could ever return to their former state of loving each other. As the doors opened, they both stepped out of the darkness of their past into the rooftop display of lights and hope for a brighter future. This was a perfect setting for Alexei and Cassandra to reconnect, review and release the past.

This was also the meeting place for the origin of a joint business that would eventually bring healing and closure to the emotional pain felt by the entire Melanakos family.

Alexei ordered the most expensive champagne to share with his beloved sister. She asked about his wife and children, assuming that by this age he had been happily married for many years with a family of his own. To her surprise Alexei revealed the heartbreak he had experienced from losing the sister he had loved and knowing it was partially his fault. He told his bewildered sister: "Oh my precious Cassie, I only lashed out at you to prove my manhood to the men in our family, our father and your macho brothers. I tried to hide the pain it caused me. Remember when I first took off my belt I only hit the bed? Remember? I really only wanted to pretend I was hitting you. And then I realized that if I did not hit you and prove it to everyone, by tearing your clothing, ripping off your panties and making sure you looked beaten, that Damion or Stefano might have hurt you much more seriously. In my own distorted way I thought I was actually protecting you from worse harm. But it broke my heart. I don't know if you saw the tears in my eyes as I lashed out at you. That was the hardest thing I have ever done in my life. And I learned a severe lesson as a result."

Alexei continued by explaining what had happened next: "That evening, Stefano and I went searching for you all over town. Believe it or not, Stefano was the first one to speak up and defend you when he yelled at all of us: 'What are you all crazy? Cassie may have done something terrible but she is still part of our family and we have always loved her. She has always been such a good girl until now. I'm sure she can explain to us how this happened, with whom and why she let it happen.' He had been set straight by a few women he had spoken to at our father's club. But the rest of us took a little convincing before we finally realized how crazy our actions toward you had been."

Alexei continued explaining what happened next. "Suddenly feeling frantic, I told everyone I would go to search for you. Both Damion and Stefano volunteered to join me but, as you know, my Fiat only fits 2 passengers. So Stefano came with me to begin searching for you. We thought it would be easy, that you could not have gone too far without a car or your bicycle. Stefano and I raced out of the house and I quickly drove down the path to go where we thought you might have gone. First, we stopped first at the church and spoke to Father Petrides. When he told us he had not seen you, we stopped in town at the only restaurant that was still open. Chloe, you remember her, that cute waitress Damion and Stefano had always flirted with? She greeted us at the door. But when she said she had not seen you, our hearts sank. That's when we started to get really scared."

Alexei continued: "Then one of us, I think it was Stefano, suggested we check out that park. I resisted saying that we had always warned you not to go in there. Then I stopped the car near the park, we both got out and we started asking anyone we saw there if they had seen you that evening. Nobody claimed to have seen our beloved little sister. After that, we went to the police station to file a missing persons report for you. Later, we hired Detective Kappas. He spent months searching for you. Damion, Stefano and our father thought you had been murdered but our mother always knew you were alive. She felt it in her heart and she told us every day how much she longed to see her beloved Cassandra. We put flyers and photos all over Agapelargos Island but nobody had seen or heard anything. A few people came to us with strange stories they had made up but those stories, of course, led to nothing."

"Cassie, sweet Cassie, nobody in our family has ever been the same. Do you know that on that same night that he had been so mean to you, our beloved father, Demitri, for the first time in his life, told your mother how much he loved her and needed her. That happened right after dinner on that awful night. And he has doted on her every single day since then. He no longer pays any attention to all those sexy women at **The Cyprus Club**. To this day, he searches the obituary columns, the missing persons' reports, and police reports. He has been trying to find you every day for these entire 22 years."

Cassie wanted to know more about her other brothers. She asked Alexei: "What about Stefano? Is he married and does he have a family of his own? Alexei lowered his head for a moment and told her: Stefano has had a drinking problem which seemed to start about that time. He had always been fond of liquor and had a special way with the ladies, but it all got worse. He did marry a beautiful woman but after giving birth to their baby boy,

Sergios, his wife moved back into her family's home. And a few years later his wife's whole family took her and the baby and moved far away to a suburb of Athens. Stefano only sees his daughter once or twice a year and never by himself. He finally got into treatment about a year ago and he seems to be finally recovering. But he needs to attend his Alcoholics Anonymous meetings a few times every week, probably for the rest of his life. He was truly devastated that we could not find you. It changed his perspective. Before that night, Stefano had felt high and mighty with his sexual prowess. After that night, his sexual desire dwindled and he wanted to find true love – but he had no idea how to do that. In our family, we had not learned much about loving and nurturing. We boys had learned that we must be powerful, strong and unwilling to let any woman control us. We were taught to control and punish and make the woman subservient. You would not recognize him. Stefano is a different man now than he was when you knew him."

"And what about Damion, what is he doing with his life now?" asked Cassandra. "As you know, Damion has always had a quick and violent temper," said Alexei. "That is why I chose to be the one to beat you that awful night to keep you away from Damion. After you left, his behavior got worse. He spent time at the local pubs drinking and creating fights. He would purposely instigate a fight with someone and then ask the guy to step outside. Our father was always coming to the rescue, sometimes having to bail Damion out of jail for his dangerous actions. But it got worse. He was dating a stunning model from Uruguay, Valentina."

Alexei continued: "Damion had really loved Valentina but he could not tolerate her independent spirit. When she would disagree with him, he would often slap her across the face. And then she would cry, run out of the house, and drive to her own apartment. But he would always sweet talk her into returning. For a few days or weeks, Damion would behave like a romantic love-sick child until the next time Valentina wanted to do something he didn't approve of. The last time he was with her he beat her so badly that she almost lost her modeling contract. Luckily he did not break her nose or scar her face, but her body was covered with bruises and she had a torn shoulder cuff injury that kept her out of work for about a year. That incident led Damion into some serious trouble with the police. Our father paid a lot of money to the police department and several leading politicians to keep Damion out of prison. Then the family sent him to a treatment and recovery center in America, in Connecticut. Damion spent a few years taking medication and speaking to counselors to keep his anger from getting out of hand. It has taken him a long time to understand that he didn't have to get so angry and he didn't have to hurt people. I think you will be surprised to see how much Damion has changed. He learned that other people have a right to live their lives their own way and he doesn't have the right to beat them up just because he doesn't approve. A few months ago, he finally returned to Agapelargos Island."

Now Cassandra wanted to tell her brother what her life has been like since that fateful night. She started by telling Alexei: "You ever knew this. I had always been jealous of Damion and Stefano for having the freedom to explore their sexual desires. There was a very upsetting incident that I never told you or anyone else about. On night, they brought a woman to the house, someone they had met that night at our father's night club. They tied her to the bed totally naked with her feet wide apart. They were beating her with a strap and also fondling and raping her. I heard what sounded like a scream and someone being beaten so I rushed to the room. And I stood in the doorway dumbfounded and scared. Stefano called me over and told me to touch this woman's breasts and private parts and he whispered in my ear that this was what a woman's body feels like. He also told me that men would want to feel my body. I was only 8 years old then."

With tears in her eyes, Cassandra continued telling her story: "Years later, when my sexual urges began and the hormones surged, I was eager to have sexual experiences. I would flirt with the boys at school but Damion once beat up a boy so badly just because he said a rude word to me. So all the boys kept their distance and I wasn't really interested in them anyway. But I would purposely flaunt my sexy body, giving them a reason to desire me. I loved knowing they were fantasizing but could never touch me."

She continued: "That awful night when all of you turned against me and the garage door was locked so I could not get my bicycle, I started walking and just kept on walking. I had no idea where I should go. My body hurt from the beating you gave me and I was in a state of emotional shock. I couldn't believe this was happening to me, that my family had really thrown me out of the house. So I walked and walked and came upon that same park where I had met the man of my dreams, the one with whom I shared one amazing late afternoon of love that I will never forget. I walked toward the bench where I had met my Cyrano. There was a man sitting on the same bench where Cyrano and I had been sitting together. So, in my delirious state, just for the moment, I thought I was seeing my beloved Cyrano again. But the man's voice was deeper and his groping hands were rougher. He fondled my breasts and sucked on my nipples and pulled me toward him. When he discovered I had no panties, he pulled me onto him to have sex. And that was the beginning of my varied sexual experiences."

"Do you want to hear more, Alexei?" Feeling sick to his stomach, on the verge of vomiting, he asked her to please stop. But she refused and continued telling him her story. "Sorry dear brother. You threw me out into the world without my panties and this man used me as if I was a common street hooker. In fact, that's what he thought I was. So he invited me to stay at his hotel room that night. I was so happy to take a bath and to be in a comfortable room. But he threw away my torn and dirty clothing and gave me the hotel terrycloth bathrobe to wear. I had been taken hostage but I knew I really had no place else to go. What I didn't expect was that between that evening and the following day, Dietrich, the man who kidnapped me, had created fake passports for both of us and had booked a flight to Switzerland. His goal was to set up a brothel and I was his first working girl."

With tears clouding his eyes, Alexei begged his little sister to stop. Ignoring his request, she continued: "Dietrich and his friend and business partner, Roffe, decided to test out my sexual prowess. They each took many turns with me that first night at the hotel suite in Lucerne. They had sex with me in different positions, different openings, and using chocolate and whipped cream and lubricants. And do know what, dear brother, I enjoyed every minute. I enjoyed being the sexy object of men's attention. They were never cruel or harsh with me, like my beloved brothers had been. These two Swedish men Have always been kind and gentle, always sexually attracted to me, and they have become even kinder and more caring over the years."

"Okay," said Alexei. "I have heard enough. Please stop." But Cassandra was having a cathartic release that she had needed for all these years. She was not about to stop talking now. So she continued her story saying: "The business began the following night. They fed me, as usual, a wonderful dinner of Swiss delicacies and then they invited men to explore their sexual fantasies with me. Dietrich and Roffe had created a menu of sexual favors so that the male customers could choose the type of treatment they desired. I was the appetizer, the entrée and the dessert – for many months – until, until my belly got so large that nobody could ignore the fact that I was pregnant."

"By that time, in my 7th month of pregnancy," Cassandra continued, "I had learned enough French and German words to communicate with Dietrich and Roffe. Their native language is Swedish, so at first I could not communicate with them at all. But after a few months, they had also learned some French and German, common languages in Lucerne. So that's when Dietrich finally learned about my prominent, wealthy and well-connected family. When he learned the truth, Dietrich was truly sorry that he had misunderstood and had treated me like a common prostitute. From that point forward, he has been a devoted friend and protector of me, like a father or a brother. Both he and Roffe never approached me for sex again. And they insisted that I become the Madam or manager of their brothel, if I wanted that. They also offered to give me money and help me to set up my own business. But I had no place else to go and nobody to start a business with. So I have stayed with my kidnapper and rapist, the man who had kept me hostage and turned me into a sex slave and prostitute."

Finally, Cassandra had finished telling her story to her brother. Alexei had a look of shame and humiliation on his face. He could not bear the thought of his beloved sister behaving like a cheap street hooker, over and over, with so many different men. But then she asked him: "So, my dear Alexei, why were YOU at the **D & R Pleasure Palace**? I can see by your shame-filled expression that you are mortified to know that your little sister has shared her body with so many men in so many demeaning ways. But what has brought You to partake in this type of activity?"

That's when Alexei broke down crying and said: "After you left and we could not find you, I chose to not get close to any woman ever again until such time as I might find you and bring you home. But I never really believed it would happen. So, my body urges were still there and that led me to receive treatments at massage parlors, strip clubs and also houses of prostitution. Now that I have finally found you, I am hoping I will be able to love again and maybe stop needing the paid services of these seductive strangers."

Sitting in a corner booth looking out over the entire city of Lucerne, Switzerland, Alexei and Cassandra both felt an overwhelming sense of love and compassion for the struggles and pain that each had endured. They held hands silently with glassy eyes for what seemed like hours. There was no longer a need for conversation. Each had bared their soul and opened their heart, once again, to love.

Finally, about an hour later, Alexei outlined his plans for a new business opportunity: importing antique, designer and popular styles of watches and clocks and other time pieces to Agapelargos Island from Switzerland. He told Cassandra that this had been the purpose of his visit to Lucerne and the **D & R Pleasure Palace** had come highly recommended by his friend, Victor. Cassandra lit up when she heard Victor's name mentioned. She said to her brother: "Oh, Victor. He is such a nice man. The girls loved him. He used to spend a lot of time and lots of money here. He was never into anything kinky and he seemed to really like the girls. But then he suddenly stopped coming here and we all wondered what had happened."

When Alexei told his sister: "Oh, Victor found a girl he

really loves and decided then and there to stop paying for false intimacy. He married this girl and told me his wife is now pregnant. Victor seems really happy." Cassandra replied: "Oh how nice. That really warms my heart. There Is hope for every one of us, isn't there? No matter what we have done in the past, our future can be different. I have read some spiritual books and they all remind me that God really loves us all. We are all his children and all he wants is to bring his children back to love."

Before parting on this very special reuniting evening, Alexei pledged to set his sister up as the Swiss branch of his watch and clock importing business. What Alexei did not expect is that Dietrich and Roffe would become private benefactors, assisting in the exponential growth of this new family business. It would now be another 3 years before Cassandra would finally take a trip back to her home town on that beautiful little Greek island that she had loved so much as a child and teenager.

After this fateful meeting between brother and sister, Alexei would regularly visit and collaborate on the business progress for several days every month. Cassandra's business acumen had developed so strongly that Alexei found he could easily trust her to handle all the details – financial needs, international taxes, legal issues, staffing, and whatever else was required. They gave the business a catchy name: **Time Travel, Inc.** Utilizing her practiced negotiation skills, Cassandra was able to easily help **Time Travel, Inc**. to become an international phenomenon in just a few years.

Damion and Stefano were eager to get involved in this new family business with their brother, Alexei. When Alexei told them he had secured a private investor and a local manager, the brothers were thrilled. Keeping his promise to his sister, Alexei would not tell anyone in the family any further details about the benefactor and the manager of their new business. They just assumed it was a local person living in Lucerne, Switzerland, so the Melanakos family thought no more about it until 3 years later on Good Friday, 2 days before Easter Sunday.

28 APHRODITE TEACHES ABOUT LOVE

By Age 25, Aphrodite had become quite a well-known psychic healing celebrity. She was invited to speak and share her healing work at local and national professional conferences. Often she declined the travel in favor of having her interested students travel to Connecticut to work with her in her own home town. At first she was sharing her healing gifts with small groups in her home. But as her student base continued to expand, she rented larger and larger rooms to hold her events. At one point, to her surprise, she had 1000 attendees eager to have a direct experience with the famous healer, Aphrodite. After that event she became seriously ill, almost to the point of dying. During her private meditation she discovered that she had taken in a huge amount of negative energy and it was making her sick. She vowed to never again hold such a large and open event. All of her future classes were closed to the general public. She would get a list of names and psychically determine whether or not each person on the list was harboring some type of negative energy that would stifle the healing potential of the group. Those disappointed individuals who were not accepted into Aphrodite's small healing classes were provided with a long referral list of approved practitioners, skilled in many different healing modalities, who might work with these students privately.

One of Aphrodite's clients who had been healed of many painful childhood traumas, was aware that Aphrodite's personal life was not yet fulfilled. Her student, Pauline, had already developed her own psychic abilities with Aphrodite's help and knew that the teacher often can only help others but not him or herself. So, without asking permission, Pauline found an adorable puppy at the local animal shelter, a fluffy, Poodle/Pomeranian mixture, with soft curly white fur and a sweet angelic face that Pauline knew would instantly touch Aphrodite's heart. As a healer, Aphrodite had always practiced by herself without the assistance of anyone or anything else. But this precious little dog became Aphrodite's right hand assistant in all her future healing sessions. Even before a client would outwardly exhibit an emotional upset, Fluffy, (the name Aphrodite instantly called her new puppy), would sit by the patient's leg sending soft, sweet, healing energy. Inevitably the client, who had been attempting to hold his or her feelings inside, would have a cathartic emotional outburst. And then Aphrodite would clear the physical energy in the air and recite a Biblical or other spiritual truth. The healing would be complete.

Aphrodite was always reading something uplifting and spiritually enlightening or else she was listening to a special meditation tape or enlightened teacher speaking. She developed a set of guiding principles that kept her centered and connected to the energetic source of all that is. Through her healing practice, she continued to observe and to know, without a doubt, that we are all connected through an invisible strand of pure energy. Aphrodite was able to actually see the matrix of the universe in vibrant colors when her mind was relaxed and she had fallen into a deep hypnotic trance. That was the signal to her that she was at home. Aphrodite often believed that she did not belong in this world, that she was more at home in that other world, that place between thoughts, that moment before falling into deep sleep and dreaming, that place of ultimate conscious awareness of all that exists as pure energy. And Aphrodite knew that this pure energy was love. She knew there was nothing that could possibly exist in this world that was not created as love.

In this state of connection with the universal matrix, beholding the magnificence of all those vibrant universal colors, Aphrodite's heart would be filled with the love of God. She could only explain this intense involvement with the universal source as her connection to God. But she never pushed her beliefs onto others. Although it hurt her to realize this, she knew that everyone is not yet ready to accept that there is truly a God.

Whenever Aphrodite would hear some terrible news on the TV, radio or in a newspaper report – a robbery, rape, brutal physical mugging, murder, or even a natural disaster such as a huge storm – she knew that this was the work of God, cleansing some evil or negative energy to make room for healing. She knew that some people would heal, rising from the disaster to create and re-create a loving monument to their life. And she also knew that many others would continue to blame this disaster for ruining their life, never seeking to overcome the negativity, never choosing to create or re-create their own legacy to follow.

Over time, Aphrodite had developed her own set of healing principles based upon the many teachings she had studied as well as her personal healing experiences. Continually adjusting her words, she would add, subtract and rearrange the words in her concepts until they accurately expressed the truth as she had currently come to know it. But her knowing would continue to evolve. Her teaching was not static. It was a fluid growing and ever-expanding knowing about the truth that every human being longs to discover, the truth of our spirituality as the source of all of our good.

One of her favorite teachings was about **Forgiveness**. To Aphrodite, forgiveness is love. She would ask her students: "How can you say you love if you have not found a way to forgive? God loves you, exactly the way you are. You cannot be separated from God. You may try. You may think you have done it. But being separated from God is impossible. God is present all the time, everywhere. You are not able to be physically or psychically separated from God. The only thing that separates you from God is your own belief system. You believe you are separate. You believe there are good and evil forces and that somehow you are not aligned with the good. You believe that someone or something outside yourself is responsible for the good and bad circumstances in your life."

Many of her students would resist Aphrodite's teachings about forgiveness. It would often take them a very long time before they could comprehend that it is truly their own consciousness attracting the circumstances or the consciousness of the people closest to them. Gradually, as her students would continue to practice forgiveness as Aphrodite taught, their lives would seem to miraculously transform.

Aphrodite's teachings always returned to **Love**. One of her favorite sayings was: **"Where there is love there's a way."** Although her students did understand the power of love, they would often resist this statement. They could find all sorts of examples of loving another person only to be rejected, betrayed or unloved in return. What Aphrodite would repeat over and over again is: "Love does not bend, does not give in, and does not give up. Love leads the way to victory. Lasting relationships require undying love to remove the darkness and make the crooked places straight. Love is the gift of the universe, the most important gift that God provides. When we feel loving and loved, we are inspired to give and share what we have with another. If we fail to give love it is only because we do not feel loved, we do not feel worthy of love. How we feel about our own self creates the world around us. When we love our own self with compassion and acceptance, we find we are living in a loving world."

Aphrodite loved to teach this important concept: "Love seems to come to us from outside, from other people. But actually, we are sending out the love and it is boomeranging back to us. What we send out returns and it often builds up strength as it comes back to us. Just as a hurricane may be quite strong on the front end, it is often even stronger as it swings around and hits us again at the back end." At this point in her lectures, she would often take a break to respond to her students' eager questions. And then she would continue sharing her powerful insights.

"The problem," Aphrodite would explain, "is that so many of us are happy and feeling content in the early stages of a romantic relationship, when love and passion lead the way. However, that initial passion is only the entrance into the promised land of love.

- When that initial passion dies down and we expect the other person to fulfill our needs
- When we believe we "know" the "right" way for the other person to think, feel and behave
- When we expect that the other person will do, and should do, exactly what we want them to do

That's when we lose sight of the unbending, unwavering, always accepting and forgiving requirements of love."

Next Aphrodite would often address the concept of God, saying: "God is a jealous God. He wants you to love him and his teachings with all your heart. He does not want you to leave any room in your thoughts, your beliefs or your heart for anything that is not love. If you love something external to yourself more than you love God, you have missed the point and will not feel the power of your own spiritual being.

- If you love money more than you love God
- If you love sensations more than you love God
- If you love comfort more than you love God

- If you love material supply more than you love God
- And if you love one person and hate another

Then you do not know God and you do not know how to love."

Her students would often be squirming as Aphrodite so defiantly would tell them to give up their desires for all their material comfort, sexual pleasure, food, movies, vacations, careers and money. She would remind them that it is more difficult to connect with God when:

- Our belly is full
- We are financially comfortable
- We live in a luxurious home
- We travel and enjoy numerous leisure activities
- We have a loving family and friends around us
- We love and are loved by a significant partner"

And just when one of her students would start complaining that this is unfair and that she doesn't really understand, Aphrodite would ask them: "How many of you have spent time today to praise God, to thank God for everything you currently have?" Only a few students would raise their hands.

Aphrodite would continue: "Let me ask you this. If you went to see a doctor tomorrow and were told that you have a life threatening disease with only a few months to live, do you think you might suddenly have an interest in connecting with God?" And that's when the students would quiet down and listen more intently.

As the students now would be more intently listening to her words, Aphrodite would continue to explain: "It is impossible to love God and yet be able to not love a single man or woman in your life. If you feel animosity toward anyone, even someone who is harming you or others, then you have not yet recognized the eternal loving spirit within that person. Why do you think anyone would behave in an unloving way? Have you looked at a baby recently? Does any baby possess an evil spirit? Can you possibly believe that? No, a baby is pure love. Just watch a baby's face light up when mommy or daddy is smiling and cooing. Babies are pure love. So what happens? Why are so many adults behaving as if they do not have the capacity to love any longer?"

The students would respond to Aphrodite's questions with some typical answers. They would say that people lose that loving feeling because they have been hurt and traumatized. And they would give many apparent examples. So Aphrodite would then ask:

Do any of you know another person, maybe even yourself, who:

- Was rejected and emotionally hurt
- Was betrayed and humiliated
- Was raped and brutally beaten
- Had been sexually molested as a child
- Became physically disabled while serving in the military
- Experienced a chronic or life-threatening illness
- Helplessly observed a loved one die

Are any of these life traumas an adequate reason to forego your capacity to give and receive love?"

Aphrodite's words would cause a long, deep silence in the room. And then she would continue by saying:

"What is the difference between those people who give up, give in to the negative forces of life, and suppress their capacity to enjoy love as opposed to those who prevail and live their lives in love? I believe the only difference is **Faith**. Without faith, we can be devastated by the trials and tribulations of life. Without faith, we are like a branch cut off from the roots of a tree. Can a branch survive and flourish on its own? No, it will fall to the ground, wither and die – and it may even be stepped upon and crushed by a passing animal or human being. We are all connected to the Tree of Life, the universal source of all that is, God, who is pure Love. Those who survive and continue to overcome the battles and struggles and detours placed before them in life, are those who have an abiding faith in the goodness of God and all that is naturally provided in this world."

One of the students would often ask at this point: "But how do we keep up our faith when the world sometimes looks dark and dreary and we feel so alone and helpless?" "Ah," Aphrodite would reply: "What a wonderful question. Faith is the power to look past and beyond what is appearing right in front of you. Ignore the appearances outside of yourself. Focus only on your own connection to that inner well of knowing that rises up from deep within your own consciousness. Realize the nothingness of everything you see that appears to be bad or evil, wrong or horrible. War, fever, rape, brutality, or abuse of any kind, only exist in this world for one reason. There is some sort of negative, self-deprecating belief that needs to be dissolved within you. Let the harshness of the world teach you to have compassion and love for your fellow man, or woman, even when that person appears to be purposely intent upon harming you. And realize that although it may appear that evil is winning out temporarily, rest assured that all evil is self-destructive. All negativity only harms the person who harbors the negative beliefs and intentions. Clear your own consciousness of all fearful, negative, self-defeating and self-denigrating thoughts. **Fill your internal vessel with good food, healthy exercise, and loving assurance that this is a beautiful and loving world that you are living in NOW – no matter how difficult or unfair your current outer circumstances appear to be.**"

Aphrodite would often conclude her current lecture with these words: "Ask yourself at all times: What am I entertaining in my thoughts and beliefs? And bring your thoughts back to God, my oneness with all that is, my birthright of universal love, and the faith that love will overcome all obstacles. Believe in love no matter what and your life will bloom with joy. Forgive yourself for past mistakes. Forgive others for hurting you. Forgive God for not appearing when you ask. Discover that the power has always resided within you to find your connection with God and love, forgiveness and faith. Do not strive to get or receive anything from anyone else. Strive instead to seek your own connection with the source, to find and release the love that is stored within your own heart and mind."

Aphrodite loved to end her lectures with this simple, rarely mentioned quote from Deuteronomy 10:15 in the King James Version of the Bible:

> *"Circumcise therefore the foreskin of your heart and be no more stiffnecked."*

She reminded her students to love with an open heart, to practice forgiveness 70 X 7, and to see the good and the God within everyone they meet.

When her class had ended on this particular pleasant early spring day, the students praised their teacher and many stopped to give her a big hug. Everyone felt a warm sense of connectedness and love that some were experiencing for the very first time ever. But when the last student had finally left, Aphrodite opened a bottle of her favorite wine, cut up some small pieces of her favorite cheese, and she prepared to sit on her couch alone and contemplate the absolute loneliness of her existence. But before she could settle into her couch with her snacks, she was interrupted by a phone call that was about to change her life forever.

When she said "Hello" and heard that familiar deep male voice respond, she felt a warm tingle spread through her body. Leo, sounding different than his usual formal approach, spoke to her in a slow and hesitant way which was so unlike his usual quick and confident style. Without wasting any time, Leo told her: "I was just given two tickets to visit a quaint little Greek island. Have you ever heard of Agapelargos Island on the Southeast coast of Greece not far from Athens? We may have a special connection there that can help you enormously in your life." Intrigued, Aphrodite asked him to tell her more. But, of course, Leo would not explain the details.

He just told her: "Aphrodite, you know I have grown quite fond of you and you know I always have your best interests at heart. Can you please just trust me on this one? I know you will be surprised and delighted with this exciting adventure I have planned for us. Please, dear Aphrodite, I won't take no for an answer." And then he held his breath, fearful that she might adamantly refuse. But to Leo's delight, Aphrodite replied: "You know, Leo, I have grown really fond of you. And I do trust you with all my heart. You have always been so kind and caring to me. Of course I will come with you on this special trip. I can hardly wait. When are we going?" Leo explained: "We will arrive at the island on Good Friday, the Friday before the Easter resurrection, in just a few weeks from now. Till then, keep warm and safe my love." And he hung up the phone.

Leo had breathed a noticeably loud sigh of relief as soon as Aphrodite had agreed to go on this trip with him. And then his final words, "Till then, keep warm and safe my love," sent her mind and heart spinning. Aphrodite thought to herself: "This man likes me. I know it. He likes me more than he has ever shown. And I think I really like him too. Wow. Life is strange. Just when I was teaching all about love while feeling lonely and unloved myself, the man of my dreams has been so close to me that I had been unable to see. I think my teachings have removed the filters from my own eyes. I can't believe I am beginning to love for the very first time in my life."

That night Aphrodite dreamed about a beautiful young lady, her mother Cassandra, meeting a handsome young sailor, her father Cyrano, in a peaceful tree-lined park near the water on what appeared to be a beautiful sunny island. She had no idea that this dream was a premonition of the upcoming most life-changing moment, the actual resurrection of love, in her life.

29 CYRANO RETURNS FROM THE WAR

Cyrano Niles Maniatis had remained a prisoner in that small hole in the ground for 21 months. Not knowing if he would ever see daylight again, at first he became quite depressed. But he was also terrified of what could happen to him if he was brought outside. At regular intervals, he would hear the sounds of new arrivals, newly captured prisoners, and the inevitable torture and spectacle made of one or two of them in front of all the others. Cyrano heard the anguished screams of another man being burned alive or one being repeatedly stabbed with a bayonet. He also heard gunfire and screams from injured victims. Knowing that life would be hellish outside of his hole in the ground, Cyrano began to feel as if he was in a somewhat safe place. The guard assigned to feeding the prisoners would always stop by and provide a tiny meal of rice and some sort of protein. Often, his food would contain a number of moving insects. In any ordinary situation, he would have been horrified and refused to eat. But when you are hovering between life and death, life seems to be the most powerful call. And Cyrano chose life, just on the very remote chance that he might one day be blessed enough to lay eyes again on his beloved Cassandra.

Reminiscing about every single detail of that afternoon - that extraordinary day when he had met Cassandra, the woman of his dreams - would get him through the morning hours of each day while living in his damp and dark prison underground. Cyrano would recall seeing Cassandra for the very first time thinking the exact same thoughts he had on that special day: "She might be the most beautiful woman I have ever seen, maybe even the most beautiful woman in the world."

When the sun was at its peak in the sky, a little glimmer of light sometimes would shine down upon him, giving him a momentary sense of the power of life. He would often imagine stretching his arms and moving his body forward and back. In his small space he would attempt to move his hips and do whatever body movements the space would accommodate. Whatever he could not actually move he would move in his imagination. Cyrano discovered, many years later, that he had instinctively used his mind to stimulate his muscles and prevent them from totally atrophying.

This is the time of day, when he feeling the warmth of the midday sun would remind him of the second afternoon he had spent with his beloved Cassandra. He would relive the sensations he had felt that day: those butterflies he had felt in his stomach and the excited anticipation of knowing he was about to see this beautiful woman again. He would remember the deep longing he felt to touch her and gaze into her eyes and to merge his body with hers. And then he would feel in his body those same sensations he felt the very first time he had moved his hands down her back to feel the round softness of her firm butt and she had not stopped him, allowing his hands to remain there for several minutes. Then he would purse his lips as if she were right next to him again and his lips were pressed against hers. And he would imagine holding Cassandra as they sat together without talking, feeling content and intimately connected, on that wooden bench next to the beautiful Weeping Willow tree.

When darkness began to fill the camp and his cell in the ground, that's when Cyrano would contemplate the third and final afternoon he had spent with his beloved Cassandra. He would imagine over and over again that incredibly sexy see-through blouse she was wearing. His lips would purse as he reached his mouth forward to encompass those firm nipples at the tip of her big beautiful breasts. His hands and fingers would caress the little space around him imagining his hands were actually holding and massaging his lover's full, round, smooth, soft and luscious breasts. He would explore Cassandra's body, one small part at a time, vividly within his imagination. And even in his precarious, terrifying and life threatening situation he would often become sexually aroused and pleasure himself in his private dungeon.

Cyrano had absolutely no idea how much time had passed. He knew it had been many months for he had observed a slight change in the temperature and the atmosphere. But most of the time it was just plain hot, very hot, and humid. His guard would not often provide him with enough water but when the monsoons came his little underground cave would start to flood with water.

At that time he could satisfy his thirst without outside assistance. But there were days when the water rose to nearly his shoulders. When the storm would end, the heat of the sun would quickly dry up the accumulated water. But being buried deep in the water for hours, and on occasion for a day or two, was quite uncomfortable for his body. Yet Cyrano and many of his shipmates managed to remain alive and endure the most unimaginable discomforts for their entire prisoner of war experience. Finally, 21 month after that initial capture by the enemy, Cyrano was taken out of his underground home by the Allied Forces. Thrilled to see some of his ship mates had also survived, he was deeply saddened to learn that many others had not. He seemed to recall an incident many months earlier when he had heard one of his ship mates screaming from underground. And then he had heard some of the Vietcong guards yelling something in their own language followed by the sound someone being dragged out of his dungeon, beaten with loud knocking sounds then there was the sound of gunfire. The screaming finally had stopped and the campground area had grown completely silent for a moment.

So, on this day when the American, British, French, Greek and Spanish allied forces arrived, Cyrano's first thought was: "Oh no, this is a cruel trick. The Vietcong have decided to dispose of us and they are forcing their new prisoners to pretend to be here to rescue us." But he heard a voice and looked up into the warm, compassionate eyes of a Greek soldier. For the first time in all those horrifying months, a smile crossed Cyrano's face and he breathed a sigh of relief, knowing his ordeal was about to end.

It took 3 Allied soldiers to pull Cyrano out of his hole in the ground that had been his home for, he later found out, 21 months - almost 2 years. When Cyrano's body finally reached the earth above, he fell to the ground unable to stand on his weary and partially atrophied leg muscles. He closed his eyes because the pain of daylight was too intense. One of the soldiers handed Cyrano a pair of sunglasses that made his eyes feel more comfortable during those early hours and first few days of his recovery. Nobody handed Cyrano a mirror to see how emaciated and malnourished he was. The trauma had been great enough. The soldiers had been advised to keep all mirrors away from the rescued prisoners.

Cyrano had been carried out of the campground on a stretcher, along with his fellow survivors, to be boarded onto a plane headed for Lucerne, Switzerland, to a special hospital offering their services temporarily for injured and traumatized Vietnam veterans. It took an entire year of rehabilitation at this facility before Cyrano had regained his capacity for walking, moving his body, and fully using his arms. He had also suffered from such a lack of nutrients that he had been placed on intravenous injections of vitamins along with a hefty supply of oral vitamins. Gradually, Cyrano's physical health and strength returned as his body weight increased back up to a normal weight for his tall stature.

While recuperating in the hospital, unbeknownst to him, his beloved Cassandra was working and living only a few miles away. Cyrano had no idea that this woman who he had continually fantasized about had provided sexual favors to a host of different men. He also had been totally unaware that she had given birth to a daughter, his child, conceived during that one night of shared ecstasy. And he did not know that the incredible Madame C. he had heard about while recuperating, the manager and head mistress of the **D & R Pleasure Palace**, was actually his beloved Cassandra. Fortunately for both Cyrano and Cassandra, he did not feel well enough to engage in sexual play, nor did he have any interest in visiting, the **D & R Pleasure Palace**. Sexual pleasure with strangers was not one of his top priorities. His main goal was to return home and to see his mother and father again.

Finally, the day arrived when Cyrano was ready to return to his home in Australia. While riding in the plane his mind felt calm and at ease, as if he had never had any of those horrendous experiences. In fact, to everyone's amazement and delight he seemed to have handled his wartime experiences without any lasting negative effects. His mother was thrilled to see her beloved, only son, return home in one piece. His father, a strong, tough businessman who rarely showed his emotions, broke down and cried like a baby when he saw his beloved son again. Fortunately, his parents had not seen Cyrano when he had first arrived at the hospital in Lucerne looking emaciated, malnourished and as if he might die any moment.

Cyrano got involved in his father's diamond export business and remained easygoing, efficient and delightful to be around. It seemed as though Cyrano was right back to being the wonderful person he had grown up to be. But then it happened, all at once. A new customer came into the store, a small Asian man who seemed to be quite wealthy. Cyrano looked at the man suspiciously and then suddenly lost it. He started screaming, ran around the counter to confront the man and then he jumped on top of this poor guy that didn't know what hit him. Cyrano began to punch the man and kick him violently until his father, Kephalos, shot his hand gun into the air to startle his son. That immediately shocked Cyrano back to the present moment. When he saw himself sitting on top of this defenseless, undeserving, non-confrontational Asian man, Cyrano became profusely apologetic. The man ran out of the store, terrified for his life and did not report the incident to the police for fear that this crazy man might retaliate and hurt him again. Kephalos acted calm and suggested that they close the store for the day and return home.

As soon as they entered the house, Kephalos headed straight for the liquor cabinet and invited his son to have a spot of liquor. Kephalos poured a shot of brandy for his son, leaving the liquor bottle open for Cyrano to have as much alcohol as he needed to calm his nerves. Excusing himself, Kephalos slipped into the kitchen to quietly talk with his wife, Cyrano's mother Adelfa. Both were quite upset with Cyrano's behavior earlier that day at the shop. Familiar with the symptoms of post-traumatic stress disorder, PTSD, they were both quite certain their son had just experienced a painful flashback.

Knowing that Cyrano was in danger of harming someone, including his own parents, Kephalos wasted no time. That night he contacted the local hospital to discuss the procedure for getting his son admitted. In the morning, 3 strong men in white hospital uniforms arrived at the

Maniatis home. Despite Cyrano's best efforts to resist, he was no match for 3 strong men. The hospital aids managed to get Cyrano into the truck and the driver then headed toward the hospital. Cyrano remained in this local hospital mental ward for 7 months. During that time he received regular sessions of individual counseling, group counseling, activity therapy and even career change studies.

When Cyrano was finally released from his inpatient hospitalization, he continued to see the psychiatrist and a counselor to talk about the horrors he had experienced in Vietnam and his lasting traumatic memories. Over the next few years, Cyrano's mental state improved and he re-joined his father in the diamond export business. Although wary of his son's capacities and fearful that a relapse could occur at any moment, Kephalos helped his son to once again feel good about life. Cyrano understood the business quite well and helped to initiate and close many lucrative deals.

Many, many years after he had returned home from his military service, Cyrano was finally ready to begin dating again. It had been over 15 years since that incredible night with Casssandra on Agapelargos Island. The memory now seemed like a vague fantasy, a figment of his imagination. Cyrano dated lots of women, some very beautiful, some extremely sexy, others very intelligent or unusually creative. No matter how special and wonderful other people would say these women were, Cyrano would always lose interest after only a few dates. His sexual experiences with all of the women he met seemed to leave him feeling empty and unsatisfied. Sometimes, much to his own surprise, he would once again fantasize about that evening on that little Greek island, when he had been enthralled at the sight and sound and touch of one young lady, Cassandra Sybil Melanakos. No matter how much he tried to forget that beautiful woman he had loved, Cyrano just could not get that memory out of his mind. Then he recalled that it was the memory of that beautiful young lady that had sustained him during the darkest night of his soul in that bleak and muggy, dirty, sweaty and miserable hole in the ground.

At one point Cyrano became interested in spiritual phenomena which led to his attendance at many mystical and spiritual events. At one of these lectures, he was invited to what was called a "tape session," a meditation group where they listened to the audio recordings of many different spiritual leaders and then silently meditated together. Intrigued, he agreed to come to one of these meetings on a Sunday evening. In that very first session Cyrano had a huge awakening to his own spiritual essence. When he first entered the room and attempted to introduce himself to someone, the moderator put a finger to his lips indicating to Cyrano that he needed to be quiet. Cyrano then noticed that as each participant would arrive, they would silently choose a seat and quickly sit down. Then they would remain in silent contemplation until the evening's recording began. At the scheduled time to begin, the moderator of the evening would turn on the tape player. Each week, the recording would be a surprise to the attendees, focused on a specific topic and featuring a different healer. Sometimes the topic would continue for several weeks and the participants would hear lectures by some of the leading healers of the time talking about this same topic from slightly different perspectives.   By the time the lecture for the week had ended, and the group remained silent for another half hour, Cyrano would find himself thrust into a deep trance where his body seemed to disappear and his thoughts went blank. He continued attending these tape classes for the next 10 years.

The women he would meet in those classes appeared to have a spiritual interest like his own but they did not appeal to his senses. The women he would meet at a local pub might appear to be attractive but they did not seem to possess that spiritual essence or spiritual interest. And the women he had met in other ways rarely appealed to him at all. At 43 years of age, Cyrano had never fallen in love with another woman. Every so often his mind would bring him back to that very special night, so many years ago, on that little Greek island in the sun, Agapelargos Island, where he had found his one true love.

So, when his father told him that his grandfather, Hermes, was quite ill and was asking to see his grandson, Cyrano thought he might like to return to Agapelargos Island to rekindle those precious memories. Having no idea where the beautiful Cassandra of his dreams lived, he thought that maybe when he gets to that island he will try to find her. Of course, he had no idea that she no longer lived there. His parents told him they wanted to accompany him on this trip to visit Kephalos' father, Cyrano's grandfather, and also Kephalos' brother, Basileus, Cyrano's uncle. Cyrano's parents told him they wanted to bring the family together again because it had been quite a while. What they didn't tell their son was that they had an incredible surprise planned for him

What happened was a chance meeting between Cassandra's parents, Demitri and Lyzandra, and Cyrano's Uncle Basileus and Grandfather Hermes at a local church ceremony on Agapelargos Island. Father Petrides, who had been a pastor at the same church for many decades had finally decided it was time to retire. To introduce his congregation to the young pastor who would be his replacement, Father Anastas, the retiring Father Petrides sponsored a huge banquet. There was music, dancing, family fun and a good time to be had by all.

Stopping at the counter to get a glass of wine for himself and his wife, Demitri just happened to overhear a conversation between Hermes and his son, Basileus. Basileus casually mentioned that he not seen his brother Kephalos or his nephew Cyrano in a long time. Hermes responded by saying: "Yes, I wonder how Cyrano is doing. Remember when he was here, how long ago was it?" Basileus answered quickly, "I think it was 25 years ago. I had just graduated from college and I had heard about Cyrano's big love affair that had only lasted a few days. Remember when he called us to say goodbye, the night before his ship left our island? He told me he was really scared but that this beautiful woman had warmed his heart and that he thought he was in love. Cyrano was about to go on that dangerous naval mission to Vietnam where he was captured and held prisoner for I think almost 2 years."

When Demitri heard that some young sailor had been in love with a young lady about 25 years earlier, his ears perked up. He turned to the two men and politely asked: "Do you happen to know the name of the girl that this young sailor loved so briefly?" Basileus immediately said: "I believe he called her Cassie." And Demitri almost fell over. The boy who had gotten his beloved Cassie pregnant had been on his way to Vietnam. "No wonder," thought Demitri, "Our little Cassie had such a big heart and she probably had wanted to give this young man some love to remember and hold on to when he was in the depths of despair and fearing for his life. Oh," he thought, "If only I could see my darling daughter again." Demitri told the two men: "I believe it was our beloved daughter who had been with Cyrano that fateful day before his ship went out to sea. We have not seen her in 25 years."

The tears welled up in his eyes when he said, "My name is Demitri Melanakos. Please let me know when your grandson comes to visit. My wife and I would really like to meet him. Our daughter spoke so highly of him. We were foolhardy, pigheaded men back then and we did not understand young love. My heart aches to see my daughter again but if we could just see the man she loved, it will comfort my whole family." The men exchanged phone numbers and did not talk again that night. In a few days, Demitri contacted Basileus and promised to pay the plane fare for Cyrano to return to the island. He told Basileus to promise his nephew a special treatment that can help with his war injuries if he is not willing to come without some sort of bribe.

Demitri and Lyzandra asked Father Petrides to give them one last blessing in his back office. Together Cassandra's parents once again begged the lord for forgiveness for what they had done to their daughter so many years before. Hearing that the young sailor might be visiting their little island, Lyzandra wistfully said: "Oh how I wish I could bring our Cassie back here and bring the two of them together again to share their love for the rest of their lives. I know they have both suffered more than I can imagine."

When Alexei visited his parents the following day, he was surprised and delighted to hear that his father had connected with Cyrano's relatives. He asked his father for the phone number so he could talk with them. What Alexei did not tell parents was that he would convince Cassandra to come to the island on the same day that Cyrano would arrive. Alexei planned to orchestrate a meeting at that same park bench of the two star-crossed lovers, only this time with the family of both Cyrano and Cassandra present and consenting. He planned to encourage Cyrano's relatives to convince his parents to accompany him from Australia on this special reunion trip.

Each party in this upcoming event knew about only a piece of the puzzle.

- Demitri, Lyzandra, Stefano and Damion thought they would all be meeting only Cyrano, the man who had impregnated their beloved Cassandra.
- Cyrano thought that he and his parents would be only visiting with his Grandfather Hermes and his Uncle Basileus.

- Aphrodite thought she would only be visiting a beautiful Greek island for a special vacation with Leo.
- Leo thought that Aphrodite would only be meeting her mother and that he would surprise her, in front of her birth mother, with his marriage proposal.
- Dietrich also thought that Aphrodite would only be meeting her mother. He had no idea that Aphrodite would be meeting both of her natural parents, her birth father and birth mother, her uncles, her great uncle and her grandparents too.
- Cyrano's parents thought their son would only be meeting his uncle and his grandfather and they were surprised and excited to accept the offer by Kephalos' brother to pay for their 3 airplane tickets, insisting that they all fly together.
- Alexei thought that Cassandra would be meeting her long lost lover, Cyrano, and would once again be connecting with her parents and her brothers. He did not know that Cassandra's daughter, Aphrodite, would also be there.

The stage was set for an amazing joining together of a soon-to-be happily united family. Love was in the air once again and romance would soon be blossoming into full expression.

30 RESURRECTION OF LOVE

It was Good Friday, a beautiful spring day designating the start of Easter weekend. After 25 long, hard, painful years - years of emotional numbness, regret and loss of integrity and personal identity, Cassandra was finally ready to reconnect with her family. But what actually was about to occur she could not have imagined. At the prompting of her brother Alexei, Cassandra had finally agreed to return for a visit to her beloved Agapelargos Island, the place she had loved so much as a child and budding teenager. More than anything, she wanted to return to that park and reminisce about her incredible experience with the man she had been her first and only love, Cyrano. Her flight was uneventful and calm. When she arrived, she took a taxi directly to her hotel, a new modern high-rise. She had chosen a room on the 16th floor with a full panoramic view of the entire island she had known so well. During the short taxi ride from the airport, she said hello again to her beautiful island. "It hasn't changed at all," she thought. "Oh it is so beautiful here. I can't believe that I am back in this magical place." A bittersweet smile crossed her lips as she recalled the circumstances that had led her away from the home she had loved to be living in exile for so many years.

Once in her hotel room, Cassandra unpacked her small bag which contained enough clothing for only a few days. Not knowing how she would feel and how she might be received by her family, Cassandra had not planned to stay very long. Her return flight was scheduled for Monday morning. Now, in her room, she went into the bathroom to freshen up. Looking at her face in the mirror she could see beneath the aging lines to that beautiful innocent girl she had been way back then, before that fateful day when the family had learned about her secret rendezvous and her pregnancy. Backing away from the mirror, she checked out her body, thinking to herself: "Not bad for an older woman. I still make men's heads turn. My figure is a little more round and full but my curves still draw attention and my long shapely legs have served me well."

Today she was wearing a pale pink form fitting jersey wool sweater and a pair of elastic pants, not unlike the pants she had worn on that fateful romantic night with Cyrano. This time, however, there were no snaps in the crotch and she definitely was wearing a pair of panties. She had no illusion of a sudden sexual adventure nor would she have wanted it. Her body had been explored, examined, pummeled and fondled in every crevice and opening and in every imaginable way. All she wanted in her life at this time was to feel calm and peaceful. Love and affection, tenderness and excitement, seemed totally foreign to her, sentiments she recalled as if they had belonged to someone else.

Glancing at the clock on the night table next to her King size bed that was covered with white lacey pillows and colorful ruffled shams, Cassandra saw that it was 12:30

PM. She contacted the front desk to arrange for a taxi at 1:30 PM to take her to that little park on the other side of town, adjacent to the lake. Cassandra left her room and went down to the lovely garden café at the hotel to have a pleasant lunch. She ordered a glass of her favorite Greek wine which she sipped along with some hummus and pita chips. For her meal, she ordered one of her mother's favorite dishes that she had helped to serve almost every Sunday in their home - chicken souvlaki. She ended this meal with a demi-cup of Greek espresso with a tiny piece of sweet and sticky baklava for dessert. The maître di came over to ask if she had ordered a taxi because it had arrived. She motioned to the waiter and told him: "Please charge my meal to room 1616." Cassandra quickly signed the check and jumped up from her seat to get the taxi."

Riding in the taxi felt to her like déjà vu. Everything around her was so familiar. She had forgotten how beautiful this island is and how much she had loved living here. The leaves were starting to peek out all over the trees and budding flowers lined the edges of the street. Colorful and cheerful, the flowers reminded her of her youthful exuberance, the dreams she had had, and that wonderful secret she had held for such a brief time. Her mind was filled with the wonder of life, as she contemplated how most of us do finally return to our origins, no matter how far we travel to get away. In that state of reverie, she did not realize the taxi had reached her destination. There she was, sitting and looking out toward that same park, the park which was the location where she had experienced the most exciting and the most devastating events of her life.

At this moment, Cassandra's thoughts turned to Cyrano. She wondered where Cyrano might be living and then the unpleasant thought crossed her mind, "If he IS still living." All she could recall was that parting moment, when he told her he would be leaving the following morning and would be going on a serious mission to that treacherous war zone in Vietnam. She had heard so many stories since then of men being captured, tortured, forced into drug addiction and slavery, and so many missing in action. She also thought about all those men who were wounded in action, men who had survived with their lives but with limbs and organs missing and their life function limited. Taking a long easy breath, she thought to herself: "I know he is okay. He IS alive. But who knows where he is living or if he is married with children. He had told me to live a good life, to get married, to start a family...."

The taxi driver honked to get her attention, saying: "Lady, I don't have all day. This is how I make my living. Please pay and let me get to my next customer." Cassandra asked the driver how much she owed. Then, reaching into her wallet she handed him a huge tip, much bigger than he would naturally expect. This was a momentous occasion for her so she was feeling very generous. Cassandra had believed for so long that she would never ever see this place again. And now she was here. Before getting out of the taxi, she asked for the driver's phone number so she could call him to pick her up later if she needed him to bring her back to her hotel. Alexei had promised to meet her at the park at about 3 PM. She told him she planned to be at the park by 2 PM but she wanted to have some private time alone to reconnect with an idyllic time in her younger life.

As she stepped out of the car, Cassandra felt that same tingly sensation, that exact same familiar sense of anticipation that she had felt 25 years earlier before entering this park for the first time. She had this strange and wondrous feeling that something momentous was about to happen.

Then she spoke to herself, saying: "Cassandra, this is silly. You are acting like a foolish school girl, as if you are about to meet a man who will change your life. You met him once, so many years ago. You will never see Cyrano again and nobody could ever have that same intense effect upon you. No, Cassandra, you have known too many men and none of them have ever compared to that handsome sailor who swept you off your feet and owned your heart forevermore."

Even with those words in her mind and the apparent reality of her life so clear to her, Cassandra found she could hardly breathe. She was really excited and had no idea what was about to occur. Of course, she had always had an intense psychic awareness which was taking place at this very moment. But since her mind was filled with memories, she did not pay attention to what was happening in her energy field. Once again, this park would be the place in which her life got turned upside down or maybe this time, right side up.

As she walked along that familiar path toward the bike rack, she was delighted to see that it was still there. She missed that pretty pink bicycle that she had loved so much, the bicycle that had given her freedom and then had led to the total demise of her lifestyle and the destruction of her family's love and respect for her. Gazing at the bicycles lined up there, she wished she could borrow one to ride around feeling the breeze through her hair with a sense of carefree abandon. And then she saw it. It looked just like her pink bicycle but she thought to herself: "It can't be mine. They must have gotten rid of that many years ago." So she brushed the thought out of her mind.

Cassandra decided to stop at that same bathroom, but of course she did not plan to remove her camisole; she was not even wearing one on this day. She just wanted to repeat the steps she had made on that fateful day, almost superstitiously hoping that it could miraculously bring the man of her dreams back to her. But she realized this was foolish thinking and she dropped the thoughts from her mind. Glancing in the bathroom mirror, once again she smiled at how attractive she still was. The pale pink jersey wool sweater showed off her shapely upper torso and she noticed happily that her breasts were still firm and high. Then she leaned away, twisted and turned her body and her head to check out how she looked from the rear. Liking what she saw and feeling confident in her beauty once more, she stepped out of the bathroom and headed toward her favorite park bench.

The time now was 1:59 PM, one minute before that fated meeting time 25 years earlier. Cassandra sat on the bench, closed her eyes and felt the warmth of the sun filling her body. The sensation was wonderful and then a strange tingly feeling emerged from the depths of her belly. Before opening her eyes, she sensed that someone was approaching. Hearing faint footsteps coming from a few yards away, she let herself imagine that it was once again that glorious day 25 years earlier and that those were the footsteps of her beloved Cyrano.

Before she could refute and suppress those thoughts, a familiar deep and comforting voice could be heard from a few feet away, speaking in slightly broken Greek: "Cassandra, my beautiful Cassandra, you have returned to me." For a moment, she thought she was totally imagining this and she kept her eyes closed so the dream would not disappear. He came closer and touched her on the shoulder, saying: "Cassandra, Cassandra, is that really you? Are you really here again? Or am I having a hallucination as I have had many times before?" Reluctantly, Cassandra opened her eyes and once again saw the most handsome face she had ever seen.

Cyrano's tear-filled eyes lit up when he saw his beloved Cassandra open her beautiful piercing blue eyes and look directly at him. Her expression was one of total shock, bewilderment and even fear. For what felt like a very long time she was not sure if this was real or only in her imagination. He reached out his hand beckoning for her to offer hers. She could feel the energy swirling throughout her body. It was really him. She recognized his special and delightful energy. Next he lifted her hand ever so gently to his lips and placed a soft moist kiss on the top. Her body tingled and her heart was pounding so loudly she thought for sure that everyone in the park could hear. This time Cyrano did not let go. In that moment, Cyrano decided he would never let go of this woman again for the rest of his life. He knew he was home when he looked at that beautiful smile he had loved so many years before. That same warm and sensual feeling spread throughout his body as he held her hand.

Twenty-five long years had passed, yet both Cassandra and Cyrano felt in this moment as if it had only been a few hours or a day at most. They knew they would have a lifetime of experiences to share with each other. He knew that his prisoner of war injuries, both physical and psychological, would have an effect on their intimacy. She knew that her period of prostitution and working as a madam and being used and bartered by men would have an effect on their intimacy. And they both knew, then and there, that the past did not matter. In this moment, here and now, Cyrano and Cassandra had finally found each other again. Life as they had not yet known it was about to begin. But there was another piece of fulfillment yet to come that neither could possibly have anticipated.

Cyrano asked politely, "May I sit down beside you and join you on this lovely spring day, my beloved and beautiful Cassandra?" She replied in an equally polite and tender voice, "Oh course you may my dearly beloved Cyrano. We have so many years to catch up on and maybe we will have just as many years left to enjoy being together." And then, as if they had rehearsed it, they both spoke in unison: "I can't believe this is real, you are really here with me. I am really talking to you and touching you again. I have always wondered where you were and how your life was going. God brought us together once. He tore us apart to face the world and release our inner demons. And now he has brought us back together, still in love and even more determined for it to last."

At that very moment Cyrano looked out across the expanse of this beautiful park where he had once met the love of his life who had finally returned to him. About to turn back to give his full attention to his beloved Cassandra, he noticed a lovely young lady about 25 years old, standing with a slightly older gentleman about 100 yards away. This young girl looked very familiar. Looking at her Cyrano thought to himself: "She looks an awful lot like Cassandra." And he turned to his beloved Cassandra to ask: "Cassie darling, do you have a daughter? Did you bring your daughter here with you today?" Startled at first by his question, she was about to say: "No." Then she looked in the same direction Cyrano had been looking and got her first glimpse of her daughter Aphrodite. She knew immediately that this was her long lost daughter. Cassandra cried out loud: "Oh my God, that is my daughter Aphrodite." She gasped out loud: "Aphrodite, oh my God, Aphrodite. You are here. I can't believe it. Oh my God!"

Aphrodite heard this couple making what sounded like groaning and grunting sounds. And then she thought she heard her name being called. So she walked a little closer to hear what they were saying. Her Greek studies had helped her to understand their words. She heard her name called again and asked Leo, who was standing with her: "Leo, please wait here. I heard these people call my name. I wonder why." Leo, knowing that this would be his beloved Aphrodite's first meeting with her birth parents, complied with her request without the slightest resistance.

Aphrodite walked toward the couple on the bench immediately asking: "How do you know my name? I have never been on this island before. This is my very first visit here. I wanted to see the place where my mother had lived and where my parents had met each other. My mother abandoned me when I was just born and I never knew my father. So how do you two know my name?"

Tears welled up in Cyrano's eyes. He had no idea that he had a daughter. But just one look at her structured features, that slender tapered nose, long neck and long legs, reminded him of himself. And her high cheek bones leading up to those deep blue penetrating eyes and her long flowing wavy hair reminded him of the way Cassandra had looked so long ago. He was the first to speak.

"You are so very beautiful young lady. Your deep blue piercing eyes are just like your mother's. Your slender tapered nose, your long neck and long legs were inherited from your father. You have never met your father before but you are about to meet him now."

"Hello beautiful daughter, I am your father, Cyrano Niles Maniatis and this is your mother, Cassandra Sybil Melanakos. We have just met again today, at 2 PM, for the first time in 25 years. So you must be 25 years old. My heart is aching to know you and love you as you should have been loved all these years." With tears in her eyes, Aphrodite Maia Morgan lashed out at her mother exclaiming: "Why did you desert me? Why did you send me away when I was just a baby? I needed my mother, I wanted to know you and be loved by you. Why did you do that to me? I have spent my whole life recovering from being abandoned. It has taken me so very long to learn how to love other people and to let them love me."

Cassandra, sobbing by now, could barely speak. She blurted out her words in between sobs: "I am so sorry my beautiful daughter. You were truly born in love. Your father and I felt so much passion and desire and love that afternoon when you were conceived. Don't ever believe for even a moment that you were not loved. In fact, I loved you so much I did not want you to see me and to grow up in the seedy lifestyle I was living then. I did not want you to know about such things. My dream was for you to have a happy and beautiful childhood like I had lived before the day I was kidnapped and brought to Switzerland. I wanted a good family to adopt you, to take good care of you and to give you the love you need and deserve. How did they treat you? What was it like for you growing up in your adoptive home? Please, we want to know all about you and your life. We are here now. We are finally a family. We can love each other now without restrictions, without suffering and pain. Please believe me Aphrodite, I do love you. I always have and I have thought about you every single day, all day long, wondering how you are doing."

Cassandra suddenly wanted to share something she had never mentioned to anyone else: "Aphrodite, I have always possessed this strange psychic knowing, a gift that you may have inherited. So I was able to see you and I know that you have been using your powers, not always for good reasons, but you have been learning and growing. Let's sit together now and talk about our future as a loving family. My heart is finally filled with joy after 25 years in exile. I have the two people I love most in the world right here next to me. I don't know if these tears will ever stop flowing but finally, finally, finally they are tears of joy. God is good. He had a plan for each of us. It was not an accident that we were separated. I know now that my life purpose has been to forgive, to learn how to forgive and overcome all adversity."

Cyrano chimed in: "My life purpose has been to develop compassion for myself, to discover that my outer show of strength is not what matters most in life. It is my inner core of unwavering trust in God. So often I had doubted that God was with me. I thought I had been abandoned while living in that hole in the ground for 21 months, in the damp and darkness. But I have discovered the power of my mind, my imagination and I have learned that strength comes from within. Nobody can do anything to destroy my faith now, now that I am sitting and facing the two women I will love more than life itself forever."

And finally, Aphrodite spoke with tears streaming down her face: "And my purpose has been to love, to learn how to love and trust and surrender to life as it is, letting go of all expectations. The pain and sorrow has been intense, yet I have enjoyed many close friendships, many deep healings and I have become a healer, helping men and women heal through love. Now, finally, today, standing here proudly facing both of my beloved birth parents, at last, I am healing. I know what love feels like. I love you both and I know, for the very first time in my life, that you love me too. I have spent all these years of my life seeking love and approval outside myself, in the poor lost souls of the men who crossed my path and in the nurturing kindness of a few of my women friends. Mother and father, I have taught so many men and women how to heal their bodies, heal their hearts and minds, and heal their relationships through love. Yet I was unable to do that for myself until now, at this very moment."

And that's when Leo approached the three of them. In front of Aphrodite's parents Leo said to her, "My dear Aphrodite, I brought you to this island for 2 reasons. One reason was to assist you to reconnect with your mother but I had no idea that you would also be meeting your father. I am so happy for all of you." And then, he got down on one knee and said in a sweet yet commanding voice: "My darling Aphrodite, I have grown to love you more than you can ever imagine. It was you who helped me to heal my inner longing for acceptance and love. With your psychic knowing you guided me to get the help I really needed and you have saved me from myself. But as the veil of discontent began to lift from my sight, I was able to see you so clearly. I love you and I want to marry you. Will you be my wife, dearest Aphrodite?" Crying and smiling and laughing, Aphrodite pulled him to his feet and told him, "Yes. Yes. Yes. I am finally ready for love my dear Leo. Yes, I will marry you?"

This reunited, resurrected family sat huddled together entranced and enthralled with each other. For Aphrodite, Cassandra and Cyrano, the world as they had known it had finally, finally transformed. Each of them had worked so hard to understand, to let go, to forgive, to love and to feel free. But it was this moment of reconnection, renewal of love and resurrection of their deep family ties, that had finally healed them all. They made plans to attend church together on Sunday to rejoice in the resurrection of love in their lives.

And then they came from out of nowhere. First Alexei smiled that sweet warm smile Cassandra had always loved. But then there was Stefano, also smiling, looking older and wiser and more compassionate than she had ever seen before. And there was Damion, crying. "Could it be," Cassandra thought, "that my domineering, violent brother has really healed and is learning to love?" Then in the distance she saw her mother, Lyzandra. At this point Cassandra could no longer control herself. She ran as fast as she could and just about fell into the waiting and open arms of her mother, Lyzandra. They sobbed together knowing that the love had returned with no need to bring back the past. But for Cassandra, the biggest surprise of all was the expression on the face of her father, Demitri, when he finally saw his beloved daughter again after all this time. The sadness, regret, shame, compassion and sorrow could all be seen in the different muscles of his face. But on top of it all Cassandra could see and feel his undying love for her. She embraced him and they hugged for a long time.

Cyrano's parents, his grandfather Hermes, and his uncle Basileus had been watching Cyrano and Cassandra's touching reunion. But they were surprised and delighted to discover that they also had a granddaughter and such a beautiful young lady. Introductions continued for quite a while followed by stories of the macho men's attitudes in this Greek culture. In the midst of all the talk, Aphrodite decided to make an announcement that would make the men in her Greek family very happy. She announced to her entire new family: "According to the tradition in this macho Greek culture, women are supposed to remain pure and innocent until they marry. Well I am announcing for all of you to hear. Your granddaughter and niece is still a virgin. And I plan to remain that way until after Leo and I marry."

The applause by all the men in Aphrodite's newly discovered family was resounding. Many intense hugs and well wishes followed her announcement. They were all bustling with plans for a beautiful June wedding. Aphrodite couldn't wait to tell her adoptive parents, Chiara and David, about the reunion with her birth family. She had talked about that possibility with her mother often and had promised she would include them if this reunion would ever come to pass. Before agreeing to the wedding plans, Aphrodite insisted that she must include the wonderful parents who had taken such good care of her and had helped her to grow up in style.

Demitri invited everyone to the family home for a special meal that he had cooked and he and his sons were planning to serve. He announced that the women would not have to lift a finger. And then Alexei brought his sister over to the bike rack saying: "Here is the pink bicycle you used to love. I brought it to the park for you to see once more. We have saved it for you my darling little Cassie. I am so happy you have returned to all of us." Lyzandra looked up at the sky and pointed to a beautiful pale rainbow with a majestic eagle sitting right in the middle as if to say: "I am watching over you and all is well." They all smiled and headed toward their cars for the short ride to the Melanakos home, Cassie's return and the wonderful meeting with their soon to be in-laws.

31 EPILOGUE

Today was an ordinary day, just like so many other days that had passed and so many unlived days yet to come. She walked slowly, deep in thought, her body permeated with melancholy as she approached the path to her apartment.

Aphrodite Maia Morgan had lived in the same townhouse on Ramsey Street in Hawthorne, CT, for a very long time. Every inch of the environment had been embedded in her brain and embodied within her hyper sensual anatomy. She walked along the winding cobblestone path, aware of the earth beneath the stones welcoming her home. As she approached the modern cantilevered staircase leading up to her front door, she paused as an expression of gratitude for being alive. Standing perfectly still she allowed her breathing to slow down, consciously counting every inhale and exhale for 5 minutes. She had timed it so often that her body mind system responded as soon as the 5 minutes was over. A very deep breath filled her body, she held the breath for as long as she possibly could and then she suddenly released it with an intense grunt of relief. The 5 minutes had ended and she knew she was home.

Before searching in her purse for her keys, Aphrodite always checked the environment to be sure it was safe to go inside. Without glancing up, her body said hello to the beautiful bluebird who visited her every day. Aphrodite did not, and could not, adhere to a rigid schedule. Yet no matter what time of day she arrived home and completed her breathing exercise, the little bluebird was right there hovering above her head. The fluttering wings of her intuitive friend seemed to give her permission to leave the outside world and enter her inner sanctuary. As soon as Aphrodite's glance turned upward, the bird flew to the top of the nearby willow tree watching intently as if to ensure that it was safe for Aphrodite to enter her home.

Today, as she smiled at the bluebird, Aphrodite could feel a deep longing for love pounding in her heart. Without words, she asked the bluebird to help her to find love, to become love, and to feel the love she so desperately craved. Little cheerful staccato chirps and the sound of wings brushing through the branches caused Aphrodite to look behind her at the golden shimmering iridescence of the setting sun. The sparkle was so intense that she had to squint and close her eyes. As she opened her eyes, she was momentarily mesmerized by the beautiful pastel palette rainbow leading over the hills that stretched for miles behind her building.

As she slowly walked up the 5 steps leading to her apartment door, her senses were attuned to everything around her. Aphrodite found herself communicating with a family of ants that scrambled to bury themselves deep into the ground as they sensed her approaching on the steps above. Without words, she asked them about their world and they sent her their message for the day. Today the word was "Trust in Love." The ants reminded her to trust in the power of love to heal, to trust that the seeds of her love have already been planted, and to know in her heart that the man of her dreams is already here and loves her.

Sadness seemed to fill her heart as she realized she would be leaving her outdoor friends once she entered her home. But, of course, she knew she could always reach them with her senses since her inner world had no boundaries and nothing, not even cement filled walls, would ever block her soul from connecting with the cosmos and anyone and anything that exists.

Reaching the top of the stairs she noticed her blossoming Sweet William plant seemed to smiling joyfully at her. Sweet William beckoned her to pluck one flower and slowly savor the taste on her tongue. As soon as her saliva touched the flower in her mouth, the leaves on the plant seemed to perk up and extend even straighter than before. The entire plant appeared to have regained its sense of elegance. Aphrodite's face lit up into a sweet expectant smile as she searched inside her purse for her key chain.

There was a gentle breeze that seemed to whisper to her, repeating the words of her friend, the bluebird. All she could hear was: "Trust, trust, trust. Love is here. Love is all around you. Open your senses and feel the love. Remember you are never alone." With that renewed sense of trusting in love, she slowly turned the key to open her door to her inner sanctuary, her home.

And there he was, beaming and energized at the mere sight of her. She could feel his excitement and she knew without an inkling of a doubt that he was all hers and that he knew he belonged to her and she belonged to him. Her very presence brought him obvious delight as he smothered her face with kisses, licked her ear and vigorously rubbed his body back and forth against her. She realized immediately that he had been sitting patiently near the door during her 5 minute exercise, eagerly waiting for the moment when she would turn the key and open the door. His entire existence seemed to depend upon that special moment when she would once more hold him in her loving arms.

Yes, she was totally confident that this handsome, very special, tender and adoring man loved her unconditionally. And he was the true and only love of her life. Although her beloved man was completely content in his overwhelming love for her, she was happy but still wanted and desired more. She longed to be held in the arms of a different man, a tall and powerful hungry man. She longed to be with an adoring, loving and exuberant man whose hunger for life could only be fed by the assurance of her undying love for him.

Fluffy, her beloved Poodle/Pomeranian mutt with soft curly white fur and a sweet angelic face that could melt anyone's heart, continued to lick her cheeks and her neck as his tail wagged rapidly back and forth. And then, just as quickly as he had gotten excited, his exuberance died down and he slowly sauntered away seeking something new to attract his attention. Aphrodite smiled at the unwavering sweetness of this little man who filled her life and her apartment with so much tender love. She watched his white fluffy body wiggle away as his tiny paws made the most delicate sounds on the hardwood floor in the hallway.

And then Leo came rushing out to meet her, sweeping her up into his arms with a big hug and a warm, tender kiss on her mouth. "Darling, I'm so glad you're home. We have dinner reservations at 8 and we still have a few more details to prepare for our flight tomorrow for our wedding on your beautiful island.

Smiling to herself, Aphrodite recalled her own words spoken to herself and written in her journals during the past few soul searching years. She had always known she was not a quitter. Often extremely demanding, sometimes overly needy and clinging, she had often felt abandoned and unloved. But one thing she had known for certain. She would never give up the fight - no matter how many obstacles she had to overcome or how much pain and sorrow she had to endure. Her inner knowing would keep her focused on the path ahead and she was determined to reach the promised land of true love, in this lifetime. All of her life, beginning in her mother's womb, she had been longing for the love that she had so often been denied. Not feeling worthy, she did find some semblance or illusion of love in the hearts and minds of so many broken people who had not yet discovered their own love and felt they had very little love to provide for her.

Smiling peacefully at her beloved Leo, Aphrodite knew she had finally reached the promised land of love. And she was determined to keep that love alive for the rest of her life. As they walked out the door on their way to dinner on this special evening, Aphrodite looked back and thought: "I am leaving my previous life as I enter the promised land of love. How lucky am I? " Aphrodite heard her precious Fluffy barking approval before she shut the door on the lonely life she had lived before stepping out into her future life with the man she loved, Leo.

ABOUT THE AUTHOR

Dr. Erica Goodstone is a Spiritual Relationship Healing Expert helping men and women heal their relationships through love. As a Licensed Mental Health Counselor, Licensed Marriage Therapist, Board Certified Personal/Life and Health/Wellness Coach, Board Certified Sex Therapist and Body Oriented Psychotherapist, she has helped thousands of men and women to find their way back to love. Her book, *Love Me, Touch Me, Heal Me: The Path to Physical, Emotional, Sexual and Spiritual Reawakening* is available as a complete book and E book, as 4 smaller books and ebooks, and as 12 even smaller Kindle books. As a Diamond Ezinearticles.com Author she was selected as one of the top 20 showcased authors out of over 400,000 authors for contributing over 200 quality articles on diverse topics. She writes about creating, healing and sustaining loving relationships in your life at: http://www.CreateHealingAndLoveNow.com/blog
Receive counseling, coaching, or additional information at http://www.DrEricaWellness.com

www.ingramcontent.com/pod-product-compliance
Lightning Source LLC
Chambersburg PA
CBHW051445260626
47162CB00001B/263